Dreamscape:
Saving Alex

Kirstin Pulioff

May all your dreams turn into adventures.

First Edition
Visit the author's website: www.kirstinpulioff.com

DEDICATION

This book is dedicated to the wonderful friendships that shape my life.

To my best friend and husband, Chris—life wouldn't be the adventure it is without you...and to my childhood friend, Natalie—Whatsamattmoo.

CHAPTER ONE

I pushed the golden nuggets around my plate. It was a bribe meal. I knew it as soon as I saw the table laid out with all my favorite food. Mom was buttering me up for something. I just didn't realize it would be something that was going to totally ruin my life. And maybe, if I was still five years old, it would've worked.

I shuffled the food, pushing one of the nuggets under the mashed potato volcano until it erupted. A slow trail of chunky gravy slid down over the side of the plate.

My mom arched a brow, glancing purposefully between me and the brown puddle congealing on her nice tablecloth.

I ignored her. She had been doing it to me for years. Now it was my turn. It killed me not eating the bribe, but I couldn't do it. She wouldn't win. Not this time. As long as I didn't look at the pile of sweet rolls in the middle, I would be fine. Easier said than done. My mouth watered as I glared across the table.

My mom lowered her napkin and refilled her wine glass. "Alexis, honey, do you want to talk about it?"

I met her gaze coolly. "Do I want to talk about it? I thought we did talk about it last month, when you told me we were moving over winter break. Three months, Mom, that's what you and Dad said. Not this weekend." My teeth hurt from clenching, but if I released my jaw, tears would fall. I couldn't let that happen. Nothing would be worse than giving her that satisfaction.

I focused on the wall behind her, skimming over the sealed moving boxes until I found the corner with the torn paisley wallpaper. Bad idea. I'd never understood why they hadn't fixed it. Everything else in our house had been upgraded over time, except that. It stood out as the one imperfection. And it was my fault. Why couldn't they just fix it so we could move on? I brushed my blonde hair out of my eyes, pausing at the slight indentation of the scar at my hairline. It had been seven years now, but still, I hadn't forgotten. They hadn't let me.

With that one glance, I was nine years old again, crying in the corner. But I wasn't that little girl anymore, and I wasn't going to let her see me cry. No matter how much I wanted to. No matter how powerless I felt. I wasn't going to admit it. Admitting it only tightened the collar around my neck. No, I wasn't going to break. Not this time.

"Really Alex, try to be reasonable." Mom's voice broke through my thoughts.

"Reasonable?" I heard my voice squeak as I turned my attention back to her. My knuckles tightened around the fork. "You think I'm the one being unreasonable? When you bumped up our move to tomorrow? How did you expect me to react?"

"Civilly," she muttered, taking a sip of her wine.

I glared at her. "Why couldn't we wait until break?"

"Sometimes plans change," she said. She wrung the cloth napkin around her polished nails and pushed her plate to the side. "We have to do what's best for the family, and right now, that's moving a bit sooner. Your dad's already over there. He's been working long hours and misses us. You can't blame him or me for wanting to be together. Being apart like this has been hard for us."

"And what about me? Don't you care about how hard this is for me?"

"We do, but it won't seem so bad once we're all back together and you're settled in. Dad's already checked out the school and gotten the house ready for us. He says everyone's real nice. You'll make new friends in no time."

I narrowed my eyes and cocked my head to the side, looking closer at my mom. Her voice was calm, but the slight twitch of her lower lip gave her away. It was her tell. They had known and just hadn't told me. Well, if they thought I was mad with three months' notice, how did they expect me to handle this?

"I don't want new friends or a new anything. I just want to stay here. Can't I stay with Natalie or something, at least until break? I don't want to miss the—"

"Honey, that's just not possible." She lifted the half-emptied wine glass to her lips.

"Why not?"

"Because we've made up our minds. We want you with us. Our family's been apart long enough. Too long," she said, finishing off the glass.

"But y-you promised," I sputtered, wishing my voice didn't shake.

She didn't notice. She was focused on filling her empty glass, swirling it until it left a residue below the rim. "And we're sorry, but this decision's final."

"You're sorry? That's supposed to make me feel better? How can I believe a word you say anymore? You keep changing things so they're more convenient for you!" I couldn't help myself. Upsetting her made me feel better.

She spread her hands out in defeat. "You're right, and we knew you'd be upset."

"You knew, and yet you did it anyway?"

"Alex, you're not the only one in this family. The decision was ours. And it's final."

"But—" I floundered. She was right. I wasn't the only one in this family—just the only one without a choice.

"That's it," she said with an edge that told me we were done. She pulled her plate back in front of her, pretending the cold chicken was her favorite. "Now tell me, what happened at school today?"

I pressed my tongue against the back of my teeth, waiting until my chin stopped quivering. "You want to know how school was? Let me tell you." Anger punctuated each word as I shook my head. "Mr.

Phillips loved my sketch. I got a C on my chemistry test. Oh yeah, and Brian asked me to Homecoming." The last words spilled out before my voice could falter.

My mom stopped mid-bite and smiled. "Oh honey, that sounds wonderful. Hmm, Brian... That name sounds familiar. Is he the one from your homeroom class?"

My mouth dropped open. Was she serious? "Yeah, it'd be great if we had three months left here, like you promised. But now I'll have to cancel. How could you do this to me?" I shouted, almost falling out of my chair as I pushed away from the table. I stomped past her, avoiding her eyes. It hurt to look at her.

"We're just trying to do what's right for the family," she yelled at my back.

"Whatever," I yelled down the stairs. They didn't care about *the family*, just about them. I slammed the door and nearly tripped over a pile of boxes stacked behind the door. Did she really expect me to pack when my whole world was falling apart?

I threw myself on the bed and screamed into one of my pillows. How could they do this to me? Make me leave my friends, my school, everything familiar? I didn't care if it made sense to them. It wasn't fair to me. Where was the reassurance that the cracks widening in my heart would heal?

Tears stained the pillow, and I tossed it to the far corner. I was tired of feeling. Of being torn between extremes. Since they'd told me we were moving, the past month had been a roller coaster of emotions. Swells of fury punctuated by brief moments of relief...then I plunged into the depths of inconsolable grief. I wanted off the ride.

Tonight would be hard enough without giving in to every emotion.

Tonight... The clocked ticked down in my mind. I groaned, flipping onto my back. How could she expect me to pack my whole room, my whole life, in one night? It was impossible.

I looked around the room, the perfect time capsule of my life. Shelves, bulletin boards, and my desk overflowed with stuff. I didn't believe in empty space. Empty space meant something was missing. Beside my desk, behind a row of rock climbing trophies, a mosaic of bright colors hid the white walls. My abstract art projects curled around a still life, and the ribbons from my competitions fit together like a puzzle.

Mom and I had argued for weeks about that wall. Not too much of a surprise. We argued about everything. But that wall topped the list. She wanted to frame them, to highlight my achievements, as she called it. I refused. I knew the truth. She wanted order and control in the one place I denied it.

She controlled everything else around the house, but not here. My room was off-limits. And they had respected that, but now... now the cardboard boxes leaning against my dresser said something different. I clenched my jaw tighter.

A stray tear broke through my defenses, cooling the flush of my cheeks.

No matter how many times I replayed it in my mind, it never got better. When they told me, I lost it, in the worst possible way. Everything became their fault. It didn't matter if it was or not, I blamed them. More specifically, I blamed my dad, and he knew it as he boarded the plane.

After he left, I stopped talking to him and my mom. It wasn't worth the aggravation. I couldn't even look at them without flipping out, let alone articulate the concerns that really mattered. And anything I said now was pointless. It was too late. I was walking into social suicide, and I'd let them get away with it without a real fight. My social career was over, and it had only just begun, especially since Brian had started paying attention to me.

I smiled. *Brian.*

Everything about him was perfect. From the disheveled way his bleach-blonde spiked hair shot off in different directions to the deep blue eyes that always seemed to be on the move, I found nothing wrong with him. Even the feature he considered his one imperfection, the small patch of freckles over his nose, matched mine.

We were made for each other. But now I would never know how it would end.

I screamed into the pillows again. No matter how I looked at it, this move sucked. This wasn't the way it was supposed to go. I wanted my happy ending!

From under the pillows, I barely heard the doorbell. When it rang again, I glanced at the clock by my bed, half-hidden behind a stack of notes and photos. Seven o'clock. Who would be here that late?

Crap. How had I forgotten?

That had to be my best friend Natalie. When my parents told me we were moving, her solution was simple—sleepovers. Just like when we were kids. I had been looking forward to this all week, until my mom dropped the bombshell at dinner.

My feet hit the ground at the same time my mom yelled my name.

"Coming!" I yelled, shooting daggers at the door with my eyes. I shook my head. It didn't matter. None of that mattered. I ran down the stairs and through the house, focused on the red door at the end of the hall.

When I ran past the living room, I heard my mom's magazine ruffle. I could picture her raised eyebrows. But I didn't look. She had ruined my day. I didn't want her to ruin my night.

"Natalie," I squealed, throwing open the door.

"Geez, took you long enough," she said, waving back to her mom who was waiting in the car. "Let me in—it's cold out here. Brr." She shivered, prancing in place. Her cheerleading skirt swished back and forth as she pushed past me. I noticed her heavy eyeliner and bright lipstick; she must have come straight from a game.

"Sorry. I, uh...long story," I sighed, closing the door.

"Then it's a good thing I'm here early. We have all night!"

"Maybe not," I mumbled.

"What?" she asked, tilting her head to the side. Her ponytail flipped out over her shoulder.

I hesitated a moment too long. Mom peeked in from around the corner, her magazine bookmarked with one of her fingers. "Natalie," she said, lowering her reading glasses to the bridge of her nose. "I'm so glad you're here."

"Me too, Mrs. Stone." She shifted her sleeping bag and backpack.

"How was the game?"

"You'd never believe it. We won, but barely," she said. "I mean, the other team must have been all seniors. They were giants! We only scraped by with a last-minute field goal."

"That sounds nice," Mom said, drumming her crimson nails against the doorway. "You know, since you're here, maybe you can help Alexis with her packing."

"Mom! That's not why she's here."

"Well, it needs to be done. I'm sure she won't mind helping. Would you?" She looked over at my friend with an overly sweet smile.

"Uh, of course not, Mrs. Stone," Natalie said hesitantly, her eyes darting between us.

I rolled my eyes. "Let's go." I hurried, grabbing her stuff, turning my back to the doorway where my mom stood. That was the last thing we were going to do.

Before we reached the first step, Mom stopped us. "I'm serious. I don't want to leave it all for the movers tomorrow."

I glared back and tightened my lips.

"Yes, Mrs. Stone," Natalie said, politely breaking the silence. "I'm sure we'll be able to get some done."

"Thank you, Natalie. I knew I could count on you." With that reassurance, Mom pushed up her glasses and disappeared back into the living room.

"Come on," I said, dragging Natalie up the stairs behind me. I shut the door behind us and dropped her bags on top of the boxes. "Anytime, Mrs. Stone," I mocked, batting my eyelashes for effect.

"What?" Natalie laughed. "One of us has to know how to work

your parents."

"Then I'm glad you're here because I gave up on that a long time ago." I paused and looked at her again. "Seriously, I'm glad you're here."

"Me too. Now stop that," she ordered, pointing at the tears poised to fall.

I batted away the tears and leaned back against my door. "This is crap!" I spat, "Can you believe this? We're moving tomorrow. Not over break like they said."

"I know," Natalie said, dropping her backpack along the side of my bed.

"What? How?" I asked.

"Well, the squad was out on the field practicing, and you can see your house from there. We saw the van."

"Oh," I said. "But can you believe she just dropped the news to me at dinner and left this pile of boxes in my room, expecting me to pack up? Like it's that simple?"

"I know, it's crazy," Natalie said.

"It's more than crazy. It's the biggest load of crap ever!" I yelled.

"Shh…your mom will hear you," Natalie warned, her eyes wide.

"I don't care anymore. It doesn't matter. Nothing I say will change anything."

"Well, just don't get me kicked out. Tonight's too important. Now, where should we start?" she asked, looking around.

"Seriously?"

"Yes, really. I'm here to help and to have fun. I'm not going to let you drag it out. Now start putting these boxes together."

"Who are you, and what did you do with my friend?" I asked, moving away from the door and falling back onto the bed.

"Don't even," she scoffed. "When we planned these sleepovers, we knew you were moving."

"But it's different now," I said.

"Why?"

"Um…because I'm leaving tomorrow, not in December like I

thought." I propped myself up onto my elbows.

She pursed her lips and rolled up her sleeves. "Another reason why we need to do this now."

"What?" I asked, confused.

"Look, you and I both know your mom's going to come up here and check on you. Do you want this to take all night?"

"Ugh…no." I pouted.

"Don't give me that look."

"What look?"

"That pathetic one." She looked at me, hands on her hips, waiting for me to move.

"Ouch." I sat up. "Fine," I reluctantly agreed, moving her bags off the boxes.

She handed me the first box and tape and sat back on the bed. "What the—" she said, pulling a photo frame out from under the comforter, frowning as she handed it to me.

I glanced down at the picture, a moment between Brian and me. There was a reason it was hidden under my covers. I both loved and hated that picture. There was so much wrong with it, from the way I stared at him while he smiled for the camera, the way I leaned too far into his body—I looked love-starved. And yet, it was the only photo I had, so I refused to toss it. Natalie peeked over my shoulder and grimaced. Her eyes strayed to the ceiling.

"There's something I need to tell you, but I don't know how," she said.

The pit in my stomach opened. Natalie always knew how to tell me everything. I took a deep breath. "What is it?"

"It's about Brian." She exhaled deeply and met my gaze.

"About Brian?" I took another breath and traced his face in the picture.

"He knows."

"He knows about what?" My voice, even as a whisper, shook. With one look, I understood exactly what she meant.

"I'm so sorry," she said, squeezing my hand. "Like I said, we saw the truck stop by your house." Natalie looked back at the ceiling.

"And?" I asked in a whisper.

"Melissa saw it too, and you know how she is. She called her mom, her mom called yours…" She stopped talking and gave me a sad smile. "She found out that you were moving this weekend and told him."

My mind spun. I looked at the walls and the ground, desperate for something to stabilize my thoughts, but nothing worked. Everything was a blurry mess. Including my heart.

Natalie bit her lip and winced. "There's more."

"Just tell me." I flipped the frame upside down so I didn't see his smile.

"He asked her to the dance." Natalie cringed.

My breath quickened. I couldn't decide which betrayal hurt worse.

CHAPTER TWO

He asked Melissa.

Those three words rang in my ears. How could he do that? Ask me out one minute and someone else the next, without even talking to me? It felt like some sort of cruel joke, and I was the punchline.

I looked at Natalie, her face scrunched as she waited. I didn't know what she was waiting for. A reaction, maybe? I wanted to run and hide, cry, shout, hit something, but I couldn't. I was frozen from the inside out. Every inch of my mind stuck on those words.

His words. My mom's words. Too many words that weren't mine deciding my life.

"Are you okay?" Natalie asked.

"No…yeah…I guess," I mumbled.

"I thought you needed to know," she said sadly. "But hey, it's not all bad." She squeezed my hand and put on her best cheerleading smile.

"Not all bad? In what world?" I rolled my eyes and frowned.

"Look, you know I think Brian's a player. He's always been one. You can do so much better than him anyway. Speaking of…think of all those new guys in Portland."

"Yeah," I scoffed. "That's exactly what I want to do."

"I'm just saying. You're going there. You might as well have something to look forward to. So what do you think?" She plopped down on the bed beside me, her ponytail swishing over her shoulders. "Lumberjack or grunge?" she asked, bringing up an old joke we'd made when my parents first told me we were moving.

"Are you serious?"

"Come on, come on, come on," she urged. "Make a choice."

Her words struck me. I looked up with wide eyes. "Make a choice," I whispered, and then louder, "you're right. That's exactly what I'm going to do." I shuffled back into a sitting position, arms tucked around my legs, and bit my lower lip. "Definitely the lumberjack. I've always loved the forest." A small smile grew at the edge of my mouth. How could she do that? Turn the worst news into a joke. I guess that's one of the reasons she's my best friend.

"Awesome. Lumberjack it is, then. Let's get these boxes packed so you can go hook up with Paul."

"Paul?"

"Uh, yeah, don't tell me you haven't heard of Paul Bunyan. He's big, strong, and probably just what you need."

"Stop it!" I laughed, throwing my pillow at her. "Just watch out or I'll send his ox down to get you."

"I'm scared." She trembled. "Now, give me a box."

Just like that, my room started getting packed. Piece by piece, shirt by shirt, trophy by trophy, everything found its way into one of the boxes. Before long, my safe haven slipped away, transforming into a blank slate. The tears stung, painfully clinging to the edges of my eyes. My treasures blurred into an obscure mess as Natalie threw more and more at me.

"Oh my god!" Natalie raised her eyebrows and lifted my tiger Beanie Baby by its tail. "You still have this, really? This has got to go."

"Stop it," I said, grabbing it from Natalie's hand. "You don't know what this meant to me." I cradled Mr. Tiger against my chest. The crusted fuzz scratched my collarbone.

"Seriously?" she asked, scrunching up her face. "You need to let some of this go. You can't take it all with you."

"I don't want to leave any of it behind," I muttered, barely hearing my own words.

"Oh boy," she sighed and walked past me to the walk-in closet that overflowed with my trinkets. Boxes and bags of old dolls, papers, and crafts hung over the shelves. "Are you serious? What is all this stuff?"

I laughed. If she thought my room was bad, my closet was even worse. I didn't even know what hid in each corner.

She pulled down the first bag and peeked out the door, her exasperation replaced by a smile. "It's like a scavenger hunt in here. You never know what you're going to find. Like this. I can't believe you still have this. Wasn't it from our fifth grade holiday program?" She held the pink-sequined dress against her body. "Do you think it'll still fit?"

"Of course it will. You never know when you'll need it for a ball."

"Or when your Prince Charming will show up. I'm sorry," she said, biting her lower lip.

"It's okay. Either way, I guess you're right. I won't need it." I grabbed it and tossed it across the room towards the trash.

"That's not what…" Her voice trailed off as the dress slid over the edge of the trash can. "I meant."

"No, you're right. I can't take all of this with me. And if something's got to go, I won't need that."

We went back to silently filling the boxes, only stopping when Natalie mistook something for trash. I didn't understand it. It was perfectly clear to me what needed to be saved, treasured. Natalie just raised her eyebrows. She didn't understand. Maybe I was being unrealistic, blinded by the shadow of what things meant, not what they were, but my heart hurt.

I looked at the half-filled boxes, then the half-empty closet, and spared a final glance at Mr. Tiger, still tucked in my arms. Threadbare, matted, and void of whiskers. Had I held on to him for too long?

"How do you know when it's time to let go?" I whispered.

"Of that? About ten years ago. Here, let me help you." She pinched it out of my hands before I had a chance to stop her and tossed it into the bin. "Come on. Stop the tears. We're not throwing all this stuff away, just the things you've held on to for too long."

"It feels the same to me."

"Don't be so melodramatic. You're going to get to your new house and set most of this back up, including this poster of—who is this exactly?" She laughed at me.

"Stop it." I laughed as well. "Seriously, it's just, I see you toss these things, I—"

"You what?"

"I just wonder how quick you'll forget about me." I turned so she wouldn't see my chin tremble, even though my voice gave it away.

"Oh Alex," she said, turning me around, squeezing my forearms and searching my face. "Stop it. This is stuff. You're my best friend. I'm never going to forget you. You're right here. Always." She pointed to her heart and blinked back her own set of tears. "Got it?"

"You're right." I nodded. She usually was, but that didn't settle the tremors rattling my heart. Everywhere I looked, something pulled at me, reminding me of my past, of what I would be leaving.

When Natalie disappeared back into the closet, I walked over to the bulletin board by my bed. I thumbed through the old photos, ticket stubs, and sketches, sighing.

I turned at a crash sounding from the closet. Torn, crumpled bags lay scattered at Natalie's feet, while old wooden beads and scrapbooking stickers found their new home within the threads of the carpet. I turned away, ignoring the impulse to scoop everything back up.

"Are you okay?" I asked.

"I'm fine, but you'll never guess what I found!"

I raised an eyebrow. "What?"

She peeked out from the doorway to the closet. "First, do you think we've done enough to make your mom happy?"

A quick spin around revealed seven full boxes stacked against one wall, empty bookshelves, and a half-empty closet. How had she done so much so quickly? I choked back the tears and forced a smile.

"Um, yeah. She's going to love you even more. Why?"

"Well…" She danced around. "I found something in the back of your closet that I'm really happy you saved. Want to guess?"

"From the back of my closet?" I chuckled. "No, I definitely don't want to guess what you found there."

"Come on, guess." Her excitement was contagious. Her ponytail swished, and I knew a cheer waited on the edge of her lips.

"I don't know, really." I lunged for the hidden item behind her back.

"Not so fast," she said, darting out of my reach as I grabbed for it. "I'll give you a hint. Do you remember all our sleepovers when we were little?"

"Yeah…" She dodged me again.

"Staying up all night…"

"Yeah…" The tips of my lips curved up.

"Popcorn, jump rope, iced tea..."

"You're killing me. What did you find?"

"Dun-dun doo-bee doo," she sang.

I stared at her until it hit me. "No way!" I exclaimed. "Dreamscape? You found it?"

"Yeah," she said, a silly grin filling her face.

That was all it took. With one word, Natalie made everything better. All the bad feelings bubbling inside me popped. It was as if she had offered me the greatest treasure. And maybe she had. I joined her squeal with my own.

The knock at the door surprised us both. Natalie burst into laughter as I ran to open it. We grew silent when I looked at my mom. I gripped the doorknob until my hands turned white.

"It sounds like you girls are having fun." She took a cursory look around the room. "Natalie, I knew you could help. You're exactly what we both needed. Thank you."

"No problem, Mrs. Stone," Natalie said, shrugging when I glared at her.

"Anyway, you girls have fun. I thought you might want some of this for later." My mom handed me an overflowing bowl of popcorn. I took it silently and closed the door.

15

"Thanks Mrs. Stone," Natalie yelled through the closed door and turned back to me. "You know it's not entirely her fault," she said, grabbing the popcorn and throwing a handful at me. "Your dad's the one with the new job."

I shrugged. "It doesn't matter. Him, her—they're working together to ruin my life."

Natalie stared at me and shook her head.

"What?" I demanded. "I'll go easy on her at some point. It's just easier to be mad at her right now. She can handle it."

"Whatever you say." Natalie shrugged and let it go, settling back on the edge of the bed, hoarding the popcorn. "Here you go. Pop it in," she said, throwing the square game cartridge at me.

I blew on the edge of the disk and stared at my friend before pressing it into the old game station. That's what I was going to miss. She never made me feel irrational, even when I knew I was. I doubted I would find that again.

"Oh my god, she put cinnamon on top." Natalie fell back, disappearing under the pile of pillows. "This. Is. So. Good."

"She only does that for you."

"That's because she likes me more."

"I wouldn't be surprised if she did." I reached over and threw a handful of popcorn at her.

The game slid in easily, and after a quick tap on the screen, bright yellow letters appeared. *Dreamscape.* I couldn't believe it. This was it, the game that defined our childhood. We played it every weekend at every sleepover for years, until we knew the game by memory. And here it was again. I smiled, but that didn't even scratch the surface of my excitement.

I looked over at Natalie, busy poking through the popcorn bowl for the extra sweet pieces.

"What?" she asked with her mouth full.

"Nothing," I laughed and looked back at the game. The golden letters of the main menu dominated the small screen, colorful birds fluttering in and out of the shadows. Time had changed things in ways I hadn't imagined. I sighed. The graphics that used to impress me were now little more than a pixelated mosaic. Everything today came with a bittersweet sting.

Once the music took over, it didn't matter. I was transported back to age ten. Boys, school, moving, none of that mattered. The only thing that mattered was the silly green hero moving across the screen, and the only thing I had to do was save the queen. If only life could still be that easy.

Natalie punched me in the shoulder. "I completely forgot about the dance."

"What?" I asked, covering my shoulder, following her pointed finger to the screen.

"Wow," I laughed, watching the little green hero twirl and send an arrow into the center of the *D*. "How old is this game?"

"Old enough that I'm sure you've forgotten the dance."

"Have not," I protested.

"Then do it!" She giggled, pushing me up.

"Okay, maybe I have," I said, falling in a fit of giggles.

"No, it can't be that tough," Natalie said, standing and pulling me up. "If we're doing this, we're doing it right. All the tricks, all the shortcuts, all the fun. Got it?"

"Got it," I said. We stood there, convulsing with laughter as we tried to do the dance again. Two steps left, two steps right, turn around and swipe the sword.

"Oh, man, how did we forget about this game?" I asked, falling back to the ground. It felt good to laugh.

"I don't know, but please tell me you didn't forget the codes too."

"Nah, like I'd forget those." I raised an eyebrow and scoffed. "How many times did we play this game?"

"Only like a million!"

"Exactly. There's no way I would forget it, or all the shortcuts. You know what? I have something you have to see. I found it while we were packing."

"While *we* were packing?" Natalie asked, grabbing another handful of popcorn, ready to throw it at me. I raised my hands in surrender.

"Okay, while you were packing. But you still have to see it."

I rushed to the wall closest to my bed, still untouched, and riffled through a stack of photos on the bulletin board. Bright thumbtacks loosened from the cork as I moved the curled edges of the pictures out of the way. Some memories were stacked three or four deep, with multiple puncture holes through their tops. A bright blue pin held the one I wanted.

"Okay, promise me you won't laugh." I unpinned the photo and held it backwards against my chest, hiding the image.

"I promise," she said, although the corners of her mouth already wavered in a smile.

"Do you remember this?" I asked, spinning the photo around so she could see it.

"I can't believe you still have that!" she exclaimed, grabbing the picture from my hand. "Look at us. Look at your braids!"

"How could I get rid of it? And I wouldn't talk, Little Miss Pigtails."

"That's Queen Pigtails to you."

"Ah man, those were the days," I sighed. "It all seemed so simple back then."

"It was," she said, handing me back the photo.

I looked at it once more before re-pinning it on my wall, careful not to create a new pin mark. The two girls smiling back at us were from a lifetime ago. The only similarities left were my long blonde hair and Natalie's love of pink eyeshadow. How had time passed so quickly? I turned back to the flashing screen before the swells of bittersweetness drowned me and focused on the controller.

"Time to play," I said, punching in the codes. "Left, right, up, down, circle, circle, enter. See, I still have it."

"That remains to be seen. Let's see how many lives we lose saving the queen. I don't think we ever had a perfect game."

"I'll just be happy if we make it past level five!"

We leaned back against the bed, watching the images fade into darkness. I couldn't think of a more perfect way to end the day. "Thank you," I whispered.

"Don't worry about it." Natalie nodded and pushed the buttons on her controller.

We fell into our routine, a comfortable pace of helping each other, arguing about the hard levels, and falling back in laughter during the easy streaks. I had forgotten more than I'd thought. The smooth movements and combinations I remembered were gone, faded with time, replaced by clumsy, last-minute reflexes. That's what I was afraid of. How could I hope to remember the memories of my life here if I couldn't recall a silly code?

As perfect as it was, it didn't last. Hours felt like minutes, and, sooner than I expected, the game was over. We saved the queen and brought down the evil empire in record time.

Natalie undid her ponytail and yawned. "I'm going to bed. That game wiped me out."

I gave her an odd look and then remembered she had cheered at school before coming here. "Sure," I said, tapping a rhythm on the controller. Without the distraction of the game, nervous energy prickled through me. I wasn't ready yet. Not for sleep.

"You're not tired?" she asked, crawling into her sleeping bag.

"Not really. I have a lot on my mind," I admitted, biting my lower lip. That was an understatement.

"Do you want me to stay up?" She yawned again and laid her head on her hand. Her mascara had smeared, exaggerating her drooping eyes.

"Nah, don't worry about it. I'll be asleep soon."

"Okay, if you're sure," she said, pulling the sleeping bag over her head so only the tip of her head remained out. "I'm glad we did this. This was fun."

"Me too." I smiled over at the familiar lump of my friend sleeping on my floor. Out the window above her, the stars twinkled as they disappeared and reappeared from behind the slight scattering of clouds. I yawned, and the lights blurred.

I wouldn't sleep. My racing thoughts were like a whirlpool, pulling me down. And even though I knew how to swim, the current was too strong. I wasn't ready; I doubted I ever would be. I felt pulled in every direction.

It was hard to decide which were stronger, the memories pulling at my heart or the pang of wishing I had more. Did it really matter? The sadness filled me the same. The ache chased my heart as it raced around my insides. There always seemed to be enough time until a countdown actually began. Once that timer started, everything spun out of control.

Most of the decisions were in someone else's hands, but not all of them. I looked down at my hands, gripping the old game controller. Maybe I could still control something after all.

"Dun-dun doo-bee doo," I sang quietly, making sure Natalie's eyes stayed shut as the game reloaded from the winning screen to the main menu. I would save the queen again, and in some way, maybe myself, too.

I yawned, waiting for the hero's dance to begin. Heaviness pulled at my eyes, fighting the urge to play. I held on to the controller like it was the last reminder of my childhood and forced my eyes open. Out of the darkness, the golden letters popped up again. I typed in the code, but my thumbs slipped, pressing the wrong combination.

"Crap."

I pressed the letters and symbols again. My eyes popped wide open as I waited for the confirmation. I let out a deep breath when I saw the secondary screen. It worked.

I accepted and leaned back against the bed, waiting for the hero to dance across the screen once more. For some reason, this round took forever to load. My gaze drifted back out the window towards the stars until they became unrecognizable. I rubbed my eyes with the back of my hand and sighed.

From the corner of my vision, I saw the screen turn black. What now?

"This is ridiculous," I mumbled, stepping over Natalie and tapping the edge of the screen. It lit back up, wanting another confirmation. "Yes, I'm ready. I already told you that." I pressed the button hard.

The words on the screen burst into thousands of golden crystals.

Whoa. That was new. I stared at the eruption of yellow coating the screen. Did I break the game? I squinted and leaned closer, checking out all four sides of the TV. Nothing seemed broken. The theme song still played in the background. I couldn't tell what was wrong. I tapped the edge of the screen again and sneezed as dust flew off into my nose.

I looked back at it, but nothing had changed. It still sparkled with golden pixels. And then I saw it. A steady stream of yellow flakes spewed out of the screen towards me.

Holy crap, what was going on? I scrambled backwards until my back rested against the bed, and I froze. Nothing made sense, and the wild images running through my mind only made it worse. I had never seen anything like this before—except in horror movies. I didn't want to go there.

Everything stopped, except my racing heart and the stuff flying at me. I couldn't move. I couldn't breathe. I couldn't do anything but watch as the dust covered me. Bit by bit, it crawled its way up my body, which tingled where each glittering piece landed. I held my breath, trembling as my legs disappeared under the golden light.

No. No. No. I tried to kick the dust off me, but my legs were numb, and my arms wouldn't move. Something was happening. It felt like a nightmare. The kind where you're trying to run away, but your feet slush through the deep water as everyone else glides past effortlessly. I couldn't do anything I wanted to do. And I knew that if I tried to scream, it would sound like a whisper.

I choked back a scream and shivered. I had no idea what it was, but something inside me was changing. Light crawled up my body, pulsing to a familiar rhythm. Pins and needles spread through me like lightening until my whole body hummed. When the light rolled over my head, darkness blinded me. Vibrations shook my core until my teeth chattered.

I sat shivering in the dark for hours. At least that's what it felt like. I had no way to gauge anything, and I didn't trust my mind. It was telling me all sorts of crazy things that didn't make sense.

I shook my head, surprised that it moved. The pulsing slowly softened to gentle thumps, like a heartbeat. I kicked, swatting the golden light off me. I might have been able to move, but I still couldn't see. Blurry golden light surrounded me. It was different than before though. This light... was warm.

That didn't make sense. I shook my head again and squinted. Other colors appeared, indistinct images moving too fast for me to focus on them. I rubbed my eyes, hoping it would help, but it didn't. I twisted around, noticing the blur of vibrant, diverse colors. Even without seeing, I felt empty space and sensed a new strangeness. Fear clenched my heart.

I swallowed hard. I wasn't home. Where was I?

A persistent hum stirred deep within and around me. Hidden in the chirps of the birds and the sway of the branches, the familiar tempo repeated itself. A blurry parade of light passed in front of me, speeding up to the pulsing rhythm, and then, after a few moments, repeated. The same hum, the same movement. Everything repeated, forcing me to pay attention. I knew that tune.

My stomach knotted in a strange blend of curiosity and fear.

"Dun-dun doo-bee doo, Dun-dun doo-bee doo," I hummed to the beat.

I was in Dreamscape.

CHAPTER THREE

"Crap, crap, craaaaaap!" I flicked off the last golden specks of dust from my shin. I must be dreaming. I had to be dreaming. There was no other explanation, except the absurd notion that the game had eaten me. I shook my head. I wasn't even going to go down that road. I was dreaming, but how could I wake up? Besides the fuzzy light, I couldn't see a thing.

My imagination worked overtime; terrifying ideas ran through my mind. Whatever was happening to me, it certainly wasn't real. Call it a dream, or maybe a hallucination. I didn't know what this was, and I really didn't care to find out. I just wanted it to stop.

"Wake up!" I ordered myself, pinching my arm. "Wake up!" I gave into the tears at the edge of my eyes. I shook with despair until I heard the Dreamscape theme song again. It played in a pattern of rustling leaves, squawking birds, and the shuffling of my own toes. The air buzzed in rhythm. It was different, fuller perhaps, than the game, but I still recognized the cheerful tune. It wasn't supposed to sound like that.

I frantically grabbed the ground. Cool dirt stuck beneath my fingernails, and sharp needles poked my fingers. A strong whiff of pine and sage assaulted me. Nothing was familiar. I had never wanted so badly to smell my mom's overly sweet cinnamon popcorn in my life. But it wasn't here, and I didn't want to be here either.

I yelped and scooted back, covering the top of my foot as something sharp punctured my skin. My bare feet dug into the ground, pushing me backwards until I stopped against the rough bark of a tree. A small trail of blood trickled down my foot where I'd been attacked.

I cried, which only made my vision worse. Nothing appeared from the rustling leaves. Nothing else crept towards me. I saw nothing. Yet I knew things moved just beyond my sight. I was scared. Vulnerability pinned me against the tree.

I waited until the throbbing in my foot became tolerable and pinched my arms again. A bruise grew near my elbow. Why couldn't I wake up? The fear I had brushed off at first now exploded. I couldn't breathe, I couldn't see, and I couldn't think.

And when I finally could see, I screamed. Not a silent whisper, but a full-blown scream that shook me from within. Unfolding around me was a world only hinted at in the video game. My mind was blown.

Holy crap! What was going on?

It was ridiculous. I mean, I had played this game for years and seen some beautiful paintings in art class. But what I saw now surpassed anything I had ever seen. Rich colors and angles blended together perfectly. Unlike in the scrub forests at home, layers of greens unfolded before me—bright green, dark green, forest, olive, jade, and lime.

My fingers itched to draw, to capture the details and add it to my wall at home. My trophies and ribbons proved I had natural talent, but nothing I drew at home compared to what I saw now. Even in the shadows, vibrancy existed. Neons and pastels flashed around me as birds flew from branch to branch. When they landed, clutching onto the undersides of the branches, I swallowed hard.

No matter how I admired the beauty, it scared me.

Squeezing my eyes shut, I made a wish. I didn't want much. I just wanted to wake up in my bed. When I re-opened them, I saw red and purple splotches on my arm from my manic pinching. It hadn't worked.

Something beyond my control was at play. I needed more time to figure it out, but I didn't think I would get it. Time was my enemy, at home and here. I had to move. Sitting here pinching myself wouldn't get me home and that's what I needed to do. Find a way home.

I thought back to freshman English and reading "Alice in Wonderland," and even further back to watching "The Wizard of Oz" when I was eleven. I wasn't the first girl to get stuck in a fantasy. Granted, I was real, and they were in stories…but it was all I had to go on. If Alice and Dorothy could find their way home, so could I. This would be a piece of cake. If this was Dreamscape, I already knew all the twists, turns, and crazy creatures here.

I cracked my knuckles and tightened my ponytail. It was time to play the game.

A parade of puff birds that had inched closer to me with each repetition of the song were now within reach. I barely recognized them. On screen, they were nothing but rolling yellow balls. Here, they reminded me of wobbling puffer fish with needle-tipped feathers and inflated bodies. The rhythmic stabbing of their spiked beaks into the ground interrupted their slow walk. I saw a bird with a bloody beak and pulled my feet in, covering the fresh wound on top of my foot.

"Stupid bird," I mumbled, standing and brushing the dirt off myself as I watched the strange creatures. They moved in a pattern, shuffling from the edge of the forest towards the field to my left.

I started a countdown—three, two, one, jump.

As I landed, a shrill scream echoed beneath me. The bones of the bird crushed easily, like cracking knuckles, when I flattened its body to the ground. A pool of red surrounded me, turning the golden feathers dark. I shrieked and jumped back, flailing my arms until I hit a tree. The rough bark grabbed at my hair and scratched my back. The other birds squawked a warning before puffing into balls and rolling away down the hill. I covered my hurt hand and looked around nervously.

This wasn't real, this was a game; it couldn't be real. But the knot in my stomach and tears falling down my cheeks told me otherwise. This was real, too real. I was losing it.

Only a few minutes in, and I had killed an innocent creature. I felt sick. Did I really expect it to burst into a puff of feathers, disappear, and deposit golden coins in my pockets like in the game?

I looked over at the lifeless bird with the sick feeling of guilt in my chest. How was I going to survive in this world? I thought about the most dangerous levels. Any advantage I'd thought I had just disappeared.

I plucked a yellow feather from my heel, looked to the ground where the trampled bird lay, and sighed. No matter how I felt, I had to move. Waiting would only bring the birds back. I didn't want another punctured foot or reminder of my cruelty.

To the right of me, the forest grew together. Branches intertwined, limbs crossing at all angles, blocking the light from reaching the ground. It was dark. Darker than I'd imagined, but that was where the first level of the game started.

I glanced in the other direction, noticing the birds twisting and turning, flying in random directions over a treeless, grassy hill. Patches of red wildflowers sprinkled the green meadow.

I bit the inside of my cheek and glanced between the forest and the meadow. If this place was real, maybe I didn't have to follow the rules of the game. The crimson puddle haunted me. I didn't want to follow those rules.

Turning away from the trees, I walked towards the field. Warm sunlight settled over me. My smile stretched across my face. I broke into a run across the grass. It seemed so perfect—the pristine beauty of the hill in comparison to the dark forest, the warmth of the sun, and the silence. Halfway up the hill, I paused mid-step and looked around.

When had the birds stopped singing?

Oh crap. Something was wrong. The grass tangled my legs. Warm gusts of wind pressed against me, slowing me down. The small patches of wildflowers gave way to larger pockets of red poppy-like flowers. Their delicate fragrance turned sickly sweet.

A burning sensation rushed across my leg. When I moved the tall grass out of the way, I saw a trail of blisters along my shin. Behind me, a bright red poppy whipped in the wind.

"Dragon weeds," I muttered, recognizing the flower. This threw in a new angle. Biting fuzz birds, burning pollen—the dangers were the same and yet they caught me off guard. I blew cool air onto my shins and, using a blade of grass, carefully scraped the poppy pollen off before more blisters grew. One thing was becoming painfully clear—I'd have to keep my eyes open.

My steps slowed as the ground softened to mud the further I trudged up the hill. Wind blew my hair into my face, blinding me just as I stepped on a loose rock. My feet slid out beneath me, slamming me into the muck. I flailed at the grass, trying to stop my slide back down the hill. A sharp pain shot up my legs as the blisters broke open.

I dug into the ground, pulling, grabbing anything to slow my descent. I glanced down the hill. Darkness waited for me past the floating pollen and whipping grass. The edge. My heartbeat doubled. I seized the closest bundle of poppy stems, ignoring their burn as I lurched to a stop and curled into a ball. Pollen covered my hands, and new blisters swelled immediately, but I only felt relief. Five feet down, the hillside dropped off in a sheer cliff.

Even from a distance, the abrupt edge terrified me. I could see myself freefalling over it. But then again, maybe that would get me home?

I threw a handful of rocks over the cliff, watching them fall, then disappear through a layer of haze that blocked my view of the bottom. My foot slipped, sending smaller rocks over the edge, bouncing off the walls. My heart thundered in my chest. Maybe not. I didn't want to be like one of those rocks.

Reality, dream, or insanity, it didn't matter. I didn't want to die. That meant one thing. No more messing around. I had to play the game, level by level, until I saved the queen.

There was only one problem. I'd never won without my codes.

CHAPTER FOUR

I was in trouble. Barely into the game, and I already had to start over. How many chances would I get? Probably not enough.

I slid my palms down my bare legs and looked down at my white t-shirt: dusty, torn, and a bit too short. I wished I had slept in something different. It didn't matter though. I couldn't change it.

The wind no longer beat against me but stayed at my back, helping me along the path back towards the forest. This time I managed to stay on my feet and avoid the patches of dragon weeds by weaving through the field. Their red petals flickered like flames.

I sighed when I reached the edge of the forest. The dark puddle that surrounded the crushed bird was still there, directly in front of me. I couldn't avoid it.

Seeing it all again didn't make it any easier. In fact, my unease grew. I felt sick. Whatever this was, it wasn't a game. I'd already killed a defenseless animal. What more would I have to do? I shook all over. How could I possibly keep myself alive, or sane?

If I entered the forest, I was committed to this game. Even knowing the tricks and shortcuts that awaited me didn't calm me down. I also knew the dangers, and what was required to win. Everything here was real, or real enough to make me second-guess my actions. Could I do what I needed to do to survive? But what other choice did I have if I wanted to get home?

Home. Where was that exactly?

It seemed like nothing more than a dot on the map. The home I wanted didn't exist anymore, packed away in cardboard boxes. But even if I didn't have a home, I had a world to get back to. And I didn't want to waste what little time I had left in some fantasy childhood game.

A shudder ran down my spine as I looked behind the tree. Level one, the dark forest.

Go big or go home. That's what my dad always said, but here, I surmised, I had to go big to go home. I smiled, surprised to hear his words in my mind. I usually hated his cheesy one-liners, especially the last couple of months. But now, it made me smile. I wished I could hear his voice.

I wished for a lot of things, especially that my path home didn't start in the dim light. From the threshold of the trees, every direction offered shadows, one darker than the next. It seemed like such an ominous beginning. I held my breath, taking a hesitant step forward, carefully avoiding one flock of puff birds creeping closer from the forest, and then another.

The trees grabbed at my shirt, tearing more holes through the thin fabric. My heart drummed against my chest, drowning out the sounds of the birds and the now-forgotten theme song. The chill of the darkness engulfed me, and then I ran.

I ran until my chest burned and felt like it would cave in, which wasn't very far. Another one-liner filled my mind. This one I didn't miss. The condescending tone of my mom's voice: *Some people are more suited to the arts than sports.* The words had left a deeper imprint than I wanted to admit.

My steps slowed, pulled by an invisible weight. Even here, I couldn't get far without my parents' voices souring my thoughts. It must be a parent thing, knowing just the right combination of helpfulness and ridicule to sting.

I yelped as tree branches whipped against my cheek, cutting my pale skin. A drop of blood smeared my fingers when I wiped the scratch. I had to let the distractions go before they killed me.

Thankfully, between the moving shadows, birds darting from branch to branch, and my own efforts at keeping my shirt pulled down, my attention wandered back to the path. The trail, made of moss, decomposed leaves, and soft bark, felt gentle to walk on. Even though my arms and legs were covered with scratches, my bare feet remained relatively unharmed. It was a welcome surprise.

I plodded through the forest, avoiding the puff birds and giving a wide berth to the dragon weeds. I dipped under low-hanging branches, scooted past rough bushes, and jumped over piled rocks, all to the rhythm of the Dreamscape theme song. The blisters along my hands and shins receded, and I found myself smiling more often than not, even humming along with the theme. It was like any other walk, except with the same song stuck on repeat. A little annoying, but it reminded me where I was. I needed that reminder in a forest like this, where increasing wonder made me forget the danger.

Shadows no longer swirled around me. Instead, the further into the forest I hiked, the more light shone down. Steady streams of sunshine followed me like a spotlight as I climbed around the larger branches. The spindly trees thickened, and the trunks twisted around each other, building wider bases until the trees blended into one another. Moss grew between the seams of the trees, creating a wall of soft, green velvet.

Roots crept across the dirt, tripping me. I slid over the smooth bark as I ran and jumped from tree to tree. The branches extended out like fingers, some draping the ground while others led into the canopy. And then I squinted, studying the trees. I squealed, sending a flush of birds off the lowest branch.

I recognized the first set of choices from the game. Maybe being here wouldn't be so different after all, especially if the challenges I faced matched up to the specifics of each level. If I could maneuver through the maze of branches, avoid the legions of puff birds, horned rabbits, and armed jugglers, and make it to the marketplace, I could put this level behind me. It sounded ridiculous, but doable. In fact, the longer I thought about it, the more certain I became. I could do this. I knew the secrets, the shortcuts, and the tools I needed. I could win!

I jumped on top of a branch and scampered higher. The bark scratched my feet. They itched to climb. A new sense of lightness settled on me the higher I went. Shrugging off the invisible weights holding me back, I pressed forward farther than I should have.

Thin and smooth, most branches fit perfectly in my clasped hands. I tested my weight, swinging lightly forward and back until enough momentum flipped me over. My confidence grew as each swing synchronized with the theme song's underlying rhythm. For the moment, I let it all go and spun around again. The contradiction of finding freedom by losing control felt right.

The branches swayed, bending with my weight. I jumped from one branch to the next, and then the next, disappearing between them as I swung.

I grinned. Maybe there were worse things than being stuck in a video game. This could be fun.

I stopped, but the world kept spinning. Leaning against the main trunk, I closed my eyes in contentment, waiting for my balance to stabilize. When I re-opened them, birds sang to me, and the breeze brushed short wisps of bangs off my forehead. Within the sparse branches, tiny forest animals played peek-a-boo. Small yellow flowers grew off patches of moss. I pinched off a bloom and brought it close. The sweet smell of honey tickled me. Apparently this world held treasures I wasn't aware of. I tucked it behind my ear.

I sought out other treasures hidden within the web of green stems, hoping for another glimpse of the delicate yellow flowers, but didn't find any. The branches thinned as I climbed higher, and the bark peeled at my touch. I had gone up too far. I climbed back down to the branches that were thick enough to walk on, and something glittery caught my eye.

As I leaned forward and looked closer, I saw it. A sparkling object hid under a mess of crisscrossed branches. I grabbed onto the limb above me for balance and swung out, kicking the stray branches away. They snapped back into their natural position, revealing a hidden box. I almost let go of the branch in my excitement. I knew what was in that box.

I balanced across the thinner branches, holding my breath as they dipped beneath my weight. Doubts crept into my mind. Greed had never overshadowed my rationality before—I didn't understand why I was letting it do so here. Yet that treasure with its glittering markings called out, and I had to have it. I jumped.

"Yes!" I grabbed hold of the box, grateful that, at the last minute, I decided against striking it with my head like in the game.

The strength of the vines held for a moment, and then they cracked. I clutched the box to my chest and closed my eyes as I fell. A pile of decomposing leaves and chunks of moss caught me. I opened my eyes slowly. The small thrill that I was still in the game surprised me, then magnified when I saw the wooden box in my hands.

Brushing off the damp leaves, I examined the box. A dark red stain outlined the golden spirals around the edges, softening its crude appearance. It reminded me of my first paintings made at recess with fallen fruit from the olive trees. This was much better, designed with a purpose. When I flipped it over, any similarities I saw to my own art disappeared. Masterfully executed leaves, flowers, and bursts of fireworks covered the wood. Only an artist could create something of this quality, but why hide it deep in the forest? It didn't make sense. Something this beautiful needed to be shared and admired.

I flipped it back over and unwound the trailing vine from the wooden knob. The box opened, and coins trickled into my palm. The money jingled in a pile, threatening to fall out of my hand. I awkwardly spread my fingers to keep the coins from slipping through, but there were too many. Pieces slipped through the gaps between my fingers. This much gold could only mean one thing—I was rich!

With this much money, I could buy everything I needed to make it through this game with ease. My mind raced over my options. The coins collided in my hand, and my smile grew wider with each jingle. All I needed now was to find a marketplace and I would be set.

Marketplaces had everything—weapons, clothes, food, maybe even a shortcut home. My stomach grumbled at the thought of food.

I hadn't stopped running or climbing for long enough since getting here to really feel anything but fear and exhaustion. Adrenaline had quieted all my feelings except the obvious bursts of pain from the burns and scratches. That made sense to me, but for some reason, the grips of hunger twisting my mid-section were unexpected. Hunger threw in an unnerving level of reality. Pain was normal in dreams, but hunger? Hunger was something from real life. Accepting that was harder.

Luckily I knew where the main marketplaces were, and as soon as I left the dark forest, I could fill that void. I balanced a gold piece atop my forefinger and flicked it up with my thumbnail. The gold glinted in the sunlight. It felt good to be in control of my destiny.

I loaded the coins into the wooden box and stared at the carvings once more. The craftsmanship astonished me. It seemed elaborate for something as simple as a money box, and leaving it in the forest didn't seem right. Beauty like this needed to be appreciated.

I tied the vine from the clasp around my wrist as a makeshift purse. The weight pulled my arm down, but I didn't mind. The substantiality of it lightened my spirits. The more reality I could grab ahold of, the better.

But the clasp didn't hold, and before I had taken three steps, most of the gold coins had fallen to the ground, rushing out in a steady stream before quieting in the soft dirt. My heart sunk as I watched my wealth disappear.

"Crap," I said. In my mind, I had already spent those coins. I spared a moment to look around before dropping to my knees. Sharp rocks cut me from beneath the layer of dirt. Without the sun shining on them, the corroded gold blended in to the soil, making my search twice as difficult.

My frantic shuffling of leaves hid the sound of breaking branches until a burst of laughter rang out. I froze for a second, then snatched a single coin and the closest stick before running to hide behind a tree. Its bark scraped me as I folded into the tight grooves of the trunk. My quick reaction did little to minimize my vulnerability. If they looked in my direction, my white shirt flashed in the darkness like a flag.

The people grew louder. How could I have missed them? I pursed my lips and dug my nails into the tree, hoping to get a glimpse of them. There were only so many characters in this game, and I couldn't think of any I wanted to meet weaponless in the dark forest. I bit my lower lip.

Judging by their voices and heavy footsteps, I counted two men. They sauntered along the trail, oblivious to me or any of the forest creatures as they trampled over bushes, stomping a flurry of puff birds and horned rabbits underfoot. They didn't hesitate at the screams of the animals or at the crunch of bones beneath their boots.

As they passed in front of the tree where I hid, I heard a soft jingling. I lost my inner battle to refrain from looking. Surely nothing that jingled could be that bad. Peeking around the trunk, I saw them and inhaled sharply.

Two cloaked men passed by with their faces hidden in the shadows of their hoods. Swinging from their hips, a collection of weapons flashed as they marched in unison. Axes, knives, and pipes hung from the rope belts around their waists. That's where the similarities between them ended. The dark, woven cloak devoured the taller man, excess fabric twisting around his exposed calves. The second man's stocky frame filled the breadth of the fabric but hung low, dragging behind his feet. He paraded forward with his hands on his hips, exposing a multi-colored suit and exaggerated collar. I exhaled as all the pieces of their costumes came together in my mind. Armored jugglers.

"Hold up," the shorter man said, grabbing his friend's dark sleeve. "Someone's back there."

"You couldn't have heard anything," the tall man said in a wiry voice, reading my mind. I had barely moved.

"My ears," the first man said, pushing back his hood. His shaved head and rigid face contradicted the jovial outfit he wore. A scowl pressed his eyebrows together, highlighting the dark circles beneath his eyes. On his right ear, a mechanical wheel rotated. He turned in my direction, and I bolted behind the tree, pressing back into the grooves.

"There! Someone's hiding."

I couldn't see his arm, but I assumed it pointed at me. Suddenly, the axes and knives hanging from their belts seemed very sharp.

The knots in my stomach tightened, pulled taut at the ominously slow jingle and shuffling bushes that revealed the men were drawing closer. And I'd been afraid of poisonous flowers and pecking birds. My chest burned with terror. I closed my eyes. The crunching of leaves and thumping of my heart deafened me. Puff birds scurried by on the path.

"Are you sure, Deakon?" the tall man asked in the same wiry voice. "We don't have much time to waste here."

"If I'm right, it won't be a waste of time. You know we can't risk any more spies," he said. He was on the other side of my tree.

"Hurry with it, then. I don't want to be late again." His words matched the pace of my heart. "The trip north to Berkin took longer than you thought."

"Yes, but it was worth it. Just think if we hadn't gone. We'd never know… we'd never've seen…"

"Maybe that wouldn't have been such a bad thing."

"Hush, Pipes. You know that's not true. No matter what, we needed to get the word out. You know this is serious now. Without King Helio…"

"You're right. You always are. I don't want to talk about it anymore. It just brings back that awful memory. I hope to never see something like that again. Hurry with this so we can be on our way."

"It shouldn't take long," he said, and then his gruff laugh assaulted me from behind. His breath warmed my neck, sending chills down my spine. "They're not all that skilled at hiding." Deakon pulled me out from behind the tree and threw me to the ground.

CHAPTER FIVE

I cried out as my knees struck the gravel and my palms ripped open. Red drops appeared on the ground, and I bit back my tears. This wasn't in the game. All my previous worries about getting hurt or being found disappeared as my survival instincts kicked in. I needed to get out of there.

"Who's that?" the taller man squeaked.

I crawled away while the shorter man answered. "She's our spy. Who knows how long she's been following us or what she's heard. You're not getting away that easily." He lunged forward and yanked my legs back. Fresh wounds tore open next to the dragon weed blisters along my shins. I screamed and kicked, twisting out of his grasp.

He silenced my yelp by curling a rough hand around my face, covering my mouth with sweat and dirt. The other hand pressed me down. Rocks dug into my thighs. I shrunk under his strength.

"I swear, I'm not a spy," I pleaded in a muffled voice, gagging between short breaths of air. My eyes shifted from the weapons swinging at his hip to the rotten teeth poking out from beneath his sneer. "I haven't heard a word, I promise. Just let me go. You have the wrong person!" I struggled to break free.

"Deakon!" the taller man yelled, his voice suddenly strong as he lifted a shaking hand to cover his mouth. "Let her go."

"Are you crazy? We can't let a spy go, even if she's a girl. She's dangerous, and besides, the cause can use the money, you know that."

"Deakon, look at her. Her hair…" His voice trailed off and his eyes widened.

My hair? I lifted a hand to it out of reflex, wincing as it stuck in a tangled heap. I pulled a branch out and looked at the tall man again. Surely my hair wasn't messed up enough to scare him. I'd take it though. Any excuse to escape.

Deakon shook his head and leaned closer. "I don't know what you're talking about."

"Pull out your glass," Pipes said. "Now! What have you done?"

The exchange between them startled me. Pipes obviously knew something the other guy didn't. I just didn't know what it had to do with me, or how I could use it to my advantage.

The shorter man fumbled with his pocket and pulled out a large sphere of glass. With one hand still pressing me down, he used the other to lift it to his eyes.

"In the queen's name, it can't be!" he said, dropping the glass. The pressure on my shoulders released, and I fell back to the ground, staring at the men. What just happened?

"Please forgive me," Deakon said, dropping to his knees, pressing his forehead to the dirt.

I shuffled back and my heart slowed. "Forgive you?" I repeated, watching him grovel on the ground.

"We didn't know it was you," the taller man said, pressing his hood back and bowing at the waist.

"Good grief man, show some respect," Deakon said, knocking out the back of the taller man's knees. "She's not royalty, she's...she's..." Every time his eyes darted to me, they sped back towards the ground.

His friend fell with a grunt and shook his head, regaining composure before he looked at me and joined his friend with his forehead to the ground. "I meant no disrespect, my lady. We just didn't expect—"

"Didn't expect what?" I asked, afraid of their response. Who or what did they think I was? I ran through the list of characters in my mind, holding my breath. Was I the princess, a rogue, another juggler—

"The Golden Hero."

An image of the game's opening sequence popped into my mind, a little green man shooting an arrow. The Golden Hero, of course. Why would I think I could go through this world unnoticed?

"Of course. Yes, I'm here," I said, pulling my shirt straight and brushing away the dust while I tried to settle my mind. "Please, there's no need for that." I pointed to their prolonged bowing and then flipped my hand over, gesturing for help up. If they thought I was the Golden Hero, I was going to work it to my advantage.

The taller man scrambled to his feet and helped me up. "My lady." He bowed again.

"Thank you…" I stalled and raised an eyebrow in question.

"Pipes, my lady. My name's Pipes, and this here is Deakon. And we're humbly at your service." As a quieter aside to his friend, he said, "Can you believe it? She's here. She's really here. Do you know what this means?" His eyes lit up.

Deakon turned to his friend and opened his mouth to speak.

"What does this mean?" I interrupted their private conversation.

"Nothing," Deakon answered softly.

"Nothing?" Pipes cried, his excitement overflowing. "Deakon, this means everything! Everything we saw done is no longer a waste. King Helio's death can be avenged, and Queen Elin can be saved! The rebellion has a chance."

I smiled in reassurance, desperately trying to figure out what he meant. For playing this game my whole life, I felt like this was my first time. Nothing made sense. None of these names were familiar, but Queen Elin had to be the pink princess the hero always saved.

"There's a chance now, right, my lady?" Pipes asked again. The hope in his eyes was palpable. My heart raced again. Smashing his hopes would be almost as bad as trampling the bird.

"Yes," I mumbled, avoiding his eyes. "Of course there's a chance now. That's why I'm here." I brushed the last bits of dust off my shirt and unhooked the box from my wrist. Indentations marked my

- Dreamscape: Saving Alex -

forearm where the corner had hit me during my fall.

Pipes inhaled sharply. "That...you...box..." he stammered, pointing to the broken box in my hand.

"This?" I asked, walking closer to him. "What do you know about these boxes?"

"That the prophecy is true," he whispered, biting down on a fist. Deakon dropped to his knees and pressed his forehead to the ground again.

I rolled my eyes. This was going to take more finesse than I'd thought. I had to change directions. "Deakon?" I asked sweetly. "Do you think I can borrow your glass?"

"Of course, my lady, whatever I can do to help." He fumbled around the ground in front of him where it had dropped and handed it to me.

"Thank you, my friends. You surprised me, and I dropped most of the coins from the box. Do you think you could help me find them? I will of course pay you for your efforts. I think that'll help the cause, right?" I asked innocently.

Deakon scratched his forehead. "We can't take that money, my lady. We need to make sure it gets to where it's needed."

"W-well, of course I'll get the money where it's needed. I just thought you might need some as well," I stammered.

Deakon stood by my side and held out his hand in offering. "You'll have our help regardless, my lady. We're humbly at your service. Just tell us where to go."

I smiled and pointed to the tree from which he'd grabbed me. "I'm afraid it's not very far, just difficult to see in the dim light and overgrown brush. I appreciate your kindness." I batted my eyes and walked purposefully to the back of the tree.

The sunken impression of my fall marked the soft ground. I stood in front of it, hoping to block their view of my clumsiness. The Golden Hero shouldn't make mistakes.

"Here?" he asked, pointing to the ruffled leaves and debris.

I nodded and knelt by his side. Before long, a third pair of hands helped clear the ground and uncover the dark coins. I heard them whistle as the box filled.

"Thank you," I said, breaking the silence between us. "So, I gather you're on your way somewhere special?"

Deakon blushed and continued shuffling while Pipes took the opportunity to stop searching through the leaves.

"Yes, we're on our way to the new capital for tonight's demonstration," he said, checking to make sure all his weapons and tools were secured on his belt.

"Hmm?"

Pipes took the invitation and continued: "We were called away when we got word of the execution. We barely made it there in time."

"Or out in time," Deakon said.

"Yes, or out in time," he admitted, lowering his head and covering his heart. "Bless the king. I wish he didn't have to go the way he did."

"How was that?" I asked, already knowing I didn't want to hear the answer.

"Berkos," he answered grimly. "He had him killed. Publicly, no less." He hung his head. "It's a travesty."

I looked between the men. I still had no idea who these people were or how this information could help me get home. "Is there anything we can do?" I asked.

Both their heads jerked up as they looked at me, then each other. Deakon responded, "Of course, my lady. That's why we're in such a hurry to get to the capital. We have to spread the word and make our plans. You already have something in mind, no doubt."

I nodded and looked back to the ground. Ideas ran through my mind, but they had nothing to do with these men or their cause, and that unsettled me. "I think we've found all the money we're going to. Thank you," I said, flipping a coin to each of them. Their faces registered a range of extreme emotions until settling on grateful tears.

"My lady, we're forever in your debt," Deakon said, touching the ground with his forehead once more.

"No," I said, laying my hand atop Deakon's. "I am in yours. And I'm afraid I still need your help."

Deakon exhaled and lowered his eyes. "Of course, my lady, whatever you need. It's just—" He pursed his lips and looked back at Pipes.

"Just what?" I asked with an exasperated sigh.

"It's just that we need to get to Lindle before nightfall. We're the entertainment," he said, exposing the bright clothing beneath his cloak proudly.

I smiled at the exaggerated costume, and then glanced at the growing shadows in the forest around us. "You're right. Of course, we'll need to be on our way then."

"We?" Pipes asked.

"Yes. We. I'm coming too. I need to know more, and you need to get to Lindle. It seems we can do both at once. Do you suppose there's a market there?"

They exchanged looks again and burst into laughter. "Oh yes, my lady. Only the most extravagant market you'll ever see. The new capital is full of shops, food, entertainment, and more luxury than you'll find anywhere else in the kingdom."

"Well then, it's settled. We'll go to Lindle, and you can tell me more along the way."

"But my lady, I don't think we should," Pipes said, running his fingers through his hair. "Lindle's not…"

"Not what?"

"It's not…" He hesitated and looked to Deakon for support.

"It's not that we don't want to help, my lady, but the capital may not be what you're expecting," Deakon said.

I looked between the two, wondering what they were leaving out. Danger or not, I needed that marketplace. "I think I know where I need to be," I said, hardening my gaze.

They averted their eyes. Pipes dragged his feet through the pebbles, and Deakon sighed. He looked up and shrugged. "I suppose you know what's best."

"I do know what's best. Thank you."

Pipes held out his hand with a slight bow. "Then we are humbled to be your guides."

With that, I took his hand as he led the way.

Their stories of the world and familiarity with the woods sped the remaining journey. They flushed out the puff birds and trampled the dragon weeds without concern as we marched down the path. By the time Pipes finished his tale, I had more details of King Helio's execution and their trip than I wanted. Worse, after hearing about Queen Elin's extended confinement, I had no doubts about what they wanted me to do as the Golden Hero. They expected me to save the queen. I shouldn't have been surprised; I had played this game for years. But knowing something intuitively and hearing it aloud can be different.

We walked the rest of the way in silence, but inside, my mind screamed. How could I give them what they wanted when it risked my life and my chance at getting home? Besides, I wasn't exactly hero material. I glanced between my companions and bit my upper lip.

Pipes opened his mouth, and the lightest trilling poured out. A trail of birds crowded behind us, streaking above our heads. Blended together, his voice and the birds grew to a symphony. I heard the familiar theme song burst through the hidden notes.

"We're almost there," Pipes said.

I nodded and smiled, hunched over to regain my breath.

The forest ended sooner than I expected. The canopy opened, and the distance between trees grew. Cobblestones formed in the dirt, creating a modest road. The stones curved around the thinning trees until flag posts replaced the trunks. A heavily fortified fortress of wood dominated the landscape, more imposing than the simple market I had expected. I scooted close to Deakon and peeked over his shoulders. Planks of knotted wood alternated in a pattern up the broad face of the building. At the top, a wide pathway guarded with armored men marked the space between the decorated towers.

"Welcome to Lindle," Deakon said. "Everyone, put on your

happy face. It's entertaining time."

My companions removed their cloaks, draping them over their left arms, revealing the bright outfits I had glimpsed earlier. They touched their right hand to their chin, then forehead, and then reached out in a strange salute to the guards.

A guard's gaze drifted over to me, and I froze. A lazy, yet expectant stare met my confusion. My heart choked me. What was I supposed to do? The guard narrowed his gaze and barked an order to another guard at his side. My fingers twitched. I didn't know what move to make next.

Pipes whistled and broke through my hesitation. I heard the beginning of the theme and hastily followed his previous gestures. I held my breath. Had I done it in the right order? It was like punching in the code all over again. Everything depended on the right combination.

The guard hesitated with a long look at me, and then jutted his chin towards the other guards spaced evenly across the tower ledge. The steel gates protested as they separated. A strip of light burst through the narrow opening, blinding me. I blinked away the golden haze and bit the inside of my lip as I waited for my vision to clear. The creak of the chains slowed as the guard pulled it taut. Behind the massive gate and bleak tower, a masterpiece of music, color, and scents awaited.

My mouth dropped. The game had not prepared me for this.

CHAPTER SIX

The guards narrowed their gaze as we passed by. Nothing, not even their clunky helmets, could hide the accusations in their scrutiny. The same initial shock of recognition that I had noticed in Pipes and Deakon now stood on the faces of the guards. But they didn't seem as pleased to see me. I tried to ignore it but couldn't. The hair on the back of my neck stood on edge, and every muscle in me tightened. I wanted to run and hide. I walked, slower than I thought possible, not wanting to give them any more reason to question me.

I held my breath as we walked across the wooden bridge and entered the busy marketplace.

"Good luck," Pipes whispered, brushing past me.

"Huh?" I asked, dumbfounded by my surroundings.

"Good luck," he repeated, leaning closer. "Heed my words: get what you need and get out. Lindle's not a safe place, especially now. Especially for you, even if you know what you're doing," he said. He bowed theatrically and patted Deakon on the shoulder. Their painted smiles didn't erase the concern in their eyes.

Deakon nodded in agreement and gave me a solemn look. "If you need anything, look for help within the trees." He pointed to a small patch that I hadn't noticed before sewn into the cuff of his costume. It was a large oak with a castle at its base, the Dreamscape logo.

"No, you can't leave me," I said, grabbing the sleeve of Pipes' cloak.

They exchanged a glance and then Pipes looked down to where I gripped his sleeve.

"I only mean that I don't know my way around the market yet. I should have an escort," I corrected myself, letting go of his sleeve and pulling my shirt down.

"I suppose we can do that my lady. We need to get ready for our show, but our stage is on the other side of the square. We can show you on our way there."

"Perfect. I'll follow you for now."

Deakon hesitated, glancing around at the crowd.

"I know what I'm doing, remember?" I raised an eyebrow.

Pipes shrugged at Deakon and held out his arm. "My lady, we go this way."

"Why thank you," I said with a smile.

Deakon grunted and sped through the crowd, vanishing into the throngs of merchants along the outer edge.

Pipes pulled me back. "Not quite yet. Let him go ahead. There's no telling what's waiting for us at the stage."

"What aren't you telling me?" I narrowed my gaze.

"Nothing more than you already know. We may have left out a few details, though."

"Like what?" I asked in a whisper, forcing a smile.

"Well, when we heard about King Helio, we left in a hurry. A few of the shopkeepers were upset at that."

"Why?" I asked.

"We do drum up a bit of business for the town with our entertainment. Let's just say, a few were a bit upset when we left unannounced."

"How upset?" I asked.

Pipes adjusted his collar and chuckled. "Their henchmen followed us for a few miles into the woods."

"And then?"

"Well, we are trained with our weapons," he said.

"So, you just—"

"Defended ourselves, my lady. That's all we did. Seems it's all we've been doing lately. I hope you're here to change that."

I swallowed hard. "We can hope. Can we go yet?"

Pipes scoured the courtyard and nodded. "Follow me, but take notice of what you need and where to go. Once we reach the stage, Deakon and I are committed."

A cobblestone pathway wound through the open square in a curved fashion between shops, vendors, and gardens. Rickety old carts and brightly painted wagons were squished together, lining every inch of the route; their owners stood in front, barking out orders. The cacophony of voices excited me. Amidst the laughter and bartering, I sensed a rhythm. Items were traded with speed and merchants' smiles increased in proportion to the gold exchanged. Some things seemed universal.

I shook the wooden box and smiled as the coins clinked together. It was almost time to shop.

Where to begin? Carts overflowed with freshly baked goods, flowers, and fabrics. Strewn petals littered the ground, tossed by quick bursts of air from the opening gates. A flock of puff birds gathered around the base of the bread carts, stealing crumbs while avoiding the stuttered kicks of a merchant who couldn't seem to decide which he wanted to do more: kick the birds or sell his bread.

Dancers twirling saffron scarves weaved in and out of carts, urged on by whistles and cheers. They moved down the pathways, rolling their hips as they wound around the crowd. Some of the busiest carts stood in the shadows of the square. I tried not to image what a disheveled man picking at his teeth with a knife sold, but his cart had a steady line of customers.

I hardly noticed the stares and strangled protests of the people maneuvering around me until the dust from their frantic pace choked me.

"Outta my way, lass," a deep voice commanded.

I jumped in surprise. The commotion had hypnotized me for a moment. I shook out of the trance and mumbled an apology as a burly man clothed in a wool tunic passed by me. A small herd of winged sheep tromped in front of me, kicking up enough dust to hide them in shadows. Unable to catch my breath, I coughed, drawing the attention of the people passing by.

Women dressed in opulent gowns glared at me over their bags of rolls. Children pointed and laughed, stopping mid-bite. Surely my cough wasn't that loud. Why were they all staring?

Then I looked down and saw my torn shirt. My cheeks melted with embarrassment. I hastily pulled it down and slinked into the shadows along the side of the square, behind the rows of carts. I ran to catch up with Pipes, now a dozen steps ahead.

"Care for a trinket? Pretty jewels for a pretty lady," a melodic voice called out. I turned to answer, but he wasn't talking to me. I shrunk deeper into my shirt.

As I walked further along, I listened to snippets of conversation and watched the interactions.

"… But two golden coins is the best I can do," one woman said, batting her eyes and tilting her head to the side, ogling a dragon necklace in her hand.

"Sold. Here you go, my lady," the merchant said, sliding behind her to clasp the jewelry onto her neck.

"Fresh bread!" the baker called out, waving his loaves overhead. My stomach rumbled, but I didn't want to spend my money yet. Not until I knew everything that this market had to offer.

"No. All sales are final," another peddler said, pushing a woman's items away.

From the darkened shadows along the outer edge of the path, I could only see the items placed along the sides of the carts, but that was enough. My eyes grew wide at the sight of decadent chocolates. Baskets of ripened berries flipped my stomach, and my hands twitched with a desire to hold the soft fabrics and scarves draped and billowing in the wind.

Not every cart held the extravagance I had expected. Hidden between the opulence, older carts sold smaller trinkets. Worn leather books propped up the broken leg of one cart, while small flies swarmed over boxes of overripe fruit. I stepped up onto my tiptoes to peek at a nearby wagon.

"Sssomething yous like over there, my dear?" a voice rasped from behind me.

I jumped and whirled around, hiding my startled gasp. "What?" I asked, trying not to stare at the grungy man leering at the hole in my shirt. The setting sun glinted off the edge of his knife's blade as he rolled it over his cheek. Dirt smudged his forehead, and crumbs stuck in his matted beard. When he smiled, my stomach turned. His rotten teeth and rancid breath were nothing compared to the twisted gleam in his eyes.

"I's can get yous anything yous wisssh, my dear. Yous name it," he offered, taking one step closer.

I tightened my grip on the wooden box behind my body and stepped closer to the crowd. "I don't have any money, sir," I whispered.

He wiped the blade along his tattered shirt and slowly lowered his gaze. When he met my eyes again, his smile sent a shiver down my spine. "Paymentsss are negotiable."

I turned and ran into the crowd, knocking over a display of Lindle souvenirs and banners.

"Watch it!" a woman grumbled as she hastily grabbed her items.

"Sorry," I said, stumbling forward, anxious to get out of their sight. It seemed every move only made me stand out more. Pipes' words came back to mind. This place wasn't safe. I shuddered and ran my hands down my arms. I hadn't thought about any non-game dangers.

My heart jumped when I caught a glimpse of neon fabric mixed in with the crowd. How had I let him get so far ahead? Ignoring the jeers and stares, I hurried forward, only briefly glancing at the carts and dancing girls.

This city seemed to accept the darker exploits with ease. I bit my inner lip and continued trailing my new friend. I couldn't see any more flashes of the bright costume he wore. My heart sank. In this crowd, how could I hope to find a single person?

Through the noise of the crowd, I heard a single bird chirp. Then another joined in, followed by a soft whisper.

"Where'd you go my lady?"

"Pipes," I cried, grabbing his forearms. "I'm so glad it's you. Some of these people..." I didn't finish the thought.

He looked down at me with concern. "Are you all right, my lady?"

"Yes," I answered sheepishly, suddenly remembering who he thought I was. Straightening my back, I pulled my hands away and forced a smile. "Yes, I was just surprised by the size of the market. I wasn't expecting all of that."

"Of course. It takes a moment to absorb everything here."

I nodded. He had no idea.

"We're almost there. The stage is just around the corner. Hopefully Deakon's not made a mess of all our stuff. He does that sometimes, you know." Pipes winked at me.

"I can't wait to see it all," I said, reaching for his hand. I didn't want to lose him in the crowd again.

The far edge of the square was quiet. Wooden benches lined the wall, curving around small pockets of trees and flowers. Pipes pulled me forward before I could comment on anything.

"Wow," I whispered, turning the corner and seeing the stage.

Pipes beamed and ran ahead. "Let me present to you our humble arena." He bowed and covered his chest with one hand.

Wooden planks and iron benches lined a semi-circle around a lopsided stage. Rotten beams leaned against the distressed posts. When I looked up, a tangled maze of beams and pipes held the structure in place. A crumpled sheet of velvet crowned the top. The older man struggled across the theater with an armload of banners and poles.

"This is... big," I said, searching for the right word. "It's no wonder the vendors were upset when you left." I rushed ahead and grabbed a handful of metal pipes from Deakon.

"This is nothing, my lady. You should've seen it before we left. Signs, ribbons, torches, we had it all. Now, this is all that remains." Deakon sighed, dropping his armful of banners by the scaffolding near the front of the stage.

"All that remains?" I asked.

"I've already cleaned up a bunch." He grunted and nodded towards a corner overflowing with shredded debris. "I'd say they weren't too happy with us."

"Then tonight we must put on an even better show," Pipes said. He grabbed the edge of a banner by Deakon's feet and stretched it between his arms. "We'll have this stage back in shape in no time."

I admired Pipes' enthusiasm. "Let me help," I said, reaching for the other end of the banner.

"No, no, no," Pipes argued, shaking his head. "You've already done too much to help us. You must be on your way. You've seen the market. Get your goods and go. Before anything happens."

"No, I insist. I'm not going anywhere until I help you set up for tonight. After all, you were delayed because of me." I grabbed another banner from the stage floor and held it out, reading the scrolled letters. *Juggling for the Cause.* "Is it safe, announcing your support like this? I mean, you just said that this town is full of Berkos' men."

"If subtlety worked here, my lady, we'd go that route, but it seems to be an excuse to ignore us and our message."

Pipes stopped hammering and leaned over the rickety scaffolding. "We won't be ignored any longer. The rebellion needs more support, and this is one of the only ways we can recruit for it."

Deakon grabbed the other end of the sign. "I'll take that, my lady."

He climbed along the rickety scaffolding that held the upper portion of the stage together and hammered one edge of the sign into the rotten planks.

A loud bang came from above, followed by a clattering of metal. Deakon stopped hammering and dove into me, pushing me off the stage.

When I recovered, I swore and massaged the spot where my hip had hit the ground.

"Deakon!" Pipes exclaimed, jumping onto the stage, waving through the dust.

I clambered up, brushing off the dirt as I limped to the stage. Where I had just stood was now a pile of metal beams and wooden supports.

"Oh no! Is he…" I let the question linger.

Pipes turned around with a tight smile. "No, he's going to be fine. Just a small cut on the head. He'll be better in no time."

Deakon sat up and picked splinters out of his hands. A trail of blood slid from his forehead down his cheek, and red blotches stained his face and arms where the beams from the stage had struck him.

"Are you sure?" I asked. He didn't look fine to me. I climbed onto the stage and walked closer, glancing at the beams wavering above us.

"Yeah, I'll be fine. It's not like this is the first time some stuff's fallen down."

"Deakon, how can you say that?" How could he act like this wasn't a big deal? "This is more than just some stuff falling. Y-you sa-saved me," I stammered, falling to my knees at his side.

"Don't give him too much credit," Pipes laughed. "He probably just knocked you out of the way on accident."

I knew it was more than that. I was lucky. And Deakon was lucky. Sharp metal edges poked out of the beams at all angles. If he had fallen even a foot further to the side, this accident could've been fatal. I was about to say that when Pipes gave a low whistle.

"This wasn't an accident, though. This was sabotage. The planks were sheered," he said, holding out one of the fallen pieces of wood in disgust. The clean lines of a saw were visible on its edge. "This is just more proof you need to leave."

"Why would someone do this?"

Deakon rolled his head forward and rested it in his palms. "It's simple. You know who we are, or at least who we're loyal to. So do they. They want to stop us."

"They who? And why stop a simple performance?" I asked, dusting off Deakon's cloak and placing it over his shoulders.

Deakon rolled his neck side to side. "You know who I'm talking about. The traitors. The ones who switched sides without a thought. The ones who think money is more important than integrity or loyalty. You'll see them around the capital, wearing Berkos' dragon with honor."

"Berkos' dragon?" I asked.

Deakon raised an eyebrow. "For being our hero, you sure seem to have a lot of questions."

I tucked my lips together and stayed quiet. He was right. I'd done a poor job of hiding it.

He shook his head sadly. "When Berkos took control, he drove most of King Helio's supporters away from town. Berkos' castle is only a day or two north of the city, so he naturally changed the capital from Flourin to here. His followers run this town and wear the dragon in support. If you see one, watch your back. Dragons strike with more than just fire."

"But why stop you? You're just performers."

"Just performers," Deakon laughed. "That's like saying you're just a traveler. We're all more than what we pretend to be."

I blushed, but Deakon didn't notice. "These shows, they're in support of the queen and the rebellion. Whatever money we earn goes straight to the cause. The capital tolerates it because they get money too. But I'm doubting their level of tolerance now." He reached back and shook his head, examining one of the boards. "It's time you left. Before it gets too dangerous here."

I swallowed, glancing behind me. A few heads peeked from behind the buildings. Pipes and Deakon were right. This town wasn't safe. The longer I stayed, the more I endangered myself, them, and their cause.

Pipes reached out and squeezed my arm. "We all play a part for the cause. Ours is here. It's time you found yours."

I nodded and felt my insides harden like lead. As their hero, I shouldn't have to be reminded or directed. Why couldn't I control my destiny in a video game?

"You're right," I said with a sigh. "I just need to find some new clothes first."

Deakon handed me his cloak and pointed behind me. "Go to Auntie Quinn's. She's the best tailor in town."

"She's the only tailor in town now," Pipes said with a frown.

Deakon shrugged and adjusted the mechanics on the spinning wheel at his ear. "Best, only... same difference. She'll have all the supplies you need to get started. Just don't forget our warning."

"Thank you," I said, turning away as they started to move planks and beams out of the way. Even with the danger, they would not stop.

But neither would I.

CHAPTER SEVEN

Heaviness pulled me down as I drifted back into the square, seeking supplies. It was more than the extra weight of Deakon's cloak. The longer I stayed here, the more threats seemed to pop up—dangers, evil kings, traitors, and now sabotage.

Surviving high school was tough enough for me, and they expected me to save their kingdom. I wasn't cut out for that. Insecurities rattled around in my mind, but I knew they were insignificant. Social awkwardness wasn't oppression. An evil king trying to kill citizens and sabotage a rebellion…the enormity of what I had gotten involved in struck me. And the most dangerous thought of all was the ease with which Pipes and Deakon placed their blind trust in me. What did they see that I didn't? I needed to find a way home, and quick. I wasn't a hero, and I didn't want to be.

A wave of people blocked my path. I moved in the shadows, pressed against the stone walls as I peeked into every store window. The capital seemed to have everything it needed, yet Auntie Quinn's clothing store eluded me.

I pulled the cloak tighter around my neck and crossed the main road. It was better than the torn nightshirt I had been wearing but was still not enough to keep me from notice. The thick fabric created a trail as it dragged on the ground behind me, and its bulky size generated the impression that I was playing dress-up.

If only this were a simple game of my imagination that I could leave at any point.

I wasn't sure what it was yet. I had spent almost a whole day here, and yet I was no closer to any answers about how to get home or where to go from here.

"It's her," a soft voice whispered from behind me.

"What?" I asked, turning around. Dust swirled up from the ground, blocking my sight.

"See? I told you!" A child snickered.

"Who's there?" I asked, shielding my eyes from the sandy onslaught.

"No, it can't be."

"It is, just look."

"Ouch," I cried, covering my arm where a rock hit me. The hood of the cloak slipped back, revealing my face and hair. A group of young boys ran off into the crowd, laughing. I fought my growing anger and raised the hood again to simmer in the shadows.

"I promise, Ma. Look," a young girl cried, pulling down on the skirt of her mother's dress with one hand while pointing at me with the other.

"Hush child. She can't be, that's just a fairytale," the mother said, pulling the girl forward.

"No, it's her, I swear it. Look."

I rolled my eyes. No more. I turned away from the street, determined to reach the other side of the square and its shops. As I walked forward, my cloak stiffened and then slid off my back, revealing my torn shirt again. I spun and stared at the girl, no older than seven, holding on to her mother's dress. Wide eyes stared at me from beneath a mop of red hair as she guiltily stepped off the edge of the cloak.

"See, see, see? I told ya!" she said, pointing at me. The older women scowled and pursed her lips before grabbing her hand and yanking her away.

"Stop her," another voice called out.

I had no clue if they were talking about me or the other woman, and I didn't want to find out. I ducked behind the nearest cart and threw open the door to the first shop I saw. Leaning against the back of the door, I heaved a sigh of relief. When I opened my eyes, the shop owner was staring at me, one hand draped across her chest, her face pale.

She stood in the back corner of the shop, half-hidden by shadows cast from piles of fabric. I must have interrupted her mid-hem. She struggled to remove her hand from a red and gray tunic.

A flicker of embarrassment at my appearance hit me. Her open-mouthed stare only added to my discomfort.

Well, at least I had found the right kind of shop.

"I'm sorry. I didn't mean to startle you," I said, smoothing out the front of my shirt. "I'm glad I finally found you."

The old woman raised an eyebrow and plucked the needle from her lips. "Is there something I can help you with?"

"Um, yeah. I need some clothes," I said, readjusting my shirt. The wooden box shook in my hands.

The woman smiled at the jingling of the coins and composed herself. She lowered her hand and secured the needle in the tunic before giving me a warm smile. "Then you've come to the right shop. What can I help you find today?"

Her welcoming words stopped the moment she cleared the back counter and stepped into the light, taking a closer look at me.

"Good grief. Have you gone mad? You're walking around in nothing but that undergarment?" Then her mouth dropped and she rushed to my side. "Oh my dear, what have they done to you?" She tsked and held up my arms, examining the bruises I had forgotten. Thankfully the blisters had gone back to normal. Besides the few fading bumps and bruises, I thought I'd fared pretty well for my first time traveling through the dark forest.

"Oh no, no one's hurt me," I said, avoiding her stare and pulling the hem of my shirt down.

She furrowed her brows. "There's no need to be ashamed. It happens more than we like to admit these days. Don't worry one bit. Auntie Quinn will take care of you."

Finally something seemed to be going in my favor.

She reached out towards me and waited. I stared at her outstretched hand to find each fingertip sparkling with a thimble. She frowned as she appraised me once more. Then with a loud sigh, she wiggled her fingers. "Take my hand, dear. We haven't all day to get you presentable."

"What do you mean?"

"Well, I'm a tailor, not a magician." No matter how sweetly she said it, the words stung. Just how bad did I look?

I hesitated, then put my hand in hers. The floorboards creaked as she led me to an overstuffed chair situated beneath the largest window. The tight black leather belied its comfort, and as soon as I sat down, it swallowed me. I stifled my laugh, fighting my way to the edge of the seat.

Auntie Quinn smiled. I suspected she had done the same thing. "The chair's a hit with the children, and the older gentlemen too. Not that there's much of a difference between them, really." She winked. "Just relax. First things first, let me see if I have the right oils to fix you up."

I smiled back at her. "Thank you, Auntie Quinn. I appreciate it."

"It's nothing, my dear. Just sit back and relax. I'll be back soon, and we can talk about what you need." She handed me a booklet of yellow parchment and pointed to extras on the table beside me.

Her generosity surprised me. Deakon had told me to find her, but I didn't expect such immediate concern. So far this world had done nothing but throw challenges and danger my way. This break was long overdue.

I glanced down at the papers she had handed me. The stiff parchment popped as I turned each page. Across the top, in fancy calligraphy, were the words *Lockhorn News*. Lockhorn? Where was that? I scanned the first few headlines, but nothing made much sense. I was about to ask about it, but when I looked up, I saw Auntie Quinn gesturing out the window.

When I looked at her profile, the softness I'd seen at first disappeared. I readjusted my body in the chair and looked at her more closely. When she clenched her jaw, a set of tense lines appeared around her eyes and down her neck. Pointed crochet sticks pinned her hair in a severe bun on top of her head. A few stray strands had fallen from the bun, streaking her face in silver. Unease stirred my insides. Something didn't feel right.

When she looked back at me, she gave me a warm smile, but the edges were forced. I recognized that expression. My mom was a pro at forced politeness.

"Be right back, my dear," she said, retreating into the back storeroom.

I watched her disappear and shook off the unease. She hadn't done anything but show me kindness. I had to stop projecting my feelings onto other people. She just reminded me of my mom; that was all.

I leaned back, letting the soft luxury of the fabric surround me. I sighed, falling further into the chair. It had been too long since I had let anyone take care of me. Here, I didn't have to apologize or admit anything. I could just accept the no-strings-attached hospitality.

But did it really come without strings?

I needed a plan before it was too late, and the simple thought of playing through the game didn't seem sufficient.

A jingle alarmed me, and my eyes shot open. I turned to the door, but relaxed when I saw that it was still closed. Auntie Quinn returned from the dark storeroom with a tray of glass canisters and steaming cups. The glass jingled as she inched around the counters and tables, careful to avoid spilling the liquid.

When the dimming sunlight hit the cups, small bursts of light reflected over the room, especially on the golden embroidery of her apron. An oversized "A" was sewn into the upper edge, and when I looked more closely, the image of a dragon lurked behind it.

I swallowed hard. I wasn't out of danger yet. I shuffled to the edge of the seat and rolled the packet of papers together to keep my hands busy. I couldn't let her see my fear.

She lowered the tray to the table and handed me a cup of tea.

Green liquid seeped over the edge as her hands trembled. She began dressing my wounds while I regarded the tea with skepticism.

"Thank you," I murmured, tucking the papers by my side and pressing the cup to my lips. A sour scent warned me, and I only pretended to drink the steaming liquid. "Mmmm. You do seem to know how to make a person feel better."

"It's nothing, my dear. I'm an old woman. Some things you learn over time, and some things you just know. A hot cup of tea cures most ailments, especially the ones that don't break the surface."

"Hmmm," I said, staring out the windows. She pressed a lavender-soaked cloth against my arm. I stiffened at the intense burn I felt.

"It has to hurt to heal, you know," she said briskly.

I nodded. The sting eased as the soothing aroma of lavender filled the room. Through the dusty windows, I heard the commotion of the courtyard. Above the wagons, golden banners swayed, and rings of smoke rose from the butchers' carts. Shadows danced along the bricks below the watchful eyes of the guards. A shiver ran down my spine.

The harder I looked, the more the facade seemed to dim. Between the golden banners, worn ridges and dilapidated bricks threatened to fall from the walls. I smiled, recognizing the technique. I had a few posters hung strategically in my room as well. When the damage wasn't visible, it was easy to ignore. I just didn't understand why, here of all places, the walls would be broken.

"Is it always so busy out there?" I asked.

"Oh yes, especially this time of year."

I smiled, forgetting my earlier unease. "Summer's a great time to celebrate."

She stopped for a moment and re-dressed my arm. "It's not quite summer yet, my dear. This spectacle is for the rebels and their pitiful refusal to accept the inevitable. They'll be parading around like fools all month."

I jumped up and walked to the window, holding the rag in place.

I watched the women twirl, coins glittering at their hips, and thought back to the deliberate destruction of Deakon and Pipes' stage. The hand that held the cooling rag to my arm slipped.

"The rebels?" I whispered. "Whose side are they on?"

"You must've hit your head in that forest," she said, chuckling, waving me back to the chair. "The rebels are against King Berkos, of course. Some of these peasants still hold out for the past. They're convinced the queen will be freed. But I know better. I hope you do too." She began mixing a bowl of crushed apples and colored oils. "I won't deny things were different under King Helio and Queen Elin, but times have changed. Like my papa always said, you can either jump on the cart or get trampled under its wheels. No, when they let King Berkos in, they should have known what was coming. The signs were there. Had been for years."

She reached for her vials and mixed the blue and green oils with something smelling of vinegar. The mixture dripped off her fingers. "You can't blame someone for acting the only way he knows. I never blamed King Berkos for taking over. You don't turn your back on a snake. No, my dear, he's been good to his supporters, provided safety and trade opportunities. I won't turn my nose up at that, and certainly not my back on him. Everything has to change at some point, even the good." She waved her hand towards the celebration out the window. "All of that's foolish. You can't eat dreams."

"Why do they do celebrate, then?"

"In remembrance of the queen, so they say. But some things are better left forgotten, or unspoken. Now, let me work on your hair," she said. "It's not right, someone as young and beautiful as you walking around like this. What does your mother think?"

I shrugged. Auntie Quinn covered her mouth. "Oh no," she said. "She's not—"

"No, no, nothing like that. We just haven't been talking lately."

"Well, perhaps if you talked more, you wouldn't be dressed like this in public."

"Ouch," I protested as she rubbed the dirt and dust from my

head.

"Sorry dear, there's quite a few branches tangled here. This mixture will strip the mud. Just a moment more. Now, where did you say they assaulted you?" The steadiness left her hands when she yanked out the branches. The longer she worked on my hair, the more strained her demeanor became.

"I wasn't assaulted," I replied cautiously. "I was just lost in the woods."

"The dark woods, you say? That's a dangerous place for a girl to be out wandering. Don't you think?" It was rhetorical and accusatory at the same time. "I'd take better care about where you go and who you meet."

"Thanks for your concern, but I made it through fine," I said, pulling a leaf out of my hair and brushing her hands away. "I'm better now. Thank you." I stood, confused at the stifled anger in her voice. No longer comfortable with my back to her, I turned to face her. "I must be going. Can you help me with new clothes?"

"Will you pay for them, or should I just hand them over?" Her voice was too sweet, the saccharine that dripped accusations. Whatever kindness she had shown had disappeared.

"Of course," I said, fumbling for the wooden box and dropping the money on the counter. "I don't expect charity."

Her eyes widened, and she slid the gold into a pouch in her apron as if it would disappear. "Right over here," she said, glancing behind me out the window before leading me to the corner filled with gowns.

"Thank you," I murmured, already losing myself in the soft velvets. I didn't notice her leave, but heard the clinking at the counter as she counted her gold.

I caressed the rich fabrics, appreciating the embroidery along the bodices. Auntie Quinn, no matter what I thought about her, certainly had a talent for tailoring and draping. Getting lost in the fabric was easy. The smooth finishes of the dresses brushed against me, and I wanted to throw one on. My fingers lingered before I lowered my hand and let go of that thought. I didn't have a ball to go to anymore. In fact, even as I shopped, draping the lavish gowns over my arms and watching my reflection change, I knew this wouldn't work.

I scanned the rest of the room, reluctantly leaving opulence for practicality. Unless I found a quicker way home, I knew what journey lay ahead. Auntie Quinn's eyes narrowed in on me.

I hurried around the store, looking at every table. The shop was bigger than I had thought. Tables wound around the room, creating niches and corners for clothes and accessories. Auntie Quinn sold it all, from men's tunics and hose to traveling attire, peasant smocks, work aprons, and gorgeous gowns. When my eyes tired of fabric, they found sparkling jewels, bags, and hats. I grabbed a leather travel bag from the edge of a table and continued my search.

At last, I found it. In the back corner, partially hidden beneath the wool coats, the costume came together. Something in my mind clicked, and as I grabbed the green cloth, I knew my fate had been sealed.

The leggings fit snugly, and when I tucked my white shirt beneath the dark green tunic and looked at my reflection, my lingering doubts subsided. The costume was a literal translation. I looked like the hero. I finished the look with a pair of leather boots and stuffed a woolen cloak, pointy hat, the papers, and my empty money box into the travel bag.

The bells above the door jingled, and I felt a burst of air. Auntie Quinn stood in the shadows, clutching the gold to her chest. She nodded at the men blocking the door and then looked at me.

"Auntie Quinn?" I asked, watching my only escape disappear behind a pair of towering guards.

"Nothing personal, my dear, but I knew you weren't who you said the moment you walked in. Money's money, and if I can get yours and theirs, eh, I can clean up the mess later." She smiled as the gold coins clattered together. "Boys, just watch the jewelry. And make sure King Berkos hears of my loyalty."

They smiled as she retreated into the back storerooms. We were alone. My heart sunk when one of them slid the locking mechanism on the door and it clicked into place.

I grabbed a dagger from a display case on one of the tables and held it up, wishing it didn't shake. Cupping it with my other hand steadied it, but too late. The men had seen it, and their laughter decimated what little bravery I had. They unsheathed their swords. I finally knew a sound that was worse than nails on a chalkboard—the steely grate of certain death.

The floorboards creaked under their weight. I threw the bag over my shoulder and grabbed a couple bottles of perfume before I pushed the table over, jumping to the side as the remaining bottles shattered. The momentary commotion worked to my advantage. I catapulted over the table and landed beyond the slick ground. One of the men dove for me, narrowly missing my legs, and slid across the oily puddle. The other approached more cautiously, tip-toeing around the fallen items, cracking his knuckles. Each pop sounded like a small explosion. The first assailant regained his footing, and I found myself caught between the two of them. The air tightened as they closed in on me.

The bottles of perfume in my palm gave me a new idea. I threw one on the ground in front of me and skidded into the rose petal oil, slipping under the man's legs. As I stopped on the other side and glanced back, I saw him, bent over, looking between his legs. The other man stumbled over him.

Jumping to my feet, I ran to the door and pulled against the metal lock. It didn't budge. The wooden door seemed cemented in place. My desperate attempts at escape amplified.

"Let me out! Help!" I screamed, pulling on the decorative steel rings and banging the rectangular window at the top of the door.

A cackle grew behind me.

When I turned around, evil intent radiated from their manic grins. They came closer, giving me a better look at them. None of the clothes in this shop would have fit them. They stood taller than the average man, with much thicker arms. Brute strength was in their favor.

My options for fighting vanished. I had to outrun them. It was my only chance, and a slim one at best. My hope for escape was the window on the opposite side of the shop.

I juggled the remaining perfume bottle and saw their steps falter. A plan burst into my mind. I lobbed the bottle high in the air between them, smiling as one fumbled and tried to catch it. The other tripped over his feet and slipped in the residual oils.

They grunted as I ran around them, jumping over the fallen table, and dove through the window. Shards of glass sliced into my forearm as I broke through and landed in the middle of the pathway.

The crowd outside stopped. Their momentary confusion quickly turned to whispers as everyone backed away from the broken window and huddled together. Their eyes darted between me and the men now peeking through the shattered window. I heard Auntie Quinn scream, and I bolted through the marketplace before someone caught me.

"Stop her!" I heard from behind me.

I knocked over carts, tossing apples, bread, and trinkets into the road, anything to slow their pursuit. My chest burned before I even made it out of the main square and around the corner. I scanned the wall for a back gate and my heart sunk. The walls were solid. There wasn't any way to escape. My only chance lay with the two men hammering away on the stage. The screams behind me grew.

"Pipes, Deakon, help!" I yelled, alerting them as they nailed the wooden planks back into position.

Pipes took one look at me and dropped his board. A look of panic spread across his face as he waved me to the back of the stage.

"Hurry, quick," he said. "I'm guessing they found out about you?"

"Ha," I replied. "Like you said, this place isn't safe for me. Or you, either," I added.

"We know."

"You can come with me," I said.

He shook his head sadly. "We all have a part to play, and ours is here."

"But I don't know what I'm supposed to do! I'm no hero!"

"We have faith you'll figure it out. But you won't find it here." He led me to the back of the stage and pointed up the scaffolding. "You'll have to climb out."

"You want me to climb up there?" My voice cracked as I stared up the tangled web of planks leading up to the sheer edges of the walls.

"It's the only way out," he said.

"Hurry up, before they come," Deakon grunted. "They won't stay back there for long. Your only hope and ours is if you get out of here unseen."

I stared at him.

"We're in enough danger as it is. Go!" he yelled, and then ran down the street with his juggling knives in hand. "You're early for the show. I'll show you some stuff while you wait," he said, slowing the mob.

I shook my head and placed my hands on the planks. It was my only choice. I was beginning to hate that. It seemed as if all my actions were spurred by the only available options. When would I get to truly decide?

"Thank you," I said as I pulled myself up to the next plank. "I'll see you again."

"I hope so my lady. I truly hope so." He gave me a quick salute and cartwheeled down the street towards Deakon.

I looked up the wavering length of boards and crossed my fingers, hoping the scaffolding would hold.

CHAPTER EIGHT

With each plank I climbed, my heart screamed in fear. I wasn't afraid of climbing; I did that weekly at the gym at home. But the possibility of falling almost paralyzed me. On the rock walls at home, the handholds and footholds were secure. The only times I fell were from miscalculations, and that was rare. And my harness always held me secure.

Here though, I had already seen the deliberate destruction of the stage, and the haphazard way the boards had been re-secured. Falling didn't seem that farfetched a possibility. I didn't want to find out what would happen if I died. Even if it transported me home, it would hurt, and my pain tolerance wasn't that good. And besides, what if it didn't? Getting home by winning the game still seemed the easiest and least painful option.

My palms slipped on the metal beams, but I didn't stop. I paced my climb to the rhythm of the theme song, audible through Deakon and Pipes' impromptu show and the muffled outcries of the crowd. My fear subsided until I reached the top of the scaffolding and balanced against the worn bricks of the outer wall. I squinted towards the sky. Still another fifteen feet to go to reach the top of the wall. The first bit of the climb was partially hidden by the stage, but this last part was exposed. I had to climb quickly or risk giving my friends away.

Deakon and Pipes held back the restless crowd. Their juggling knives and axes flashed in the air. As hypnotic as their routine was, I didn't know how long it would hold off the mob.

Now was the moment of truth. A layer of dust flaked off the wall as I ran my hands over the rough stones. Using the dust as chalk, I covered my palms and tightened my grip within the worn edges. The holes were not as big as I would've liked or as stable as I was used to, but I scampered up the side of the wall.

It took the last of my strength to pull myself over the top edge, and when I did, I melted onto the cold bricks on the other side. A wide hallway of sorts opened up, which I imagined the guards paced regularly.

The commotion of the crowd escalated below me, and I was certain they had broken through Deakon and Pipes' performance. I wanted to peek over the edge, but I didn't dare. Their malicious obscenities frightened me. How could they think I was the bad guy?

I sat up and propped my back against the bricks, remaining low enough to stay out of sight. The rise and fall of my chest mirrored the erratic beat of my heart. This place was driving me crazy. Red blood stained the sleeve of my new shirt. I no longer doubted the reality of this world. I could only be beaten, cut, and attacked so many times before I had to believe. I was stubborn, not stupid, and I needed to start playing smart. I had come too close to game over too many times

I plucked the remaining shards of glass out of my arm and opened the leather bag to see if I had any sort of bandage. Waves of disappointment rocked me. For one moment I had been rich and could have bought anything I wanted. But when I tipped over my leather bag, all I had to show for it was a dark green cloak, a leather belt, a jewel-encrusted dagger, and a few other limited supplies. So much for a shopping spree. My wounded pride spent everything in a flash.

I pulled out the dagger and thrust through the air. The hilt cooled my hands, the sun flashing off the blade. It wasn't the beautiful jewelry from the gown table, but it would serve me better. Maybe it wasn't all a loss. At least I'd gotten the basics I needed to start. I had the costume and a weapon, and I had to believe that I would run into another market soon. They were in several levels of the game. I just had to figure out how to find it.

I pulled my hair back and tightened my ponytail. Whether or not I ended up doing what Deakon and Pipes expected by helping the rebellion didn't really matter. That was a side issue. I only cared about getting home, and that meant I had to win the game. No more fear, and no more letting someone get the better of me.

My stomach growled, startling a couple of birds perched along the outer edge of the tower walls, closest to the outside world. I covered my belly and swore. If I could have gone back and changed one thing I'd done in the market, I would have bought out the bakery cart before meeting Auntie Quinn. I looked at the one bird remaining on the edge, pondered, and then dismissed the idea of eating it. The memory of killing the puff bird still darkened my heart.

Instead of hunting, I hummed the theme song. Even though I sung off-key, the bird scooted closer, joining in harmony. Its iridescent feathers blinded me. I reached forward, drawn to its irrefutable beauty, and snatched my hand back as a new gleam caught my eyes. The feather tips were razor sharp and nearly sliced my hand.

I balled my fingers into a fist and bit my knuckles. Nothing here came without danger. I kept forgetting, and once again, I almost got hurt. I needed to keep moving. Deakon and Pipes bought me time, and I couldn't waste that gift. Scrambling to my feet, I felt the dust and mortar from the worn bricks shift under me, and I tripped forward, landing halfway over the outer edge of the market's wall. The songbird flew away, its melody fading to nothing.

"I'll sing with you again." I sighed, glancing back down at the edge of the wall. "What's this?" I asked, finding a small hidden ledge and compartment between two of the bricks. Something glittered.

I straightened, threw all my items back in the bag, and leaned over the wall. I wasn't leaving without this.

"Jackpot!" I mumbled, reaching further over the edge for the box of money stuck between the worn bricks. It didn't budge. My stomach grumbled. I needed money, and this time I wouldn't spend it until I found some food.

As I leaned towards the ledge, I felt my balance shift. The edge of one of the bricks crumbled beneath me, jolting me back to my senses. With a desperate grab, I dug my nails into the wooden sides of the box and ripped it from the wall as I fell.

I screamed for a moment, and then smashed into the ground. No leaves softened this fall. My only saving grace was that the back end of the town was built into a hill, so my fall was half the distance of the climb. It may have saved my life, but it sure didn't stop the pain that wracked my body.

The edge of the box bit into my ribs as I tumbled down the hill. Rocks dug into me. I felt fire down my side, and my screams sounded like groans. I wanted to cry, give in to the pain, but the hill refused to let me go. Over and over I tumbled, until light and shadow became one. My neck and cheek burned with dragon weed pollen, but I held on. I plunged into the cold river, still struggling for breath.

The icy water stung. I struggled against the current. Treading didn't help; nothing seemed to help. My racing heart forced the air from my lungs. Once my body numbed, I gave in and let the current take me.

The river pulled me past the marketplace. From the outside, no one would have guessed that there was a festival of dancing and celebration inside the square. Auntie Quinn's distaste for the rebels and their futile attempts at defiance filled my mind. Would Pipes and Deakon's demonstrations really make a difference if no one knew about them? And did they even realize that their celebrations were concealed under the containment of the king's market?

My heart broke for them. They were risking their lives for nothing. I closed my eyes. It hurt too much to cry.

I floated past open fields and a meadow, similar to the one I'd first walked through when I arrived that morning. Had it really only been one day? It seemed like a lifetime's worth of pain.

My earlier resolve to win the game died out. How could I possibly win with all the dangers that I knew—which were formidable on their own—mixed with perils I couldn't expect? The novelty of this place wore thin, sprouting seeds of loneliness. Instead of the theme song, one question ran on repeat through my mind: Where was the game over button?

Just as the sun set behind a range of jagged mountains, the river bent and deposited me along its gravel edge. A subdued palette of orange and blue painted the sky as I hung on to the sharp rocks at the bank. I watched, but the beauty escaped me.

It took every ounce I had in reserves to pull myself out of the river. Even numb, I knew I couldn't float forever. I wanted to cry. I wanted to let the world of Dreamscape know it had hurt me, but I settled for weak protests. Anything more required too much effort.

I flipped over, shoving my bag under my head, and adjusted the wet tunic. The sky softened, and after a slow progression, the blues faded dark, and a blanket of stars covered me.

Stars. I had lamented losing them when we moved, and yet here, in this new world, they shone the same. Spread across the sky in constellations that looked oh-so-familiar, they offered me comfort. I grabbed onto it. It didn't matter if they were the same stars or not; it was enough for me.

Out of the corner of my eyes, a burst of yellow broke my thoughts. Despite the pain in my ribs, I propped myself up onto my elbows. Fireworks. After a handful of deep explosions, the sky erupted into color. Streaks of red flames were followed by blue sparkles, and then yellow stars filled the sky.

I leaned back and laughed. Fireworks symbolized one thing—level one was over.

CHAPTER NINE

The last, lingering moments of sleep were my favorites.

When I was trapped in that ethereal place between wakefulness and sleep, my biggest dreams of adventure came true. For a few blissful moments, I thought that Dreamscape was nothing more than a dream. Befriending armed jugglers, narrowly escaping murderous thugs, and finding glittery money boxes made sense. Dreaming of a video game was normal.

Being stuck in it wasn't.

I made a new wish in the last tendrils of sleep. Not for another adventure, but to be home, in my own bed. I could almost imagine being there, if I ignored the sharp rocks digging into my ribs, the quick breeze that froze my damp clothes, and the pain pulsing through my body.

Nope, I couldn't even pretend that I was home.

I flipped onto my side and swore as the gravel found new spaces between my ribs to poke. Sleep didn't offer me a reprieve from pain. The longer I rested, the more my body protested. Sharp spasms ran through me at the slightest of movements. Breathing hurt, pushing myself up onto my elbows burned, and when I sat up and hunched over, every muscle screamed at me.

I leaned forward and brushed a few small rocks off my cheek. Small puckers covered my face where the gravel had dimpled my skin. I hung my head in my hands. I wasn't ready to deal with another day here.

Even with my eyes closed, the theme song nagged me. That

infuriating tune bore its way into my head until even my inner thoughts sung on cue. I despised it. I pulled the cloak up over my head, but it was no use. The melody infiltrated everything, from the water lapping up on the shore to the birds' song. It didn't matter where I looked, I saw and heard the programming of the game.

It felt like a subliminal message, like my mom's snide remarks; always giving me a gentle reminder about who was in charge. I discounted the messages at home, or at least I tried to, but could I afford to ignore them here? It seemed pretty clear this place had a plan, even if I didn't know it.

Wait! I was the Golden Hero.

I picked up a larger chunk of gravel, tossed it into the river, and watched miniature waves appear, altering the rhythm and sound of the water rolling up onto the shore. I picked up a handful of pebbles and tossed them all in, forgetting about the pain, and smiled as the underlying rhythm faltered.

My eyes widened with a new idea. I could make my own choices here! If I tried hard enough, I could alter the underlying programming and maybe return home. Trying certainly couldn't hurt anything.

But where would I go? Taking control meant actually knowing what I was doing. And I had no clue.

I plunked more rocks into the river, along the shoreline. As the water settled back to normal, the song recalibrated itself in the background. Maybe the key wasn't in fighting the inevitable, but in working with it. Fumbling through the levels hadn't gotten me anything but pain. Maybe if I crafted a plan, I might actually stand a chance.

I took the leather bag I had used as my pillow and dragged it across the ground in front of me, smoothing out the pebbles. With my blank canvas in front of me, I took out the jeweled dagger and dragged the blade through the rough ground. The rocks didn't move as smoothly as I would have liked, but this wasn't an art project. It was a strategy. Visual clarity helped me. I had to get all these little pieces of information out of my head to really see the big picture.

What I knew from memory seemed small in comparison to the forest and marketplace I had already gone through.

I scribbled triangles around all four sides of the makeshift map to represent the woods. Dreamscape's great forests were filled with giants, colossal trees, cacti, and sand traps. There was no telling what I would find in each section. Passing through the dark forest had proved difficult enough. And the shortcuts I relied on back at home…well, I didn't even know if they existed here.

After the forests, I drew a jagged line across the middle. A mountain range I only knew as the ice world split Dreamscape in half. In the other direction, the river that swept me away from the marketplace divided the terrain.

I sat back and appraised the map. Dreamscape seemed so undeveloped in comparison to the maps I knew from school. Exotic and diverse, but simple in construction. In the most basic sense, it was forests transected by a mountain range and river, with a few towns, castles, and manors thrown in.

I placed the dagger tip on the edge of the western forest and drew a straight line east, mimicking my route with Deakon and Pipes. I stabbed the knife in deep and leaned behind me to grab a couple of larger rocks. I placed the biggest rock next to the blade. That was Lindle, the capital. And from what Pipes had said, I knew Berkos' castle wasn't much further north.

I wrapped my arms around my knees and stared. Could it be that simple? Even though there wasn't much to the world, I knew my path would be so much more difficult than just walking up to the castle. No one skipped straight to the end of the game, even with shortcuts. I was missing some key points, I knew, but none came to mind. I'd have to fill in the blanks as I went.

As I went…the thought lingered in my mind. How long could I stay on the shore? I tucked the box into my leather bag.

As if reading my mind, a bright red bird swooped low, dragging its feet in a line across the river's surface as it approached. Then the rest of the flock arrived, lining the river's edge like an out-of-bounds warning. It was time to go.

I grabbed the bag and threw it over my shoulder, flinching as the edge of the wooden box slammed into my back. Since sleep hadn't healed me the way I expected, I needed something more, like a healing potion.

If only I knew how to get one. The game simplified everything— collect coins, get food, collect more coins, buy a potion, get healed. Survival was secondary to the adventure.

I doubted that a medicine hut or the red liquid of a healing potion would materialize out of thin air. The possibility of making one flashed through my mind, but I quickly dismissed it after glancing back at the dragon weeds on the shore. Red petals and berries spotted the forest bushes, but I wasn't sure which to use. There were too many variables to consider. The red liquid I needed could be made from anything.

There was only one thing to do. Keep moving and keep my eyes open. I had no doubts that something would happen soon. Something always happened.

I hobbled over to the trees that lined the entrance to the forest and stumbled forward from tree to tree until I found one with a low-hanging branch. A rattling sensation grew in my chest as I sawed through the thick wood, fashioning a walking stick.

With the new support, I moved a bit more quickly and entered the forest, careful to keep my breaths shallow and even. I couldn't be distracted today. Not when I had no idea where the river had deposited me. I could be anywhere, and worse, I had no clue what hid in these woods. I glanced around at the towering trees, waiting for the overwhelming dread from yesterday to return. It didn't. These trees seemed arbitrary. Nothing stood out to pinpoint me at a location or specific level.

Light flickered down through the forest canopy, teasing me with warmth. I stretched out my arms, hoping it might dry the last bit of dampness from my clothes. A steady stream of leaves fluttered from above as animals skittered through the branches. The tree bark broke into thick vertical fissures, covered by varying shades of green moss. Vines spiraled from the top of the canopy where yellow birds sang.

Hardly any branches swooped to the ground, meaning I wouldn't be able to climb here. Not that I could have climbed anyway.

I wandered for what seemed like hours. Except for the noise I made tripping over the occasional puff bird or horned rabbit, everything seemed quiet.

And then a slow rumble, like a distant storm, sounded ahead. It grew until the raging thunder turned to wild thrashing. Along the path ahead of me, something crushed the bushes and sent the puff birds scrambling. A flock of bright birds squawked above me as they took to the air. Twirling feathers fell with the leaves, and the vines swayed ominously behind them.

"What now?"

CHAPTER TEN

I threw myself down behind the closest bush. The branches stuck in my hair, but I hardly noticed. The thundering mass rolling towards me had my attention. What was this new challenge? My mind spun with Dreamscape's dangers: magical creatures, dragon weeds, puff birds, monsters, thieves, armored knights, and giants. And those were just the ones I knew about.

The noise rose in crescendo as underbrush and vines fell onto the trail, trampled by the incoming threat. The moment the beast broke into view, I knew my hiding spot would not protect me.

Giants.

Why did it have to be giants?

I didn't have time to wonder. Hiding wouldn't save me from two steamrolling giants. Even if they didn't roll over me, they'd track me down with their heightened sense of smell. I'd have to fight. My heart hammered in my chest, and the dagger slipped in my grip.

I cursed and jumped out from behind the bushes. A lone man running in front of the oncoming giants sped past me, sliding to a stop as soon as he caught sight of me.

"It's you!" he cried, doubling back and grabbing my arms. "I found you!" His voice softened, and he disarmed me with his smile. He hunched over to catch his breath, then glanced back up at me. "You have no idea how relieved I am to see you. Hide your hair and get behind me." He turned back to the giants. His intense eyes, half-hidden beneath his dark hair, distracted me as they darted between the path and me.

It took a moment to comprehend what he'd said.

"What?" I asked, my hands flying to my hair in confusion. What a strange request.

"Hide your hair, Goldy, and move away," he said before turning back towards the rumbling forest, brandishing his sword. "Things are about to get dangerous."

"Hide my hair?" He was concerned with my hair when his stuck out in all directions? I ran my fingers through my tangles and threw one of the broken branches at his feet. My lips curled up in defiance, and he stared at me in disbelief. Then his mouth dropped as I limped forward next to him, gripping the dagger.

"Yes, your hair." He raised his eyebrows. "Don't tell me you're really going to fight."

"Don't underestimate me. I can take care of myself," I retorted, ignoring him to focus on the giants tromping closer at a deceptively slow pace. The ground shook with every movement. I looked over at his smug grin and tightened my grip on the dagger. It was too late to back out now.

"Goldy," he whispered. "I don't think you know what you've gotten yourself into."

"I could say the same for you," I said, refusing to take my eyes off the giant, although he may have had a point.

"Suit yourself." He chuckled. "Have you ever fought a giant before?"

"What?" I asked, barely able to hear him over my heartbeat. "No, I've never fought a giant." I wanted to add that we didn't have unicorns or dragons either in the real world, but I bit my tongue. While we didn't have mythological creatures, arrogant teenage boys seemed universal.

He gave a slow whistle. "This will be fun then. Watch me if you can. Their weak spot is on the side of their head: aim right above the ears. And be careful when they turn around. They move quicker than you'd think, and one strike from their fist will knock you out cold. Trust me, I know." He rubbed his cheek.

I swallowed hard and nodded.

"And if you get too tired or it looks like he's going to win, just play dead. I'll come by to save you." He laughed as if he'd told a joke.

I couldn't tell if he was laughing at me, the situation, or just staving off his own anxiety. "Oh, I won't need saving," I said. "But remember your own advice, you might need it."

"Oh, Goldy, this *is* going to be fun."

I tightened my jaw. "Stop calling me that."

"What?" he asked with an arched brow.

"Goldy. It's not my name."

"Sorry, my lady. I didn't mean anything by it. Just seemed fitting."

"Why, because of my hair?" I snapped, refusing to be swayed by his softened tone. He lowered his sword.

"No, my lady," he said in a grave tone. "Because you're a treasure."

What? My annoyance melted. Was he serious? I couldn't focus on it. There were giants coming at us. Giants! I turned away from him and pointed my dagger towards the trail.

"They're almost here," I said.

"This is your last chance to leave. Seriously, just move to the side. I'll take care of them."

"No way." No one was going to tell me what to do anymore, especially when I was supposed to be the hero. "Just stand back and watch me. You might learn something," I said, twisting my left arm around one of the long vines at my side. After double-checking that it would hold, I ran and jumped, kicking off the tree. I arched through the air, racing towards one of the giants.

I had never been in a fight before. I'd fantasized about it, of course, but had never followed through. I channeled that energy into art or climbing. As I swung through the air, none of that inexperience bothered me. Pride had a way of silencing everything else, especially sound judgment.

My feet connected with the side of the giant's head, knocking him to the ground. Just like in the game, a quick kick to the head, and he was done. My moment of relief was short-lived. By the time I landed and unwound the vine from my arm, the giant had regained his balance. And he was mad.

Now what? I thought about running away, but couldn't. Even though I couldn't see him, I knew the mysterious man was watching.

I ran to one side and then lunged to the other, ducking under a fallen log. The giant followed. His thick steps slowed in the brush, but when he cleared it, leaving a trampled mess behind him, he grinned at me. Pointed teeth gleamed under his wide mouth as he licked his lips. A shudder ran through me.

I looked back and saw the man leaning against a tree, a wry expression on his face. No. I wouldn't give him the satisfaction of watching me fail. I ran back towards the giant, dove beneath his legs, barely avoiding his swinging fist, and darted around him once more. My chest burned. I couldn't keep this up much longer.

Nothing I knew from the game seemed applicable. All I had to do there was jump on top of their heads. I had already done that, and it didn't work.

I ducked, skimming past his fist a second time. The whoosh of air sent my heart racing. I ducked again, and sidestepped to the left. He swung, but I dodged it again. When he stepped towards me, I moved back. Then the familiar routine struck me. A smile grew on my face, and I winked at the giant. Perhaps I could win after all.

The rest of the ridiculous moves from the Dreamscape dance sequence flooded my mind.

"Hey Giant!" I called. "It's time to dance."

My feet moved to the rhythm. Confused, the giant struggled to grab me, and after a moment, he fell, tripping over his own feet. I jumped on top of his back, straddling his neck with my legs.

"It looks like you missed a step," I said, squeezing my thighs until his face turned red.

He sputtered and stirred, coughing up chunks of blood, giving me a split second to decide. How far was I willing to go? I squeezed my legs tighter until his head fell to the side and a drop of blood slid down his cheek.

My legs trembled when I tumbled off him. I took a closer look at his features, noticing a surprising softness to his bumpy face. His pointy teeth didn't look as menacing with his tongue slipping out the side of his mouth. I felt his shallow breath and the quick pulses of his heart. The longer I looked, the less convinced I became. Which one of us was the monster?

I wiped dirt over my leggings, trying to cover the blood, but it seeped deeper. I felt sick. How much of myself was I giving up here? First killing the bird, and now this. It seemed I couldn't survive without sacrificing my integrity.

I looked away. Maybe if I ignored it, I could pretend it didn't happen. Doubtful...I knew the guilt would stick with me. It usually did. A quick yelp broke through my thoughts. When I looked up, the mysterious man ran into view, battling it out with the other giant.

He ran up the trunk of a leaning tree and flipped through the air, striking the giant on his back before landing in a crouched position. His sword followed the giant's awkward attempts to spin around. When they faced each other, the man dove beneath the giant's gangly arms. Dark stains covered his knees as he rose on the opposite side. His tan pants hugged his muscular legs, hinting at impressive strength.

I couldn't look away. Unfortunately, he noticed me watching him before re-engaging the giant. My heart skipped a beat when he grinned in that annoyingly hypnotic way. *Stop staring*! I commanded myself, but my eyes wouldn't obey.

He glistened with exertion, and each swing of his sword accentuated the muscles rippling along his arms. Vibrant feathers hung from buckles on his vest. They fluttered against him, revealing an arsenal of weapons tied to his chest and strapped to his side.

With that many weapons, why was he taking his time? As he spun around the giant and ducked beneath his flailing arms, poking into his side again, I realized he wasn't fighting. He was playing. What had taken all my strength was mere child's play for him. When he had enough, he silenced the giant's outcries with a swift kick to the back of his knee, knocking out his legs. The giant fell with a mighty crash, taking out a few saplings with him. The mystery man knocked his sword hilt across the giant's head, then turned and smiled at me.

I noticed every detail about him.

He swaggered with a measured and deliberate pace, re-sheathing his sword at his side. At ease in the forest, he leapt the fallen logs without hesitation. His unruly hair fell in short waves across his forehead. The intensity of his dark eyes still hit me, but behind the initial curiosity, something else stirred. Respect, maybe?

That look left me weak; thankfully, I was already sitting down. I didn't trust my legs anymore. I was powerless over them and the silly smile that stretched my face.

He dropped to a knee in front of me and took my hand in his. My fingers trembled as he moved them closer to his lips. A faint twinge of spice swirled around me.

"Ah…there's nothing quite like slapping around a giant child to get your blood moving. Nice moves, by the way." He winked, then kissed the top of my hand. "I'm sorry for the rough introduction. I didn't mean to startle you."

I stared at him as the top of my hand warmed with his gentle touch. "You didn't startle me," I whispered in a weak, stilted voice. "What do you mean, giant child? Those weren't full grown?"

"No," he laughed, lowering my hand. "I thought you knew that. Isn't that why you didn't kill him?"

I didn't kill him?

He cocked his head to the side before continuing. "They escape from the north all the time, but I don't think I've ever seen them this far west. Something must be happening up there." He paused in thought.

I didn't press him. Truth was, I didn't know what to say, and even if I did, the words seemed to twist together on my tongue. Silence was fine with me.

He shrugged, handing me back my dagger, which I'd dropped by the giant's side. "You know, that was pretty impressive back there," he said. "I've never seen anyone use the vines that way."

"Thanks." I grinned. It was pretty impressive, considering I had never done something like that before. Pushing some buttons on a controller and actually swinging through the air were quite different. I looked back at him, and another whiff of spice hit me.

I was in trouble, there was no denying it—he smelled like cinnamon.

"This isn't going like I planned," he said with a rueful smile. "I had envisioned our first meeting differently. I hope you can see that I mean you no harm. It was blind luck finding you here, but I'm glad I did." He rubbed his forehead and then held out his hand. "My name's Arrow."

"Arrow, like the weapon?" My momentary weakness disappeared. With a name like that, I couldn't pretend he was anything more than a character in the game.

"Yes." He winked at me with a little grin. "I hit all my targets."

My heart jumped and the weakness returned to my knees. Was he flirting with me? I didn't know how to deal with that. The photo of Brian and me came to mind as I cleared my throat. No matter what, I refused to be that pathetic, fawning girl again.

"I'm Alexis, or Alex, whichever," I said, trying to appear calm as I reached forward to shake his hand.

"What are you doing this far west?" he asked, brushing his hair out of his eyes once more. It didn't hold and flopped back down onto his forehead.

"I, uh, must've taken a wrong turn somewhere. I left the market in a hurry, and now I don't really know where I am," I said, feeling warmth rise to my face.

His smile returned. "I'm glad I came along then. I can't allow a beautiful lady to wander these woods alone. Dangers lurk everywhere."

"Yeah," I laughed. "I figured that out the hard way."

"Lucky for you, I'm an expert in these woods, and I know exactly where I'm going to take you."

Warning bells sounded in my mind. Cute or not, I was not going off with a guy I had just met. I hadn't lost my senses.

"Wait, back up buddy. I don't know you. I'm not going anywhere with you," I said, holding up my hands in protest.

Disappointment flashed in his eyes before he lifted his hands. "You misunderstood, my lady. I mean you no harm. I've been looking for you. Everyone's been looking for you. I'm just glad I found you first so I can lead you to safety. I'm not understating the dangers of staying here."

"Why should I take your word?" I asked.

"My word's all I have. That'll have to be enough."

He waited for me to respond. I looked him over carefully, deliberating. How could I know who to believe here? If armed jugglers were my friends and old seamstresses despised me, where did a handsome and rugged giant fighter fit in? He looked sincere, and if he had wanted to hurt me, he could've done it already. I had given him more than enough chances. Then again, I gave Brian the benefit of the doubt too and sorely overestimated his feelings.

The silence between us grew awkward. How long could we just look at each other? Okay, who was I fooling? I could look at him all day.

"I don't...I...wait!" I exclaimed as he lifted his arm to brush his hair away from his eyes. He stopped mid-sweep, and I grabbed at his wrist to look closer. "You...you're part of them."

Arrow chuckled. "Yes, I suppose you could say that. You know about our cause?"

"Yeah, yeah, sure...save the queen, destroy the evil empire..." I rambled, reciting the mission of the video game. I traced the tree on the inside of his wrist. It was the same emblem sewn into Pipes' and Deakon's costumes, yet here, tattooed on his skin, the ink made it seem more significant. More personal.

"You don't seem concerned about the dangers involved. I knew we wouldn't be disappointed with you. Your talents are exactly what the rebellion needs to win. We really need to be going though." He glanced meaningfully down the path behind me.

"You wouldn't happen to have a healing potion on you, would you?" I asked with sudden inspiration.

"A healing potion? I didn't think the giant hit you."

"He didn't, but I ran into a few problems at the market, and if we're going to be walking very far, I really need to get something for these," I said, pointing to my bruised arms and legs.

His eyes darkened as he looked at my arms and torn leggings. "Who did this?" he asked, his fingers drifting towards his sword.

His concern sent a shot of heat through my belly. I reached out for his arm and pushed his sword back in its sheath. "No one did this to me. Well, not directly. I just made a few wrong moves and trusted some people I shouldn't have."

"I bet they got a surprise when they realized they messed with the wrong person." His laugh broke through his tight-lipped concern. "Who were they? I won't let anyone hurt our hero."

My head shot up. "Hero?"

Arrow nodded. "Of course. News about you has been spreading throughout the kingdom."

"O-oh?" I asked, swallowing hard. "W-what kind of news?"

"Don't worry about that. Let's just say you've caused quite the commotion since you've been here."

"What's that supposed to mean?"

"You stand out in a crowd. People have taken notice and spread the word. With everything going on, your appearance changes things. Surely you know that?"

"How can you be so sure? I mean that they're talking about me?" I asked, feeling my insides tighten like a spring.

"Are you serious? Any doubts I had disappeared the moment you leapt through the air towards the giant. Only our hero would be that brave and reckless. You're the one we've been looking for, I'm certain. Besides, look at your hair."

He was back to obsessing over my hair again. I ran my fingers through my hair a final time, pulling out the last few stuck branches and tying it in a ponytail.

"What's wrong with my hair?"

"Nothing's wrong with it."

"Then why do you keep bringing it up?"

"What can I say? It's distracting."

"And you're infuriating," I shot back. His serious expression cracked with a smile.

"Have you noticed anyone else with hair spun from gold?"

His words gave me pause, and as I thought back to everyone I had met, I realized he was right. Everyone here had dark hair except for me.

"You're special. Now, what I want to know, Goldy, is who did this to you." He motioned to my bruises again.

"I already told you, most of this was my fault. Of course, I was set up," I admitted. "But the rest is just from the clumsiness of my escape."

"Who dared do such a thing?"

"Auntie Quinn," I said, the name souring my tongue.

He grimaced. "Auntie Quinn's a danger to us all. She was one of the first to turn. Let me look." He dropped to his knees and traced the welts and bruises. His fingers were softer than I'd imagined, and when he leaned in, his scent curled my toes.

"All of this on such a small girl," he murmured.

"I'm not a small girl," I said, pulling my arms back. The insult stung coming from him. I didn't want his pity. "I've taken care of myself just fine, even before you came along."

"It doesn't look that way."

"Oh no," I said, blood rushing to my cheeks. "I made it out of the market and dealt with a giant without your help."

"It was a child."

"A giant child," I hissed.

"It doesn't matter. You still need healing."

"Anyone would after dealing with what I've faced," I retorted.

"And you're no older than me, so don't give me that crap. I can make my own decisions just fine, thanks."

He bit his lower lip and glared at me before masking his face in cool politeness. "You're right, my lady," he replied tensely. "I apologize for any insult I've caused. It wasn't my intention. I just want to get us to safety. We mustn't stay any longer."

"I'm sorry," I said, chastised by his tone. "It's been a long couple of days, I didn't mean—"

"No need to apologize, my lady. Your feelings came across clearly. I'll keep my concerns to myself. I shouldn't second-guess our hero."

"That's not—"

"It's fine, my lady. Like you said, before we continue, we'll need to heal those wounds. The paths ahead hold more danger than young giants, no matter how brave you are."

I cringed. The amusement and warmth from earlier had disappeared. I had ruined any sort of friendship before it even had a chance to begin.

"That's all I was asking for," I said. "Do you have a potion or know where the nearest marketplace or healer is?"

He unsheathed his sword and came towards me.

I fell behind the rock, fumbling to release the dagger from my belt in a sudden panic. Was he going to hurt me? He turned to the right, giving me his back for one moment. By the time he spun back around, I had the dagger pointed at his throat.

"Stop there!" I cried.

"What?" he asked with wide eyes and a face contorted in confusion. "Here," he said, throwing a handful of cut vines at my feet. "Tighten those around your wounds. They'll heal in a few hours."

"What are you talking about?" I whispered.

It was silent—agonizingly silent—and then I heard his loud sigh. "The vines. You wanted a healing potion."

I closed my eyes and wished the embarrassment away. The pile of vines curled around my feet. "Oh," I said. "I see. I don't—"

"The way I see it, Goldy, you have two choices. You can listen to me and take my advice, or you can continue to fight me for no reason. Either way, make your choice. We can't stay here much longer. And when I say to hide your hair—hide your hair. This isn't a game. If you don't want to wind up in Berkos' dungeon or dead, you'd better start listening. Do you want my help, Goldy?"

My eyes stung as I unsuccessfully tried to blink away the collecting tears to no avail. Within moments, ugly sobs racked my body. I couldn't take it anymore. I felt broken. This had to be the worst first impression ever, and now, I had to ask for help.

"Yes, please help me," I whispered, tugging at the tangled vines, afraid to meet his eyes.

He knelt beside me, patiently spreading and slicing the vine so it splayed evenly. Where it made contact, the red interior of the plant cooled my injured skin. I choked back a combination of tears and laughter. The healing potion had been hanging in front of me all this time.

I twisted my hair, turning the ponytail into a bun and tucking it up under my hat.

"So what did you mean about my hair?" I asked, trying to break the ice that had frozen between us while he continued winding the vines up my legs. "I mean, it's unique here, I guess, but why is it dangerous to wear it down?"

"It's nothing," he said. "It just sends the wrong message to some people. If you want to save yourself more trouble, keep it hidden."

When he finished binding my legs, he worked on my arms in the same fashion. The crisscrossing vines relieved my sore limbs in a healing salve. I hated to admit that I already felt better.

His hand gripped mine and pulled me to my feet. Unprepared for his strength, I stumbled into his arms. The warmth of his body surprised me as I stalled against the soft leather vest. The tips of his lips lifted when I pushed off him.

This was a video game; he wasn't real. But no matter how much my mind tried to convince me, his arms seemed substantial enough. Did it matter if he was real? This was a danger I had not anticipated.

"Where are we going?" I asked.

"To rescue the queen," he said, pressing my hands down to my side before heading down the trail.

"Of course," I mumbled, sighing, and followed him into the overgrown brush.

CHAPTER ELEVEN

Silence comes in three sizes—comfortable, pointed, and bitterly intolerable.

The first two, I wore easily enough for the first hours of our journey together, but the third didn't settle right. I wanted to apologize for earlier, but his dagger-sharp glances told me he didn't want to hear my excuses. The growing hush suffocated me. I only liked solitude when I chose to maintain it.

I struggled to keep pace with him, trampling bushes and flushing out animals on the bramble-crowded trail. Every step I took seemed to announce our location. Arrow glared with annoyance as he motioned for quiet.

"The whole point of taking this trail is to remain hidden," he snapped, disappearing into the lush vegetation. "Keep the noise down."

"I'm trying," I hissed.

"Try harder," I heard from ahead.

I scowled as I stepped over a fallen log blocking the path. He acted as if I was making noise on purpose. Keeping pace with him was hard enough; doing it quietly was impossible. What he called a trail was little more than a worn path winding between bushes and thorns. I certainly did not fit in the small clearance. Sharp brambles grabbed my legs with each step, threatening to pull the healing vines off me.

Branches swung in the distance as he ran ahead. I couldn't figure him out. He puzzled me in the most frustrating way. One minute he's kissing my hand and I melt under his charm, and the next he acts as if I am nothing more than a nuisance. Even looking back to the video game was no help. I could place the jugglers, even the market merchants, but not Arrow. He didn't match up to any of the characters I knew.

He had every right to be upset with me. I did almost attack him with my dagger. But in the middle of the woods—after beating up giants, for heaven's sake—how did he expect me to counteract his sudden movement? How could I not be wary of a stranger in an even stranger world? Help was the last thing I expected.

"Stop," he commanded, lifting his arm.

I dutifully followed his request. I could do that much, at least. But when I looked past him, to where the forest opened to a small clearing, I faltered. Tall grass rippled in the wind, with no signs of danger. After hours of trampling through close vines and brambles, I wanted to run through it and enjoy the open space. Why couldn't I? There was no one here to stop me.

"Arrow, this is wonderful!" I cried, moving past him to twirl into the warm meadow. He reached for me as I bounded forward, but his hand slipped off my wrist.

"Goldy," he said, then stopped with an amused grin. He leaned against the nearest tree as I spun in circle after circle. "When are you going to start listening to me?"

"When are you going to start listening to me?" I countered playfully, my arms extended to the sky. "This is amazing. You have to come out here. I can't tell you how good the sun feels."

"I'm good right here," he said. "You might not want to—"

"Seriously, can't you just enjoy a moment of fun?"

"Do you think we're here for fun?" he asked, one of his eyebrows shooting up.

"Everything can be fun if you want it to be," I said. "You get to make the choice, right? Just like I do. And I'm choosing to have fun."

"I'm fine right here," he said with a smirk. "You go have fun."

"Suit yourself," I said carelessly, advancing further into the sun-filled meadow, "but I'm not missing out."

Arrow's eyes lingered on me as I went, watching me enjoy the silky grass blades on my palm and the sun on my face. Too soon, however, my movements slowed as the ground softened to mud.

"Just my luck," I muttered, trying to step back to no avail. The sludge trapped my boots, pulling me deeper into the goop with each step. It slid over the edge of my boot, warming my shin as it slid down my leg.

"Arrow! What's happening?" I cried, grabbing my shin and attempting to pull my foot up. The warm slime clung to my leather boots. Every bid at escape forced the sludge higher, until it covered my calves, and my feet were cemented in the ground. Arrow's deep laughter interrupted my rising panic.

"Ah, Goldy," he chuckled. "You're right. Everything can be fun. I had no idea this trek would prove so entertaining."

"Stop laughing," I snapped, struggling to hold back my own smile.

"Sorry, my lady. It's just that I haven't seen someone try to traverse these pits since my youth."

"The pits?" I asked.

"Let me introduce you to the Pits of Wonder." He spread his arms in introduction. "It's one of the highlights of the Western Woods."

"Pits of Wonder? That's a joke, right?"

"Ah, 'tis no joke, my lady. You'll find most of these woods are riddled with mystery and danger." His voice dropped in an ominous tone. Only a small twitch at the side of his mouth gave away his sport.

"Stop it, Arrow. I'm seriously stuck. Help me out of here." I stopped flailing and matched his grin. Somehow I knew he would rescue me.

"I was just having a bit of fun. Isn't that what you suggested earlier?" He couldn't stop the twinkle in his eyes.

"Arrow," I pleaded. "I really want to get out of here," and then I said in a smaller voice, "you were right. I should have listened."

"Did I hear you clearly? Did you say I was right? Are you saying you need my help again?" He draped his hands behind his head. I glared at him. He was enjoying my discomfort a bit too much.

"All right, I won't make you ask. Stay there, I'll be right back." He disappeared into the brush we'd just hiked through, snorting to contain another laugh. After what seemed like hours, he emerged with an armful of wooden debris. Vines draped over his shoulders, and a carefully stacked pile of sticks and leaves teetered in his arms.

"Please hurry," I said.

"Good things take time, Goldy," he said, not bothering to look at me, focusing instead on the pile of wood and vines he dropped to the ground.

"As long as this good thing doesn't sink to death," I muttered.

He rolled his eyes. "You don't need to worry about sinking. The pits are…uh…more of a trap than a sinkhole."

"A trap?" I asked, glancing around.

"Yes. You see, there are reckless creatures that tromp through the meadow without noticing the signs and find themselves stuck."

"What happens to them?" I asked, feeling fear clench my heart.

"I couldn't really say. I'd imagine a variety of things. Some might escape, others may starve to death, but the birds help themselves to the majority of them."

He casually looked back at his pile and began sorting the items. I frantically searched the sky.

"Then get me out of here!"

"Are you afraid of a few little birds, Goldy?"

"No," I said. "But the idea of being pecked to death isn't exactly comforting."

"I'm almost ready," he said, tying together a few vines. I stared in disbelief as he held up two ovals, cross-woven with vines, their reinforced edges made from bent branches.

"How did you do that?" I asked, staring as he slipped an oval over each of his feet.

"Let's just say I'm good with my hands…and I may have seen

someone else do this before," he admitted with a smile.

"Who?" I asked.

He cleared his throat and sat down to secure the woven mats to the bottoms of his boots. "It's not important, Goldy. What's important is that we get you out of there."

I nodded and pressed my lips together to stifle my laughter. No wonder he knew about the pits in this meadow.

Once the makeshift shoes were in place, he hobbled over to the edge of the pit and made a move as if he were going to jump. I closed my eyes in anticipation, but no splash followed.

"Don't worry, Goldy, I wouldn't do that to you." He winked.

"I'm not quite so sure!" I giggled at his antics.

"Really?" he asked, tilting his head. "It seems there's a lot you're unsure about."

I bit my lower lip. What did he mean? Hopefully he wasn't second-guessing my usefulness again. He didn't seem to give it a second thought as he stepped into the pits. Soft mud surged around his shoes, and I held my breath as he came closer. Displaced mud rippled out from under his steps. Thick muck sloshed over the top edge of my boots.

"Ugh, I think I'm going to get sick." I gagged.

"Don't do that, Goldy. I'm almost there."

"Hurry!"

"Hmm, I don't know anymore. I wouldn't want to interrupt all this fun," he teased, lingering slightly out of reach.

"You want fun?" I asked. Narrowing my eyes at him, I scooped up a handful of goop and tossed it at him. I missed, but it sent him into fits of laughter. He was definitely enjoying this too much.

Now, in addition to the mud stuck to my boots, dark slime dripped down my forearm. Slow, like syrup, and with an acidic smell that burned. I hadn't noticed it when I first walked in, but now the stench overpowered me. "Why didn't you warn me? This stinks." I plugged my nose with my clean hand while Arrow bent over to catch his breath.

"I tried Goldy, I tried. This is too good!" He pretended to duck as I reached for more goop. "Okay, okay, here you go," he said, throwing the pile of branches and the extra pair of woven shoes to the ground in front of me. "Line the shoes up, secure them with one of the branches, and then tie them together. You'll want to attach them to your legs, like I did."

I looked down at the sticks and vines and cursed as my feet stayed in place. "I can't move my feet."

"Relax. We have to go step by step. If I started swirling the mud before you knew how to tie the shoes, it would be pointless."

I took a deep breath and tucked my lips together. Relaxing was the last thing I wanted to do, but I tried. "Okay, I'm ready. What's next?"

"Now this may sound strange." He stopped as I stifled a chuckle. What wasn't strange here?

"Sorry, go ahead," I said.

He raised his eyebrows, but I remained silent. "To get you unstuck, I need to alter the movement of the ground below. Don't be afraid," he said, stopping my protests. "It's not as bad as it sounds. You'll feel the ground soften around you first, and then you'll be able to pull your feet out."

"What are you going to do?" I asked nervously.

"Stir up the ground."

"Stir up the—no!" I yelled, then cursed under my breath. There had to be a different way. A way that didn't involve me tumbling backwards into this goo.

Arrow winked and ignored my concerns, dropping a large branch onto the ground. He swirled small circles first and then larger ones closer to me. The ground trembled, and I dropped a couple inches. I shifted my boots and recovered.

"It's working," I said.

He didn't answer, continuing to stir in front of me, and then to the side, and then around behind me. The mud softened, and when my legs broke free, I almost fell backwards. What now? Arrow's instructions flew past my ears while I stared at the sinking pile of twigs and vines.

"And you better do it before everything sinks or the ground solidifies around you. Are you sure you have it?"

"Uh-hmm," I said, collecting the sticks. "Thank you, I really mean it."

"I'll see you on the other side, Alex," he said, sliding by effortlessly.

I held my breath. My heart raced. My fingers refused to listen to the simplest of instructions. He said my name. Alex. Not Goldy, and not with a sneer. It slid off his tongue like honey, smooth and deep. I liked it. He looked back at me still fumbling with the sticks and smiled. The ice between us had finally thawed.

I followed his instructions, and before the sludge covered my knees, I had the woven shoes attached to my boots. The first few steps threatened to knock me back into the mud. I wobbled out of control and then managed to trudge a lot less gracefully than Arrow across the quicksand pit.

Luckily Arrow didn't press me to keep going on the trail. In the time it took me to maneuver over the wobbly ground, he had started a small fire and prepared lunch.

The smell of warmed bread and oranges bowled me over. I dropped to my knees, remembering that I hadn't eaten since arriving. I crawled across the dusty ground, ignoring the dirt that stuck to the residual slime on my arms and legs.

"You made it," Arrow said as I crawled past him.

Whatever had guarded his eyes before had transformed into an amused twinkle. I pulled myself up with his help and hobbled to the log where he sat, carefully pulling off my caked boots. It took more effort to strip my arms of the slime, and when he offered a branch for scraping, I accepted it.

"You can put your boots by the fire to warm. Once the mud dries, it'll flake off. No one will ever know. Except me, of course," he said with a sly wink.

I stared at him, my words frozen in my throat. Why was talking to him so difficult?

"You don't have to be afraid," he said, offering me a warmed slice of bread and an orange. His grip lingered for a moment before he released the food, and our eyes connected, sending my heart spiraling out of control.

"I'm not afraid," I said, glancing away.

"What is it then?"

I shrugged. The feelings stirring inside me weren't fear, but something just as terrifying. Silence gave me the illusion of control over my emotions. I bit into the bread.

It melted in my mouth. I closed my eyes and let the world disappear. At that moment, nothing mattered except the bread as each piece fed my insatiable appetite. I took the second offered slice and leaned back against the log, closing my eyes. The orange had a tang that I relished, especially when the sweet citrus slid down my throat. Hunger made everything taste better, and despite the two slices of bread and the fruit, my stomach still grumbled.

The birds sang as Arrow poured a drink. He wasn't close enough to touch, but even with my eyes closed, I sensed his proximity. The clarity of the details I recalled of his face startled me, from his strong jaw to the hair that fell across his forehead, just barely covering his eyes.

Those eyes.

The look of admiration he gave me after I knocked out the giant, and then the confusion when I drew my weapon on him came back to me. Now that I had eaten, everything seemed so clear. Why had I ever doubted him?

When I opened my eyes he was prodding the fire with a stick. He added another log to the fire and a spray of embers highlighted the clumps of dried mud that fell off the bottom of his boot.

I kicked chunks of goop off my leggings with my foot, wishing I could kick off the entire costume. Why was being the hero so difficult? When I first put the costume on, I thought I knew what I was supposed to do. Obviously I didn't. All this pretending twisted my insides.

"So, Goldy…" he stopped mid-sentence as I shook out my hair. I let it fall loose, embracing the one thing about me that remained unchanged.

"You really should hide your hair. Someone might notice," he mumbled, locking his gaze on me.

"Maybe I want someone to notice," I said with a direct look. My heart raced. Why had I said that?

He stopped drinking and appraised me. The cup covered most of his face but not the mischievous gleam in his eyes. Oh crap, what had I done?

"So how come I've never heard of you before?" I asked quickly, bringing the conversation back to safe ground. My hand shook as I reached for another piece of bread. "I'm pretty sure I would remember a name like yours."

I'd definitely remember his face.

He shrugged. "I don't know. I'm pretty well-known around here, especially in these woods. What about you? Where are you from?" He sliced an apple with his knife and let the blade hang by his lips. I took another bite to buy time. How could I possibly tell him I was from a different world? A real one. I couldn't. I only had one reasonable option—lie.

"Um, pretty far from here. Further north, I think."

He stopped prodding the fire and arched an eyebrow. "From the north, huh? I would have guessed further away."

"What do you mean by that?" I asked, scrunching my face as I took an additional bite of bread.

"Nothing bad," he said, appeasing me with a quick gesture of surrender and pointing to the vines crossing my body. "I'm not one to question how or why you're here. I just noticed that you weren't aware of the Wounded Woods."

"Wounded Woods," I said. "I guess that's a fitting name. I needed the vines, that's for sure. You never did tell me what you were doing there today."

"Besides rescuing you from giants?"

"Funny, I seem to recall handling mine just fine," I said, relieved to joke about something that had pulled us apart before. "No, seriously though, what were you doing there? Was it just random luck that we found each other?"

"I don't believe in random luck." He shook his head and reached for my hand. "This was more. I was meant to find you."

My heart leapt. "I…"

"The rebellion needs you."

Just as quickly, my heart sank. The rebellion. Those two words defined my purpose to these people. How could I forget about that? He was looking for the hero, not for me.

"Do you have any more bread in there?" I asked, changing the subject again. I scooted forward, within arm's reach. Why did I do that? He could see my heart beating for sure.

"Just a few slices, but we should ration those for later. I'm down to the last two apples as well," he said, sliding off the log to sit by my side and opening his bag for me to see. His proximity clouded my mind, making it hard to remain level-headed or breathe. I grabbed for my bag out of reflex and opened it.

"Nothing in here either," I said, leaning forward to share my bag with him.

"Wait!" he said, placing his hand over mine. The speed in his movement and alarm in his voice surprised me. "Can I?" he asked, pulling the bag from my grip.

Startled, I nodded. What could have caught his attention? There wasn't much in my bag to begin with. *Except those*, I thought, watching him pull out the carved wooden boxes.

"Why did you take these?" he asked, shooting an accusatory glance my way.

"Take them? I just found them in the woods. Someone must have left them there. They're just money boxes," I snapped, clutching the bag to my chest.

"Just money boxes," he muttered, cracking his neck in exaggerated motions.

"Yes. If I didn't, someone else would have."

"So you just took the money?"

"Yeah." I hesitated, put off by the accusation in his voice.

"You stole the money?"

"No," I said. "It's not like that."

"What do *you* call it when you take money that's not yours?"

"But that's not...that's not fair," I stuttered, flustered by his insinuation. "I needed the money."

"So you just took it? What about the people who it was intended for. Don't you think they needed the money?"

"I didn't know," I said weakly. His words rattled in my head like a trapped beast trying to find a way out. I'd done it again, ruined things before I knew what had happened.

He looked at me for a long time before speaking. "What's done is done, but why did you take the boxes? You could have just left them there," he said in a quieter tone. I looked at the way he traced the designs on the wood. He must've recognized something I hadn't.

"They're too beautiful to be left to rot in the forest," I said, pursing my lips and dropping my gaze to the leather bag in my lap. My hand shook as I felt around along the bottom and clutched the money from the second box. I dropped the coins into his hands. "Here, take it. I don't need it, and I didn't mean any harm by taking it."

I held my breath as he considered my offer. He put the money back in my hand and closed my fist around it, shaking his head.

"I'm sorry. It's just, there's so much you don't seem to understand," he said, stiffening, refusing to meet my eyes.

It was more than just Dreamscape that confused me. Every piece of me ached for Arrow's warmth. No matter how much I shouldn't have, I reached out for his hand.

"Can you help me understand?" I pleaded. "You're right. I'm not aware of all the rules here, and I wish I had a good reason for that.

But I want to learn."

When he looked back at me, my heart fluttered. So much emotion raged behind his eyes, and I didn't understand half of it. He scooted closer, knocking a chunk of mud off with his heel.

"Sorry," he said and moved even closer. The side of his thigh touched mine. I forgot how to breathe. Did he have any idea what he did to me? I recognized the first box he held out. The stained swirls and carved craftsmanship still captivated me.

"See? It's too beautiful to leave for no one to appreciate."

He sighed so loudly I knew he was almost out of patience, so I bit my cheek and waited.

"They are beautiful," he conceded, "but they're so much more than that. Look closer. This mark here," he said, pointing to the tree carved into the outside, "that's a mark from the royal army. This box was intended to pay for a month of supplies for the queen's army."

"The queen has an army? Auntie Quinn said a king ruled."

His jaw tightened. "Yes, Berkos is in charge, but the rebels still fight to free the queen. This money was for them, to aid in the rebellion."

"And the other box?" My voice trembled.

"This one," he said, juggling the boxes in his arm to focus on the second. He exhaled. "Where did you find this one?"

"Just outside the marketplace." I closed my eyes as if that would shield me from his answer.

"Open your eyes," he said, nudging me hard with his elbow. "This isn't a game."

I opened my eyes, but he had nailed the underlying problem. To me, this was a game.

"This money was meant for medical supplies," he said before swearing under his breath. His dark hair covered his eyes as he shook his head. "Now they won't get any of this." He cursed again and dropped the box in my lap. "Did you get your money's worth?" he asked. "No, don't answer that. I'm sorry. It's just that now, more than ever, we need every bit of help we can get. You're nothing like I expected. I only wish…" his voice trailed off as he looked at the fire.

"Wish what?" I asked timidly.

He gave me a sideways glance and sad smile. "I only wish I knew what to do with you."

My heart doubled its pace. I bit the inside of my lower lip as my thoughts raced. How could I regain his trust? I sighed. There was only one way. If he wanted a hero, I would have to step up my game. It was my only way home, after all. I reached forward, tapping him on his shoulder, and gave him my biggest smile.

"You said you were looking for me, right?" I asked. "That I'm the one here to help the rebellion."

"Yes, but all of that seems ridiculous if you don't understand even the most basic of principles."

"I'm your hero, Arrow. Don't doubt me because I've forgotten a few things. You have to remember that heroes go on many quests. They're all kind of jumbled in my mind right now. Help me sort them out, and you'll have no more doubts."

His forehead scrunched in concentration as he thought about what I said.

"Help me understand?" I asked.

"There's so much—"

"Then we better start now," I said. He poked at the fire again.

"Ah, Goldy, you don't give up, do you?"

"Never," I said, winking and reaching behind him to grab my leather bag. "We can start with these," I said, pulling out the packet of worn parchment from Auntie Quinn.

"Where'd you get this?"

"From Auntie Quinn. Why?"

"Lockhorn News," he spat, reading the title. "This is trash." He handed the papers back to me. "You won't find anything useful in there."

"Maybe not," I said, opening the pages of the book and stopping at a picture of a man dressed all in black. "But there's still some stuff I need to know about what's in here."

"What?"

I flipped back to the front. Where to even begin? None of it made sense. "Okay, like this for instance. Lockhorn News. Where is Lockhorn, exactly?"

He gave me a sad glance and looked away. "Goldy, if you don't even know that, then I don't know what help this is going to be."

"Help me," I said, shaking the papers in front of him. "I need to understand what we're facing if you want my help."

He shook his head, but remained silent.

"So, Lockhorn. Where is it?"

"It's all of this," he said, staring at the fire.

"All of this," I said. "I thought this was..." but I didn't finish my thought. Dreamscape was just the name of the game, not the places within. It made sense. "Okay, so this is the news for the whole area. It says here that—"

"It says here that Auntie Quinn won tailor of the year, that Lindle has been awarded the national trade award for its fifth year in a row. There are advertisements for the local vendors and news that the rebels have been driven south of the capital into the woods. What more do you want to know?" He turned the page.

"I...uh...I don't know," I said, taken aback at his anger. "What about this one?" I asked, pointing to the one headline he had skipped.

He shook his head and stood up. "Like I said, my lady, this is trash. News twisted to their agenda. I haven't read it before, and I refuse to now, even to humor you. It's time to go," he said, dumping a handful of sand over the glowing embers.

"I'm sorry," I said. "I didn't mean to upset you again."

"You haven't, my lady. But the longer we sit here, the more upset I'll get, I fear. Let's go."

"Okay, but where are we going?" I asked, leaning over to grab my boots. Dry chunks of mud flaked off at the slightest touch.

"We're headed back to the camp at the Grove to finalize plans, but we have to make a quick stop along the way. Do you think you're up for it?"

"Of course. I can handle anything you throw at me. Where are we going?" I asked, maybe too eagerly.

"Baron Marix's estate," he said, ushering me ahead.

My heart practically leapt out of my chest. I had to restrain myself from looking too excited. I didn't know who Baron Marix was, but I knew my way around all the barons' estates. For once, I could help!

As Arrow finished extinguishing the fire, I glanced at the one headline he refused to read: *King Berkos Wins the Election by a Head.* I exhaled and stuffed the papers back in my bag before Arrow saw.

"Are you ready Goldy?"

I nodded, not trusting my voice to hide my excitement.

"Let's go," he said, leading me into the woods.

CHAPTER TWELVE

Walking beside Arrow rather than playing catch-up behind his manic pace was nice. Smaller details of the forest, which I'd missed on my own, took my breath away when he pointed them out. The woods teemed with beauty I had overlooked.

The delicate nature of this world grew on me. Increasingly, I found myself enjoying the beauty rather than comparing it to its two-dimensional equivalent. Some things just didn't transfer. I had seen only a fraction of this world, but I felt like I had lost out on so much over the years. Dreamscape was a pale imitation of Lockhorn.

"How do you know all of this stuff?" I asked as he pointed out the erratic patterns of pollen on the underside of dragon weeds.

"I grew up not too far from these woods. Once you get burned once or twice by dragon weed, you tend to take notice."

"Tell me about it." The burns were still fresh in my mind. He chuckled and reached up to pull some vines out of our way.

"Over the years, I've learned a lot from these woods. This, here," he said, folding up the cuff of his sleeve and pointing to a scar across his forearm. "That's from my first pet horned-bit."

"Pet horned-bit?" I asked. I'd never heard of such a thing.

"You laugh, but I was serious as a child. I begged and begged for a pet, but my parents refused."

"So what'd you do?" I asked.

"What any reasonable boy would do. I tried to tame one of these wild beasts on my own."

"No, you didn't!" I covered my mouth.

"Oh, I did. And as you can see, he didn't like it one bit. He rammed his horn right through my arm the first time I tried to pick him up. Sad to say, my days of pet ownership were very short-lived. Any time I asked again, all my parents had to do was point to my arm."

"Oh Arrow, I'm so sorry," I said, tracing the small scar that ran across his forearm.

"These woods, this world...it leaves its mark on you," he said solemnly. I didn't know what to say. There was a depth of emotion behind his words that I wasn't prepared to handle.

"Did you have any pets?" he asked, rolling down his sleeve.

"Flipper," I said with a smile.

"What?"

"Flipper. I had a rainbow fish when I was ten."

"A rainbow fish? That sounds like an odd creature. What happened?"

I looked up, searching for the memory, and frowned. I had almost forgotten. "My mom gave him away."

"Why?"

"Just another time she decided things for me," I muttered. "We were going on vacation, and she arranged for someone to take care of him. But when we got back, she didn't want to pick him up. She said life was easier without a pet. Less to worry about, less to clean. Like she had ever taken care of him." I rolled my eyes.

"Seems like our parents liked to think they know best." He rubbed his forearm. "That's sometimes the case, but not always."

"Not always," I said, exhaling deeply before meeting his gaze. "So what else would surprise me about these woods, besides the obvious danger and strange animals?"

"I never called them strange."

"A horned-bit; come on. Those are pretty strange looking, if you ask me."

"I never noticed," he said.

I shrugged. Maybe they weren't that strange to someone from

this world. "What else?"

"Never turn your back on a fly trap," he said, swooping me forward into his arms.

"What?" I asked just as something slammed shut behind me. Wind from the forceful snap blew my hair off my neck. I stared at a pair of light green petals and overlapping thorns that had closed where I'd stood. Where poison dripped from its open petals, steam shot up in bursts. "Thanks," I whispered. My hands slid against the cool leather of his vest, tangling in the feathered fringe along the pockets. His heart beat as rapidly as mine.

"My pleasure," he said. "I can't have you hurt before we really need you."

A lump caught in my chest. I couldn't help but feel bad for leading him on. What would happen when I found my way home and the rebellion had to fend for themselves? That wouldn't happen. This world wasn't real—when I got myself out of it, it would vanish. Wouldn't it? I shook the guilt out of my head.

"Speaking of when you need me. What exactly are we looking for at the baron's?" Each level of the game ended with a special token. If I knew what he wanted, I might be able to pinpoint the exact level.

"How do you know we're looking for something?"

"Believe it or not, I know about these manors." I felt smug.

"Really?" he asked, even more skeptical than before.

"Yes, really," I said, putting my hands on my hips. "Now, what are we looking for exactly? I want to make sure I know which one we'll be in."

He exhaled. "You know more than one?"

"I know a lot you haven't given me credit for."

"That will change, my lady. I'm truly sorry for any misgivings. You are our hero, and I'm proud to accompany you on this journey."

I hid my blush by looking away.

"Anyways, we're on a reconnaissance mission of sorts."

Now it was my turn to be skeptical. "Reconnaissance? What are we looking for?"

"The rebellion needs information from Baron Marix."

"So we're going to talk to him?" I asked. There had to be more to the story. No tokens that I knew of related to just talking.

"Not quite," he said, softening his gaze as he looked at me.

"What then?"

"The information we need is hidden in his paperwork."

Paperwork, paperwork, paperwork. My mind raced until it landed on an image of ancient scrolls. Of course we had to go to the hardest manor of them all.

"And you know where we can find it?" I asked.

His smile wavered in a crooked grin. "In his safe," he said.

"Wait a second," I said, stopping mid-step and grabbing his arm. "Are you really telling me after you just got mad at me for stealing that you've been planning to do the same thing?"

"I wouldn't call it stealing."

"What do you call it when you take something that's not yours?" I asked, feeling amused and annoyed at the same time.

"You got me there, Alex." He feigned defeat and held his arms out in surrender. "I have to hope stealing from the baron is less offensive than taking money from ailing children."

I twisted my lips. He had me there. "Fine," I said. "So we're looking for papers and maps? That's all?"

"You make it sound like a small matter."

"I just want to make sure I know what we're getting ourselves into. The fewer surprises the better. Can I ask what type of information you're looking for?"

"Let's just say it's worth the risk."

I let it be. He could keep his secrets; they didn't change what I needed to focus on. I had more secrets than I ever wanted to share. "Okay, I trust you," I said, falling into step beside him.

"Really?" he asked, furrowing his brows as he looked at me.

"Yes, really," I said with a sideways glance. "Don't you trust me?"

He matched my smile and nodded. "With my life."

We hiked east for hours, traversing the Wounded Woods until we reached the foothills. I tried to recall the map I had hastily drawn at the shoreline to envision where we were now. Lingering pieces of this world floated around my mind, and pinning them down would free me to concentrate on other things.

Like how to get us out of the baron's manor alive.

I hadn't lied about knowing Baron Marix's manor. I did. Natalie and I struggled with that level and had to repeat it often, sometimes several times in a game. We often ran out of time in the passageways; other times, the fire dancers killed me. When we made it to the end, we still lost to the baron more times than I wanted to admit. Knowing my way around the manor didn't ensure our success. My mind churned, flashing awful images of our imminent death. Add that to the new ominous song the birds chirped, and the oppressiveness of dread became unbearable.

"Why do they do that?" I asked, shuddering at the reverberating timbre in the song.

"What?"

"The birds," I said, pointing to the trees. "Why do they sing that way? It was different before."

He followed my gaze and shrugged. "Different birds, different songs."

I looked up and saw he was right. The bright, colorful birds that had been with me since the beginning weren't here. It took me a moment to spot the new creatures, and once I did, I wished I hadn't. Black birds covered the trees like leaves, shrouded by darkness. Wings and beaks stacked atop each other, blocking out the night sky. Large red eyes bulged beneath crowns of feathers. Their bleeding eyes stalked our every step, mocking us with their insidious song.

I jumped into step with Arrow and watched the darkness brighten as we withdrew from the forest and summited the peak. The moon illuminated the night, and bright speckles dotted the vista. The birds stayed behind the tree line, but their song haunted us, bass tones giving way to reverberating chirps and clashing squawks. I knew the melody too well. Reserved in the game for castles and the end of the hardest levels, it only added to my reluctance. Nothing good awaited us down the hill.

"Do you think we can stop to eat before we enter the manor?" I asked, looking up at the stars. Arrow stopped and opened his mouth like he was going to argue but then changed his mind.

"Of course," he said. "Will here work?"

I nodded and dropped my bag to the ground. My neck ached and muscles I didn't know I had screamed.

"I'm not used to all this walking," I said, rubbing the indentions on my shoulders where the bag's straps dug into my skin.

"Even with all your journeys?" Arrow asked, pulling out a quarter end of a loaf of bread and an apple.

Whoops. How many times was I going to forget I was the hero here? I rolled my neck and looked him square in the eyes. "There's usually more fighting than walking." It was only a half-lie. I certainly fought with my mom.

"There's not much further to go, I promise. We should be there within the hour. It's just over this ridge," he said as he handed me a small slice of bread.

I swallowed hard and accepted the bread. Had we already traveled that far? The first bite of bread melted in my mouth again. It tasted just as wonderful.

I crossed my legs and wrapped my arms around my folded knees, looking back at the sky. Even here, the twinkling lights put me at ease. The keepers of wishes and unfulfilled promises. Would my wishes be answered in a fantasy world? It didn't hurt to try. I found the brightest and made a wish.

"Have another," Arrow said, throwing me a slice of bread.

"Are you reading my mind?" I asked.

"Ha, I wish that I could, my lady, but your mind is a mystery to me." He sliced the apple in half and then paused. "I'm sorry—" he began as he sliced the apple again and nicked his finger.

"Arrow, are you okay?" I jumped to his side and wrapped his

thumb with one of the old vines trailing across my arms.

"Yes, I'll be fine now," he said, covering my hand with his.

I tentatively smiled and sat back down. A flurry of butterflies flickered through me, and my hand tingled where his skin touched mine. What was happening to me? I couldn't do this. Not here, not with him. I didn't have imaginary friends as a kid; I couldn't have a fictional boyfriend now.

I took another bite of bread and twisted my hands around each other. "What are you sorry for?"

"For my behavior earlier today. It was uncalled for," he said, dividing the apple into pieces and handing me half.

"Oh geez, please don't do that. I won't let you justify my actions. I'm just glad we've moved past it. Right?" I raised an eyebrow at him.

"Yes, my lady."

"Look, if you want to apologize for anything, let it be for calling me that all day," I joked. He looked at me with a strange expression. "It's not that I don't like it," I said quickly, "but I'd rather be called Alex."

"Of course, my…er…Alex."

"Thanks. I like that," I said, biting into the apple.

"I like it too." He smiled. "So what's our first move?"

I glanced behind him to the dark forest. "You said it yourself. We go through there and down the hill."

"When we get there?"

"Ah, that's where the fun begins. This manor's set up pretty straightforwardly. If you stick by my side, you'll get through with no problem." I embraced the arrogance. Right now, it felt better than fear. Maybe if he believed it, I would too.

"Then I won't leave your side."

We finished our apple, and when I went to find my bag, I stumbled over a fallen log. "Crap," I said, rubbing my shin. His face lit up, and he reached around my leg for my bag.

"Do you mind?"

I shook my head and watched him pull out the two wooden

boxes. "I noticed this when you first showed them to me," he said, pulling out two thin envelopes that were pasted to the top interior of the box. "They might come in handy for us now."

"What are they?" I asked, leaning in towards him.

"Just wait, you'll see." He winked at me and tipped the first package towards my hand. "Put your hands together."

I gasped as a stream of yellow dust filled my palms. The soft powder illuminated the area. "What is this?" I asked in a whisper.

"Another thing you don't know about?"

I ignored his joke, watching the light grow as I squeezed my hands together and fade as I released them. "Really, what is this? It's fantastic."

He pulled out the second package and slipped it into one of the pockets on his vest. "It's luminance powder. It might help us maneuver down the hill and inside."

"How does it work?" I asked, fascinated by the rolling light. It was as if the stars had fallen into my palms.

Arrow cupped his hands around mine. The same jolt of electricity ran through me. "Change the pressure on the powder, depending on the amount of light you want." He demonstrated by pressing my hands together and then letting them fall open again.

"Like this?" I asked, letting the light roll along my palms. Each grain of powder flickered, and when condensed, brightened. I created small snowballs of light in each hand.

"Not too bad for someone from the north. I actually think you might know what you're doing." We laughed together.

The excitement behind his eyes deepened as he looked at me. I loosened the powder to hide the red rushing to my cheeks and slid half of it into the envelope, tucking it away inside my bag.

"Don't give me too much credit yet. Wait until we make it out of there. Speaking of, we really should be going. Ready?" I asked.

"At your command, Alex," he said, brushing the dirt off his legs, stepping into line behind me. "Lead the way."

Something about his words struck me. I hadn't thought about

being in control. Now it was like a spotlight shone on those words. It was all I heard. I'd never had complete autonomy before.

This could be fun.

I smiled as I made my first decision and stepped into the forest. The stars hid above the dark branches, and when I looked up, the silhouettes of the birds followed me into the bramble-lined forest.

The farther we marched, the more thorns bit into the thin fabric covering my legs. Ducking into the thorn bushes didn't help, and a nagging pressure bordering on pain poked my ribs. Sharing space with the heavy branches hurt, but also gave us the best vantage point into the valley below. The damp ground soaked through my leggings, and my teeth chattered. Arrow draped his cloak over my shoulders, but it wasn't that kind of chill.

My breath looked like the layer of fog surrounding the already ominous building. The Marix estate stretched across the bowl of the valley, backed up against the foothills opposite us, and rested near a small pond to the east. I could see the strategy of its design. With only one entrance to the manor, the baron effectively kept his enemies at bay by watching every arrival.

I wanted to leave. Every fiber of my body screamed *danger!* Terror choked me from the inside. My heart pounded in my chest, keeping me from breathing deeply. Could I really do this? Face the multitude of dangers lurking in those long hallways?

Before my fear could paralyze me, I stood up. Arrow's cloak slid off my shoulders. I had to remember I wasn't doing this for the rebellion. Papers were not worth this risk…but getting home was.

"You're sure you know this place?" Arrow piped up from beside me. His voice didn't give away the glint of doubt in his eyes.

"Like the back of my hand," I said, keeping my eyes glued to the building. My heart hammered against my chest. I shuffled forward through the brush, only hearing snippets of what Arrow said. I glanced in his direction and saw him checking the fastenings on his vest and tightening his bag.

"…Armored knights, poison darts, fire balls…"

"Mmmm hmmm."

"...Explosives, trap doors..." he continued, rattling off the list of known dangers.

"Yeah, I know all about them," I said, moving closer to him.

I wasn't ignoring him on purpose, but his nervous energy was killing me. I was well aware of the dangers awaiting us at the castle. Having them listed off did nothing but escalate my heartbeat, and if it drummed any faster, I would need more vines to heal broken ribs.

"Look, Arrow, no more talking about the dangers. Unless you're trying to talk me out of this," I said, raising my eyebrows at his silence. "I didn't think so. I promised we'd get your papers, and we will. We'll be out of there in no time. Together."

"Before we—"

"No. We leave now," I stopped his thought before he said something that would change my mind. "Stick close to me. We might not be able to stop once we get in there."

Arrow didn't flinch, falling silently into line behind me.

From a distance, the illusion of the game continued. As a tiny speck on the horizon, the manor hardly presented a threat. Even as it grew to the size of my palm, I felt in control. It wasn't until we reached the bottom of the hill, hiding behind the bridge's stone pillars that the pit in my stomach opened.

A sensation of nausea, exponentially worse than how I felt before every art contest, crept up my throat. I had to move. Experience taught me not to let it linger. I cracked my knuckles and tucked the ponytail underneath the edge of my hat.

Time to play the game.

The manor was close enough now for me to see it in detail. Shadows blended into the stones, creating a wall of varying shades of gray. Charcoal stained the walls where the torches had been extinguished. Even the Marix crest, a black stallion, melted into the nothingness. The manor stood several stories high. On each level, torches created a beam of light across the base of the hills, briefly illuminating the multitude of guards defending the estate.

My breath caught in my chest again as I counted men inside rushing past the windows, dimming the light with their movements. An isolated light shone from the top of a tower.

The baron's quarters. That's where we needed to go.

We hunched over, skimming the damp ground as we crossed the bridge, hiding ourselves in silence and shadows. The only sign of our presence, the small triangles of our wet footprints, slowly faded away.

At the threshold of the door, I paused, my hands scraping the rough stone. Arrow's eyes remained alert, watching for my signal. "Are you ready?" I asked, cursing the slight warble in my voice.

"As ready as I'll ever be. I won't leave your side," he said, tightening the buckles on his vest one last time.

"That's what I'm counting on," I said, offering a warm smile.

"And I'm counting on you."

No pressure.

"Arrow, there's one thing you should know," I said. "I have a good idea of some of the dangers we'll face in there. I'm not afraid, but if it comes down to it, I'm not sure I can kill."

There was a long silence. "You may not have a choice."

The sadness in his voice caught my attention, and when I looked back, his eyes had darkened with their familiar, guarded expression. How many choices had been taken from him? I frowned and turned back to the manor. That discussion would have to wait until we were safe.

The cold, black handle of the door chilled my hand. A loud click sounded as I leaned my weight against the handle. It didn't budge. This would not be the stealthy entrance I'd hoped for.

Arrow hissed at me and nodded towards the end of the path. I followed his gaze and saw a dark mass flutter in and out of a window. I ran to the window, carefully peeking around the curtains. No guards, light, or loud clicking noises from the door to alert anyone. My heart leapt. There was still a chance we could miss some of the threats.

With my dagger in one hand, I straddled the windowsill before

114

dropping into the room. Behind me, Arrow followed. It was too late to change my mind now; we were committed. The room echoed with silence. I rolled my fingers over my palm and activated the luminance powder. Through the dim light, cold, hard grimaces peeked through the shadows.

"We're in the statue room," I whispered, walking tentatively forward.

I shook my palm, loosening the powder to create a broader light. My breath caught in my chest. Marble statues stared at us from around the room. Each was carved with great skill, showcasing details down to the razor edges of the swords. I walked silently past the figures at first, but the artist in me couldn't resist them. A thick layer of dust collected along each bust. It was a shame that no one enjoyed or took care of this art. No wonder they didn't notice the window was open. I blew off the dust, apologizing as Arrow sneezed.

"Is there something in here?" Arrow's question brought me back to the present.

"No, sorry. I was just looking at the statues. So much underappreciated beauty. Who are all these people?"

He clenched his jaw. "They're the new ruling class. Berkos and his minions. Let's go."

"I'm sorry. I didn't know."

"Now you do. Where do we go from here?" He stepped in front of me, and a flash of red caught my eye.

"No!" I yelled, pulling him back towards me as an explosion shook the room. Chunks of marble hit my legs as we rolled away from the statues underneath the window. Dust covered us, making it hard to breathe. The blast had turned over statues, breaking some in pieces. On others, new scars marred the hard surfaces.

Not exactly the stealthy entrance I had been hoping for. Every guard had now been informed of our intrusion. It wouldn't be long until they arrived.

I stood slowly, yanking a chunk of marble from my thigh. Blood soaked the upper edge of my leggings; the rest hung together in tattered shreds. I bit down on my dagger and tied my belt around my leg. I hated blood, and now it coated my free hand.

"Arrow," I said, shaking his still body, curled underneath the windowsill. "We have to go."

He stirred with protest, and rested his head in his hands. A trail of blood rolled down the side of his head, clearing a path through the layer of dust. His dark eyes stood out in his pale face as he looked me over. "Are you hurt? How did you know?"

"No, the explosion missed me. Don't forget, I know this place," I reassured him, hoping to calm the fear in his eyes. "The statue's eyes flashed before it blew. I'm just glad I saw it in time."

"Me too." He coughed and bent over, grabbing his ribs.

"Look Arrow, this is your last chance. We don't need to do this. We can just jump back out the window like we were never here," I said, seeing the pain on his face.

"We're not going back. I need those papers," he said, gripping my hand and standing up. "At whatever cost."

"Then we have to go," I said, helping him up and wrapping my arms around his back. I just hoped the cost wasn't more than I wanted to pay. Together we hobbled around the edge of the room, avoiding the now-obvious trip wires. As we passed each statue, red flashes warned me of their activation. With that one misstep, we'd armed the entire estate.

I kept my eyes focused on the flashing lights on top of each statue. One wrong step would cause another explosion.

CHAPTER THIRTEEN

We hobbled out of the statue room and slid against the stone walls in a darkened corner of the hallway. Guards ran past us, their armor echoing through the corridor as we shrank further into the shadows. I pulled the cloak over us, grateful for the invisibility of the unlit hall. In our condition, we weren't prepared to fight any of them.

I leaned over Arrow and glanced down the connecting hallway. Every second we lingered put us in jeopardy. His breath sounded in my ear, shallow and strained. When I leaned back, I noticed his arms protectively cradling his ribs. I held back my instinct to hold him, to try to make him feel better. In all the scenarios I had run through my mind, Arrow getting hurt had never occurred to me. The consequence of my actions, or lack thereof, moaned at my side.

"Did you break something?" I asked, dreading his answer.

"I'm fine," he said, wincing as he adjusted his position against the wall.

"That didn't answer my question. Do you have any more vines?"

"There's a few more, but I'm saving them, just in case."

"In case of what?" I demanded. Too loud. I forced my voice to be quieter. "You're hurt. You need them."

"No, not yet. I'll be fine." He pulled his bag to his chest, wheezing with effort. "We should save them." He raised an eyebrow and managed a small smile. The vines were for me.

I gave him a hard look. "There's no point in saving them if it costs you your life. This mission is for you. Not me. I don't need the papers to do my part."

He kept his bag closed.

"Look, I'm not playing around here. You're hurt, and my wounds are fine. The bleeding in my leg has already stopped and I can walk, but I'm not strong enough to carry you. So if you want these papers, you need to heal yourself. Otherwise, I'm walking right out that window. I'm not going to get killed because of your stubbornness. I'll find another way."

He avoided my gaze for a long time.

"Let me see your dagger," he said, pulling out a tangled heap of vines from inside his bag. I handed it over, surprised at the emptiness I felt with it out of my hand, even for a moment.

"Thanks," he said, slicing through the vines.

A scent of melon hit me. I hadn't noticed it in the forest, but in these stuffy halls, the crispness was overwhelming. I was about to say something, but the words stuck on the tip of my tongue as he undid his vest and lifted his shirt to wrap his bare stomach. Strong muscles hugged his body where his fingers tied the vines together. I couldn't look away, I couldn't stop my heart from beating, and I couldn't find the words I had planned to say. I froze, my cheeks flushed.

He caught me looking before he leaned against the wall, closed his eyes, and sighed. "You were right." A content smile reached across his face. "I'm sorry I was so stubborn about it."

I mumbled incoherently, still tongue-tied. He opened his eyes and gave me a crooked smile.

"What?"

I still couldn't remember what I'd wanted to say. Even worse, his playfulness told me he had an idea why.

"If you're better, it's time to get going again. Every second we stay here is an extra chance to be caught," I blurted out.

"I live to follow your orders, Goldy," he said, winking. "Give me a couple more minutes for the vines to soak in." He leaned back and closed his eyes again. "Thanks for saving me by the way. I guess that makes us even."

"Don't thank me yet. Not until we get those papers." I reached for my hair, brushing away the loose strands around my face and down my neck.

As I waited for him to heal, I turned my attention to the dusty floor and dragged my fingers through the dirt. A clear line appeared under my fingertips. I quickly outlined the castle formation and the rooms we'd pass through on each level.

"Can you see this?" I asked.

"What's that supposed to be?" He covered his ribs as he leaned forward. The pain still resonated on his face, but he wasn't as pale as he had been a few minutes ago.

"It's the manor. Or at least the parts I can remember. We're here," I said, pointing to where I had drawn two stick figures. "And we need to get over here." I trailed my finger through the dirt to the top room of the tower.

"It can't be that simple."

"Oh no, it's not simple at all. We have hidden passageways to go through, traps to avoid, and guards to elude. The temptation to fall for the traps will be great. These manors were built to kill. Don't forget that for a moment. The thing that tempts you most could be your undoing."

"I doubt that," he said, his gaze lingering on me.

"Don't test it. You said the woods were full of danger? This is so much worse." I stared him down until he looked away. He was already hurt. I didn't want to get him killed too. I knew just enough for it to be dangerous.

"With you leading, Goldy, I don't worry. My life's safe in your hands."

I didn't want his life in my hands. Trying to save my own was tough enough. His cavalier charm was great when our lives weren't in danger, but now it added another level of responsibility I didn't want.

"Let's go," I said.

Rocks scuffled behind me, and Arrow's arm encircled my waist for support as he struggled to stand. When I glanced down at his hand resting on my waist, I wondered if all my nerves were from the manor.

"I'm ready. Where do we go from here?" His deep voice brought my mind back to the present.

"Stay close. Remember what I said about traps?"

"I won't leave your side," he whispered.

"You already promised that."

"This time, I mean it." He peeked beyond me into the hall. "I think it's clear."

My eyes lingered on him for a moment before following his gaze to the corridor we had to take. "Okay, let's do this." We plunged through the darkness, hoping against hope that we wouldn't run up against any more guards.

After a moment, we left the dim hallway and entered a larger room on the other side. Bare walls encircled us, a blank canvas of gray broken by the occasional torch and a row of evenly spaced doors. Flames danced across the tops of the torches, the only movement in the still room. As our eyes adjusted, we saw, hidden in that darkness, displayed in niches between the doors, bouquets of dragon weed in brass vases. Half of the poisonous flowers wilted over the edge. My palms burned just at the sight. I looked more closely at the faded, red doors that lined both sides of the room. Chipped paint revealed hints of hidden designs underneath.

We marched through the room, ensuring that no guards followed us. When we passed beyond it, we entered another chamber, nearly identical. The only differences were in the doors. Instead of faded red, a mosaic of colors stained the wood.

"It's beautiful," Arrow said, straying from my side.

"You can't always see the biggest dangers. Don't underestimate anything in here," I whispered, pulling him back to my side. "These men don't fight fair or by the rules. If they trick us into submission, that's fine with them."

Each door called out to me. Hidden images flashed beneath the bright paint. The designs played peek-a-boo with the light. Even knowing the traps hidden behind these doors, I fought the temptation to draw closer. I wanted to know what they held.

"What is this room?" Arrow asked as I reached for the first door. I didn't need to look at him to see the wonder rushing through him. I felt it too.

"The room of promises," I said, tracing the delicate designs on the door panels. Light blue paint flaked off at my touch. I gasped and covered my mouth. When the faded paint flecked off the door, an image appeared.

My room.

Contrasting art pieces intersected along my wall, creating an indecipherable puzzle, showcasing my triumphs and struggles. Cardboard boxes were nowhere in sight, and my favorite treasures remained untouched on my shelves. The sheets on my bed bunched together creating an odd shape, and I saw popcorn lining the floor. Was that me, tangled in the sheets?

My hand tightened around the handle. If I opened this door, I could be home. Re-enter my world. That's what I wanted, right? What I had been searching for since waking up here. This was it, a way back. The metal handle jingled under my trembling hand. Why was I hesitating?

The longer I looked at the room, the more unsettled I became. Something didn't feel right. It was my home, yet it seemed different. This wasn't the room I remembered, the one I was pulled away from.

This wasn't real. The vision offered to me was from a lifetime ago. It was what I fantasized about—going back to a time before moving was even an option. My unease increased. It was a hollow dream. If I grabbed it now, I would be stuck in a prison of the past. My trance broke.

It was a trap.

I let go of the handle and stepped back, turning just in time to see Arrow at the green door next to me. His hand was poised to turn the handle in front of him.

"Arrow, no!" I yelled, running at him and slapping his hand off the knob.

"I have to go in there! He needs me." He pushed past me, and I grabbed his wrist.

"You can't. It's a trap."

"I don't believe you," he said, fighting against my pull.

"You have to. This whole manor is nothing but a trick. You can't give in to it," I begged, pulling him away with all my weight. "I tried to warn you before. None of this is real. Your door's the same as mine was; nothing more than your deepest hope."

"It can't be," he whispered with tears glistening in his eyes. He backed away from the door and me.

"You have to believe me. This is the room of promises. It pretends to give you your greatest desire. But it's just a ruse. If you open that door, you'll be trapped forever." I looked at the fading image of two boys on his door. "Who are they?"

"No one," he said, turning away. "Like you said, it's nothing more than a memory."

"It looks like a good one," I said, letting my hand linger until he pulled away.

"It was." He walked straight to the doorway at the end of the room. I met him there, watching the personalized images on the doors fade. A stab of loss hit me when I turned around. Walking away from a dream, even if it was a trap, wasn't easy.

"Wait for me."

He stopped, but didn't meet my eyes.

"Did you want to talk about it?" I asked, reaching for his shoulder.

"I just want to get out of here. There's nothing good in this place," he said, shrugging off my offer.

I couldn't agree with him more. We walked through another room, a replica of the one we'd already passed. Everything was the same, down to the wilted dragon weed bouquets. The only differences were the colors of the doors—saffron, silver, violet.

"Are you sure we're going in the right direction?" he asked. His hands balled in fists at his side and tension strained his neck.

"I know it seems odd," I said. "But you'd be surprised how many people pass the first test, only to fail the next. Beating one temptation doesn't mean it goes away. Don't lower your guard until we're out of here."

He nodded and followed me through the room. We stayed in the center, refusing to reveal the hidden images on each portal. Not knowing made it easier.

We found ourselves in a new chamber with more doors. Arrow pulled me back when I strayed close to the walls again.

"Don't worry. I know what I'm doing this time," I said, counting out the number of doors until I reached the seventh and stalled with my hand on the knob. Arrow placed his hand on top of mine. I saw the question in his eyes and nodded. "This is the one we go through."

"Our deepest hope?" he asked with a straight face.

"That's debatable," I said with a dark chuckle, "but it will lead us to the baron, eventually."

"Eventually—" The darkness greeting us from behind the door stopped him.

"Eventually." We stepped into an abyss of darkness. The door slammed shut behind us as we let go. "Arrow, please tell me you have more of that luminance powder handy," I whispered, fumbling to find the edge of the room.

After a few moments of shuffling, a small ball of light appeared in his hand, illuminating his haunted face. Just as my eyes adjusted to the new light, he screamed and dropped the powder.

"No!" he yelled, disappearing into shadows. The walls thundered with the pounding of his fists.

"Arrow, wait!" I shouted, scrambling after the dispersed luminance powder. Without that, we'd be consumed by darkness. I pressed the granulated flakes together and scooped them into my hands. When I looked up, a mutilated face with gouged eyes and sunken cheeks smiled down on me.

I screamed, dropping the powder again. The rough floor cut through my leggings when I tripped over my feet, crashing to the floor. I skidded backwards until I hit the wall. The sound of Arrow's pounding fists disappeared under the hammering of my heart.

"Arrow, where are you?" I screamed. "We need to get out of here!" The silence responded for what seemed like an eternity.

"I'm right here." He picked up the fallen light and cupped my shoulder.

"D-did you s-see him?" I asked, grabbing onto him.

He exhaled slowly. "I saw him, and the others."

"Others?" My heart hammered as I furtively looked over his shoulders.

"They're all here. Brave men," he said sadly. "They won't hurt you." He pulled me up, keeping his arm wrapped around me, holding the light forward. "They won't hurt anyone anymore."

My heart broke as Arrow lifted the light to the wall. Behind a glass enclosure, the remains of an army faded to dust. All I could see were faces frozen in misery, hands outstretched towards the clear wall, ivory bones encircling steel bars, searching for a way out.

"You knew them?"

"Some of them. Do you see the crest on their shoulders? That's the Great Oak. These were men of the rebellion."

"What were they doing here?" I asked.

Arrow's lips tightened. "The same thing we are."

I stared at the men, trapped by a wrong step or temptation, and the reality crushed me. The consequences here...

Failure led down one path—death.

I couldn't stand it anymore. The walls of this estate bore down on me. Nothing in here hinted at the fun I remembered from my childhood. The simple maze of hallways and doors I had memorized over the years had transformed into a labyrinth of death and terror. I had to get home before I turned into one of them, defeated by a futile journey.

I gave the feathers on Arrow's vest a quick tug and nodded to the door at the far end of the room. "It's time to go."

"But what about them? We can't just leave them here. We have to get them out, give them a proper burial," he protested.

My heart ached for him, it really did. If they were my friends, I probably would've wanted the same thing. But they weren't. And the pressure on my shoulders told me time was running out.

"We can't. Not right now. Once we're out, we can tell someone about it," I said.

His eyes cut into me, and I knew he didn't understand. Sometimes the harshest news needed to be delivered quickly.

"I promise you'll have a chance to make sure no one else gets trapped in Marix's manor, but for now, you need to trust me."

He nodded and pulled his hood over his face. I sighed as his eyes became unreachable. The more time we spent together, the more similarities I found between us.

"It'll be better once we leave here," I said, but the reassurance sounded hollow, even to me.

We hid in the darkness. Arrow followed close behind me as I darted down hallways, going through one set of doors only to pass into another room of promises. Each room looked the same as the last, bare except for dragon weeds, painted doors, and burning torches. I knew it couldn't last much longer.

I had traversed these halls enough to know that once one challenge was conquered, the next awaited. When we turned the corner into a brightly illuminated hallway, I knew we'd found the next danger. I stopped. Sometimes knowing what came next wasn't an advantage.

"What is it?" Arrow asked, peeking around my shoulders at the empty stone path, then searching my face.

"Our next challenge." My voice shook. "I'll need some rope."

He tightened his lips, looking like he wanted to say something. His hands lingered on mine as he handed me the rough twine.

"Be careful," he said.

I wished that were possible. Before I turned back to face the bright corridor, I looked into Arrow's eyes. "No matter what, promise me you won't let go."

"I promise."

I untied the belt from my thigh and wrapped it around my waist, securing the rope through the belt loop and around my shoulders in a harness. "You'll need to hold me and be ready at any moment. There won't be any warning." I handed him the rope and pulled away, testing his grip.

His eyebrows furrowed in concern. "Warning for what, exactly?"

"I told you this wouldn't all be easy," I snapped and bit my lip. "Just make sure you're holding on."

Tears flooded my eyes, and I turned away before he could see them or the depth of my vulnerability. Up to this point, I'd had control. Now I had to let go. I blinked hard, wishing the tears away. Heroes didn't cry.

The slight tug from the harness gave me security as I started forward. The ground would give way at any moment. This hall continued seamlessly, every cobblestone blending into the next as we wound out of view.

Besides the shuffling of our boots and my shallow breaths, an eerie silence filled the long hallway. I stepped tentatively, testing my weight before fully moving forward. Each solid step surprised me. Halfway down the hall, my fear let up a little. Soft cracks sounded as we shuffled forward, but the ground held.

I stepped again and then stopped when I heard a loud click. Sand disappeared around the cobblestone under my foot, plummeting into darkness as soon as I jumped back. My eyes locked onto the black hole inches away that had almost swallowed me.

Another click sounded, and the stone beneath me dropped without warning.

CHAPTER FOURTEEN

My screams echoed off the rough walls of the chasm, broken abruptly as the harness caught my fall.

A jolt ran through my body as I swung into the wall, feeling the breath knocked out of me. I hung suspended over a dark void, staring into nothing. The rough edges of broken stones scratched my palms. I grasped at them, stopping my body from bouncing off the wall again.

Arrow leaned precariously over the hole, his jaw clenched and brow furrowed as he tried to balance. A drop of sweat rolled down his face, and his arms shook under the strain of holding onto me.

I wasn't sure if the fluttering in my stomach was from butterflies or a reaction to my fall. Arrow had literally saved me, more than once now. And what twisted my stomach more was that this time I had trusted him to do it.

Once I stopped swinging, I stretched my arms and legs out, pressing against the outer sides of the pit and holding my position. My legs buckled beneath me, threatening to give way. Slowing my heart took longer than I'd anticipated. I looked up to see Arrow watching me. The small lines crowding his forehead looked out of place, and in that instant, my determination returned. I had to remind him that I was his hero.

"This is going to sound strange," I yelled up at him.

"I have a feeling nothing you say will surprise me anymore."

"You need to let me go," I said.

"What? No!"

His desire to protect me warmed me. "Don't worry, I'm not going to fall. But you have to let go so I can climb down."

He looked past me into the pit and raised his eyebrows. "We have to go down there?"

"Do you trust me?" I asked.

"Well, yes, but…" he stammered, tightening his grip on the rope.

"But nothing. Unless you want to fight legions of armed men, this is the way we have to go. It's the secret passageway. We'll get there so much quicker… and safer. Now let go so I can climb down before I lose my strength." I nodded towards my shaking legs.

He looked at my legs and let go. The tug at my waist released, and my weight sunk my feet more firmly against the walls.

"While you're up there," I yelled, "throw down a torch so I can see the way."

He leaned over the opening, flickering flames in one hand. The thought of descending into a raging fire flashed through my mind. "Wait! On second thought, drop some of that luminance powder instead."

He disappeared for a moment and then sprinkled the powder around me. Golden flakes glittered as they descended like snow. No, not like snow; like the golden pixels that had transported me here. I shook off a couple of flakes as they landed on my legs, just in case.

"Arrow, does this powder do anything besides create light?" I asked.

He thought in silence for a moment. "I don't think so. Why?"

"No reason," I said, starting to lower myself towards the ground. How would I begin to explain being eaten by light pixels and transported here?

"Are you sure this is the only way?" he asked, brushing his hair out of his eyes as he peeked over the edge.

"No, Arrow, it's not, I just enjoy getting stuck in pits." I rolled my eyes. "Yes, it's the only way I know how to get through alive. Now, get down here." I shook under the strain on my legs and the burn of the rocks digging into my palms. The narrow chasm seemed to stretch as I descended. He smiled weakly before lowering himself into the pit.

"I'm right behind you," he grunted.

Arrow had an easier time, resting his back against one wall and his feet on the far side. "This is terrifying," he muttered under his breath.

I glanced up and saw his hand shake as he wiped away his hair from his eyes. His wide-eyed, pale face surprised me.

"Are you really afraid?" I asked.

"A little," he said, sliding down an inch. "Why are you laughing?" he asked, skidding down further.

"I'm sorry," I said, stifling a chuckle. "I've just never seen you afraid."

"You've never seen me in tight spaces before either," he said. "I prefer the expanse of the forest to this...this...pit." Sweat beaded on his face as he looked down beyond me.

"Ah, well, you introduced me to the Pits of Wonder, I wanted to return the favor." I hid a smile as I lowered myself another couple of feet. My arms shook with pain. I cursed the fact that, even though he trembled with fear, his arms displayed hardly any exertion.

"Thanks for the wonderful gift, Goldy. I'll remember that once we get out of here. Remember, there's still much more of Lockhorn you haven't seen. I know all its treasures."

"I bet you do."

"I'll show them to you if we get out."

"When we get out."

"Hopefully sooner than later," he said. "How deep is this pit, anyway?"

"Not much further," I said, glimpsing a glint of metal below me. "Not far at all."

Sweat dripped off my face. Now that I saw the spikes, time quickened. Every twitch of my fingers and slip of my feet created a new sensation of imminent death. One mistake meant game over in an instant. My palms slickened and my legs wavered, but eventually I made it to the bottom. The exit, a small opening in the side of the wall, lay right above the spikes. If I didn't aim my body correctly, I'd be impaled.

I pushed off, diving through the small opening and landing in a heap on the hard stones. Curled into a ball, I shook, heaving, letting the emotions overflow. Being face-to-face with death yet again was too much. Dark spots marked the stones where my tears fell, and next to them I saw imprints from the fresh wounds along my palms and knees. I convulsed on the floor, trying to convince myself I'd be fine.

I didn't hear Arrow until he wrapped his arms around my shoulders. I melted into him. My head found its match in the curve of his neck, and my arms wound a path around him. His warmth surrounded me, and the slow beat of his heart calmed mine. We sat entwined, silent. His hands rolled over my back. Greed overwhelmed me.

I grabbed fistfuls of his sleeves, not caring about the dust that covered us or the thought that I might stain his shirt. I didn't care about anything. Every rational thought disappeared from my mind. At that moment, all I cared about was being alive.

Arrow responded. His hands turned more forceful, pressing me closer to his chest. His eyes swept over me, a wild range of emotions flickering across his face—fear, relief, confusion. I rose to my knees, meeting his gaze with my own. He leaned forward, his lips parting, but my inexperience wormed its way through my desire, and I hesitated a moment too long.

Arrow pulled back.

"We better go," I said, even though I didn't mean it. I bit my cheek and brushed the dust off my palms.

"Of course," he said, tightening his lips and pulling his sleeves straight.

Nothing I said could make what had just happened better. The last thing I wanted to do was admit that I hadn't kissed anyone before. He had already accused me of being little more than a child when we met. Besides, it couldn't work out. We were too different. And he wasn't even real.

I had my own mission that went beyond stealing these papers or aiding the rebellion. I couldn't forget where I needed to go. Why was it so hard to remember sometimes?

"Where do we go next?" he asked as if nothing had happened.

"What? Oh, uh, wait here," I said, running ahead to the doorway at the opposite end of the hall. Part of me still reeled from the adrenaline and our near-kiss, but most of me appreciated the distance from him. Right now, I needed to focus. I could almost touch the token at the end of the level.

Sharp staccato beats echoed from the next room. I ducked back behind the doorway's opening and caught my breath. If we could get through these next few rooms, we'd be at the baron's chamber. I inhaled deeply and peeked around the corner.

The opulence of the room overwhelmed me. The minimalism we had seen throughout the estate seemed out of place in comparison with this extravagance. Marble pillars lined the outer edge of the room. Cascading from the ceiling in a scalloped pattern, crimson velvet drapes covered the walls like flames. The edges swirled with the breeze. Perfectly framed within the window, the crescent moon winked, appearing and then disappearing behind a steady line of guards marching in formation.

Their movements shook the ground. Dark, plated armor covered their bodies, and chains and leather masked their faces. Spiked helmets crowned their heads. What was I thinking? I knew I wasn't the hero. I was a girl who freaked out over a bird! The guards would crush me without a second thought. This was insane.

"What do you think?" Arrow whispered from behind me.

"What are you doing here?" I asked. "I thought you were waiting until I had a plan."

He shrugged and peeked around me. "You were taking too long. How many are there?"

"More than I'd like. I don't know if this is such a great idea anymore."

"Ah, Alex, stop worrying. We'll be fine. I know you can get us in without too much fuss." He lifted his fingers and marked the air as he counted the lines of guards. I wished I felt half as confident as he did.

The rhythmic beat of their march grew faster, but it was still slow compared to my heart.

"There are only fifty at most."

"Only fifty. You make that sound like it's a good thing!"

"Berkos has thousands. I'd say this is manageable," he said, leaning further in as the last of the guards marched to the next hall.

How could I argue with that? "Okay, let's go, before they come back," I whispered, pressing my back flat against the wall. Arrow mirrored my position on the other side of the doorway.

"We won't have much time," he whispered. His gaze followed the guards out of the room, and then turned back to me. "Where do we need to go when we get in there?"

"It's down there," I said, focusing on the small stone archway at the far end of the hall. Now if only we could get there without incurring anyone's attention.

Arrow didn't wait. He jumped forward and disappeared behind the first marble pillar. A moment later he appeared and disappeared again behind the next. Something unexpected rose inside me—hope. Maybe we could get through undetected.

I followed, pressing my hands against the smooth surface of the marble as I slid from one column to the next. Cautious, listening for footsteps but anxious to reach the end, we skipped ahead as fast as we could.

Arrow had already passed into the next room when the metallic beat began resounding from the far side of the chamber. I held my breath and pressed my body against the pillar. Now that the guards had returned, I would have to carefully swing around the pillars, moving just enough to stay out of sight while they walked past.

My palms slid down the marble. The guards moved down the center of the room. Red stamps covered the back of their armor, marking their kills. In the game, these marks had been simple dots, pixels of red. Here, they were figures, and I felt sick when I saw far too many small images alongside the full-sized pictures. Some things were inexcusable in any world. I simmered in silence.

Arrow waved me forward as soon as the path cleared. He glared at the guards disappearing behind me.

"Let's get out of this place," I said, dragging him behind me until the cloak of the stairwell's darkness enveloped us. We ran up the spiral stairs two at a time until we reached an ornately carved wooden door. I covered my lips with one finger. We'd arrived. I fought to suppress my rising relief.

A slit of light poured out into the stairway as I pressed against the heavy door. It protested with a deep groan, scraping the ground. We slunk through the small gap before the noise escalated. A pulsing rush of excitement and anticipation gripped me. We'd made it.

Arrow crept past me, his steps smooth. He glided from the doorway we had entered to another at the end of the foyer. Before he disappeared into the darkness, he flashed a bright smile and a wink at me. I waved him forward. I had done my part in getting us here. The rest, securing the papers, depended on him. The quicker he grabbed those, the better. I wanted nothing more to do with this place. It reeked of murder.

The quaint design of the entry room surprised me. After the extremes of opulence and minimalism we'd seen, I didn't expect modest décor and an eye for artistry. Brief hints of luxury shone in the golden frames and elegant figurines, but the room possessed a richness I didn't anticipate. Crisp, pristine furs lined the hand-carved benches sitting beneath each frame. Intricate scenes of horned-bits and winged monsters hid within the spirals and grains of the dark wood.

"Horned-bits," I whispered with a giggle, noticing the pointed antlers that were as big as the animal they belonged to. Arrow was lucky only his arm had been impaled. Why would he have ever wanted one for a pet? The thought of him brought me back to the present. Where was he? He'd had more than enough time to grab the papers.

"Arrow?" I hissed, walking past the first few paintings. Familiar faces from the statue room glared down at me. Both in stone and in paint, the artist had captured the condescending sneer of the royals perfectly. I peeked around the far doorway into darkness, but heard nothing.

"Arrow," I whispered again as I stepped into the pitch black, fumbling around in front of me. I was scared. More scared than I could remember ever being before. We were so close to the end, and I just wanted to get out of there. "Where are you?" I turned the corner.

Candles flickered in glass jars on either side of the room. The baron's private chambers. I slowed my approach to half-speed, exaggerating my steps.

What was taking Arrow so long? I looked at my wrist out of habit, but my watch wasn't there. It didn't matter. I didn't need it to tell me what I already knew from counting the beats of my heart. Too much time had passed. Something must have happened.

I tiptoed closer to the next room and held my breath. Even the whisper of my breathing seemed to echo. As I breached the doorway, a flash of light blinded me. I covered my mouth and screamed as the knife's edge flashed in the candlelight.

"No!" I yelled, stopping Arrow before he plunged his blade into the baron's chest.

Arrow glared at me as the baron stirred in his bed. Despite my protests, he raised his knife again.

"You can't kill him," I said, grabbing Arrow's free arm and pulling him towards me.

Baron Marix's eyes flew open, and as he sat upright, he pulled his sheets up to his chin.

"Didn't you just go through that manor?" Arrow said, clipping each word, shifting his gaze between me and the baron. "Didn't you see the faces of the men?"

I stared at him. He was right. The man deserved to die. There was no justification for anything he'd done. The stamps on the back of his guards' armor showed the atrocities he allowed.

Arrow's hand shook as he held the knife high. It wasn't that I didn't want the baron to die. But I didn't want it to haunt Arrow. I didn't have time to explain, though. While we locked eyes, the baron pressed an emergency alarm, and a bell sounded throughout the room.

"We have to go, now!" I shouted, pulling him away from the bed.

I ignored the 'I told you so' glare Arrow shot at me and ran down the steps. The ringing of the bell followed us. An invisible threat tightened around my heart. Our time ran short.

Behind us, the baron's incoherent shouts almost drowned out the increasing rumble in front of us—the rhythmic marching of the guards.

"We're stuck," Arrow said.

Obviously.

I pressed my body against the far wall. My hands slid against the stone, stopping against something warm. I looked down at Arrow's hand under mine and met his expectant gaze.

"What now?" he asked.

My eyes widened. I had never had to find a way out, just a way to win. The levels usually ended once I got the token. "I don't know. Did you get the papers you needed?"

"I have them." He nodded and patted his vest pocket, where I could see the rough edges of worn parchment.

I nodded and looked past him up the stairs. That wasn't an option. I had already stopped Arrow from killing the baron once. The echoes of the armor alerted me to the guards. They moved more quickly than I remembered.

They raised their swords as they approached. Moonlight flashed off their smooth helmets, and an idea hit me. It was a long shot, but it seemed like the only chance we had.

"Do you still have a packet of vines?" I asked Arrow, keeping my eyes on the glinting helmets, counting down their approach.

"Yes…"

"Enough for the both of us?"

He tightened his lips and nodded.

"Then follow me, and whatever you do, don't stop!"

I ran back up the stairway about ten steps and turned around, facing the entrance. Energy pumped through me. Just as the first guard crossed the threshold, I jumped, flinging myself forward. My feet connected with the smooth helmet of the first guard, knocking him backwards into the guards behind him. I jumped again before he collapsed to the floor and catapulted off the next guard's shoulders, leaping from one person to the next.

Before they could raise their swords to attack, I was already where I needed to be. With the last of my strength, I grabbed the velvet drapes and swung through the open window, waiting for the openness below me. Letting go, I dropped two stories to the ground.

My legs jammed and buckled underneath me as I landed. The ground shook when Arrow landed next to me, and I realized that I couldn't move. Breathing took all my energy. I knew that the moment I shifted, I would regret it.

"Did we really just jump over Marix's guards?" he wheezed, scrambling through his bag.

"I told you not to worry." I struggled to get the words out, wincing. I was right about regretting movement. "Vines?" I rasped, grimacing.

"Almost," he said. "I will never underestimate you again." And then he gave me that smile. The kind that made me weak from the inside out.

I blinked my eyes to keep the tears from falling and looked up as a firework burst across the sky. "Look at that. It's beautiful."

"We don't have much time. The baron's men will be out searching for us soon," Arrow said, slicing the vines open.

I nodded and refocused on the sky, watching the fireworks blur under my tears. Relief overcame me as the first vine took effect, and I closed my eyes.

CHAPTER FIFTEEN

I nuzzled into the warmth of a wool cloak, enjoying a moment of comfort. I refused to open my eyes, no matter how intense the sunlight was on my lids or how pervasive the sweet song of the birds. Sweet song? When had the oppressive chirping ended? My eyes shot open.

Arrow stilled my scream with a smile. "Good morning, Alex."

Good morning? Oh no. How long had he been carrying me? "Good morning," I mumbled, hiding my face in his chest.

His warm laugh doubled my mortification. What if I had talked in my sleep, or worse, drooled on him? Ugh.

"Hey, hey, just relax, Alex," he said, tightening his grip as I shuffled in his arms. "I'm carrying you for a little bit." The tone in his voice told me not to bother arguing. He had made up his mind.

He sped through the trails of the forest, twisting around low branches and high-stepping fallen logs, clearly in his element. Above us, the birds circled, following us with their melody as we moved out of the thick woods into lush meadows. Pockets of honey flowers and dragon weed intermixed in the field. Long ombré blades of grass gave way in the wind, moving in gentle waves.

Nothing seemed to slow him, not even carrying a damsel in his arms. I cringed at the thought. The years of Mom's lectures about being strong and independent came back to me. Surely saving his life kept me out of that classification. I hoped.

I sighed and melted into his arms. I won't lie. It felt good. His warmth, the way his muscles hugged me, and the steady beat of his heart, all put me at ease. I had never felt this way before. It confused me, even more than the whole 'not being real' thing.

Doubts rose to the surface, unsettling me. I couldn't shake them. No matter how much I tried to fade them out or pretend this was all an illusion, I found myself in the same predicament. To survive, I had to be part of the game instead of simply playing it. I looked up at Arrow and noticed the slight smile that rested on the edge of his lips, the dark hair swooping over his eyes. Being part of the game was more dangerous than I wanted to admit.

A contented sigh escaped my lips, and even though he kept his face forward, I saw the corners of his lips rise even more.

"I can walk now," I offered halfheartedly.

"Are you sure?" Arrow asked, his brow furrowed.

"I'm much better," I said, kicking my feet to show him, feeling for the first time the vines spiraling up my legs. I reached down to touch them out and frowned. When had he tied them? So much of last night melted into a fog, except the moments I wished I could forget.

He let me down gently, but kept his arms around my waist, looking at my downcast face.

"Alex?" he asked, tilting my head up to meet him. "What is it?"

"It's nothing," I said, shaking my head, the thoughts twisting me up. "So... about last night..." My voice trailed off.

"Last night?" he asked, tightening his grip around my waist, swinging me around. "You were incredible!"

I brushed the stray blonde wisps out of my mouth and met his gaze. "What?" He obviously remembered something different than I did.

"Last night. The way you led us through the estate. I've never seen anyone be so brave or innovative."

I let out a low chuckle. "I suppose you could call it that. I was thinking more along the lines of crazy."

"Well, that too," he said. "But worth it." He pulled out a packet of rolled parchment.

"Are those what you were looking for?" I asked, staring at the yellowed scroll.

He nodded. "Thanks to you, we got them. Thank you."

"Can I take a look?" I asked, curious to see what had almost cost us our lives.

"Sure, just be careful."

I took the papers and scanned them quickly. "These are just names," I said, disappointed.

"They're more than just names," he said, pointing to the first on the list. "Paulin Jons is a butcher from the south. Larson," he pointed to another name down the list. "He's an innkeeper in Lindle. And...no," he sighed deeply. "Perkins was an old friend."

"I still don't understand. Who are they?"

"Berkos' spies. We've lost a lot of men in recent ambushes. Now we know why. Anyone on this list is an enemy of the rebellion." He shook his head. "This changes the game for us. We now know who we can trust and who we can manipulate to our advantage. You have given us this. I don't think I can thank you enough," he said, his voice thick with emotion.

"Well, maybe you can thank me with some food. I'm starving." On cue, my stomach grumbled.

"Ah, Goldy, I wish I could, but we finished it all yesterday. We'll have to head into town to get something. Are you up for that?"

"I think so. My legs are better," I said, stretching them. I reached around for my dagger and floundered at the empty slot where it normally rested. My stomach growled again. "Do you know where my dagger went?"

"It's here. I had to take it to carry you." He pulled it out of his bag and handed it back to me. "I wanted to get as far away from there as possible before he sent his men out. We surprised him, but I don't think he'll forget about us anytime soon." He chuckled and brushed the hair out of his eyes. "I still can't believe it. I don't think I've ever had quite so much fun fighting anyone."

Fun? We had very different ideas of fun. I straightened my tunic and felt unusual ripples constricting my ribs. Peering beneath my shirt, I saw the vines crisscrossing my stomach. I blushed.

He'd had his hands around my ribs, and I couldn't remember.

"And then the way you jumped over the guards..." His voice continued in the background.

His hands were all over my stomach, and I couldn't remember.

"The way you..."

How could I forget that?

"What?" I cut in, not having paid much attention to anything he'd said.

"Last night. I just can't get over it," he said, coming closer to me.

My version of it didn't seem quite as heroic as his when I replayed the events in my mind. I remembered a lot more fear and fumbling.

I unwrapped the vines around my waist and felt his hand stop on top of mine.

"I'm sorry about that. I didn't mean to cross any boundaries," he said, nodding towards the vines.

My skin flushed. "Don't apologize for healing me. If you haven't figured it out, I seem to attract a little danger."

"Is that all you think you attract?" he asked, shrinking the distance between us.

"It seems everything here comes with some danger," I said, my heart threatening to leap out of my chest.

"Then I'll just have to make sure I stay close," he whispered, taking my hand in his.

"I thought I was supposed to be the hero," I said, looking down at our entwined hands. A blush warmed my face.

"Even a hero needs saving sometimes." He tilted my chin up to meet his gaze.

How was I supposed to respond to that? My stomach fluttered and my knees buckled. We stared at each other, the moment stretching into silence. I didn't know what to do or what to say. I did the only thing I could think of, and looked away.

"Don't do that," he said.

"You don't understand."

"Then help me understand." He raised my chin, searching my face for answers.

"I can't..." I protested, lowering my gaze. Looking at him was too difficult.

"Can't or won't?"

I twisted away. Tears stung the edges of my eyes.

"Alex, you're everything I've ever hoped for," he said softly.

"You mean the rebellion—"

"No," he said, turning me back to face him. "I mean me."

"Don't do this. I...I can't," I said, trembling. I was losing the game of tug-of-war between my heart and mind.

"Why not? There's nothing you can say that could deter me."

I stared at him for a moment. "Nothing?"

"Nothing. Whatever's in your past, is just that...your past. You're here now, with me. I hope," he said, lifting my hand to his lips.

"Arrow, it's not that easy." But I was melting.

"It can be. Let the rest go."

I wanted to. I wanted to fall into his arms, feel his embrace and the beat of his heart that matched mine. I wanted to believe...but I couldn't. How could I forget who I was or pretend that this fantasy was real? I couldn't lose myself here when I needed to get home.

"No," I said, silencing the battle within.

Arrow stepped back, his face fallen. "What?"

"I can't be what you want me to be," I said more evenly.

"I don't understand."

"I don't either. But I can't. I'm not from here," I said after a deep breath.

"It doesn't matter to me where you're from. We could make it work," he said.

"Not this far." I bit my lip. "Arrow—"

"Don't," he said, quieting my protests with his finger on my lips. "We'll make it work."

"Please, Arrow, you don't understand. I don't want to hurt you."

His eyes flickered between confusion and hurt, finally settling on disappointment. He let my hand go. "It's fine, Goldy. If you're truly not interested, I understand. You don't need to worry. I just thought I saw something back there between us," he said.

I bit the inside of my lip. That did not go how I'd intended. "Arrow?"

"Forget about it. Please, just pretend I didn't bring it up. We still have a long way to go to get to town."

I sighed deeply and nodded. Maybe some things were better not discussed. "Which way is it?"

"It's about a half-day walk over that ridge, and…"

"And what?" I asked, following his gaze to the dark plumes. "Oh no." My stomach dropped.

Dark smoke spiraled over the horizon. Beneath each spout of smoke, flames crowned the forest. In their wake, charred remains darkened the trees.

"This has to be Berkos' men. Marix couldn't burn the king's territory without permission. I should have known they would retaliate. I just didn't think it would be so soon."

"Retaliate? Against us?"

"It's bigger than us. He's retaliating against the rebellion. We may have been the spark they were waiting for."

"But how would he have even known? We just left there last night."

"He has ways of communicating quickly. He's probably been following you since you arrived. In fact, he's probably tracking us right now," he said, pausing to look around. "I hate falling into someone else's plan."

I reached for his hand, knowing that feeling all too well. "What do we do?"

He shook my hand off, grabbed his bag and then handed me mine. "We need to get more men," he said, throwing his bag over his shoulder.

"More men? Why?" I asked, dreading his answer.

"Because, Goldy, you're going to lead us to victory, and I assume you'll want more men than just me behind you." His voice held an edge.

"Whoa, what?" I asked, feeling fear's grip tighten on my chest.

"You're the Golden Hero. That's why you're here."

Crap. I knew pretending would eventually come back to haunt me. "I can't do that," I said.

"What do you mean?" he asked, exasperated.

"I mean, I'm not who you think I am," I said. "I'm not the hero you're looking for."

"We've already been over this. I've seen what you can do and what you know about the places we need to go. If you're worried, don't be. You'll have plenty of people to support you."

"No, Arrow, I mean I can't do it. Leading you to hidden papers was one thing, but I can't lead a rebellion. That's not why I'm here."

"Then why are you here?" he asked, shuffling his bag to his other shoulder.

"I'm just looking for my way home."

"To the north?" Arrow rolled his eyes and started back on the trail.

"No." I grabbed his forearm. "I lied before; I'm not from the north. I'm not even from Lockhorn."

"What are you talking about?"

"I'm not from your world."

He laughed.

"I'm serious," I said.

He stopped in his tracks and turned around to face me. "This isn't the time to go over this. If you're scared, that's fine. Most of us are, but we still do what's required. I expect the same of you," he said with a tightened jaw.

"You're not understanding what I'm saying. I'm not from here."

"You keep saying that as if it would mean something to me. It doesn't. Now let's go. We can't waste any more time on these trivialities.”

“Trivialities?” The ease at which he brushed off my concerns angered me. “Trust me, this isn't a simple matter.”

“Then explain it to me.”

“I don't know how to explain it so you'll understand,” I said slowly.

“We have to get moving, so find a way quick.”

“Okay… I'm—I'm not from this world. Where I'm from, Lockhorn is nothing more than a game.” I cringed, watching him absorb what I was saying.

“A game?” he scoffed.

“Yeah, it's just a game. We play it for fun, traveling the forest, storming castles, saving the queen. All of it…all of this, isn't real.” I tried to keep my voice even and stop my feelings from pouring out in my words. I watched anger and confusion collide on his face.

“So none of this is real to you? You don't believe in Lockhorn?” he asked again, this time with an equal measure of disappointment and comprehension.

“No,” I said, biting my lower lip. I felt bad for him, struggling to understand when I still hadn't come to grips with it myself.

“Why are you here then? Why did they send you to be our hero?” he demanded.

“I don't know,” I said. Part of me wished I didn't feel so relieved at telling the truth, when it meant crushing him. But I did. “I just want to go home, and I think I can do that by rescuing the queen. I've spent my entire life playing here, beating the king and saving the queen. In theory, I understand everything about this world.”

“In theory?” he asked. To his credit, he didn't move, didn't even flinch at the rest of my confession.

“Things are just a little different from how they were in the game. That's why I didn't understand the history or the meaning behind the boxes and stuff. In the game, you just kind of take the things you need along the way.”

“I can believe you're not from this world. That much is a given. I knew that from the moment I saw you. But to hear that this is just a game to you…that you don't believe…" He rubbed his forehead and tightened his lips. "I don't know what to say," he admitted.

"I know, and I'm sorry I didn't tell you earlier. I didn't know how to explain it. I still don't."

"None of that really matters. Magic is magic. Even if you don't believe now, or understand why you're here, I do. You were chosen for a reason."

"It's not that easy, Arrow. I don't think I can be who you need me to be."

"Goldy, you're exactly who I think you are. I don't care where you're from, you're here now. You know things, and that's what we need."

"But—"

"But nothing," he said with finality.

"Don't you care who I am?"

"I could ask you the same thing. Are you going to leave us just because you aren't from here? Because you don't understand who we are? Is that what you do in your world?"

"No, I, uh…" I stammered, shocked at harshness in his words. They struck too close to home.

"Think about it, Goldy. It's obvious you're different, but it never mattered to me, because you acted as if you were committed to us and to our cause."

"Then why are you acting this way now?" I asked, hurt.

"How am I acting?"

"I-I don't know!"

"Fed up? Angry? Hurt?" he asked, punctuating each word with emotion. "I feel all those things. But most of all, I feel responsibility for my people. I swore I would bring them the Golden Hero, and that's you."

I looked at him and pressed my lips together.

"You're our hero, Goldy. The rest doesn't matter to me."

I looked down at the ground. What if it mattered to me? I wasn't sure I could do all that he expected of me. If they put their faith in me, their lives in my hands, shouldn't I be willing to do the same for them? But I didn't want control anymore. The moments of power weren't worth their cost.

"Now grab your stuff. We have to head to the capital," he said.

"To Lindle? No, I was just there, and trust me, you don't want to go there."

"No, not Lindle," he snapped. "We're going to the true capital, Flourin. You'd better learn that while you're here for the rebellion, you're here on our terms. We're still loyal to King Helio and our history."

"Okay," I said, taken aback.

"Our time's running short, and I want to make sure we're ready. Are you with me?"

I nodded and fell into step behind him. I was with him, but I still didn't know what that meant.

CHAPTER SIXTEEN

I stumbled into town, dragging my bag behind me. I'd been reduced to incoherent mumbling, begging Arrow to slow down. My shorter legs refused to keep up with his urgent pace. By the time we crossed into town, they gave way, refusing to budge anymore. I slumped over and hung my head low, avoiding his eyes. I'd had enough.

"It's not much farther," he said, pulling my arm.

"I can't do it. I'm done. I can't move. You go, get your men, and do what you have to do. Just leave me here for a few minutes." I waved him along, keeping my gaze fixed on the dusty road.

Even though I refused to look up, his eyes burned into me. "I was going to get food first. But if you're too tired for that..."

My head jerked up, and my eyes met Arrow's mischievous smile.

"You better not be kidding," I said, narrowing my gaze. This wasn't the time to mess with me. "Help me up."

"It'll be the best stew you've ever had, I promise. Now Goldy, before we go any further..."

"I know, I know, hide my hair." I started to twist my ponytail, but he stopped me.

"No. This time, I want everyone to see who you are."

"I don't understand." I let my hair slide back down my neck.

"We've passed the point of waging a silent battle. When they see you, they'll know the time has come for action. It's time to take back our kingdom." His voice rang out triumphantly.

I rolled my eyes. I was not in the mood for a speech.

"Whatever you say. Just get me something to eat." I reluctantly stood, leaning against his arm as a wave of lightheadedness rolled over me. I hated the way my body—and attitude—deteriorated so quickly without food. *Hangry*, as Natalie called it. All my other pains seemed minor compared to the gnawing hole growing in my stomach.

My vision blurred, and I followed Arrow's gentle tugs. The brief glances I managed to take of my surroundings did not impress me. I looked around, disheartened.

Flourin seemed to be a city of monotony, forgotten under a layer of dust. The bones of the old capital were there, but I recognized nothing else from Arrow's stories. Nothing stood out to me in the deserted market. I didn't see a single person. In fact, everything Arrow had praised about this town seemed wrong. I only hoped he was right about the food.

Cobblestones tripped me, and I stumbled, barely finding enough energy to step over the broken edges.

"We're almost there," Arrow said, stopping to help me up. "I promise you, this will be worth it."

"It better be," I mumbled, grabbing at his arm.

The farther into town we went, the more I began to doubt where he was taking me. Cottages and storefronts appeared from behind the wall of dust. Instead of comforting me, the evidence of disuse and neglect added to my discomfort. Gusts of wind shrieked through the broken windows, signs creaked, swinging from only one end, and dark corners lengthened into dark buildings.

It was a shame, really. These cottages, if repaired, could belong in one of my mom's magazines. I sighed, watching half my reflection disappear in the cracks. Neglect was a formidable enemy, always underestimated.

A knot, bigger than hunger, twisted my stomach. Who did Arrow hope to find here?

He stopped in front of a rundown building. The faded sign had twisted on its hinges. The letters spun, indecipherable, but the bread and bowl etched into the windows told me what it had once been.

"Arrow?" I hesitated as he pulled me forward. "I don't think we should go in there."

He laughed and walked to the door. "I thought you were hungry. Are you coming?"

I stood there, frozen in place. "I don't think it's a good idea."

"It's fine. Trust me," he said, shaking his head as he disappeared into the dark abyss of the tavern. I bit the inside of my cheek, cursing him. But I did trust him, even if this place gave me the chills.

"Wait for me!" I said, trying to catch him before he disappeared. There was no way to know what lurked in the shadows. If it was anything like what I had seen so far in Lockhorn, it couldn't be good.

I blinked as I stepped through the door into the dingy tavern, letting my eyes adjust to the dark. The smells knocked me off guard. Thick smoke mixed with wine, choking me. I couldn't breathe, I couldn't see, and I felt like I was going to get sick. The dim lighting only made things worse. When I couldn't see, my imagination worked overtime, giving me nightmarish visions. Visions I didn't want to meet for real.

It was too late. The loud thump of the door closing behind me echoed in my soul. I swallowed hard and closed my eyes. I didn't need to see clearly to know that everyone stared at me. The moment the door closed, all conversation stopped. Not in a casual, lull of conversation way, but in an abrupt halt, where whispers sounded like echoes. They were all staring at me. I no longer wore my nightshirt, but I felt just as exposed.

"It's her," one man whispered.

"She's so young," a woman said.

"What does this mean?" another piped in.

The silence grew into frenzied murmurs. I didn't know which was worse. Both twisted me up on the inside. I spun around, choking back the instinct to be sick. My fingers slipped over the greasy door as I groped for the handle. I had to get out of here.

"What did I tell you? She's a showstopper." Arrow's deep voice came out of nowhere, an instant comfort. I turned back around and squinted through the tavern until I found his smile.

"I told you not to worry," he said, taking my hand and leading me away from the door. My gaze lingered on an etched window beside the entrance that disappeared under the haze of freshly blown smoke.

"No, you didn't!" I whispered.

"I didn't? Must've been an oversight. There's nothing to worry about, we're all friends in here." He laughed as we walked through the crowd.

I forced a smile, trying to ignore the stares as I banged into tables. People stopped mid-sip to watch, glasses resting on their lips. A man in the corner kept his eyes on me as smoke rings rose above him. Every eye turned to me, even those that had been leering down the blouse of the server moments earlier. The attention weighed on me. I hated that feeling.

"Arrow, get me out of here. I'm not that hungry anymore," I said, leaning in towards him.

"And miss all the fun? Alex, remember, I promised to show you more highlights of Lockhorn. This, here, is one of them!" His voice grew louder, commanding the crowd's attention. "What do you say? Let's give Alex a warm welcome!"

I shrank under the attention. Around me, the room erupted in cheers, and mugs clanked together in celebration.

"On the house," the server called out over the din, refilling the outstretched mugs, and with that, everyone returned to normal as if nothing unusual had happened. Except the man blowing smoke rings in the corner. His eyes never left me.

"That's how you make friends here," Arrow said, pulling me over to the far corner. "Not that they wouldn't have followed you anyways. Now, you are guaranteed their devotion."

I sat down beside him and leaned in over the table. "I don't understand. How is *this* possible? The town looked deserted," I asked, careful to keep my voice low.

Arrow laughed loud enough to draw the attention of the table next to us. "Looks can be deceiving."

"Obviously," I said, glaring at him. Now that my nerves had settled, my stomach growled, recognizing the smell of food. "So why haven't they rebuilt the outside? They've clearly reinforced the interiors." I traced the inside of the windows, void of any of the broken shards visible from the road.

"If they did, Berkos would just return with more men. This way, he thinks he's won."

"Hasn't he?"

"No, we're just letting him think he has. Besides, if we fixed it, the memory of that battle would fade a little more every time we looked at the new bricks. Newer supporters might be aware of the history, but they wouldn't see the full impact of what Berkos has done. No, leaving it deserted and dilapidated is a good reminder to us too, and the fact that it keeps him from coming back is a bonus."

A light bulb went off in my mind. I smoothed down my hair, tracing the small scar on my forehead. That's why my mom had never fixed that wall in our dining room. They hadn't wanted me to forget, and it worked. I shook my head, defeated. I had been played.

"I'm hungry," I said, although that memory of my parents soured my stomach.

Arrow tossed something to me and leaned back to assess the room. I caught the hard roll and broke into it, looking more closely at him. Something was different. Ever since we'd entered Flourin, he seemed to have more confidence. His eyes had lightened as if the worries he'd carried all day had disappeared, and a smile played at the edge of his lips. He seemed at home with these people.

I opened my mouth to say something, and then noticed the woman coming towards me with the steaming bowl in her hands. The yells, stares, and stench all became inconsequential to me. I was desperate for food.

When she dropped the bowl in front of me, I almost wept. Arrow hadn't underestimated the stew. I gave her the warmest smile my hunger would allow before diving into the bread bowl full of chunks of potato, beef, cheese, and carrots.

Spoonful after spoonful filled my mouth until none remained, and then I broke into the bread until only the smallest of crumbs flaked onto the table. I licked my fingers to pick up the last crumbs, and cringed as they stuck to the table. It was gross, but not enough to keep me from doing it again.

"Are you ready for another?" Arrow seemed amused.

I shot him a look, but nodded and handed him a gold coin from the box. He slid it back to me. "Not this time, Goldy. This is my treat."

I didn't argue. I watched him return to the bar and took another look around the room. Maybe my first impression was unfair. Sure, they were unruly, stained, and crude, but that didn't make them bad people. No one had insulted me, chased me, or tried to kill me. Compared to my experience in the rest of Lockhorn, they seemed to be the good guys.

In fact, since I'd sat down, no one paid me much attention. No one except the old man in the corner. Even in the dim light, I saw his eyes gleam. We locked eyes.

Arrow broke through our stare by dropping two mugs on the table, red foam frothing over the rim.

My heart plummeted. The few times I'd drank before hadn't ended up well. Hours of holding my hair back and embarrassing confessions never seemed quite worth the effort. I looked at Arrow and then beyond him, wishing for the distraction of food.

"It's carrin root tea. A little bitter, I admit, but it's the best we have now. And there's enough diced vines in it to heal a village," he said, as if he understood my discomfort.

"Thanks." I sipped the tea, unsuccessfully hiding my distaste.

Arrow's deep laugh made me smile. "I take it you haven't had this before either?"

"No, nothing like this," I admitted. Although as I drank it, I couldn't help but think it looked like the red healing potion I had been searching for earlier.

"In that case, to new adventure—in drink and more." He winked and raised his mug. I hit his mug with mine and choked down another sip.

The next bowl of food arrived, identical to the first, and I grabbed it. It filled me to a new level. I was stuffed. Happy and content, I leaned back and closed my eyes.

"Are you ready?" he asked.

"Ready?

He looked at me expectantly.

"Sure, whatever." I would have agreed to anything at that moment.

I should have figured it out when the smile widened on his face. Or when he stood and straightened his vest. But the warning bells didn't ring until he jumped on top of the table. What had I just agreed to?

"Men, women," Arrow called out, swinging his mug through the air as he walked the narrow table. "You too, Boris," he said. The room erupted in laughter. I frowned as tea splattered my leggings.

"I don't know if you noticed the woman I came in with today." He winked. "She's quite remarkable."

I blushed and straightened my hair as the rush of attention flashed back to me. I hated it when people stared. It felt like everyone knew something I didn't. The air tightened around me, and my stomach clenched with nerves. I shifted in the chair.

The rush of whispers escalated as they glanced between Arrow, on top of our table, and me, slinking as far into the shadows as possible. An uncomfortable lump settled in the pit of my stomach, and I tried to keep from getting sick. I hoped Arrow knew what he was doing, because I was in no position to stop him.

"But most remarkable is that we found her before Berkos," he said. The room shook with cheers. More carrin root tea spilled over the rim of my cup as my grip tightened and my fingers shook. I wanted to disappear into the shadows, but I couldn't move.

"She's given me quite the adventure so far. See, I even have scars to prove it." He raised his shirt, showing the scars crossing his defined abs. The server howled with delight, and my heart raced. He winked at the server before dropping his shirt. "But I have discovered something interesting. Not only is she brave, and stubborn," he looked at me, "but she also has insider information about Berkos' castle."

I swallowed hard. What was he doing? I shuffled uncomfortably as every person in the room turned to look at me. I wanted to hide. My face paled; sweat beaded on my temples. My palms slid over my sleeves, and I pulled the collar of my tunic away from my neck, hoping for fresh air. Nothing worked to calm the anxiety clawing at me.

Arrow stomped on the table, quieting the room. "You all know what we've been up against these past five years. It's not getting better. In fact, even as we speak, Berkos is making final plans to stomp out the rebellion. Why do you think the Golden Hero is here now? It's time, men. Time to finalize our plans and strike before he does. Let's take back Lockhorn for our queen."

"But what about King Helio?" the server piped up, "We heard news..."

Arrow's eyes darkened. "You've heard correctly. We won't be able to save King Helio. He's gone. But his kingdom is not, and the queen is not. We can still rescue Queen Elin and reinstate the order they created."

The air thickened as everyone shared glances of stunned silence. I wondered about the shift, and saw the man in the corner narrow his gaze on me.

"We're not doing this alone anymore. We have our hero to lead the way. With her guidance, we maneuvered through Baron Marix's manor and successfully retrieved his list of spies. Her information saved us from capture, and I have no doubt that had I gone alone, I would not be here." His voice quieted. "She risked her life for me and our cause, and she'll do it for you as well. The scrolls told the truth. Our Golden Hero is here, and so is the time to act."

Every mug in the room spilled, clinking in agreement while I tried to make sense of his words. He promised what I wasn't sure I could give, the very thing I'd warned him about. My stomach soured, and I regretted that second bowl. If this continued much longer, I was going to be sick.

Arrow raised his hand for silence and continued before I had the chance to move.

"Berkos knows of us. He knows we broke into Marix's manor, and he has already taken revenge on some of the smaller villages on the outskirts of the forest. We saw the plumes of smoke on our way here. There's no way of knowing where he'll attack next. The only thing we're sure of is that he will."

"What do you want us to do?" asked the man in the corner, taking a moment to blow another ring of smoke.

"Thank you, Cale. We need to regroup and get ready for attack. Time's running out, and if we want to save the queen, we need to move now. We're here to get all those who are ready and willing to fight. We'll reconvene with the rest of the army at the Grove and make our final plans." Arrow held his hand out to me.

I shook my head, but he curled his fingers towards me, beckoning me to join him. Everyone followed his gaze. What could I do? I couldn't say no. I didn't have time to think things through. Arrow reached down and grabbed my hand, pulling me up beside him.

I straightened my shirt and looked around the room. His arm slipped to my waist as he pulled me closer to him, and the jumbled nerves I'd fought before tumbled out of me. I was a mess. Hardly able to stand on my own, let alone do what he suggested.

"Meet Alex, our Golden Hero!" He lifted my arm into the air. The room broke into resounding cheers.

"What does she have to say about all this?" Cale asked, inhaling smoke, once the cheers wound down.

They looked at me, their eyes hungry for confirmation. I looked at Cale, then back to Arrow. What could I say? Did I dare argue with

Arrow's declaration or share my fears?

"Tell them how you've done this before." Arrow nudged me. "Tell them about the insider information you have, the layout of the castle where they're keeping the queen, the traps. Tell them."

"Well yes, it's true, but..." I stammered, balling my hands into fists.

"You know the king's castle?" someone yelled out from the crowd.

"Well, yes—"

"And you made it through Marix's manor?" Boris asked from up front.

"Yes, we made it out, but…" I said, trying to find the right words to minimize my expertise.

"You are the hero," the server exclaimed, refilling the mugs around the room. "Another round of drinks on the house!"

The cheers cut off the arguments resting on the tip of my tongue.

"Let her speak," Cale said.

Finally, someone who shared my hesitation. "Yes," I said, "I know these things, but that doesn't mean I can lead you to the queen." I met the old man's eyes.

Arrow pulled me back as the grumbles began. "She's a bit hesitant, but make no mistake. She's the one the scroll talked about. She knows what we have to do. Tell them."

My eyes pleaded with Arrow. I looked back to the crowd. How could I lie to them?

"If you can do it, you have my sword," Boris said. "Since they took my wife and my farm, my life doesn't mean much anymore. I'm ready."

Arrow jumped down and patted Boris on the back. "Any others?"

"You have me too," another voice piped up from the crowd.

"I believe the scrolls. I'll follow wherever she leads," said another.

One by one, they promised their allegiance. I watched them turn from Arrow to me and shrank under the weight of their hope. How could they blindly put their future in my hands? Didn't they understand I couldn't even control my own life, let alone theirs?

Cale grumbled but took off his hat. "If what Arrow says is true, you may be our only hope. If destiny's on our side, I can't argue with that."

My voice cracked. Their blind devotion angered me. "Listen, I know the king's castle, but there are dangers that I can't begin to imagine. I've seen it firsthand in the north, in Lindle. I saw some of the demonstrations. Berkos knows who you are. I've already seen what his thugs do to supporters of this cause. Whatever you're planning, it won't be a surprise."

They looked at each other and smiled. I glanced at Arrow, suddenly angry. Why didn't they understand? Even if I knew a few tricks, there were more dangers they weren't aware of. Their efforts wouldn't go unnoticed.

"No, you don't get it," I yelled, angry at their lack of concern. "He allows your rebellion. I've seen it myself. He knows about all of this, all of you. He will be expecting it, waiting for you in ambush. It's more than the rebellion at stake. It's your lives."

Arrow walked over to me, smiling. "We know. We're hoping he feels that confidence."

"I don't understand," I said. "If you know he's aware of you and what you have planned, why go through with it?"

"Goldy, this plan isn't a spur-of-the-moment decision. We've been building towards this for years," he said, jumping back to the top of the table beside me. "And we're already at risk."

"But—"

"We've deliberately let him believe that this is all there is to the rebellion. If he's too busy watching the fireworks, he'll miss the preparations for the real attack."

"Then you know he knows?" I asked, confusion clouding my mind.

"Yes, we've made it quite obvious," he said.

"Then what do you need me for if you have a plan?"

"We have a plan, but with you, our success is guaranteed," he said, reaching for my hand.

"I can't guarantee that for you. Just look at the people who've already died," I whispered, remembering the faces of the men trapped in Marix's manor.

His smile faded as he looked around the room, then back to me. "We're all aware of the price. That's why we can't give up now, or ever. Their lives can't be wasted."

"What you're asking me to do is crazy."

"Maybe, but it's our only hope. You're our only hope," he said, squeezing my hand.

"There has to be another way," I pleaded.

"But you've already said it, you know the way through the castle. You can get us in unnoticed," he said. "You've already done it once."

"Yes, but—" I pulled my hand back, aware that he was no longer listening to my arguments. He had made up his mind.

"You know how to defeat the king." His tone didn't allow for any disagreement.

I shot Arrow a harsh look. Was this why he'd wanted to come here? "But what I know isn't real," I said through my teeth.

"It's what we have to hope for. You can't let us down. We've been waiting for you."

"I don't know what you've heard or how to make you understand, but I'm not your girl." We stood in silence, staring each other down.

"In the end of times, a Golden Hero will present herself," Cale recited from the bar, breaking the awkward moment. The hoarseness of his voice added a level of authenticity to the ancient words. "Brought from the darkness to the world of light, the Golden Hero will fight to preserve humanity and restore freedom to the land. Place your trust in her in the darkest of days. She may be your only hope."

Wasn't that what the back of the game said? I twisted my hair, tucking it into my cap and looking from face to face as their hope and faith weighed on my shoulders. Did they really believe this?

"You're our only hope," a young boy said from near the front.

I looked behind him to the other people. Their solemnity surprised me. The older men bowed their heads in respect. Others stood tight-lipped.

I looked around uncomfortably. "Arrow," I whispered. "I can't do this. You have to understand."

But he didn't, and in a voice louder than any of my protests, he raised my hand and, for a final time, proclaimed me their savior. One look at him, and I knew he wasn't listening to my refusals.

Tears stung my eyes. My mind spun. There didn't seem to be enough air to breathe. Didn't they understand that blonde hair did not qualify me to be a hero? It had to be a mistake. I was a sophomore in high school, not a hero.

Fear gripped me. Without a thought, I spun around towards the door and ran.

"Alex!" Arrow yelled.

I didn't turn back or stop. I ran until my chest burned, and then slumped over to catch my breath.

"Alex!" I turned and saw Arrow catching up to me.

I took a deep breath and jogged forward, away from him.

"Stop! We need to talk about this," he said, grabbing my hand.

"Let me go," I begged, leaning forward.

"No. I won't let you go until you talk to me. Why'd you leave like that?"

I stared at him, the confusion in his dark eyes partially hidden by the hair sliding down his forehead. "What did you expect me to do? You practically told them I would defeat the king by myself!" I yelled.

"With our help."

I shot him that look again. "Do you think that makes it better? I don't know how to fight. I know how to win a game, not kill an evil king. Those are two *very* different things, and you know it. You can't just sign me up for your rebellion without asking. All I care about right now is getting home and getting out of this game."

"Isn't that all life is, though, a game? Aren't we all just trying to find a way through?"

"Yes, this is just a game. One that I desperately need to get out of."

"This may just be a game to you, but it's our lives. Don't let the fear of being the hero keep you from doing what's right."

"But this isn't real. None of this is real."

"What's more real than the things you can touch and feel?" He reached out and pressed his lips to my hand. "The things that touch you."

"But—"

"Stop fighting and listen. Not to me, but to yourself. You know you want to do what's right."

"Arrow, there's more to it than that. You can't put your hope in me." I turned around so he wouldn't see the tears streaking my cheeks.

"We already do. I don't understand why you can't." He grabbed my wrists and turned me back around. "Look at what you've already done. You're more than just a hero."

"Let me go. It was one thing going along to get your papers, but this—" I said, pointing to the tavern. "This is too much. Did you see that little boy? I can't be responsible for his life. What if I get him killed? I didn't ask for any of this. I'm tired of people expecting me to do things without asking."

"Then what do you want?"

"I want to go home. I'm sorry for ever giving you the idea that I could do more. But them?" I pointed back to the tavern. "They need a real hero. That's you, or your men. At some point, I have to stop pretending before someone gets hurt. I'm not a hero. This is nothing more than a costume. I won't let that boy, or any of them, put their faith in an imitation, not when they need something more."

"You're more than you realize."

"I'm nothing here. This isn't real. You're not real," I screamed, pushing him away. "I can't pretend anymore."

His eyes hardened. "I had hoped I'd mean more to you by now. I can understand you're afraid, but I don't understand how you can be so self-absorbed. You can't just push us away, telling me that we're a game. What do you think happens when you're not here? Do you think we disappear?"

"I-I don't know!"

"Let me tell you—we don't. This isn't a game. This is a fight to reclaim our kingdom. I can't tell you why you were sent as our hero. And honestly, if you can't find a way to put someone ahead of yourself, I don't know what good you'd be. I'm done wasting my time. If you want to go home, then go."

"Now you're not being fair. You're twisting my words to make me look bad."

"Goldy, I don't need to twist anything to do that."

I slapped him, then balled my fist to my mouth, cringing as I waited for his reaction.

He rubbed his cheek and turned back to me with a spiteful grin. I held my breath as he came closer. "Did that feel *real* enough for you? What about this?" He reached behind me and pulled me near.

My protests stopped as his lips covered mine. Everything gave way to his demanding kiss. My knees weakened, and I fell further into his arms. I grabbed his sleeves, pulling him closer, feeling my greed resurface. And then he pulled back and unhooked my hands from his sleeves.

"Was that real enough for you?" He wiped his mouth with the back of his hand and retreated into the dusty town.

I watched him leave, feeling a pang of longing with every step he took. My chest heaved, refusing to hold anything but my shattered heart.

"Yes," I whispered, feeling the lingering of his lips and the burn of regret.

CHAPTER SEVENTEEN

The morning sun attacked me with its blinding light as dust swirled around me. I rubbed my eyes, wiping away the sleep and dirt. After our fight, I didn't dare return to the tavern. I couldn't. There was nothing more for me to say. I would have to wait for Arrow to lead me to the highway, and then we'd go our separate ways.

I'd slept outside, curled up in my cloak under a fallen sign. The shrieking wind had jolted me awake throughout the night, providing a much-needed break from my troubled dreams.

The doors to the tavern burst open. The men barreled past me with surly grimaces and grunts. The few that pretended not to see me scuffed up dirt or kicked my cloak on their way across the street.

After the sleepless night, I didn't have the energy to fight their accusing eyes as they lined up. It didn't take much effort to guess what they thought about me. It came through loud and clear. I had transformed from hero to traitor in one day as if I bore a scarlet "T" stamped on my chest. If I wasn't the bad guy here, why did I feel so guilty?

Arrow marched through the dusty street, his hair falling in front of his dark eyes. He stopped in front of me and dropped my bag at my feet.

"What's this?" I asked, cautiously squinting up at him.

He ignored my question and looked over to the men gathering across the street. "I would stay over here until we're ready to go," he said. The anger left over from last night simmered beneath the surface.

"I'm sorry," I said, pursing my lips.

"So am I."

"Is there anything?" I asked, letting the thought linger.

He scoffed and brushed his hair back. Dark circles surrounded his eyes, and deep lines etched his forehead. "No, you've done enough."

"That's not what I meant," I said, shaking my head.

"Meant or not, Goldy, it's the way it goes," he said, turning away.

I nodded and watched him leave. His shoulders softened as he walked back, as if the weight of dealing with me had been lifted. Really, though, it had just been transferred onto my shoulders. I sunk deeper under my cloak and clutched the bag, teetering on the line between denial and complete devastation. I hadn't felt this alone since waking up in this world.

The warmth on my hands surprised me. Peeking into the bag, I breathed in a rush of steam from fresh rolls, which warmed my cheeks and turned my stomach. Everything else was there: a new cloak, money boxes, the remains of the money I'd taken, and, tucked underneath it all, an oversized package of vines. The gnawing hole in my stomach doubled in size, and tears welled up in my eyes.

How could he do this? This generosity confused me. Everything about this world confused me.

I leaned against the gate, closing my eyes while I waited. Maybe if I had told Arrow earlier, this could have been avoided. Could it have, though? He seemed just as determined as I to have things play out on his terms. I thought back to the manor, the missteps and close calls. Both our agendas twisted around each other.

I sighed. Replaying the past wouldn't change anything. One thing I knew from playing the game was that when you finished a level, you couldn't go back. Whatever level Arrow belonged in was finished. It was time to move on.

The wind picked up, and Arrow and his men formed a line. My breath caught in my chest. They walked past me without a glance. I jumped into line, leaving a significant distance between us. Dust swirled up from the ground, and I covered my face, trying to keep from choking.

We walked for hours away from Flourin, crossing northwest of the woods Arrow and I had taken to get to Baron Marix's, through miles of meadows and marshy grasslands. Their pace challenged me, but I didn't dare say anything. They didn't owe me, and I didn't want any favors. I didn't even want their attention. For the first time since being here, I faded into the background.

It didn't feel the same as I remembered.

I tightened the cloak, braving the brunt of the wind. I was out of breath when we stopped at the crossroads where the mountains met the wetlands.

"Goldy!" Arrow yelled.

"I'm coming," I said, cursing the slight quiver in my voice.

"Well, here we are." Arrow clenched his jaw. Sadness haunted his eyes, even though the rest of his face was emotionless.

"Thank you," I whispered, breaking eye contact. If I stared any more, I didn't think I'd be able to leave. "What will you do now? Where will you go?"

"We'll continue with our plan. With or without you, it's time to settle this battle."

"Is that safe? I mean, you could wait for another hero."

He gave me the same look he'd given me when I slapped him. "It doesn't work that way. I already told you, you were our only chance."

The silence stretched between us. "Arrow, I'm—"

"No," he said, cutting me off. "It's all been said." He pointed to the intersecting trails. "The trail to the right will take you around the mountains. The one on the left will take you to the wetlands, and if you're looking for the shortcut home, go straight up the cliff." That sent his men into a fit of laughter. "Goodbye Goldy. I hope you find your way home, I really do."

"Good luck to you too, Arrow." A tear slid down my face, blurring the line of men. I turned away, trying to ignore the sadness drowning me from the inside, and looked up towards the cliff. It was time to end this game. He may have been joking about the shortcut, but this was a video game. He might have told me something important without realizing it. And with a shortcut, I might be able to get to the final level, and home, sooner. I'd try the cliffs.

The enormity of the cliffs crushed me. Taller than anything I had seen before, sheer walls rose hundreds of feet, vertical cracks breaking the smooth surface. Fallen boulders filled the long crevasses. Clouds collided with the stone, breaking into a river of mist at the top. I swallowed hard and wiped my palms along my thighs.

Climbing came naturally to me, but this stretched my limits. I dusted my palms and caressed the walls, searching for the right hold. I found it. A narrow crevasse surrounded my palm like a glove. The next one fit just as perfectly. One handhold led to another. Prickles of anticipation shot through me. I climbed up the first twenty feet easily, finding holds and ridges perfectly aligned for my height. That's what I loved about climbing. I chose my own path. Only I could see where to go next. And when I reached the top, it was always worth it. The satisfaction I felt reinforced my resolve, and I did something I shouldn't have. I looked down.

Never look down. It was the first rule I was taught, and the most important. Besides the obvious threat of disorientation, I had a bad habit of second-guessing the path I had chosen. Hindsight was my enemy. The world spun, and my fingers slipped against the smooth rock. I couldn't find any more obvious handholds, and I cursed my impulsiveness. There was nowhere else to go. I had started in the wrong place.

Tightening my grip, I climbed down, and when I reached the ground, I folded my arms across my chest and looked up. The shortcut had to be here. I was sure of it. Trees and vines always marked the shortcuts between levels, and fifty feet up, a tree jutted out from the sheer walls. If I climbed there, I knew I'd find my next move.

I dragged my hand along the rough stone, walking over fallen boulders and scattered bushes until I stood directly underneath the tree. I pushed against the stone wall, applying different levels of pressure. Nothing happened. The shortcut wouldn't be as obvious or simple as an unwinding vine from the game—or would it? My fingers slid across something smooth tucked inside a vertical fissure between the rocks.

"Jackpot." I curled my fingers around the twisted plant. After a quick test to make sure it would hold my weight, I climbed.

The rope swayed with bursts of wind, and my feet slipped, losing traction along the gritty wall. Sweat dripped down my face, rolling over my arms, but I didn't stop. I climbed until I reached the ledge where the tree grew and pulled myself over. The vine continued higher up the cliff, disappearing into the cloud of mist above.

I leaned into the trunk, letting the shade cool the sweat beading at my temples. Resting my forehead against the rough bark, I studied the horizon. From above, the details disappeared. Life didn't get in my way like it did when I was on solid ground. But climbing this mountain was different. There was so much to see, and yet I couldn't focus. I stared out over Lockhorn, and details that I couldn't ignore popped into my head.

The bark scratched my arms as I held on to the tree, struggling against the forceful wind. Small rocks slid out from the cracks surrounding the tree, echoing off the wall below. I followed the rocks as they fell until I saw the trail I had started on. It was farther down than I thought. A lump formed in my throat.

The dusty trail curved through the landscape. My gaze followed its meandering path through the green land, marveling at how the wetlands painted the earth below me. Shades of blue and green bent around each other in an intricate pattern that I could just barely make out. I followed the sweeping lines until I found a cluster of moving dots. That had to be Arrow and his men.

The lump in the bottom of my stomach pulled me down. I sighed. What was I doing here? In the game, shortcuts were easy, quick ways to reach the end. Now it just felt like cheating.

I banged my head on the tree. It seemed so stupid. On the list of the dumbest things I had done since arriving, this would top it. Given the choice of having an army at my back or fighting on my own, I chose myself. Why?

That was the million-dollar question. Why hadn't I just stayed with Arrow and offered my help? Weren't our plans pretty much the same? We both wanted to save the queen. We both needed to get to the castle. I'd said I couldn't be responsible for their lives, but that didn't make sense. If I thought they weren't real, then it didn't matter. And if I did believe, then why didn't I want their protection or support? Either way, neither of us would succeed without saving the queen.

The longer I sat there, the more obvious it became. I was an idiot. Hindsight, my biggest enemy in climbing, got me again. I sighed and looked the other way.

The charred remains of trees lined the forest. Dark patches intermixed with the lighter greens, winding in a design reminiscent of the paisley wallpaper in our dining room. The memory forced its way into my mind.

Natalie pressed down on my shoulders to peek around the corner. "Are you sure?"

"Positive." I smirked and pointed to my mom, hidden behind her favorite magazine in the living room. She wouldn't notice us, and Dad was still at work. "Coast is clear!"

Natalie snickered behind me and gave me a push. "I want the strawberry one this time."

"I think I ate all those. What about grape?"

"Sure, whatever." She shrugged.

It was our third popsicle of the day and our second box that week. Stealth was necessary.

I tiptoed away from our hiding spot towards the kitchen. Water dripped from my bathing suit to the floor, turning the narrow hallway into a slip-n-slide. Then my feet slid out from beneath me, throwing me into the dining room instead of the kitchen.

trust her," he said again, turning around.

I bit my tongue. Now was not the time to lash out.

"Tell me, why are you here?" Arrow insisted.

"They're coming," I choked out, hunched over and out of breath.

"What? Who's coming?" he demanded, motioning for his men to lower their weapons.

"Marix…Berkos…I'm not sure. Army. On their way," I said, gasping between words.

"And you came to warn us—why?" His hand still rested on the hilt of his sword.

I gave up and fell to my knees. The groundwater drenched me as I searched his face for understanding. "Because I may not be your hero, but I don't want to see you hurt. You're right. I can't ignore this, no matter how much I tried. I don't know what I can do, but I'm all in—with you, the rebellion, with everything."

He opened his mouth to say something and stopped, jerking his gaze beyond me. "How many are there?"

"I-I don't know. They were just a bunch of black dots moving across the forest. Maybe fifty? Maybe more. I knew they'd be on you if I didn't—"

"I got that part, Goldy. Listen, we don't have much time. They're here."

"That's why I'm back," I said. The beating of my heart drowned out the frantic running of the men.

"Boris, Cale, the rest of you, we have to go now. Goldy's right, they're on their way. Hide!" he yelled.

He pulled me down the path. My legs protested but didn't stop. The ground rumbled beneath us. I ignored the sneers from the other men as I ran alongside Arrow. I'd have to fix that later. If there was a later.

The cold water stung my legs when we waded through it. Arrow pulled me around the next bend, and then slid beneath an old wooden bridge. I skidded across the rocky shore, spraying rocks around us before hiding behind a curtain of reeds. Blood seeped through my leggings and into the gravel below. I bit the inside of my lip, cradling my shins.

The rest of his men caught up to us and huddled underneath the bridge, careful to crowd in from the edges. Boris took a long look at my leg and tore off his sleeve to tie around my wound.

"Thanks," I mouthed, but he looked away without a word.

"Thank you for coming back," Arrow said, wrapping his arms around me, pressing me down against the rocks.

Tears welled behind my eyes as I folded into him, biting my cheek. I hoped it wasn't too late.

"Hey, hey, it'll be all right," he said, cradling me in his arms. "You're safe now. We're all safe now," he said pointedly to the other men. "Remember, we're in this together." He looked me in the eyes. "I still mean that."

"What?" I whispered.

"We're in this together, you and me, saving Queen Elin."

"That's what I thought you meant," I said, looking away.

CHAPTER EIGHTEEN

The ground shook with the approach of Berkos' army. We froze, watching the shadows flicker as they crossed the wooden bridge above us. The rotten planks bowed under their weight. Rocks skittered between the planks, blanketing us in dirt. I held my breath.

The rumbles seemed to last forever. I closed my eyes and felt like the ground was shaking long after it had stopped. My body trembled. We stayed hidden, cramped behind the curtain of reeds until Arrow was certain the danger had passed.

"I don't like hiding," Boris grumbled, peeking through the long grass.

"We don't have a choice for now," Arrow said, kneeling beside him. "They're here, we're here, and we're not ready for a fight. I just hope we're not going to the same place."

"Do you think they could be heading to the Grove?" Boris asked.

"It's hard to say. We know they have some spies, but thankfully none that are within the camp. Berkos' men could simply be heading back to the castle," Arrow said.

"We can hope." Boris nodded.

"It may be our only hope," Cale grumbled, pulling cloves out of a small leather bag and stuffing the edge of his pipe. It hung limp in his mouth after a sharp look from Arrow warned him not to light it.

"Don't be so sure, Cale. Alex is back, and that means something." Arrow offered me a smile.

"You're right, I almost forgot. Men, let's show her what we do with our traitors." Cale grunted, grabbing the weapon at his side.

"Since she's not a traitor, but our hero, we don't need to worry about that," Arrow said, holding his arms out to calm the other men. "Why don't we all get some air? The army's passed, and we won't be leaving until this evening so we can guarantee safe passage. There's no need for us all to squish under here."

The men looked at each other and grinned. It was as if Arrow had given them a gift. But really, he'd given the gift to me: he might have just saved my life.

Boris was the first to step out of the confines of the bridge and stretch towards the sky. He nodded to Arrow for guidance. "What do we do now?"

"Whatever you want, my man," Arrow said, slapping him on the back. "Hunt, fish, play cards. Have at it; just be ready when I call…and stick close to the bridge. There's no guarantee that someone else won't be following them," he said. "Now go."

I watched as man after man filed out from the under the bridge, slapping Arrow on his back as they passed him. Whatever hope they had originally wanted to place in me found a better place on his shoulders.

Staying tucked into the shadows under the bridge, I watched Arrow systematically grab each man's bag, lining up the packs near the water's edge. He tested the straps, peeked inside to count supplies, and even wove long strips of waxed grass through any tears.

The more I watched, the more it seemed clear: he cared for these men. This was his team, and he took that responsibility seriously. I thought about the full bag that he'd given me that morning. He had felt the same for me. He had accepted me, even after I'd told him the truth.

My stomach turned over, a swarm of insecurities plaguing me. What had I ever done to deserve that trust? The reality was, up to this point, I hadn't deserved it. But that would change. That had to change. I'd made that decision when I climbed back down the mountain. Rejoining Arrow came with a commitment that I couldn't back out of now.

I leaned back against the edge of the bridge and watched the couple dozen men that had joined Arrow. It was an odd collection. Older men with just as many scars as wrinkles sat at the river's edge, sharpening the tips of their swords with rocks. Younger, more boisterous men took turns using a slingshot to knock down the birds circling above. And out of sight, but just on the other side of the bridge, Cale sat, smoking his pipe. Clove smoke swelled and wafted around the corner of the bridge. He was closer than I wanted him to be.

I ducked deeper under the bridge and untied the shirt sleeve protecting my wounds. My leggings peeled back slowly, sticking to the dried blood. I gasped and looked away when I saw my shins. Puckered holes spotted my legs, and a jagged gash crossed just below my knee. I should've grabbed the vines, but I didn't want to appear weak, not with Cale around the corner.

I picked out a few sharp rocks indenting my skin and threw them down by the river. I rolled my leggings down and leaned back, watching the particles of dust slowly descend through the rays of light passing through the bridge beams.

Arrow turned when one of the rocks I threw narrowly missed him. "Hey, Goldy, no need to attack me."

Oh crap, I hadn't meant to do that. "I, uh, I wasn't," I stammered, looking away.

"It's a joke, Alex," he said, tossing his head to the side. "A bad one, but just a joke." He sat next to me. "You know, you didn't have to come back."

I wrapped my arms around my knees and raised my eyebrows. "Really?"

"No you didn't. So why did you?" He searched my face.

"I don't know," I said. "These past few days have thrown me for a loop. I've been lost in the woods, beaten by guards, practically drowned in the river, and then you throw me into a rebellion I'd barely heard of." I took a deep breath. "I guess it just all piled up, and then when you wanted me to be the hero for everyone, it was too much."

"I'm sorry. I could've handled it better. And I should have. But how do you tell someone that they're the hero everyone's been waiting for?" he asked with a small smile.

"Probably the same way you tell someone you're from a different world," I said. "You don't unless you're forced to."

"Yeah, but I shouldn't have forced you into this." He tossed another rock into the water.

"You didn't force me to come back today. When I was up there and saw the army approaching, I didn't really think about it. I didn't have a choice. I couldn't let them hurt you, not when I had a chance to stop it."

"Even if we're not real?" he asked, pausing before tossing the next rock.

I let out a deep breath. "I don't know what's real anymore. These cuts on my legs tell me that it's not as simple as I first thought. That's why I came back. I couldn't risk being wrong. Do you think they'll forgive me?" I nodded towards the men, who kept their backs to me.

"Give them time. It's hard to be introduced to the hero, abandoned, and saved all in one day. It took me a while to get used to it too."

"But I came back. That kind of redeems me a little, right?" I cocked my head to the side and threw a pebble at him.

"You don't need redemption. You just need to be yourself. You're more charming than you give yourself credit for."

"What?" I wanted to argue, but the sudden thumping in my chest stopped my words.

"And you're so blissfully unaware," he said, coming closer, reaching for my face. My cheeks warmed where his fingers brushed my skin. "It's as if the golden dust they created you with fell over your face."

Did he mean my freckles? I blushed and threw another rock into the water.

175

"I'm glad you're back, Alex, more than you know." He stood and moved to check on the other men.

"Me too," I whispered, watching him go.

I plunked more rocks into the river, watching the splashes ripple out, and then leaned back and closed my eyes. The sleepless night caught up with me instantly.

"Hey, Alex, wake up," a deep voice whispered in my ears. "It's almost time."

I smiled at the voice and flipped over to my other side. The deep tones sounded like a dream. A wonderful dream that I didn't want to lose.

"I have food," he sang, and the scent of warm bread made my mouth water.

My smile grew, and I slowly opened my eyes. I grabbed at the roll dangling in front of me. I wasn't sure how long I'd been asleep, but it wasn't night yet.

"Ah, I knew that would wake you," he said, sitting by my side, biting into his own roll.

"You think you know me so well," I said, propping myself up onto my elbows.

"I'd never claim that, Goldy. But what I know, I'm happy to use to my advantage." He winked and then nodded towards the men playing cards by the river. "Do you want to join them?" he asked.

I looked at the men, a tight circle enclosed around a small fire. Shadows danced across their faces as they laughed. I shook my head and took another bite. "Not tonight."

"All right," he said. "In that case, come with me. I want to show you something." He stood and pulled me up next to him.

"Where are we going?" I asked, brushing the rocks off my pants.

"To get a better view of the fireworks. They're almost ready to start."

I looked over my shoulder and saw a red wave swell up over the mountains. How had the day disappeared?

Arrow pulled me away from the bridge, towards the trees swaying in the breeze. The rocks crunched beneath our feet as we made our way into the darkness.

"You can climb, right?" he asked.

I rubbed my hands against the rough bark and smiled. He had no idea. I didn't bother answering and scurried past him to the top, staring in amazement when I crested the canopy. In a few moments, he made it to the top and sat beside me.

"This is beautiful," I said, watching the sky transition to twilight. In all the sunsets I had seen here, this was the first I really took in. Stars sprinkled the sky, and the song of crickets filled the background. "Thank you for this."

"I could say the same to you."

"You know what I mean. It seems that since I've been here, we've been plagued by one danger after another."

"And you don't think we are now?" he laughed.

"Sure, I guess we are, but for a moment, I can breathe," I said.

Right on cue, the first firework streaked the sky. A burst of red erupted followed by gold and blue sparkles. I gripped the branches beside me.

"All of this is for the queen?" I asked softly.

Arrow nodded and picked at the leaves. "It's just a small tribute for all she's done."

"And even with her locked up, you still continue?"

He gave me a sad smile. "It seems strange, doesn't it?"

I shrugged and twisted the leaves by my side. "I don't think I'm qualified to say what's strange here."

He chuckled. "Good point."

I scrunched my face and threw a leaf at him.

"No, these displays are just a reminder of what she's done. When King Helio and Queen Elin ruled, this kingdom was different. It flourished."

"How so?" I asked, looking back at the sky.

"Everything was different. We traded with all regions, there seemed to be something to celebrate every night, and most importantly, peace filled everyone's heart," he said choking up. "Elin did that. She gave us all a piece of hope. This is just giving a little back to her."

"With fireworks?" I asked. "It seems like an odd tribute. Don't get me wrong, beautiful…but odd."

He laughed. "I suppose if you didn't know her. But," he sighed, "this is perfect for her. She loved fireworks. They were always her favorite way to end each occasion. So this, even though we can only save enough for a month of each year, is all worth it."

I watched Arrow's face, noticing the softness that came over him when he talked about her. "She sounds amazing." The leaf snapped between my fingers.

"She is," he said, glancing up at the stars.

"So tell me," I said, brushing the broken stick off my thigh. "Why are we really doing this?"

"What do you mean?" he asked, turning my head to see a blue flame shoot across the sky.

"I mean, you've been through so much. How come nothing's happened before? Why now?"

"That's simple. We didn't have you before." Even in the darkness between fireworks, I saw his smile.

I scoffed and looked away. "So just like that. Boom, I'm here, and now we're going to act? It's more than that. I can see it in you when you talk about responsibility and the queen. What motivates you? Not the rebellion, but you. Is it the queen?" I asked, holding my breath for his response.

"The queen?" He gave me a strange look. "Sure, I'm devoted to her, but it's more than that."

I exhaled, surprised at the relief that washed over me.

"Berkos had my brother," he said.

"Oh Arrow, I didn't know. We'll get him back, I promise," I said, reaching for his hand.

"Had."

"Had? I'm so sorry." I folded my fingers between his.

He looked down. "I meant what I said back at the tavern. I won't let any of their lives go to waste."

"I won't either. Look, I can't promise that I'll be the hero you've been waiting for, but I can promise you that I'll do my best."

"That's all I ever wanted, even if I went about it in the wrong way. When you arrived, all I could think about was freeing Lockhorn and bringing back the way things were before. I wasn't thinking about you, and I'm sorry. Our freedom won't mean anything if it comes at the cost of yours. Help us, and I promise to help you."

"You have my word."

He squeezed my hand and pointed to the next firework. I turned away but not before I saw him wipe tears from his eyes.

We sat there in silence, content to watch the fireworks race across the sky. Blues, greens, and reds streamed in perfect succession, each chasing the next across the horizon. When the last firework faded into darkness, Arrow slipped a package into my hand.

I looked at the glittering lights rolling around my palm and the soft shadows lighting Arrow's face. I licked my lips, waiting for courage to surface, to grab the moment.

"It's time to go," he said, breaking my thoughts.

CHAPTER NINETEEN

Darkness hid our steps as we drifted through the wetlands and then back into the forest. Arrow and his men blended in, seamlessly mimicking the rustling of reeds as we traveled. Naturally, my stumbles overrode their stealth.

What I couldn't do covertly in the daytime became even more obvious at night. I trampled bushes, got stuck in branches, and tripped over every large rock or dip in the trail. The luminance powder didn't seem to help either; it just broadcast my clumsiness to the group. The darkness concealed my embarrassment and their glares. That was all right. In the night, their silence didn't seem as insulting.

My legs hurt, again. Even walking more slowly through the night, the distance wore on me. It didn't surprise me that when the sun rose over the horizon I could barely keep my eyes open or my legs moving straight. If I'd had any doubts before, this journey solidified the fact that heroism did not actually suit me.

The sun rose over the horizon, and the isolation of night diminished. I shook the few grains of luminance that had stuck to my sweaty palms into the dirt below and caught up with the group, which had stopped in a small clearing in the woods quite a bit ahead of me. They sat together, tracing designs in the ground. Now was my chance to ease back into the band.

They stared at me with unhidden contempt as I entered their circle. Any inclusion the darkness of night offered disappeared with their first look at me. Dark circles sunk their faces, amplifying their bloodshot eyes. Their matted and tangled beards overflowed with forgotten branches and displaced leaves. Each face hid a different expression, ranging from weariness to annoyance. As I looked from man to man, I recognized a common theme—they didn't trust me. Betrayal had a way of pulling the heart down, and I saw its sting.

I looked for Arrow, but he wasn't with the men. I thought about asking for him, but dismissed the idea. He couldn't be my solution. I made this mess on my own, and I would fix it. If only I knew how.

"Phew," I said, trying to catch my breath. "You guys are quick." Hunched over, I got a good look at the designs they had traced in the dirt.

They turned their gaze from me back to the ground where someone had drawn a hasty map. Lines intersected systematically on the ground in front of them, but I ignored them. What caught my attention were the two large crosses marked in the forefront of a castle.

I combed through my hair, pulling out a few thorns before I spoke. "So... when do we stop for breakfast?"

Arrow ran back to the circle and laughed at my question. "Is it always time to eat for you?"

"I have to keep my energy up!" I felt relieved to see his warm smile.

He tossed me a roll and jerky and pulled some out for the men. "I guess this is a good enough time to make our arrangements."

I dropped my bag to the ground and took my first bite. Its soft warmth had disappeared, but it still quieted my growling stomach. I waited until the other men had gotten their food and looked more closely at the map. It resembled the one I had scratched on the river's edge, but had more details.

"So this is all of Lockhorn?" I asked Arrow, taking a quick bite.

"Most of it," he said, leaning over and nodding. "Some of the smaller villages aren't there."

I saw Flourin marked with a star, the river that had taken me away from Lindle, and several estates similar in size to Baron Marix's.

The more I looked, the more familiar it seemed. I knew this place from deep in my core. Lockhorn finally made sense.

"So where are we going?" I asked, grabbing for another roll from the pile near the map.

"We're going here." Arrow pointed with a stick to a tree symbol below the mountains. "This is the Grove, where we'll meet up with the rest of the rebellion." Arrow dragged the stick from the first 'X' to the tree. "This is our route. We should be there by this evening as long as we don't run into any other problems."

I nodded and looked around at the other men. They seemed distracted, either looking at the map or the forest. Their gazes seemed to always skip over me. I sighed and took another bite.

"I haven't noticed any signs of the army. They must be on a different trail," Boris said, pointing to one of the marked paths on the makeshift map.

"That's good, right?" I piped in, my mouth full of bread

"As far we can tell. We should be able to get to camp without any more issues," he said, refusing to meet my eyes.

"The only issue we have is already with us," Cale muttered.

I jerked my head towards the surly man as he puffed a ring of smoke at my face. I waved the smoke away and glanced at Arrow.

Arrow took a quick bite of his jerky and smacked Cale on his shoulder. "There's no need for that this morning."

Cale grumbled something under his breath and blew another ring.

"Stop that!" I coughed, swatting at the rings of smoke.

"Is it too much for you, little girl?" he snarled back. "Do you want to run away again?"

"Cale," Arrow said, moving between the two of us. "This isn't helping anything."

"No, Arrow, it's fine," I said, stepping around him. "He obviously has something he wants to say. We might as well get it out now. I'm tired of seeing the glares. From everyone," I added, moving forward. "So what is it Cale? What's your issue with me?"

"Alex," Arrow said, grabbing my arm. "I don't know if—"

"I have to know what his problem is with me. I came back. I'm here. Either he accepts that, or I don't know what." I brushed Arrow's fingers off my wrist. I didn't want my hand held; I wanted to fight.

Cale choked on his smoke, but still managed to exhale a perfect circle. "Fine, girly, you want to know why I don't like you? It's simple. You're like spoiled cheese—only parts of you seem good."

"Spoiled cheese?" I put my hands on my hips. "That's the best you can come up with?"

"I don't need to come up with anything. It's the truth. I'm just not afraid to tell you."

I looked around at the other men, noticing how they looked away. "Is this how you all feel?" Heaviness sank my heart. I hadn't imagined they'd all agree. One or two or five, maybe, but not all of them.

Arrow stepped in and pulled me away from the group. "This isn't helping anything. It's been a long night, and we have a full day ahead. Just give them some time to come around. You're back. That's what matters."

"Too little, too late," Cale said under his breath. The familiar words stung. "Let me spell it out for you, Goldy. You only came back for Arrow. You know it, and we know it. You don't care about the rebellion or our lives. Do you?" He blew another ring at me, waiting for my response.

Had I really been that obvious? I looked away and tore into the strip of jerky before I said something I might regret.

"You must be getting senile in your old age," Arrow said with a tense laugh. "Like it or not, Alex's one of us. She came back to warn us about the army. We should be grateful. We owe her our lives."

"I still wonder. If it had been just us in trouble, would she have come?" Cale asked, blowing a final ring before turning his back on me.

"I could still leave you behind, don't forget that. I don't have to take this," I snarled, throwing my bag over one shoulder.

Arrow grabbed my arm. "Where are you going?"

"Anywhere but here. I need some air. I'll meet you at your camp," I said, starting to walk away.

Arrow tightened his hold on my wrist and pulled me back gently. He raised an eyebrow high. I met his gaze and clenched my jaw. He must have seen my determination, because he nodded.

"Don't get too far ahead. These woods are teeming with bandits and other creatures. It's not safe to travel alone."

"It doesn't seem all that safe here right now either."

"I'll give you that. If you're going to go ahead, follow this path, but promise me you'll stay within sight." He didn't release my arm until I nodded.

"I'll see you in a little while," I said, turning away.

"Alex," he whispered.

I turned and gave him a questioning look.

"I'm glad you're back." He brushed his floppy hair away from his eyes.

"Me too," I said with a small smile. I didn't want him to worry about me again. "I'll meet up with you soon. A little space will be good for all of us." I looked behind him to the other men. The months of fighting with my mom reassured me that after a little break, the awkwardness would be gone. I wasn't going anywhere, and once they recognized that, the rift would heal. I hoped.

His hand lingered on mine as I twisted away. The chill that hit me when he removed his hand surprised me. I covered my wrist as I walked away, and then I burst into a run. I knew I wouldn't get too far ahead. With my short legs and questionable coordination, the rest of the team would catch up when I hit my first obstacle.

The cold air stretched my face, tightening my skin. I ran, jumping over bushes, flushing out droves of puff birds and horned-bits. They squawked in protest. I smiled and sped up. My cheeks began to relax as warmth pulsed through my body.

The path narrowed the further I went, branches crowding in,

scratching at my arms and back when I ducked low. The slower pace allowed my mind to wander. Distracting thoughts surfaced.

When was I going to realize that my stubbornness only led to exhaustion? I had lived in a state of defensiveness for so long, and what had it gotten me? My stubbornness hadn't changed anything that I didn't control. It just destroyed my ability to enjoy the moment. Even here in Lockhorn, so much of the joy I remembered from the game fell victim to my attempts to leave.

That had to stop.

I paused and rested my head against a tree. My fingers shook as I gripped onto the small grooves in the bark. Small patches of moss cooled my skin, and sweat rolled down my temples. I wiped the hair off my forehead with the back of my hand and took a deep breath, enjoying the silence.

Oh crap. Silence meant danger here.

It wasn't completely quiet. The faint rustling of the branches sounded above me, as did the infrequent caw of a bird. Not the cheerful trilling that had followed us through the morning. The more I looked around, the more dreadful things I found. Dragon weeds popped up around me, burning through the underbrush with their bright petals, and dark, quiet birds circled above, like silent stalkers.

They dove and perched above me on spindly branches. Their beady red eyes bored into me.

Pushing myself off the tree, I ran again. The need to evade their eyes pushed me forward. I ran until my sides ached and my knees pounded with each step. They followed me. When I looked back up, they mocked me with the rough fluttering of their wings. I dropped to my knees and narrowed my eyes.

"Caw," I squawked under my breath. "Crap!" The birds snapped their beaks and launched off their branch.

I'd made the wrong move. They screeched through the air, tripling in size as they dove towards me, their fully extended talons reaching for my head. I stumbled forward and took off running, barely jumping out of the way as they snapped at my hair and then disappeared in the tight branches above.

I didn't stop. If I did, I knew I wouldn't start again. I ran until the small trail opened onto a larger road.

The highway didn't impress me. Deep puddles and patches of rock covered most of the muddy road. Only one good thing stood out to me—no overhanging trees for birds to lurk in. I hunched over to catch my breath, pulling my ponytail tighter. Loose strands stuck to my neck, matted from running.

I riffled through my bag, looking for one of the rolls Arrow had packed. Most of them were gone, but a few elusive morsels rolled around at the bottom. I reached for one and hastily ducked when a blackbird dove at my shoulder, screeching as it disappeared down the trail.

Shaking my head, I shuffled my bag and brought it up for a closer look. The last roll hid behind the sleeve of my cloak. I bit into it and relaxed as I heard stomping from behind me. I was sure Arrow had more food.

"Arrow, do you have any more rolls? I can't find any. And, about the animals here, don't you guys have any that are nice? A bird just attacked me. No wonder you wanted a horned-bit for a pet."

"Not all animals are bad. We value our pets," a husky voice said behind me.

I stopped chewing, and the roll slipped out of my grasp. My hair stood on edge. I could feel his breath on my neck.

"Let me show you," the stranger's voice rasped. His rough hands encircled my throat and pressed me to the ground.

An involuntary gasp escaped me as he tightened his grip to choke me. I twisted around and caught a glimpse of his crazed eyes, half-hidden behind his greasy hair. My chest hammered as I saw the sides of his mouth rise. He enjoyed this.

"Don't fight it, li'l one. Papa'll take care of you and give you a new home."

I fought against him, but my nails slid off his skin.

"I take care of all my pets. Hush…just sleep." He shook me until my breath choked out in short gasps and my eyes closed. Blinding light flashed in my head as he slammed me against the ground. The ringing in my ears deafened me. Everything seemed out of focus.

When the ringing subsided, I heard laughter. I strained to see what made the noise and saw the blurry outline of two large men. My pulse raced. Even at my best, I didn't know if I could subdue them. Sure, I had handled the thugs Auntie Quinn had summoned, but I'd had a store full of impromptu weapons. Even when I fought the giants with Arrow, rage bolstered my abilities. Here, I had none of those advantages.

The longer I stared, the clearer my vision became. Bound in a cage next to one of the thugs, three young girls, barely ten years old by the looks of them, reached towards me with looks of desperation. Dirt stained the rags that hung over their bodies, and small patches of red stained the bandages from old wounds. Their faces hid under welts and bruises, masked by a layer of dust. A stream of dried tears cleared a path down each cheek. The girl in front screamed as a rod smashed into her knuckles.

I reached down to my side and tightened my grip on the dagger hilt, hidden beneath my body. No one deserved to be treated this way. Least of all, children.

"Now, now, pretties. Make room for a new friend," the bandit said, poking his spear into the cart, forcing the girls to the opposite end. Then he turned back and faced me, digging the blunt tip of his spear into the ground.

He yanked on my hair and dragged me across the highway, dropping me on the ground at the base of the cage. Keys jingled above me as he struggled to open the door.

"Don't forget to mark her. We don't want to lose another," the other man said.

"Good idea. Hand me your knife."

I swallowed hard and forced my body limp as he grabbed my hand. I needed more time to come up with a plan. Under the cart, through the rickety spokes of the wheels, clumps of dragon weed caught my attention. If only I could reach one of them or a large rock.

White hot fire shot through me as the blade sliced my palm. I screamed into my fist as the man went back to unlocking the cage door. Blood collected in a warm pool around my arm.

The keys stopped jingling above me, and I knew my time ran short.

"Time to join your new friends," he said, flipping me onto my back. A glimpse of red on my other side caught my attention as he turned me over, and I dropped my left arm nonchalantly in that direction. I closed my eyes and tightened my grip around the flower.

Fire shot through my arm as the prickles along the stem punctured my wound. I tightened my fist and pulled it free from the ground as he lifted me up. The acid blistered my palm, but I didn't flinch. I couldn't. This was my one chance at freedom. I hadn't died up to this point, and I wasn't going to let some brute capture me.

His putrid breath assaulted me as his lips scraped mine. "I'm looking forward to this."

"Not as much as me," I growled, opening my eyes and smacking him across the cheek with the dragon weed. His eyes widened, and he dropped me to cover his face.

Our screams rose together in a fit of agony. I cradled my hand, feeling the blisters swell and burst. My palm slickened with acid. I kicked him in the stomach and turned around in time to see the other man approaching.

I didn't have time to think. Every inch of my body screamed as the toxins invaded my bloodstream through the cut on my hand. It was unlike the small blisters I'd gotten before; the acid raced up my left arm, throbbing in rhythm with my heart. My body weakened. The dagger hilt slipped in my right hand, and my eyelids drooped.

The other man lunged at me in slow motion, his face contorted as he screamed obscenities. I clenched my fists together and leaned forward, feeling the impact as he hit me. His eyes widened, and he paled as he clutched his abdomen. Blood seeped out between his fingers. I stared at him blankly, watching him fall backwards to the ground.

The pressure against my hands relaxed, and I dropped them to my side. My head pulsed with the beat of my heart, clouding my perception of everything.

I looked down at my hands, sticky wetness dripping off my fingers. It stained my skin even after I wiped them on my leggings. What had I done? The words screamed in my mind, but I didn't understand. Nothing made sense to me. I floated from one dull sensation to another, lost in a nightmare that I knew was real.

I fell to the ground, the cool dirt soothing me for a moment as it coated my open wounds. Dark lines raced up my arm where the wet dust settled, hiding part of the red web of poison. I bit my lower lip, feeling it tremble as a stray tear slid down my cheek. This was it. What would happen when I died here?

Another voice joined in my cries. Through my blurry vision, I saw an arm stretch out. Thick, red blood stained her fingers. No, those were mine. I was imagining things. I dropped my head and heard the voice again. This time when I opened my eyes, I saw the wagon and the girls.

I wasn't done. If I was going to die here, it would be saving these girls.

My fingers screamed as I dug them into the ground and pulled myself forward. It felt like ages, sliding inch by inch forward. When my hands hit the spoke of the wheel, I cried out.

My palms slipped along the bars of the cage as I hauled myself up and stumbled around to the door. I twisted the keys and leaned into the door, falling through to the floor of the cage. My eyes swelled. I couldn't keep them open much longer.

The girls swarmed around me, their screams muffled as they yelled through the strips of rags binding their mouths. They lifted me back up to a sitting position. I understood their indecipherable moans perfectly. Their outstretched arms trembled as they waited.

I tried to untie the restraints from their wrists. My fingers fought against the demands of my mind as black crept in from all sides of my vision. The ropes tore new holes in my blisters, and my left arm began to tingle before numbing altogether. It became worthless. I bent over and bit into the rope, tearing with my teeth until I remembered my dagger.

My hand shook as I reached to my belt, but it wasn't there. I stared at my blood-soaked hands, uncomprehending.

The tallest girl's eyes widened as she poked me and nodded behind me to where the spear rested. With my last burst of energy, I pulled the rusted weapon inside the wagon and used the pointed tip to saw through the cord.

She fell into my lap as the restraints broke.

"It's done," I said, smoothing her hair, letting her dry her tears on my shirt. I leaned my head back against the bars and closed my eyes. "I won't let them hurt you again, neither of them. You're safe. I swear on the queen's name, you're safe."

I held her until her sobs subsided, and then she moved to help the other girls.

I fell forward and hit the wooden floor. Through my swollen eyelids, I saw Arrow and his men walking along the highway. Arrow removed my dagger from the bandit's chest as Boris tied the acid-burned man to one of the trees. Cale placed his hat over his heart and lowered his eyes. His mouth moved, but I heard nothing.

I surrendered to darkness.

CHAPTER TWENTY

"Wake up, Alex, we're here." Arrow shook my shoulder.

"What?" I jumped. I didn't remember falling asleep. One glance at Arrow's heavy eyes and the girls sleeping a few feet over from me told me we had traveled longer than I'd thought.

I rubbed my eyes. "What happened?" My voice squeaked as I looked down at my arms, covered in vines and blood.

I tried to shake off the vines, and noticed a pile of withered ones beside me. My face paled. "Arrow, what happened?" I repeated more insistently.

He knelt by my side, covering my hands with his. "Shhh…it's all over now," he said, helping me untangle the vines.

I bit my lower lip, but couldn't stop the tears from welling up. "I…I…thought I was…" The words wouldn't come.

"I wouldn't have let that happen to you. You know that, right?" he asked, tilting my chin up.

I wiped the tears with the back of my hand and nodded.

"When we saw the welts racing up your arms, we knew the acids in the dragon weed were in your bloodstream. We weren't sure we'd be able to heal you. How do they feel?" he asked, looking at my arms, then my face. "You scared me," he said, pulling me to his chest.

That was all I needed to hear. I fell into his arms and wept. Tears ran unbidden down my cheek. All my frustrations and fears blended together until every pain, sorrow, and question I had felt for the past month flowed out of me. My tears knew no discrimination, and I shed them until every ache that I held inside screamed at its release.

"You're going to be all right, Alex, I promise you," he whispered, brushing the hair off the back of my neck.

I pulled back and looked into his eyes, wanting to believe the sincerity staring back at me. I nodded towards the vines. "Do you think you could help me with one more wrapping?"

He reached behind me to where a fresh pile lay. Seizing the moment, I wiped the tears away and blew my cheeks dry.

"Does that feel any better?" he asked, looking at me expectantly as he wound the vines up my left arm. My arms soaked up the healing salve of the plant, and I relaxed.

I shook my hands and pinched my skin, forcing a smile. Besides a faint tingling sensation in my left arm and in my stomach, I seemed fine. I brushed the pile of vines out of the way to stand up. "I don't think we collected enough."

"I don't think the forest itself would be enough for you." He laughed. The tight lines on his forehead eased as he offered his hand for support.

"You're right. I'll probably have to live closer to the Wounded Woods." I matched his grin, and then my cheeks burned. What was I saying? Had I already forgotten where my home was?

"I'm sorry you had to fight those men on your own. I should've been there," he said.

"It was my own fault. I'm the one that ran ahead. But it's over now, and at least I've proven myself to your men."

"You've nothing to prove. We believe in you."

"Tell that to Cale," I said. "Your men needed to see that I'm committed to them and to the rebellion," I said, scrunching my forehead.

"Yes, but to risk your life—"

"You do it every day."

"Yeah, but I'm their—"

"And I'm supposed to be their hero," I said. "This at least paves the ground for them to accept me a bit more."

He tilted his head and looked at me thoughtfully before speaking again. "You're different than you were when you first arrived."

I shrugged and looked down, balling my fists so I didn't see the faded specks of blood. As the stupor that had clouded my mind wore off, I replayed my actions in my mind with vivid clarity. I had changed, and processing the differences hurt.

"You did what you had to do," he said, cupping his hand over my shoulder. "You saved yourself and those girls. Don't doubt yourself."

I nodded but looked away. "I don't want to talk about that right now," I whispered.

He held out his hand to help me stand. "What about something a bit more pleasant?"

"I'd like that." I smiled, taking his hand and stepping off the wagon, careful not to wake the other girls. Without the terror behind their eyes they looked younger than I'd first thought.

"Were those Berkos' men back there?" I asked.

"Probably. This seems like the sort of things he has been doing for the past few years. Ever since he took control, our youth have disappeared—kidnapped, forced into slavery, and worse."

"Worse?" I whispered. My heart overflowed with emotion as I looked longer at them. "I'm glad they're free now. Where'd everyone else go?" I asked, noticing that the rest of Arrow's men were nowhere to be seen.

"They've gone ahead to camp. I wanted to make sure you and the girls rested."

I arched an eyebrow. "So you woke me up?"

"What can I say, I'm impatient," he said. "Come with me—I want to show you the camp." He pulled me away from the cart.

"What about the girls? We can't just leave them out here alone."

"Don't worry. I brought someone to watch them," he said, pointing to a boy I hadn't noticed leaning against a tree at the edge of my vision. "Everything's taken care of. Now, let me show you the Grove."

I glanced at him curiously and then at the dark forest in front of us. The eagerness in his voice intrigued me. Where exactly was he taking me?

"This time, I'll follow you," I said, stepping to the side of the trail.

He winked back at me. "Promise you'll stay close."

I crossed my fingers and tucked my lips together. My earlier angst disappeared when he smiled at me. He led me several hundred feet away from the cart, past where the boy sat.

Wispy branches intertwined and draped to the ground, creating a curtain of variegated greens. Arrow pulled the screen of branches to the side and motioned for me to step through ahead of him.

"May I present to you my humble camp, the Grove." He bowed and held his arm out flamboyantly, letting the leaves fall behind him, blocking out the forest we had just hiked through.

I stared at him, and then back to the camp, and then back at him again. "A grove is a simple gathering of trees. This…this…" I stumbled for the right words. My composure slipped away, and my knees buckled.

He jumped to my side and held me steady for support. "This…is my home."

"Arrow," I whispered. "This is amazing."

"Do you like it?" he asked.

"I've never seen something so incredible," I said, squeezing his hand.

He beamed, and I knew I had said the right thing.

I wasn't lying; I hadn't seen anything like it before. Hidden within the forest, Arrow's camp blossomed in the shadows of the trees. Built around the base of each tree, quaint cottages welcomed us. Worn by time, their white paint had begun to peel, and moss grew in the small spaces between the wooden planks. Delicate flowers and trailing vines cascaded over broken window boxes, and small rounded stones at the doorsteps finished the charming entrances. On the rooftops, ladders stretched high into the canopy above, where a suspended bridge system weaved through the forest. My feet prickled with a desire to climb those branches.

He must have read my mind. "Over here," he said, leading me over to one of the houses.

"What are you doing? You can't just walk through someone's house," I said, resisting his pull.

"Alex, your concern is sweet, but this isn't a house."

"It's not?" I asked with a raised eyebrow, looking over at the flowers and welcome mat. "You expect me to believe this is what, a store?"

"No," he said, amused. "I just expect you to believe me."

"I, uh, I'm sorry. You're right," I stammered, feeling the blush rise in my cheeks.

He laughed and opened the door beside him. "You can see for yourself, it's empty."

"No, I believe you," I said, but the dark room behind him eased my fears.

"Now, come on. Trust me. There's so much I want to show you."

"Up there?" I asked, trying to hide my confusion.

"Alex, when are you going to trust me?"

I didn't know how to answer him. Didn't he already know I trusted him? I pursed my lips and frowned. "Right now," I said.

His footsteps sounded behind me as I climbed the rough ladder. Twine and vines twisted together and wound around long sticks, creating a crude stairway. The ropes creaked under my weight, swinging through the narrow opening in the ceiling.

I propped myself up and paused as I breached the opening. My hands slipped along the moss growing on top of the wooden roof, and I fell backwards.

"Whoa," he said, grabbing my waist, pressing my legs onto the small edge of the ladder. "You okay?" he asked.

I looked down at his arms encircling my waist and suppressed the butterflies flitting inside me. "Yeah, I'm fine," I murmured, unable to speak above a whisper.

Everything seemed heightened here—every emotion, thought, and touch. My gaze lingered on his hand before I pulled myself back through the ceiling and onto the roof. I wished I could pass it off as an ordinary slip, but it was more than that. Maybe it was what had happened with the girls, maybe it was the beauty of the Grove, but everything I saw threw me off center. The simplicity of the game-world I knew from home had disappeared, replaced by something as real and complex as anything I'd known before.

"This is the only way to see the Grove properly," he said, gliding across the wooden planks to an archway of tangled branches. Beyond the threshold stood a wooden bridge suspended above the ground, a walkway through the trees.

"I see what you mean." Walking past him, I grabbed ahold of the vine railing. My palms slid over the slick vines, and the wooden planks creaked with our movements. I looked skeptically at the old strips of wood holding the bridge together and the gnarled limbs and branches that twisted to make a railing. Despite Arrow's confidence, I wasn't sure I trusted the strength of the vines and branches.

"This gives you a better idea of the camp without getting lost in the details," he said, leaning over the edge of the railing. "I forget that sometimes."

His words struck me. I let go of the railing and furrowed my brow as I stared at him. That was exactly why I loved climbing so much, but I never knew someone else would feel the same way. I took a step closer to him and noticed the people wandering around below us. I let out a happy sigh and met his grin. "Show me more," I said.

I found myself matching his enthusiasm as we walked along the bridge. The creaking faded away when we moved deeper into the Grove, replaced only by the soft rustling of leaves. The trees thickened, and larger branches held the bridge in place.

As we moved closer to the center of the village, I noticed streams of braided fabric flowing through the air, tied to the largest branches and to the supports of the bridges. Waves of purple and blue turned the Grove into a blossoming garden of color.

Arrow pointed out the buildings and tents as we walked—homes, shops, and medical huts. The camp had everything they needed to survive. He even pointed out the training fields, where I saw the familiar faces of his men mixed in with strangers. I picked out Cale from the crowd immediately. I couldn't ignore him if I wanted to. Smoke rings encircled him like a bull's-eye.

It seemed everything had been accounted for, even the mobs of people. Without notice, the simplicity of the quiet homes exploded into a flurry of activity, men racing through the camp below.

"I don't understand. How is this all here?" I spun around, watching men weave in and out of buildings and tents, their arms full of supplies. "How does a village like this stay hidden in the middle of the forest? Not just a village, but an army?" I listened to the rhythmic pounding of a blacksmith forging armor and the clanking of metal as swords and shields were stacked along the outer edge of the longest building.

Arrow shrugged. "It had to, I suppose. Necessity forced us to rise to the occasion. Do you remember what I told you about Flourin?"

I thought for a moment and nodded. "About it being the capital, or Berkos destroying it?"

"Both. You see, after Berkos burned down Flourin, most of the people had nowhere to go. They were afraid to regroup in the big cities, so we offered refuge here."

"That's an amazing thing to do," I said.

He shrugged. "Not really. It's just what we had to do. It's not that special."

"It is," I said. "You just don't understand that. I've never seen such teamwork or generosity."

We stood in silence for a moment, watching the flurry of activity. I finally broke the silence. "Thank you for showing me all this. I mean it. This camp, your home, it's truly special."

"You're welcome. But there's more."

"More?" I asked.

He answered my question with a mischievous smile. "Much more," he said, leading the way to the nearest tree and grabbing ahold of the rope ladder. He climbed down through a small opening between the bridge and the tree and looked up at me. "What're you waiting for?"

I shook my head and climbed down after him. The noise increased to a roaring din around us. I nudged Arrow and plugged my ears.

"Another reason why I enjoy it up there," he yelled. "It gets loud down here, especially now with the preparations."

"Preparations?" I asked.

He pulled on my sleeve, bringing me closer.

"On your right," a man yelled, carrying an armful of shields as he clanked past us.

I twirled and saw more men scurrying by with piles of armor and weaponry, the elders barking out orders. Sweat rolled down their red faces as they stacked boxes and rolled barrels in front of the stockrooms. Children barely old enough to walk followed the older boys, dragging spears behind their wobbly legs. Everyone seemed occupied with their tasks, but none of them were so busy that they couldn't stop to stare at me.

"Don't forget, we all got word that you were coming. They're naturally as excited as I've been."

I bit my lower lip and regarded them more closely, noticing the smiles tugging at their lips and the way they tried not to be obvious with their stares, quickly turning when I met their gaze.

"Don't make that look," he said. "You knew this was coming."

"Yes, but…"

"I told you that you'd have all the support you needed. This should put you at ease."

I swallowed hard and forced a smile. "You're right. It'll be fine." But everything inside me screamed that I was in over my head.

"Now let me finish showing you camp. Over there, next to the practice meadow, is the stables, and on the other side are the quarters."

"Uh-huh," I said, trying to listen to everything he described. Half his words slipped over my head as I soaked in my surroundings.

He grabbed my hand and raced across the pathway to the other side of the camp. The practice meadow was an open field surrounded by hay bales, stacked two and three high, with old wooden barrels overflowing with spears, arrows, and swords. At one end, a group of men gathered, adjusting their bows, while at the other end, two younger boys adjusted new targets—hand-painted caricatures of a man with a dark mustache and black crown.

"Over here," he said, pulling my attention away from the field. "This is your tent. I hope you don't mind that I had them set it up for you. It's not much, but it should have everything you need. And if anything is missing, just come find me. I'm right next to you."

"Thanks," I said, hoping my face didn't look as red as it felt.

"It's nothing. I just figured after everything…" His voice trailed off.

When I looked up, he was staring behind me with an excited grin. I turned to look, and my stomach dropped. Three heavily armored men walked towards us. Their armored breastplates swung in sync with the weapons hanging from their sides.

"I want you to meet the generals." He waved the men over and pulled the package of papers we had stolen from Baron Marix out of his vest pocket.

"Generals," he said, warmly clasping hands with the tallest of the armored men. "It's been too long."

"Well worth the wait," the general said, nodding at me. "Is this who I think it is?"

"Yes. Generals Amos, Tanner, and Gerding, please meet Alex, our Golden Hero."

"My lady," General Amos said, kneeling and lowering his head. "It's an honor."

The other men followed suit, their armor clanking as their knees hit the ground.

I spared a quick glance at Arrow. A slight grin quivered on the edge of his lips.

"Please don't. It's my pleasure." I reached forward and grasped General Amos' hand, blushing as each man took a turn kissing the back of my knuckles.

"Now that that's taken care of," Arrow said, "General Tanner, has there been any news from the north?"

"There have been rumblings from everywhere, not just the north. You've heard the rumors?"

"They're not rumors," Arrow replied, his lips tight.

"I'm so sorry. I was afraid of that," General Tanner said. "We have another issue too. We've heard from more than one group that the money didn't reach their targets."

I gasped at his words and covered my mouth. Could he be talking about the boxes I'd taken?

"That problem's been solved. It was all a misunderstanding. Everything's in place now," Arrow said.

"Are you sure?" the larger man asked, rubbing his forehead. "We can't have many more mishaps."

"Amos, don't worry. Everything's in place."

"But the word from the north says Berkos is on the move," Amos said.

"Then we have nothing to worry about. We're ready. For the first time in five years, I feel we have an honest chance."

General Gerding smiled and patted him on the back. "We never doubted you, Prince Atiro. We knew you'd find her and bring her here."

"Prince?" I whispered, jerking my gaze to Arrow.

Arrow shifted his weight to his left leg as he looked at me. "I can explain. I didn't—"

Prince...my mind rolled over that thought until my voice found something to say. "Didn't what? Why would you keep that a secret?"

"Does it matter?" he asked, searching my face.

"Well, no," I said, wanting to scream 'yes!' I couldn't help but think of all the things I had said, all of my stubborn outbursts. Humiliation didn't even begin to describe the feelings rushing through me. I wanted to hide.

"I told you they'd had my brother. That was all that mattered," he said.

"You never said he was a prince," I countered in disbelief. Was he really trying to downplay this?

"The king, actually. He and Queen Elin ruled the kingdom together before Berkos imprisoned them."

"King?" I squeaked. "Didn't you think I needed to know?" General Amos coughed.

Arrow glanced over at the generals and rubbed the back of his neck before looking back at me. "Well, now you do. Alex, we'll have to finish this later. Men, let's go over the details in my tent."

The generals nodded and followed Arrow down the dusty path.

"Now I know..." I mumbled, watching the dust settle behind them. I stumbled to my tent in a daze, securing the tent flap behind me and leaning against the pole, throwing my head back. "Now I know..."

Who was I kidding? I knew nothing.

CHAPTER TWENTY-ONE

A prince? The thought left me stunned and sick at the same time. I sat down on the cot at the far end of the tent, trying to articulate what bothered me most. Was it that he hadn't told me? There were plenty of secrets I had kept from him. I could hardly hold something against him when I was just as guilty of it. So if it wasn't that, what was the issue?

I took off the green hat and twirled it around a finger. Deep down, I knew what the problem was, and I hated to admit it. Here I was again, attracted to a guy completely out of my league. After Brian, I swore I wouldn't do it again, but I couldn't deny that I was falling for Arrow.

It was bad enough that he was so good-looking, but a prince too? If he were a warrior, like I'd thought, I could deal with that. There were plenty of cute football players at home. Even if he were a builder or a tradesman, I could wrap my mind around it. But a prince? That was beyond me. I wasn't some princess or damsel in distress for him to rescue. Not even close.

I threw my hat behind me and ran my fingers through my hair, jerking through each tangle faster and faster, until the luster of my hair shone. A quick glance in the mirror told me not to stop. I didn't recognize the girl staring back at me.

Deep lines circled my eyes, and my freckles hid under a layer of dirt. My clothes, frayed from the journey, looked exactly like I felt. Faded and broken. I was tired of feeling inadequate. It was time to change. First, I needed out of the costume.

I unhooked the dagger from my belt and shook myself out of the tunic. It dropped with a thud by my feet. I kicked it under a table with my foot and took a closer look at my leggings. Ripped at the knees and dotted with holes along the shins, they weren't worth trying to save. The dagger sliced easily through the thin fabric. I cringed as I peeled the pants off, wincing as they clung to old wounds.

As I stood there in nothing but my torn white shirt, I still didn't recognize myself. I wondered if I ever would again. The girl from home and the girl who entered the dark forest were mere shadows of who I was now. Tears slid down my cheek, but it took too much energy to stop them.

My vision blurred, and my gaze strayed around the room. Arrow had been right. Everything I could've ever needed was here. The table beside me held a full basin of water and lavender oil soap, and next to it sat a stack of green and gold fabric.

When I reached for it, the fabric slid across my hands, luxuriously soft in a way the first set was not. Golden thread work detailed the deep collar on the tunic and the hem of the leggings. My mom always said that clothes made a person. It turned out that she was half-right. My first outfit was nothing more than a costume, perfect for dress-up. But this one was different. It felt right, and I was ready to wear it...when I was clean. I rubbed out a smudge from below the delicate trim and put it back on the table where I'd found it, grabbing a cloth from the edge of the basin.

A strange satisfaction rolled over me as the water darkened. I scrubbed, watching the suds clear a path across my face. My freckles peeked out, and I smiled. I scrubbed until my face and arms were raw.

The clothes felt as luxurious on me as they had between my fingers. The smooth silk slid over my body, and the golden threads glittered in the mirror's reflection. I still didn't know who looked back at me: Alex or the Golden Hero, or some magical blend of the two. It didn't matter.

I grabbed two oranges and a couple of rolls off a silver tray and peeked out the tent door. Did Arrow remember that was the first thing he'd offered to me, or was it a coincidence? It had to be coincidental. I peeled and bit into one of the oranges before my doubts could sour the sweetness.

The Grove continued along its frenzied pace. People walked by with loads of armor, and kids giggled as they chased each other on the field. Everyone had a place to be or a job to do. The ebb and flow of their movements and the soft rustling of the branches above me lulled me into a hypnotic state.

The moment of peace surprised me. I hadn't felt such calm since arriving in Lockhorn, and I refused to squander it. For the first time, nothing—not my parents, not the game—dictated what I needed to do. I could sleep, I could explore, I could do anything. The possibilities rattled in my head. What to do first?

I peeled the second orange and looked up at the trees. As rickety as the bridge was, I wanted to cross it again. I finished the orange and let the tent flap close behind me. It felt good to have a plan of my own making.

I jumped into the crowd, weaving a way through the rowdy kids and around the busy shopkeepers, barely missing a larger man as he stopped in front of me with a wooden barrel.

"I'm so sorry," I said as I passed him. His back tensed as he released the barrel and stood up.

His demeanor changed the moment he saw me. His anger melted into an apologetic gesture. "No, my lady, it's my fault," he said, waving me along. "I'll keep better watch next time."

I stared at him, puzzled at the sudden change.

He bit his lip and covered his heart with his hat, timidly approaching me. "If it's not too much, my lady, may I ask a favor?"

"Of course," I said.

"When it's time to go, can I ride alongside you?"

"When it's time?" I asked, confused.

"When it's time to ride, I'd be honored to be by your side."

I nodded. "Yeah, of course. If it's up to me, I'd be honored to have someone of your strength with me." His smile stretched his face, and he beamed with childlike enthusiasm.

"Thank you, thank you, my lady," he said, bowing as he walked away.

This hero thing amused me. It still didn't make much sense, but I supposed if my life had been devastated like theirs, retribution would be my main focus too, and I'd embrace anyone I thought could help. Luckily for me, it wasn't, and my focus still remained on that bridge, dangling at the far end of the path.

I bounded past the edge of the training field, noticing how one end had been commandeered for wagon repair. It was hard to miss Boris's loud laugh as he swiped the wagons with dark green paint. Trilling around his loud bursts of laughter, softer giggles drifted towards me. I covered my mouth when I saw their source.

Three girls ran around the wagon, dragging braided vines behind them. They wore smiles and new dresses, and I almost didn't recognize them. Almost. The bruises and scars on their arms told a story their smiles couldn't hide.

"That's not what I meant, and you know it," a voice boomed behind me.

I spun around. "Arrow?"

"Prince Atiro, wait!" General Amos yelled, running onto the path behind him. "There's still much to discuss." He stopped and crossed his arms.

"There's nothing more to discuss. I've given my orders." Arrow's words rang clear on the quieted path.

General Amos scowled and threw his arms up in frustration before turning back towards his tent.

Arrow's eyes hid beneath his dark hair, but I could see the scowl in his tightened jawline. I looked up at the bridge and sighed. That could wait.

"Arrow, wait up," I yelled, racing back across the street towards him and the training field.

The path cleared before him as he jumped over the hay bales surrounding the field. Men and women scattered to the outer edges, and the group painting wagons at the other end stopped to watch, leaning against the hay and propping themselves atop wooden barrels.

Arrow's anger transformed into focus. He grabbed the closest bow and pointed down the field. Even without a posted target, his arrow flew straight. One after the other, blinding shafts of color flew through the air, toppling the highest bale with the arrow's force. He seamlessly turned and focused on the second target, knocking it over with the same accuracy and speed. And then the next, until all the targets were turned over.

The crowd grew until the entire outer edge overflowed with spectators watching him annihilate his targets. Everyone wanted to see their leader in action. I leaned against the closest hay bale and bit my cheek. Stray strands of hay poked into me. Without thinking, I pulled them out and braided the edges, holding my breath and watching as General Tanner stepped out onto the field.

I half-expected him to instigate an argument like General Amos had, but he surprised me by embracing Arrow and taking hold of the bow. The sun glinted off his armor as the targets were restacked.

"Tell me, which arrow is the right one?" he asked, smiling at Arrow.

Arrow stepped back and leaned against the hay stacks. An amused grin lit up his face.

"Do we want the strong and silent type?" he asked, holding up a black-shafted arrow. "Or perhaps something a bit more whimsical and fun?" He picked up a red one. "Hmm, I'm still not sure. Maybe this one?" he asked, offering up a green one.

The crowd yelled out all three colors. General Tanner waffled between his choices until Arrow shook his head in laughter. "Choose the green," he said.

"There's only one arrow I trust," a woman's voice purred.

The crowd hushed for a moment, and then burst into louder yells.

"And what Melody wants, Melody gets," General Tanner announced to the crowd's delight.

I looked around for the mystery woman who called for Arrow's attention, disappointed when she remained hidden. I tried to ignore the pit that opened up inside me as another layer of insecurity hit. I hadn't thought about anyone else being interested in him.

"I think we can all agree, we want an arrow strong and true." General Tanner fit the green-shafted arrow into the bow. Methodical and precise, he let go, and the arrow sliced through the air, hitting its target. "Right on target. What do I get?" he asked and pulled a woman from the edge of the crowd, planting a kiss on her cheek.

"Oh, General Tanner," she said, covering her chest theatrically. As she stood, she brushed dark waves of hair out of her eyes. The deep blue of her vest accentuated her eyes and the mischievous twinkle that grew in them when she laughed. The tone of her voice entranced me. No wonder they called her Melody—she sounded like liquid music.

I narrowed my gaze, trying to find an imperfection, but could see none.

"Right," he said with a laugh, setting her down. "Maybe my charm will work on another woman. Anyone else willing to bolster this general's ego?"

Melody laughed. "When you put it that way, how could anyone resist? How about I give you a challenge instead?"

General Tanner raised an eyebrow. "I like challenges. What'd you have in mind, sweet lady?"

"Just a simple challenge of skill."

"No one can best you with the bow." He bowed.

"No one can best me at anything," she retorted. "But a brave man tries…if the reward is worth it."

"And what are you offering, sweet lady?" He leaned towards her.

"Something of value, of course, good sir. How about the winner gets a date?" She licked her lips.

His eyes lit up. "You have a deal, my lady. After you." He bowed as she strutted forward.

If anyone had missed the earlier exchanges, they were here now.

Even General Amos stood at the edge, towering over the crowd.

Melody paraded forward, using the crowd to her advantage. They whistled at her indecision as she stroked three different shafts before choosing a red one. "One can never be too hasty," she purred.

The crowd murmured their agreement.

She pricked the tip of the arrow as she walked to the middle of the ground and licked the tip of her finger. General Tanner leaned against Arrow, practically drooling over her performance. Her outfit looked like Arrow's, except for the sharply angled cut on the vest and the way her leather pants clung to her curves. The bright blue vest caught the fading sunlight, sending a shadow of feathers and a flutter of light in all directions. I gasped at the selection of knives sheathed around her vest. She wasn't one to mess with.

I found myself splitting my gaze between Melody and Arrow. He seemed amused at her performance; a slight smile played on the edge of his lips. I couldn't blame him. She had a way of commanding attention. The lump in my throat grew. If I didn't think I stood a chance with him as a prince, I knew I didn't stand a chance against her.

"General Tanner, are you sure you don't want to shoot with me?" she asked with a sideways glance as she placed the arrow in her bow. "It gets lonely out here by myself."

"It's a difficult choice, my lady. It's a joy to watch you prepare…but, alas, I am compelled to answer your every request."

"Thatta boy," she said as he jumped into position beside her.

The crowd grew silent.

"On my count," she said, turning her attention to the stacked hay at the end of the field. "Three, two, one," she said, releasing the bowstring. Both arrows whooshed across the field, striking the targets. Only one penetrated the inner circle.

General Tanner bowed in defeat, wrapping one arm around his stomach and outstretching the other towards her. "As usual, I defer to your talents."

"One of these days you'll get the best of me, good sir. I have faith in you." She patted him on the back before turning her gaze to the crowd. "Now, for my prize."

"A date, I believe, is what you requested," Tanner said, adjusting his armor.

"Yes, a date. But not with you, dear boy," she said, patting him on the chest.

He stumbled back, his lower lip pouting, hand draped over his chest like he had been hit, until he ran into the stacked hay bales. A deflated expression filled his face.

"I knew your offer was too good to be true. Outplayed by your talent and wit again. I stand no chance against you." He readjusted his breastplate and bowed with a wink.

"Oh General," she laughed. "I outplay you here so no one gets the better of you out there. Think of it as training."

"By the master," he said.

"Would you want to be trained by anyone lesser?" She walked along the outer edge of the field. All eyes followed her, curious to see whom she chose. We didn't have to wait long. She stopped in front of Arrow.

Crap. I knew it. Of all the people here, of course it would be him. I held my breath and waited. She leaned in, whispering in his ear. Arrow tossed his head back and chuckled. Melody brushed her hair off her shoulder and continued walking. I exhaled and fought my growing smile.

"Time to choose my date," she mused, still walking slowly around the field, twisting the strands of feathers on her vest. Sighs of disappointment came from each person she passed by. Whatever game she played with them, she played it well. They all leaned forward in anticipation.

I glanced over my shoulder to where the ladder to the bridge was tethered. Now was my chance.

"I choose you," her smooth voice called out.

I looked up to see whom she had chosen, surprised to see her only a few feet away, staring at me.

CHAPTER TWENTY-TWO

"What? Me?" I choked out. A lump grew in my chest. "You're joking, right?"

"I don't joke," she said gravely, and then the corners of her mouth lifted. She held out her hand expectantly.

I looked over her shoulder at Arrow, who simply shrugged, and then I skimmed over the rest of the crowd that eagerly awaited my response.

"I don't... I, uh, sure," I said, reaching for her hand.

"Don't be shy. No matter what rumors General Tanner spreads, I don't bite," she said with a wink. "Now come on in here," she insisted, pulling me into the field near the weapon barrels. "We don't have all day, and I don't want to go back to work without a little fun first."

"But, I-I don't..."

"Don't tell me you don't know how to have fun?" She arched an eyebrow and let my hand drop. "I had higher hopes for the Golden Hero."

"Hey, wait, I didn't mean that. I know how to have fun. It's just..." My words lingered as I looked around, watching the crowd disperse. The spots that had been so crammed with people grew empty. It seemed everyone else had somewhere to be. There was nothing I had to do, nowhere that I needed to be. I sighed.

Melody watched me curiously, leaning against the barrel of arrows. "It's just what?"

"It's nothing," I said.

"That's what I thought." Melody flipped her dark curls behind her shoulder and pulled out a handful of arrows, filling two quivers.

Arrow approached from the other side of the field. "Treat her nice, Melody," he said. "We'll need her later."

"My prince, I'm offended at your suggestion." She batted her eyes and curtsied.

"No, you're not." He laughed aloud.

"Ah, you know me too well. As you wish. She'll be returned unharmed and in one piece. Care to join us?" she asked.

Arrow glanced between us and then over his shoulder to the general's tent. "I can't. There's some unfinished business with General Amos I have to take care of."

"Ah, that old man doesn't know how to have fun." She pouted.

"This isn't all about fun," he said.

"Well this is." She waved Arrow off and turned her attention back to me. "Are you ready?"

"I, uh, sure," I said, wiping my hands on my tights.

Arrow reached for me, his hand sliding down my arm and stopping at my wrist. "Are you sure you're okay?"

"What?" Melody jumped in. "I don't think so. Your precious hero will be fine. Go, off with you. Do whatever you and your generals do in that tent. It's my turn with her." She pushed him away.

He raised an eyebrow.

"I'll be fine," I whispered. He shrugged before leaving the field.

I watched him leave and sighed. When I turned back around, Melody arched an eyebrow and handed me a full quiver.

"So what's the deal with you and our prince? You seem close."

"I…uh…what?"

The smirk on her face grew as I fumbled for words. "You don't need to worry."

"Worry about what?" I asked.

She kept her gaze low as she looked through the weapon barrel. "About him," she said, pulling out a black arrow.

"I don't know what you mean," I said, too quickly. I bit my inner lip as she smiled.

"I haven't seen him this happy in a long time."

Relief flooded through me, and I fought the smile threatening to take over my face. "Oh, we're not—"

She interrupted me with a hearty laugh. "Trust me. He's my cousin. I know every expression that passes across his face. He's interested, and I'd wager the same for you." She pulled back on her bow, focusing down the field. "You may be our hero, but you're not a very good liar." She released a perfect shot.

He's my cousin.

Three words never sounded so good.

"So what did you have planned for us?"

Melody leaned back against the barrel and ran her fingers over the edge of the feathered shafts. "I thought we'd find out just what you're made of."

"That's not vague."

She threw her head back in laughter. "I like you, Alex. You're not afraid to tell it how it is."

I fought against the grin growing on my face. "What can I say? It's hard to be anything but blunt here."

"You speak the truth, and you're not afraid to fight. No wonder they sent you," she said.

"Look, not everything you've heard about me is true."

"I've heard a lot, we've all heard a lot, and I wanted to tell you something. That's why I chose you."

"What's that?" I asked.

She brushed her long hair off her shoulder and looked me straight in the eyes. "Thank you."

"Thank you?"

"You sound surprised," she said, throwing me a bow from the pile of weapons. I barely caught it before it hit the ground.

"It wasn't what I expected you to say," I admitted, looking over the bow. "Most of my first impressions haven't gone over too well."

"I've heard that, too," she said, smirking. "None of us knew what to expect when we heard of you. History and legend didn't quite give us a clear picture."

"I can imagine," I mumbled.

"But you're here, and some of the men told me what you did. Coming back to save them, and then those girls. That was nothing short of heroic."

"Who told you that?" I asked.

"Boris told me everything. Even grumpy old Cale had something nice to say about you."

"That surprises me."

"Me too," she said. "But those girls and our men owe you their lives, and we owe you a debt of gratitude."

"Is that what this is supposed to be?" I lifted the bow awkwardly.

"Something like that. Do you shoot?" she asked.

"A little." I hedged my bets. When my mom was late picking me up from the gym after climbing, I'd tried archery a few times. I was pretty good for a beginner, but I couldn't do anything like what she had done.

She gave me a crooked smile. "This will be fun. Head closer to the target, and we'll practice a bit. You never know when it'll save your life."

I followed her lead and mimicked her stance. The smooth shaft slipped in my palm as I adjusted to the heavier weight of the wooden bow. I hadn't shot in months, and I wasn't in the mood to be embarrassed.

"Good, good," she said, looking me over. "Relax your shoulders and loosen your grip on the arrow. This is supposed to be fun, not torture."

I listened but didn't respond. Not everyone had gone back to work, and I felt their eyes on me. My grip slipped on the bow. I readjusted my hands, ignoring the giggles from the side.

"Don't worry about them. Block them out and focus ahead. On my count. Three, two, one, release."

My arrow sliced through the air. The fletching wobbled as it skewered the outer ring on the target. It wasn't a bull's-eye, but it was good enough for me.

Melody ran to remove the arrow.

"Looks like you can shoot after all. Let's see how good you are." She stepped back to where she had shot earlier with the general. "Think you can hit it from here?"

I joined her and took my aim. Her competitive nature was contagious. "Without a problem," I said.

The awkwardness between us disappeared after that next shot, replaced with something I had missed. She reminded me of Natalie. I bit my lower lip. It was bittersweet, thinking about her. Of course, nothing could be the same as my relationship with Natalie, but having a new friend felt good.

We fell into a routine of alternating our shots. I took her suggestions to improve my form, and my arrows began to land closer to the center.

"How did you become such a great shot?" I asked.

"Do you want the short or long story?"

"Short, I guess."

"Years of practice. I need to be good enough to kill my father." She released the arrow and it skewered the target.

I lowered my bow and stared at her. "Okay, back up. I guess I want the long version."

She sighed and brushed her hair over her shoulders, pulling her leather vest to the side. A jagged scar stretched down a few inches from her collarbone. "My father gave it to me for my fourteenth birthday."

"Your dad did that? How? I mean, why?" I asked. Sure, my parents had stabbed me in the back before, but not literally. I couldn't even imagine.

She pushed her sleeve back into position, covering up her collarbone. "I don't think he wanted to kill me, just send me a message."

"What message was that?"

"That not even his daughter was more important than the throne."

"His daugh—" I covered my mouth. "Wait! Your father's Berkos?"

"Yup."

"Oh my god, what did you do? I mean, I can't..."

She shrugged. "Given the choice between running away or being killed, I chose to run. Thankfully, Arrow found me hiding in the woods while he was out hunting with his men. They took me in and taught me everything I know."

"They did a good job."

Melody shifted her weight and set her next arrow. "Revenge can be a powerful motivation. Look, I'm not here to reminisce. The past is past. Done. I only focus on the future now." She fired her arrows off in quick succession. All of them landed in a vertical line, splitting the targets in half.

Whoa. She was one girl I didn't want to mess with.

"All righty, then...Can you show me how to do that?" I asked.

She appraised me and chuckled. "I don't think you're ready for that yet."

I gave her an exaggerated pout and reloaded my bow, taking aim down the field. My arrow missed the target by a foot. I laughed as I ran to get the arrows.

"I guess you're right. So what else can you teach me? What do you do for fun?"

"Are you saying you're not having fun?"

"No, no. I am," I said. "But what else do you do here?"

"I don't know." She shrugged and released her next arrow. "Probably the same as you. We hunt, weave, draw, explore, train."

"Yeah, just like me," I muttered.

"Oh come on, you know what I mean. We have fun, but we don't dare lose sight of our goal."

"To save the queen," I said.

"No, that's Arrow's fixation. For the rest of us, it's not just that.

We're fighting to save ourselves." Her face softened. She lowered the bow and looked at me. "The Grove is our home now, but before," she said, "before, we could go anywhere, do anything. We had opportunities, lives, and loves. We fight to get that back. I'm not an idealist like Arrow. I love the queen and want her to be safe. But I really just want my life back."

I nodded and looked down at my quiver. I knew something about not wanting to let the past go.

"Anyways, you're not bad at this. With more training, I'm sure you'd be my equal."

"I don't know about that," I said. Then I added more quietly, "I don't think we have time for that."

"Speaking of time, as much fun as this has been, it's getting late. What do you say we call it a night?"

I shrugged, looking up at the dim sky. Part of me wanted to sleep, but I didn't feel ready. I had a friend again and didn't want to let that go.

"If you're up for it, I'd like your help tomorrow," she said, reloading her quiver with arrows. "There's a lot to do around here, and we could use you. That is, unless there's something else you have planned?"

"No, there's nothing planned, at least not that I know of."

"Then we're settled. Tomorrow morning I'll come find you. And, if you have any questions about anything or anyone, all you have to do is ask."

"Good night," I said, watching her glide over the hay bales with ease.

The short walk back to my tent did little to quiet my mind. As I lay on my cot, looking up at the white ceiling of the tent, I wondered if I would ever sleep through the night again.

CHAPTER TWENTY-THREE

I stirred at the gentle lap of the tent door whipping against the rigid fabric. The quiet shuffling of footsteps swelled and faded as people walked by on their business. The birds harmonized with the soft trilling insects, and piercing bright light snuck in through the half-open door. I flipped over. Even if the camp woke this early, I didn't have to.

I sunk back into my dream, replaying the events from yesterday. From the first moment I'd entered the Grove, my feelings about Lockhorn had changed. The endless loop of canopy bridges, the army of people living and working together in harmony, the feeling I got plucking the bow against my fingers, and the thrill as I struck the target. The Grove filled a void I hadn't realized was there.

The shuffling got louder, alerting me. I tightened my hands into fists and slowed my breath as the sound grew closer. The pounding of the tent flap, the smooth whoosh of fabric, the footsteps on the ground—I wasn't imaging it. Someone was in my room.

Before I could grab my dagger, a hand tugged on my shoulder.

"No!" I yelled, flailing my arms. I flipped over, striking something hard. When I opened my eyes, I gasped and covered my mouth. "Melody, I'm so sorry!"

Red frothy liquid raced down her leather pants. "Good morning to you too," she muttered, shaking the excess liquid off her hand.

"Oh no, I am so sorry," I said, standing to hand her a washcloth. "What are you doing here?"

"You said you'd be up for helping me today. I was just coming by to get you. I didn't realize you'd still be sleeping." She threw the washcloth over her shoulder. I watched it arc towards the edge of the wash basin and slide inside. I shook my head; this girl could not fail at anything.

"Here," she said, holding out a now half-full mug of tea.

Peering over the glass, I caught a familiar acrid scent off the steaming red liquid. "Carrin root tea?" I asked, sticking my tongue out.

"I see you've had it before," she said. "It's good for you, though, and will heal any residual aches from the other day. Trust me, I wouldn't steer you wrong."

I raised an eyebrow and gave her a skeptical look.

"Anyway," she continued, ignoring my look. "I'll meet you outside."

"But I didn't say—"

"You don't want to help the rebellion?" she asked.

"That's not what I'm saying."

"Ah, Arrow was right. You are amusing to poke fun at. I'll see you in a few minutes." She turned and walked back out of the tent.

My face flushed as I watched the tent flap close. I glanced down at the warm blankets and sighed. No more dreaming for today. I threw on my new green outfit and straightened my hair in the mirror. Melody didn't seem the patient type, and I didn't want to miss spending the day with her. I grabbed an extra roll and ran out the door. The bread worked wonders at soaking up the residual bitterness of the tea. Good for me or not, that tea tasted awful.

The harsh sunlight blinded me as I exited the tent and stopped on the dusty pathway. It seemed like I was the only one who'd slept in. People rushed by with their arms loaded with supplies. Through squinted eyes I saw Melody waiting across the street. Leaning casually against a wooden fence, she twisted the feathered fringe along her vest as she leaned forward, whispering into General Tanner's ears. A dark shade of red flooded his cheeks before he ran off.

I weaved through the busy street and met her with a curious

look. "What did you tell him?"

"Who, General Tanner? I was just telling him a little secret," she said, straightening the fringe on her vest.

"Must have been some secret."

"Don't look at me that way. It wasn't *too* scandalous."

I looked down the pathway. Even from a distance, the red in his cheeks stood out.

"Sure…" I said sarcastically.

"Okay, maybe it was. Just a little." She winked. "Harmless fun."

"Is that fair? I mean, at the field yesterday, he seemed sort of taken with you."

"All the more reason for it. With the sacrifices we've all made, the least I can do is set his heart aflutter every once in a while. It's innocent…for the most part," she said, shifting against the fence.

"Does he know that?" I asked. "It might be fun, but what happens later? It's not fair to lead him on like that."

"Don't get worked up. It's not all a lie," she said, looking down the road. "But with his position, any relationship would be more of a burden than a pleasure right now."

"You can't honestly feel that way."

"I have to. My feelings don't outweigh the greater good of the rebellion. We can't afford for one of our generals to be distracted." I heard a twinge of sadness in her voice.

"You sound like your cousin," I said.

"Not really. He's a smart leader, but we don't always agree." She gave me a direct look.

Silence stretched between us, and I looked away. I couldn't ignore her hint.

"Enough of this," she said, pulling her vest straight. "There's fun to be had. Ready?"

"Absolutely!"

She led me further down the dusty road past the training field, where a group of archers practiced. Younger boys lined the edge, captivated as General Amos shouted out orders. Deep lines marked his face, and his arms remained firmly folded across his chest.

I sighed and turned my attention back to Melody just before she moved around the edge of an old wooden barn. Green paint peeled off in strips, revealing worn planks and empty holes where the birds had nested. The smell of freshly turned dirt and warm hay wafted towards me. It was heaven. I took a moment to peek inside the building, amazed at its simplistic beauty. Rays of sunlight burst through the holes in the rotten planks, and horses half-hid in the shadows, their manes sending flurries of dust through the air as they pranced around the edges of their enclosures.

I wished I had my art supplies. This was a painting waiting to be created.

"This is it," Melody said, breaking my reverie, gesturing around the corner. I peeked around and saw an open field where a set of long tables overflowed with groups of women and men.

"What do we do?" I asked.

"We join in the fun." She pulled me forward through the tall grass. A few heads lifted as we came closer, but most stayed down in concentration. "What do you want to do first?"

"I don't know, what are my choices?" I asked, looking down the long tables. Excitement buzzed from every station. I leaned closer to Melody and whispered, "What're they doing, exactly?"

She pulled me down the open space. "We're putting together some of our weapons and defense mechanisms to prepare for battle. Here," she said, pointing to the table in front of us, "is where we're making packets of dragon weed pollen and vials of its oil."

I balled my fists together and shook my head. "No dragon weed." I had been burned enough. Even the sight of the dust sent a wave of prickles down my spine.

She pursed her lips but didn't question it. "No dragon weed— got it. Then here at this table, we're sewing feathers onto vests."

"Feathers for defense?" I laughed.

"Of course. They make the perfect camouflage. Why'd you think we wore them?" she asked.

I blushed but met her gaze. "They're pretty."

She stared at me for a moment, then smirked. "Moving on," she said, pulling me to the next table. "How about doing a little welding?"

I looked at the brown and copper components on the table and then back to her. "I've seen these before. What are they?"

"They're acoustical enhancements—"

"Hearing devices," I said. "That explains it!"

"Explains what?" she asked with a furrowed brow.

"It's nothing," I said, shaking it off.

"No, tell me." She placed her hands on her hips. "I'm curious."

How could I tell her without the embarrassment of admitting my early capture? I grabbed a couple of the wheels from the table and balanced them in my palm. "Some of the people I ran into in Lindle had one."

"Who?"

"Just some people." I shrugged.

"People from Lindle? They had one?" She grabbed my hand, her face paling.

"Yes…"

"This is awful. They're not supposed to have any of these devices. What do we do now?"

"What's wrong?" I asked.

"What's wrong?" she asked, giving me an incredulous stare. "If the enemy has their hands on this, then they know one of our advantages."

I turned to face her and grabbed her hands. "No, not the enemy. The people I met, they were performers—rebels like you, me, and everyone here."

"Are you sure?"

"Positive."

"Who were they? Did you get their names?" she asked.

I was sorry I had brought it up at all. Turning our day into an interrogation wasn't my plan. "Deakon had the ear thing, and his friend Pipes was traveling with him."

Her look softened. "Pipes? You saw him?"

"He was one of the first to recognize me, and he helped me escape the capital."

"It's not the capital," she said, reflexively. "How did he look? Was he all right?"

"He was fine. Wait," I said, giving her a sidelong glance. "You didn't...Pipes?" The lanky man I remembered and the poised beauty before me seemed like an odd pairing.

She looked off towards the trees. "It was a long time ago. Did he sing for you?"

I pressed my lips together and smiled. It made complete sense. "Yeah, he did. What happened between you guys?"

"I'm sure you know how these things go sometimes. We had different callings, in life and in the rebellion. I'm glad he's alive," she said, looking back at me with a smile that didn't quite reach her eyes. "Now that that's taken care of...do you want to make some of them?"

I hesitated. This seemed like something I could handle, but I didn't want to make it awkward for her. "What else is there?" I asked, looking at the crowd gathered around the last table. Even from a distance, I saw sweat beading around their temples and tense exhaustion on their faces.

"That," she said with awe, "is our newest weapon."

"Weapon?" I asked, taking a hesitant step closer.

"Our reclamation team scavenged an electric whip last week from the woods surrounding Berkin. They've been busy reverse-engineering it ever since. Do you want to take a look?" She didn't wait for me to respond.

I crept up behind her, finding a spot near her side where I could peek over a shoulder. Most of the people had their fingers twisted in a web of wires. Small metal chips and bits of wire littered the table. Women inserted spark plugs and electric circuits into a metal cylinder. Next to them, a second team twisted and secured copper wire around a long strip of leather. Sparks flew from the far edge of the table, where a few people hid under a haze of smoke, soldering the pieces together.

Melody bit her lower lip and smiled, but I knew the power these weapons contained. Even the lowest voltage meant death. This was not good.

I wiped my hands along my leggings and tugged at one of the feathers on Melody's vest. "I've made my decision. I want to work on the ear things," I said, pulling her back.

"What?" she asked, reluctantly prying her eyes away. "Sure, if that's what you want." She glanced back once more before joining me.

"It is," I said and strode back to the last table. The workers only casually glanced up as we took two of the empty spots at the far end of the table. They were entrenched in a web of wires and wheels.

"What do we do?" I whispered.

Melody smiled. "Just follow my lead. Once you put one together, the rest are easy."

A tangled mess of bright gears and coiled wires flashed from the center of the table. I watched Melody, grabbing the same materials she did until I had a small pile in front of me.

She inserted the copper wire between the gears and folded the electrical pieces behind a leather strap. I followed her movements, a step behind, until the first pieces were connected and a loose but complete device sat in my hand.

"Easy, huh?" I asked, stifling my laugh. "I seriously hope no one's counting on me to create these things."

"No, we're counting on something much bigger," she joked. "Besides, it doesn't need to look good, it just needs to function." She twitched her nose at the botched device in front of me.

I smiled but looked away, drawn to the table behind us. A loud cheer erupted, followed by a buzz and a crackle. I stood on my chair to get a better look, and my sense of dread tripled. A blast of blue light erupted at the table. Streams of electricity spiraled around the whip, sparking with sporadic bursts of blue flame.

"Yeah! You did it!" Melody cried.

Half the people from our table rushed over for a closer look.

I didn't share their feelings. They didn't know what power they wielded, and that disturbed me.

"What's everyone looking at?" a deep voice asked from over my shoulder.

I jumped, then exhaled deeply. "You scared me," I said to Arrow.

"I didn't mean to startle you," he said. "What's going on?" He peeked behind me, pulling out a strip of jerky.

My mouth watered when he took a bite. Had that much time passed?

"They figured out how to make the electric whips work," I said, returning my focus to the table. "I don't think it's such a good thing."

"Really?" he asked, surprised. "Why not?"

"They're bad."

"Bad for us or them?"

I gave him a half-smile. "Both."

"Hmm," he said, shrugging. "Sometimes we have to take risks. Most of our devices started out as dangerous. Dangerous doesn't have to be bad if it can be channeled rightly."

"Who decides that?" I asked, looking back at the blue flames.

"That's a good question. I guess I do."

"Then I hope you know what you're doing. They don't." I cringed as the whip lit one of the chairs on fire. "Turn the lever off!" I yelled, waving my arm.

I turned around as the fire leapt to the next chair. "Do something," I said, pushing him towards the crowd.

Arrow laughed and covered his chest. "They have it under control. And now, I have this," he said, grabbing the wiggling ear device from my hand.

"Arrow, no!" I yelled, chasing after him as he darted towards the stables. "Give that back."

"You lowered your defenses. That's not a good idea." He

couldn't hold back his grin.

"It's your home, I'm supposed to be safe here," I said. "Now give it back!" We reached the stables, and I leaned over to catch my breath.

"I'm happy to hear that," he said, lowering his voice to a whisper. "I'm glad you feel safe here."

"What?" The pounding of my heart threatened to drown out his words.

"I'm glad you're enjoying your time here. I was worried it would be boring after all we've seen the past few days."

"Boring? I don't think anything here could be boring, especially with your cousin keeping me company."

Arrow flashed his charming smile. "Ah, Melody. She's a handful," he said. "Come to think of it, that makes her a perfect fit for you."

"Hey, take that back," I said, making a grab for the hearing device.

He caught my hand and lowered it to his side, pulling me closer. "I meant it in only the best of ways." His voice deepened as he looked at me.

"I... uh..." The words escaped me again.

"Let's see what you've been doing this morning," he said, slipping the device over his head.

"Please, no," I said, reaching for it, stepping forward into his arms.

His grip on the device held and his body pressed close to mine. I froze. The mischievous gleam in his eyes twisted my stomach.

"What are you afraid of?" he asked.

My heart drummed. At that moment, only him.

"I'm sure you're mechanically inclined. It'll work. I'd bet my life on it," he said, turning the lever on the bottom.

I couldn't stop him. I could hardly breathe, let alone move quickly enough to grab it.

"Alex, you did it! Want to give it a try?"

I grabbed it a little too quickly, bringing that warm smile back to Arrow's face. "I take it you didn't get a chance to test it yet?"

My head stopped mid-shake, and my eyes popped open. I could hear everything down to my heartbeat, including its rapid increase when Arrow touched my elbow. Nothing remained private under the microscope of this machine. Flushed and embarrassed, I turned to see Arrow smiling.

I pulled the piece off my ear, and everything returned to normal. "That's amazing. I've never seen anything like it. How did you come up with it?"

"We have a collection department that scours the countryside and forest for useful items, and our engineers are remarkable. Anything from the most basic, outdated technology to the newest intelligence devices that we are lucky enough to get our hands on comes back here. We try not to let anything go to waste."

"Clever," I said, handing it back.

"And effective. These were originally used to help the elders hear like they used to, but over the past few years we amplified the acoustics and adapted them for reconnaissance."

I put the earbuds back in and squinted in the distance, weighing their value as I tried to recognize the distorted sounds. The shuffling of feet blended with the electric hum, and the exaggerated exclamations from the people at the tables melted into an indiscernible roar. I imagined with time, sorting out the sounds would be easier, but it gave me a headache. At least I finally understood how Deakon had heard me.

Booms echoed in my ears when Arrow tapped me on the shoulder, and I pulled the device off. He brushed his hair off his forehead and looked behind me. "I'm glad you're settling in nicely. I just wanted to check in to see how you were doing today, but I can see you're in good hands."

I turned to follow his gaze and saw Melody squint as she watched us intently.

"I'd like to talk later, if that's all right," he said.

"Oh? What about?" My cheeks felt warm. I hoped I wasn't reddening.

"I don't want to go over it now, but there's some stuff I should tell you. Things we should've talked about earlier. Just come find me when you get a chance," he said, looking past me again.

"Yeah, sure, later," I stammered. What did he want to talk about? My mind raced, but couldn't settle on anything specific.

I watched him run off, and when I turned back, Melody stood behind me, a smirk on her lips as she unhooked a device from her ear. "These things," she said, "you never know when they can come in handy. So...you and my cousin...I was right."

"What? No, it's not like that," I said, feeling my cheeks burn again.

"You say that, and yet I heard something much different. And my eyes don't deceive. Look," she said, leaning in. "I'm the last to judge, and frankly, it's none of my business."

"It's complicated," I said, trying to find the right word.

"Complicated?" She snorted. "That might be the biggest understatement I've ever heard."

"What do you know about it?" I retorted, rubbing my fingers together. "Like you said, it's none of your business."

"You got me there. But how much do you know about what you are?"

"What do you mean?"

She sighed heavily. "About being the Golden Hero. What do you know?"

"Not very much," I admitted, feeling a lump gather in my chest.

"You see," she said, leading me to the edge of the stables. "We know more about you than I think you know about us." She sat down and picked at the flaking paint on the edges of the stables beside her.

"What do you mean?"

"I don't know how to say this in a way that will make sense," she said, changing positions to fidget with her feathered fringe. "You see, Lockhorn has a long history of summoning the Golden Hero when we need help. In the past, the Hero appeared at each crisis point to aid us." She stopped tugging on her vest to look at me. "We've been waiting for you for years now."

I tried to ignore the accusation in her eyes, but my stomach dropped. How was I supposed to know?

"So when we heard that you were finally here, Arrow went out in search of you. Didn't he tell you this?"

"We didn't really talk much," I said, pulling handfuls of grass out of the dirt so I didn't have to look at her.

She leaned back against the wall. "Do you even know how you got here?"

"I won't be forgetting that anytime soon," I said with a scoff. Being eaten by light pixels wasn't the sort of thing I'd easily forget.

"Not what happened to bring you here, but how you were summoned?"

"There's a difference?"

"Yes, a big difference. No matter how you get here, one thing is always the same—the summoning. There's only one way a hero enters our world."

"And that is?"

"By a death spell."

"A what?" I asked in a whisper.

"A death spell," she said. "It's our strongest magic. It's the only magic we have left, really. We didn't have the foresight to preserve the wisdom of the ancients. But the death spell…it transcends all worlds and all rules. When it's cast, nothing can stop it."

I stared at her, feeling my face pale and a piece of grass fall from my shaking hands. "How does it work?" I asked, although I didn't really want to know the answer. Anything called a death spell couldn't be good.

"That's the tricky thing. It only works for some, and only with a sacrificial death. Only in the direst of situations has anyone tried to cast it."

"So to get me here…" My voice trailed off as my mind wrapped around the meaning of her words. "Someone had to die."

"You're starting to understand. But not just anyone died."

"Who?" I asked, closing my eyes to avoid the answer.

"King Helio," she said, "Arrow's brother."

I inhaled sharply.

"Yes, so before you get too close to him, try to remember the price he's already paid," she said, a bit too pointedly. "And there's one more thing we know about the heroes."

I looked up.

"They never stay."

I stared at her, letting the implications of her words sink in. "Thanks, Melody. I wouldn't have known."

She nodded and walked away, leaving me alone with my thoughts. The last place I wanted to be.

CHAPTER TWENTY-FOUR

After Melody left, I wandered aimlessly around the camp, my mind jumping from insult to accusation, circling around the inevitable conclusion. His brother died for me. How could I even begin to make up for that?

Dust swirled as I walked back towards the entrance to the Grove. I hadn't recognized how far I had walked until I saw the abandoned wagon by the quaint cottage. The door to the wagon opened easily, allowing me to slink back into its far corners. I gripped the wooden bars, feeling comfort in the symbolism. Even with the door open, my feelings imprisoned me.

I briefly thought about leaving again, then banged my head against the bars. I couldn't do that. That would be the deepest betrayal. His brother's death would be in vain.

No wonder Cale didn't forgive me. I could hardly blame him or the rest of the men for how they'd reacted. They'd lost their kingdom to Berkos, and then their king to bring me here. And I'd refused to help.

I felt sick. No number of vines could heal the pit that opened inside me. I hadn't really thought about anyone but me, and I'd never thought a game could be so complicated. I banged my head against the bars until the pounding dulled my thoughts.

Then I remembered that Arrow wanted to talk to me. Whatever it was about, it couldn't be worse than what Melody had already told me. I clenched my jaw and walked back into the village. The knot in my stomach twisted until my entire body turned into pins and needles. The slightest of sounds unraveled me, even though I couldn't put my finger on what it was that worried me most.

My feet guided me forward until I spied movement on the training field. I sighed and made my way over to the edge of the field, resting against the stacked hay bales. The dry edges of the straw scratched my arms. I pulled out the offending pieces, peeling them in half as I stared at the field where Arrow taught some of the youth how to shoot.

A group of boys no older than ten crowded around him. Casually slung over his shoulder, Arrow's black bow glinted. He walked in front of them and pointed to the different areas of the field. I tried to imagine what he was telling them, but I didn't understand his gestures.

That was okay. Watching him was entertainment enough.

His deep laugh rang out as one of the smallest boys lifted a bow twice his size. Arrow tossed his bow to one of the older boys—I thought I'd heard them call him Ronan—and grabbed a smaller wooden one from the barrels. Ronan stared at Arrow's bow in disbelief. I knew that look.

Arrow didn't seem to notice, fully involved with the younger child. He stood behind him, helping him string the arrow and aim at the end of the field. The muscles in Arrow's arms tightened as they pulled back and released. I held my breath, watching the wobbling arrow strike its target.

The boy jumped up and howled as he ran to retrieve it.

The other boys scampered over to the barrel to find a bow their size. When they all had their new weapons, Arrow lined them up carefully, youngest to oldest, and waited for the other boy to return. The hay bales towered over him as he jumped to retrieve the arrow.

Arrow ducked down and put his finger to his lips to tell the others to be silent. He tiptoed down the field and grabbed the boy, throwing him onto his shoulders. Even from where I stood, I could hear the child's giggles. When they turned around, everyone cheered. Arrow lifted the little boy's arm up in victory and handed him the arrow from the target.

I couldn't contain my laughter. Moments like these made Lockhorn feel like home. My heart grew watching him—that's the only way to describe the ache that pulled me from within. The knots in my stomach seized. I didn't have to worry about any of the things I had done when I first arrived. My biggest concern now was what I wanted to do, having heard Melody's warning.

He must have heard my laugh; he turned in my direction and smiled. My knees gave way, and I melted. He ran back to the line of waiting boys and dropped the child in line with the others. General Amos, who had been watching from the other side of the field, nodded and took Arrow's place as he ran over to me.

My hands scraped against the rough straw as I wiped my palms on my leggings.

His hair bounced as he approached, falling in front of his eyes. I wanted to reach out and move it for him, but he beat me to it.

"Did you come for a lesson?" he quipped.

"Melody taught me quite enough—or at least reminded me that I can't claim archery as a skill."

"I thought you did pretty well," he said.

"Pretty well won't save the rebellion."

"Good thing you have other tricks, then." He winked, then glanced back at the boys, who continued practicing under the general's guidance. "What are you doing here?"

"I, uh, was looking for you," I said. "You said you wanted to talk."

"I did. I mean, I do." He scrunched his face as he looked behind him at the field. "I think General Amos can handle it from here."

"Are you sure?" I asked, looking back as the boys ran in circles around the old general.

Arrow chuckled and grabbed my hand. "It'll be good for him. Are you up for a walk?"

I bit my lower lip and nodded.

His smile lit up, and he pulled me forward towards the cottage where the ladder led up to the bridge. "I haven't had a chance to relax since we got here. I hope you don't mind the bridge."

I couldn't hold back my grin. He had read my mind. "It's perfect," I said, walking in front of his outstretched arm to climb up first.

The planks creaked under our weight. I stopped when I reached the first bridge. It hadn't changed, but it seemed so much more alive. The planks didn't just creak; they rejoiced under our steps. The vines swayed with their own mysterious breeze, and an echoing silence surrounded us. Before, I had concentrated on the Grove below and had missed the beauty of the bridge and the canopy of the woods.

The cool vines slid under my palms as I walked forward, making room for Arrow to climb up behind me. I peered through the wooden archway leading away from the tree. "How did I not see this before?"

"It's amazing what we miss the first time we see something," he said, right behind me.

"I'm glad I get this second look then," I whispered, my eyes flitting between his face and the trees around us.

"Me too." He pulled me forward. "Follow me."

"Where are we going?" I asked as we passed under the archway.

"I want to show you something. Remember? I promised to show you all the wonders of this world." His boyish grin charmed me. How could I resist?

"Wait up!" I yelled as he ran further ahead. His long legs skipped multiple planks as he conquered the bridge in a few leaps. I followed, more tentatively, refusing to let go of my grip on the railing.

He didn't stop, only slowing down briefly each time he crossed onto a new bridge. We climbed through the canopy and around to a part of the Grove I hadn't seen.

The view below me was dizzying. Without the reference points of people and places, the ground seemed miles away.

"Arrow," I called out. "Can you slow down a bit?" I wasn't afraid of heights, but the thought of getting lost in this tangled web of bridges and trees unsettled me.

"Sorry, I'll wait for you here. I just wanted to make sure we got there in time."

"Where?"

"I'm not giving up the surprise that easily," he said, reaching for my hand as I struggled with my steps. "It'll be worth it, I promise."

"Didn't you say that about the Pits of Wonder, too?"

"Oh no, you can't blame that on me. You discovered that one all by yourself." He smirked.

"Fine, but how much further?" I asked, leaning against the railing to catch my breath.

"We're almost there."

"Okay, let's do this," I said, waving him forward.

I stumbled behind him, wearily moving from bridge to bridge until we stopped. "Are we there…" My voice trailed off as I looked up and lost my train of thought.

"What do you think?" Arrow asked, moving to the side to give me a clear view.

I stepped slowly, brushing past him without a glance. My gaze focused on a long staircase that led up to a delicately carved gazebo overlooking the top of the forest.

The bark was cool under my fingertips. I caressed the smooth designs carved into the side of the tree and the handrail. The scent of pine came through more strongly as I climbed closer to the tree. Boughs of pine needles swooped over the staircase as a natural cover.

I stopped at the top of the staircase and turned around in awe. I wanted to speak, but I had no words.

"You can come in," Arrow said, stepping around me, pulling me in with him.

I looked around him at the woven limbs that encircled us in the wooden structure. They intersected seamlessly, creating a natural barrier above and around us. Tucked between the leaves and branches, nature painted a masterpiece. Patches of moss filled deep crevices in the bark, and portions of gnarled wood twisted into spirals around us. Yellow flowers grew along the outer edges of the roof.

I gasped.

"You like it?" he asked, reaching for my hand.

"I've never seen anything like this before," I said, tightening my grip on his hand.

"Then it's perfect," he said.

"I don't understand."

"You don't have to. I just wanted to share it with you," he said, pulling me to the far edge of the gazebo to see an unrestricted view of the forest. We leaned over the edge of the railing, and the tops of the trees swayed in rhythm in the breeze. I exhaled and propped my arms along the woven branches, watching the blue of the sky lighten to orange.

In a world of so much beauty, I wondered why I had been in such a rush to leave, to get home. Melody's warning flashed in my mind, but I brushed it aside. I might not be able to stay, but I wasn't leaving anytime soon. Winning the game, finding my way home…it no longer compelled me.

I placed my hand atop his and looked him in the eyes. "I might not have to understand, Arrow, but I want to. I've pretended long enough that what I know from my world explains this one. It doesn't. I want to know the truth about this place, about you."

He searched my face for a moment and then settled his gaze back over the forest. "This is one of the old guard towers."

"From before Berkos took over?" I asked, trying to fit it into the history I knew.

"Yes, from a long time before, even before my parents and grandparents ruled. These forest lookouts served as resting places during hunting parties or long travel. When Berkos came into power, this was the only place I could think of that he wouldn't find me. Even in his youth, he was always more interested in staying in the city, attending parties and banquets than roaming the wilds."

"So you ran here? It's a long way from Flourin."

He nodded. "It was the only chance I had. I had to go

somewhere Berkos wouldn't look. This tower was the one place that I knew I'd be safe. It became my second home, or rather, my new home." He sighed. "All of that seems so long ago."

"So how did it all happen? I've heard bits, but no one's really put it all together for me."

"You really want to know?"

I nodded and placed my hand on top of his. "Yeah, I mean, I was brought here to help you. It'd be nice to know."

"Well, I guess I'll start with my parents. They died when I was young, too young to really know what happened. There was some sort of accident, the doctors told me, but I still don't know if that's the truth or not. At six, I didn't think to question it, and I don't know if my older brother Helio did either. Even if he suspected something, he would have had to focus on the new pressures of leading Lockhorn, for the good of the people."

"Was he as young as you?" I asked.

"He was thirteen, barely old enough to take care of himself, let alone a kingdom or a brother."

"I can't imagine how hard that must've been for both of you," I said.

"It was, but we had some help. Helio connected with my father's advisors and continued their policies and ordinances for seven years. Life was good under my parents' reign; he didn't see the need to change any of that. Unfortunately, Berkos didn't feel the same way."

"So you knew him? I mean, I know he's Melody's dad, but how close were you?" I asked.

"We weren't close. I don't think my father ever really trusted him, to tell you the truth. But after our parents' death, Helio reached out to him. Berkos presided over a territory to the north as a governor, but I guess it wasn't enough for him. He turned my brother's kindness into an opportunity. He sat in on all of Helio's council meetings, offering his own experience and advice. In the beginning, he had great ideas, but over time my brother became more uncomfortable with the direction Berkos wanted to take the kingdom.

Helio shut him out, but not in time. Berkos had already planned his coup."

"I am so sorry," I said, taking a moment to squeeze his hand.

"I escaped, but only by luck. I'd been running around the forest all day, and he didn't recognize me under my soiled clothes. One of Elin's maids hid me as Berkos went on his rampage. Before he had a chance to detain me, I had run off. By the time I made it to the outskirts of Flourin, the news had spread. Only a handful of servants and villagers remained, and Berkos had claimed sovereignty."

"What did you do from there?"

"The only thing I really could do. I rallied my men and found loyal supporters that were willing to fight against Berkos' tyranny. It's been a long five years. Every day, I recount that devastation and plan for our revival."

"I have no doubt you'll succeed this time."

"I don't doubt it either. Not with you here. You've brought back the hope that had dwindled." I saw the conflict in his eyes.

"I don't know about that."

"I do. The moment we heard you had arrived, the whole atmosphere in the Grove, in all of Lockhorn, changed. Everyone knew that your appearance revolutionized everything. One way or another, this'll all be settled. Only with you here, our fight doesn't seem so futile."

"I didn't know that," I said, feeling even worse for the way I'd acted. I needed to change the subject. "So, since this was your hideout, you must know what we're looking at, right?"

He smiled at the redirection. "Uh-huh, you see that hill over there?"

I followed his pointed finger to a set of jagged mountains and nodded.

"Well, I used to hunt horned-bits in those foothills. The mountains beyond them separate the north from the south. From here you can easily track the movement of any giants or armies. That over there," he said, pointing off another direction, "is the Loude

River. It passes right by Lindle and handles most of the trade."

"You can really see it all from up here," I said. "What about…"

"Berkos' castle?" he asked. "Do you really want to know?"

"No, probably not," I said, shaking my head. "I'll face it soon enough, and I don't want to ruin this. The rest of the view, it's beautiful."

We stood in silence, watching the slow transition of the sky from sunset to twilight. Only the sharp chirp of a bird and the pulsing hum of insects broke the silence.

Arrow looked at me and then turned back to the forest. A sense of anxiety grew between us the longer we stared at the view. I didn't know how to articulate what I wanted to say. Conversations like this baffled me. Too many raw emotions threatened to take away my control.

I nudged him with my elbow, the friendliest gesture I could make without trembling. "You wanted to talk?"

The sides of his mouth lifted, but he didn't look at me. He rubbed his forehead and picked at the leaves from the railing. "These have been some of the longest days."

"You're telling me," I said. "I can't tell you how much I am looking forward to a full night's sleep."

He rubbed the back of his neck. "I wish I could give you that, but I'm afraid there are even more sleepless nights in our future. I can give you a roll though." He pulled a piece of bread and a couple of strips of jerky out of one of his vest pockets.

"Do you just walk around with packages of food?" I asked, though it didn't stop me from taking one.

"Sometimes," he said with a small smile. "It's seemed to work to my advantage recently."

"I can't help it if I'm hungry," I said. "It's not like we haven't crossed this entire kingdom in the last week."

"I'm just giving you a hard time. Although I won't lie, it's been nice coming to the rescue. Even if it's just with food."

I bit my cheek. What could I say to that?

"The real reason I brought you up here though," he said, exhaling deeply. "I wanted to tell you some things before they slipped out again."

"Like the whole prince thing?" I asked, raising an eyebrow.

"Yeah." He laughed. "Like that. I meant to tell you. I really did."

I looked at him. "Why didn't you?"

He sighed and stared thoughtfully into the distance. "When we met, it didn't seem to matter. There were more important things we needed to do, and then when you lied about being from the north... well, I guess it seemed like our backgrounds weren't significant."

"I'm sorry about that," I said, embarrassed. "I didn't know what to say at that point or what was really going on. You have to see why I thought it would sound crazy."

He gave me a reassuring smile. "It's not a big deal. In fact, after a while, I was happy you'd lied."

"Really?"

"Sure. It meant I didn't have to tell you who I was. And for once it was nice having someone treat me like a normal person without hidden agendas or expectations. Sometimes it's just nice to disappear."

I looked down at my green outfit and sighed. "I can understand that."

"Also, I wanted to tell you about my brother."

"Arrow, I'm so sorry about Helio. I didn't know that he... er... I mean, that to get me here, he had to... I should have put it all together sooner, but I didn't," I whispered.

He looked at me and half of his mouth curved up in a sad smile. "I'm sorry too." And then he took my hand, and the words poured out of my mouth.

"Can you forgive me?"

He cocked his head to the side. "Forgive you? For what?"

"For the way I acted in Flourin. I was childish and selfish, and I'm sorry. If I could go back—"

"Shh," he said, pressing a finger to my lips. "Please, you came back. That's apology enough. There's no need for more. This isn't your fault. There's no way you could have known."

I didn't understand it. If I were in his place, acceptance would be the last thing I offered. "But—"

"I've already come to terms with this. It was his choice, and I have to believe that he understood the bigger picture when he made it."

"How?"

"It's my only choice. Well, the only reasonable one. I could wallow but that just wastes time." I followed his eyes as he looked down towards camp. "We don't have much of that anymore."

His words pierced me. In a simple statement, he'd made my last few months of arguing at home seem immature. I didn't know what to say. A flash of light caught my attention.

"Arrow, look! We're just in time for the fireworks!" I pointed to the open expanse behind him where colors painted the sky. "They're beautiful."

"They are," he said, his voice deep with emotion as he traced his fingers down my forearm, resting them on my wrist. When he pulled me towards him, the full force of his longing hit me. "Alex, do you know what is real yet?"

I didn't resist. I couldn't. At this point fighting the desire was like fighting myself, pointless and counterproductive.

"You said before that nothing's more real than the things you can touch and the things that touch you. I think I'm beginning to believe that." I looked from his eyes to his lips. My heart pounded as he leaned in closer. "Arrow, I'm not good at all this stuff."

"You fooled me," he said before pressing his lips against mine, first tenderly, then more demandingly. I pushed my insecurities to the side and gave in to his kisses, meeting his desire with my own. He traced the outline of my face, from my ear to chin, sending a thrill down my spine. I melted into him, filling the curves of his body with mine.

"I'm glad you aren't fighting me anymore," he said, giving me a soft kiss on my forehead.

I twisted around so that his arms surrounded me as we overlooked the fireworks. "I just had a hard time believing that this was real, that I was ready for this adventure."

His chuckle warmed my ear. "You weren't sure if you were ready for an adventure? I find that hard to believe."

"Well, where I'm from, I'm hardly the hero," I admitted.

He rubbed my arms and kissed the back of my head. "I guess here we see adventure a bit differently."

"How's that?" I asked, glancing up at him.

"We don't see it as something that happens to you, but as a way of living, without fear of what's to come."

"That's beautiful. I've never heard it quite that way," I said, pulling his arms tighter around me.

"It's not really something we think about, just a standard that we've learned to live with. Whatever we know one day may change the next. You can call it adventure, but we just call it life. We've had to learn the hard way sometimes that you can't be present if you're too busy holding on to the past." He looked off into the distance. "When we first entered the Grove, I told you that you'd changed. I think that's the difference. You weren't really here before...not until you came down and saved us in the wetlands."

"I can't deny that. I don't think I was fully committed, to you or to Lockhorn, before that moment. I felt like I had to choose a side: this world or my home."

"And what did you choose?" he asked.

I exhaled deeply and shrugged. "I chose to not worry about it anymore. Whether I'm there or here, I'm still me, and that's what I ultimately have to be true to."

"But if you had to choose?"

"If I had to choose, then right now, I'm here." The truth released a weight that I didn't know I had been carrying.

"And I'm right here with you," he said, tilting my chin up for a kiss.

Fireworks popped, and bursts of light streaked the sky, but I hardly noticed.

"So what do we do now?" I asked, knowing that as nice as the moment was, it wouldn't last.

"I don't want to think about it tonight," he said, pulling me closer as another firework burst. "I want to know more about you."

"About me? There's not much to tell." I laughed and bit my lower lip. "I'm just a normal girl."

"I wouldn't say you're normal." He leaned in and tucked a strand of hair behind my ear.

"Well, pretty normal. I'm an artist."

"That explains your interest in the boxes and in the statues at Baron Marix's."

"Don't remind me," I said, trying to forget the trouble that I'd gotten us into.

"What else?" he asked, turning me around to face him.

My mind raced, trying to find something else interesting to tell him. There had to be more to me than art. Only one other thing defined me at the moment.

"We're moving," I blurted out. Why did I think that was interesting?

"It sounds like adventure follows you everywhere," he said, cupping the side of my face in his palm.

"I wouldn't call it an adventure, necessarily," I whispered, feeling my breath slow in anticipation.

"Everything can be an adventure, if you look at it the right way."

"I wish I could see things from your eyes."

He framed my face with his hands. "I'll show you how. Trust me, before you leave here, you'll embrace adventure."

The pounding of my heart matched the booms of the fireworks. I didn't want to think about that. Leaving was the furthest thing from my mind. Not now that I had opened my heart to him. I'd finally found my place, and it was here by his side. I leaned in for another kiss.

CHAPTER TWENTY-FIVE

We strolled down from Arrow's hideout. No longer in a hurry, he kept his arm around my shoulder and pointed out the small details I had overlooked, like the way vines spiraled up the trunks for sunlight and the strange calls of the blackbirds. Arrow knew every detail of the Grove, and I devoured his knowledge. This place sung to me in a way the rest of Lockhorn hadn't. Maybe it was the apparent lack of danger or the new friendships I'd found, but it felt right. Peace settled over me for the first time in a long time.

As we descended, I knew that the feeling couldn't last. When we got close to camp, the silence that had shrouded us above gave way to disorder.

"Arrow, what's going on? Is this normal?" I asked, watching the people below us run through the streets in all directions.

He frowned. "Let's go." He dropped his arm from my shoulder, pulling on my hand instead. The bridges swayed with our frantic pace. When we reached the wooden archway, he let my hand go and slid down the ladder, not bothering to use the steps.

I followed more carefully, finding the right spots for my feet as the ladder swung violently. By the time I landed, a swarm of villagers filled the gap between us. Between heads, I caught quick glimpses of alarm on Arrow's face.

"What's going on?" he demanded.

Melody pushed her way through the crowd at the same time I did. A scowl knotted her forehead, and her fingers tapped at her hip. She glared at her cousin. "Where have you been?" she asked.

"Why does that matter?"

"While you were missing, everything fell apart!" she opened her arms, gesturing to the chaos around us.

"We were up on the bridge, watching the fireworks," he said. "Last I heard, we weren't letting Berkos steal those moments from us."

Her mouth dropped. His words must have stung. She arched a brow and looked at me but answered Arrow demurely. "You're right, my lord. We're to enjoy the moments when they come. But right now, there's no time for that. We have serious business."

"What did I miss?"

"I feel like I should be asking the same question," Melody said, glancing between us.

My face felt hot, but Arrow didn't miss a beat. "Forget about it. If you don't want to tell me what's gone on, I'll ask someone else."

"There's not much to tell right now, but let me show you," she said, her voice softening.

She elbowed through the crowd, dragging him forward and pointing to the people frozen, staring at the sky.

"Melody, they're entranced by the fireworks. There's nothing new about that."

"Wait," she said, straightening her arm to stop us. "Didn't you see the fireworks?"

I looked at the ground.

"What were you...no, never mind. I warned you," she said, shaking her head. "I thought you would have been smarter about this."

I stared at my new friend and then back down at my feet.

"Now just wait a minute. She's done nothing wrong, and you know that," Arrow exclaimed.

"Except distract you from knowing when the enemy's declared war!" she yelled, pointing back to the sky.

"What are you talking about? I'm not distracted."

"If you weren't distracted, you would've seen that!" She pointed to the faint trails of smoke in the sky, outlining a dragon.

"What is that?" I asked, stepping closer to Arrow's side.

"A symbol of the enemy intermixed in our celebration," Melody huffed. "I don't believe this."

"Look, it's just a firework. I'm sure it meant nothing," Arrow said.

"Meant nothing?" Melody said. "What are you talking about? You know exactly what this means. Don't belittle it because you weren't here watching."

"What does it mean?" I asked softly.

Melody tightened her lips. "War. It looks like we're going to need you sooner than we thought."

Or sooner than I'd hoped. I looked around at the people, some paralyzed in fear as they stared at the sky, others rushing about in a chaotic frenzy.

"It's not like we didn't know this day was coming," he said. "It's been a countdown since Alex got here. There's no more wondering. It's time to act. If he's declared war, all the better."

I looked between the two, unable to settle my gaze on either.

"You're incredible," she said, rolling her eyes. "If you're not worried about that, what about him?" She pointed to the edge of the field where General Tanner tended to a wounded man who moaned, laid out over a bed of hay bales. I could hear him from where we stood. Bloodied bandages littered the ground, and fresh red droplets slid down the ragged edges of the hay. His skin a pale shade of gray, he hung limp over the edge. A faded design caught my attention.

I burst through the crowd, skidding to the ground next to him, twisting his arm to look at the inside of his wrist. Under dark bruises and smudged dirt, traces of the Great Oak peeked out at me. His cold hand fell from my grasp.

"The symbol…he's one of us," I said to no one in particular. The words sounded hollow. I found Arrow watching me with concern.

I shook out of my reverie and looked over at General Tanner, who patiently tied a new set of vines around his legs. "There's got to be some way to help him."

General Tanner shook his head.

"He's not…is he…?"

"No, not dead," he said grimly. "Not yet. Come, let us walk for a moment." He grabbed my hand and helped me up, leading me back towards the spot where Arrow and Melody waited.

"Is it bad news, then?" Arrow asked with a clenched jaw.

"I'm afraid it looks that way," the general answered, rubbing his forehead.

"Who is he?" Melody asked. "Has he said anything yet?"

"Nothing yet. He surprised us all when he stumbled in through the gates. We got him to lie down, but the spasms didn't stop until just a few minutes ago. I'm afraid he's in a lot of pain."

"Can't we heal him?" Melody asked. "There's got to be a way to save him. He's one of us."

"Nothing I've tried seems to be working. It doesn't look good. Frankly, it's a miracle he made it here all by himself. If he had gone south first, for vines, he would've had better luck. I'm afraid it may be too late for him now."

Arrow narrowed his gaze on the wounded man. "What happened? Do you know?"

"That I'm afraid is a mystery. None of the usual signs of torture are present, just a couple of strange puncture marks hidden beneath blackened skin. If I didn't know better, I'd say he was burned, but his skin…I can't explain it."

"Did you say puncture marks?" I asked, paling. Only one thing made puncture marks in Dreamscape.

"Do you know what they are?" General Tanner asked.

"I think so. Can you show me?"

The general nodded and led me back to the man, carefully lifting his torn shirt, revealing an emaciated ribcage and two round holes in his abdomen. I gasped and lowered his shirt. Even if I hadn't seen the wounds, I would know this man had suffered. Dark bruises swelled along his arms and cheeks, and above the puncture wounds, charred skin had begun to scab over.

All of them stared at me while I wiped my forehead with the back of my hand.

"Well?" Melody asked. "Do you know what happened?"

I nodded and glanced back to the dying man. "There's only one thing that could've done this. I hate to say I told you so, but…those whips were bad news." Anger tightened my words.

"Whips? Are you sure?" Arrow asked.

"I've never been more sure. On the edge of each whip is a lever. When you push the button up, it turns into a taser for close contact attacks. This poor man probably didn't know what hit him until it was too late."

"What can we do for him?" Melody asked.

I shook my head. "At this point? Nothing. General Tanner's right; he's going to die. That's why I hate them so much. If you get hit, you're dead, now or later. The electricity is too much. Maybe if he had been healed right away."

The man groaned and turned over, falling off the makeshift bed of hay. "Prince," he croaked, reaching towards Arrow.

Arrow ran to his side, covering the man's bloody hand with his own. He spared a quick glance at the general and another man, nodding for them to help him. The three of them carefully lifted him back onto the hay.

"Brave man, what is your name?" Arrow asked, forcing a strained smile.

"Not…import…ant…" he said raggedly, wheezing with each breath.

"General, can't we do anything more?" Arrow pleaded. "He's in pain."

"We've given him all we can. It's just a matter of waiting now." The general frowned and coiled a pile of excess vines.

Arrow knelt by the man's side, adjusting the vines to cover the wounds on his forearm and neck. "Tell me more. If your name's not important, what is? What brought you here?"

"Qu...Queen Elin," he stuttered. "She's in...danger." He exhaled and closed his eyes.

Arrow and Melody exchanged a look, and she quickly moved the rest of the crowd back, away from the man. One look at her fierce expression cautioned anyone from breaking through her barrier.

"What about the queen?" Arrow asked. "We can help her if we know."

I saw the fear coursing through him.

"All of them... dead..." he said, cringing.

"Who?" Arrow demanded. He softened his voice as he repeated his question. "Who is dead?"

"All of them...the queen's friends...servants...cousins...they're gone." He flopped onto his side, coughing in fits. A drop of blood slipped out from the side of his mouth.

Arrow glanced back at me, and I ran to his side. I grabbed the man's shoulder, poised to move him when his eyes widened and he focused on me. "It's true," he said.

"What's true?" I asked.

"Berkos said the...time had come. I didn't understand..." He struggled to move his hand to his forehead in salute.

"You don't need to do that," I assured him, moving his arm back to rest at his side. "Yes, I'm here. The time has come for all of this to be decided, once and for all. What you know may help me. What happened to the queen?"

"Berkos...since Helio's execution, he's been parading..." he stopped to cough up more blood. His voice grew stronger. "He's taken the queen hostage. Forcing her to choose sides. She has to either pledge loyalty to him or...he executes someone in front of her." He closed his eyes.

"But the queen?" Arrow asked.

"She's...not broken yet. I'm not sure how much more she can resist...without the king..."

Arrow blinked back tears. "We'll get her, my brave man. You just rest. We'll find her and save her."

"When the guards found out about me...too late...save her..." he pleaded, tightening his grasp around Arrow's hands before falling back a final time.

"What does this mean?" I asked, struggling to keep my voice steady as the general checked the man's wrist for a pulse.

Arrow tightened his jaw and spoke only loud enough for the inner circle to hear. "This means that our time has run out. Even if Berkos hadn't declared his intentions with the fireworks, we'd be declaring ours now. It's war."

A loud boom rattled the ground around us. I looked at the quaking trees and then at the sky. I covered my mouth.

I wasn't the only one who saw it. The village cried out in alarm and pointed to the colors streaking the sky. A new firework stained the sky. Berkos had taken the rebellion's symbol and twisted it.

Instead of explosive bursts of color, a dragon burned above us. The chilling message came through clearly.

I stood and brushed the hay off my leggings before running to Arrow and Melody.

"It's like the others?" I asked.

She nodded and stared at the sky. "It seems that times are changing."

I jumped as another boom shook the Grove. Arrow met my gaze and squeezed my hand before I could say anything. I squeezed his back and gave him a small smile.

Cale forced his way through the crowd, cursing at the top of his voice. He stood in front of Arrow and packed the end of his pipe. "What would you have us do?" He lit the pipe while Arrow contemplated his answer. Smoke rings shrouded the image fading in the sky.

"It's time to act. You all know what we've planned, what is at stake." Arrow looked at me. "We have a chance now." His message rang out loud and clear. Everyone knew what he meant and looked in my direction.

I swallowed hard and nodded. It was time to save the queen.

CHAPTER TWENTY-SIX

Arrow struggled to climb to the top of the hay bales. Hands from the crowd reached out towards him as they clamored for answers. When he reached the peak, he raised his hands, signaling for silence.

"I will answer each and every question you have, but first, let me speak. I know your minds are troubled with thoughts about Berkos, battle, and what that means for us. Let me assure you, every concern or doubt you feel, the person next to you feels, and I feel. Years of hardship and sacrifice have ingrained those anxieties into us. But stronger than that fear is a desire for freedom, to reclaim the joy and prosperity we once knew.

"When King Helio and Queen Elin were captured, the purity of our people darkened. For the last five years, an evil ruler has tried to bend us to his will, taking away our lives, loved ones, and property. We were made witness to a depth of suffering and atrocity beyond our worst nightmares, and we rebelled. We refused to give in, even to temptations of bribery and royal favor, knowing that allegiance to the dark king would cost us more.

"We now stand at a precipice, and our actions will determine whether we succeed or fail. My hope for the future, for all of us, is that our reclaimed joy will overshadow the sacrifices we've made.

"These dark years haven't been for naught. Our ingenuity has prospered, and even under the dark regime, our light has not dulled. In every dark period, there is a shining light." He met my eyes. "And we have our Golden Hero to lead us through this. I vow to you, no sacrifice will be forgotten. We will remember these losses and build upon their memories to ensure that Lockhorn will not falter again. Let us regain the joy of the past. Are you with me?"

Not one dry eye remained. Tears streamed down their faces as the painful memories of the past melded with the adrenaline of this last chance for freedom. The crowd burst into cheers, meeting his declaration with their sworn allegiance. Arrow jumped down from the bales, disappearing for a moment under the throng of people as his generals swooped in from the sides and barked out orders.

The crowd thinned out, everyone moving with purpose. The controlled chaos made it abundantly clear that a plan had been set in motion. Once the initial shock wore off, the years of preparation kicked in. I could see the acceptance in their eyes as they dispersed, sharing snippets of stories with each other. Nothing that Arrow had said had come as a surprise. Since the beginning of the rebellion, battle had been unavoidable.

I didn't know what role Arrow wanted me to play. I had knowledge of the castle, but I hadn't prepared for a battle. What did I do now?

Arrow cut his way through the few stragglers in the crowd to reach me. His smile was tight, and a pit began to open in my stomach. Heaviness weighed on him, and he didn't want to share it with me. I could see it in his eyes, in the way he avoided my gaze.

"That was quite the declaration," I said, trying to relax him with my smile. It almost worked.

"Thanks," he said, sitting by my side, leaning forward to rest his head in his hands. "You know, I've been rehearsing that speech for years, knowing it was inevitable, but actually saying the words makes it different. A little surreal. Did it sound sincere?"

"I don't think you ever have to worry about sincerity. You'd do anything for them and they know it." I rubbed his back and stared up at the sky. The faded lines of the fireworks had disappeared, leaving a map of twinkling stars. "They'd follow you anywhere."

"I just hope it's the right move," he said, glancing up at the sky with me. "There are so many variables."

"And I'm sure you've thought them all out. Don't start second-guessing yourself now. You've been planning this for years."

"Sure." He brushed his hand through his hair, resting his head to look at me. "But now it's real. There's no going back."

"Would you want to?"

"No, that's a good point. We're done hiding in the shadows of the forest. One way or the other, this is the end."

"I hope it's a good end," I said.

He leaned against my shoulder. "Do you remember when I told you that adventure is just learning to accept what life throws at you? Well, this is it, our next adventure."

"Our next adventure?" I shook my head with a small snort.

"It's one way to look at it."

"I could also call it crazy," I said, knocking my body into his side.

"Ah, Alex, I think you enjoy this more than you let on."

"Maybe," I said with a small smile.

"But what?" he asked, sensing my hesitation.

I shrugged as I tried to find the right words. "What happens when this is all done and decided? It'll be different. Are you ready for that?"

He tilted my chin up, searching my face. "Not all change is bad."

"Not bad, just scary sometimes."

"That doesn't mean we stop though," he said. "When we're afraid, those are the moments we need to press forward even more."

"How do you do that? With everything going on, you always seem strong while I get stuck on the fear."

"That's normal. Fear gets the best of all of us sometimes. When you don't have control, you cling to the things you've always known. When we first left the cities for the Grove, we lived in a constant state of anxiety. We could hardly get anything done."

I thought back to my room, the overflowing bookshelves and covered walls. He didn't know how true his words were.

"So how'd it change?" I asked.

"We had to step out of the fear and change our perspective,

focusing on what we could change. And we did. But what we did back then seems small in comparison to this." He motioned to the crowds already busy stacking items. "Ever since you arrived, the control has shifted back in our favor. You control our destiny."

"I control it?" I swallowed hard.

"I think you always have."

I looked down at my hands, covered in scars from dragon weed blisters and scratches I'd gotten in the forest. I had the control, I just hadn't used it the right way. Until now.

"So what do we do?" I asked.

"Right now, I'm going to finalize plans with the generals and prepare the battle team leaders. You need to get some sleep. If there is one thing I have learned about you, it's that, hero or not, you need your sleep and food."

I gave him a crooked smile. "Seriously? You can't think I'd be able to sleep right now. Look around, everyone's doing something." I pointed to the crowd gathering supplies and the generals hunched over maps. "Where do I fit in?"

"Besides the obvious?"

"I guess I just want some specifics."

"You *really* want to go over this now?"

"Better now than in front of Berkos' castle," I said. "We're rescuing the queen, not stealing a few papers. You may have a plan, but I need time to digest it. Believe it or not, I don't always do well under pressure."

"That's fair." He picked up a piece of hay from the ground and drew a large circle. "This is Lockhorn."

I nodded for him to continue.

He made a few marks across the realm. "This is Berkos' castle, and these are networks of his other supporters. You can see most are here in the center around Lindle, with just a few scattered down south and in the north. Thanks to the papers we retrieved, their identities are no longer secret."

"We'll be sending small contingencies to contain the threats in the south, while the majority of our people will move north. They'll strategically engage his army, pulling the defenses away from the castle, where we'll be." He drew a line far beyond, where the attacks would take place. "We'll make it to the castle once everyone is gone and free the queen."

I started to argue, but he stopped me. "The plan's been made; we just need you to execute it. Can you do it?"

I looked over the map at the web of lines he'd made and thought back to his fight with General Amos the day we'd arrived. "Is that what all the arguing was about the other day?"

"Yes," he looked down sheepishly. "I didn't realize you saw."

"I think everyone saw."

"Well, yes, we had to decide how you fit in. They wanted you to be a figurehead, leading the main battle. I knew that wouldn't work. You're more of a spy than a warrior."

"You think I'm like a spy?" I asked, amused.

"Maybe 'spy' isn't the right word. Reconnaissance expert, perhaps?" he offered. "I need you with me at the castle, guiding me through the traps."

"Okay, I'll take that," I said. At least I wouldn't have to fight in a battle. "Do you really think this will work?" I asked, twirling my finger at his drawing. "It seems like you're spreading our resources thin. Can we defeat his army with small attacks?"

"The attacks aren't meant to defeat him. They're just distractions."

My head jerked up. "Distractions from what?"

"They'll give us a chance to breech the castle and rescue the queen. Once she is free and Berkos is dead, the rest will fall into place."

"So all their lives are at risk so we can sneak in and meet minimal resistance?" I demanded, feeling the full brunt of pressure choke me. There was more at stake than I had realized.

"Yes," he said solemnly.

"So this is the plan. And all the generals agree?" The hesitation in my voice bothered me. I wanted to be the strong and confident hero he needed. Or at least look like it.

"To some degree," he said, sighing. I saw his patience running thin. "This isn't going to be a battle decided by our fists. If it were, we wouldn't need you. The winner here is the one who underestimates the other the least. These," he pointed to the X's he'd drawn to indicate skirmishes. "They'll provide some distraction, but I don't doubt for a moment that Berkos has his own ruses planned."

"So it's just a game of deception?"

"Parts of it are," he admitted.

"And we'll win by not being deceived by him?"

"Or by not deceiving ourselves," he said. "We can't afford to think, even for a moment, that we have the upper hand."

I sighed and threw my hands up in defeat. "I trust you. All this," I said, pointing to the map, "sounds complicated. I'm just going to stay focused on what I can do to save the queen."

Arrow kissed my hand. "I like your focus."

"But I have one improvement to your plan," I said, grabbing a stick to mark up the ground.

He raised an eyebrow. "Really? Show me."

"Instead of walking all the way around these areas, we cut straight through." I pointed to a portion of the map empty of lines and skirmish marks.

"You mean take a shortcut through the mountains," he said, considering my point. He shook his head. "It's too dangerous."

"For who, me? It may have taken me a while to get to this point, but I meant it when I said I was all in. This isn't about me, or you, or any of these people individually. This is about saving the queen. It'll work if we go around like you've planned, but if we cut through, we'll shave off half the time. If we coordinate it right, we can make it there with minimal loss of lives. I think that's worth the extra risk. What about you?"

I hardened my face as he looked at me. If he searched for a weakness, he wouldn't find it there.

"If you're sure, we'll cut straight through the mountains," he said with a frown. He scratched out the long path and drew a direct line through the center.

"I am." I gave him a hug and rattled off the things we'd need.

"Whoa, wait a second. We already have someone packing our supplies."

I cocked my head. "Yes, but we'll need more than the basics you're thinking of to win."

He let out a soft whistle when I finished rattling off the list of every weapon and power-up I had ever used to win. "That's a lot."

"We might not need it all, but I would rather have too much than miss the one thing we needed."

"I agree. Alex?" he asked, drawing me in.

"Yes?"

"You really do need to get some sleep. I promise, everything will be ready when you wake in the morning. Do you trust me?" he asked.

"With my life," I said, my stomach flipping.

"And I you. Now get some sleep, we'll leave early." He kissed my forehead and left me sitting there, watching him disappear into the frenzied crowd.

"Good night, Arrow." I knew sleep would be a long time coming.

CHAPTER TWENTY-SEVEN

Sleep lingered like a layer of fog, light enough to cover me but not deep enough to block out the commotion outside. I pulled the covers up, hiding in the warmth for one more moment.

Arrow's deep voice—not directed at me, but at the men and women scurrying outside—brought me out of my cocoon. I groaned. I should be helping. I threw off the covers and dressed, securing my dagger before peeking out of the tent flap. The progress shocked me. Nothing that I had heard prepared me for the lines of supplies and packed horses.

The sun, still partially hidden behind the trees, bathed the boxes of food along the main street in orange highlights. An arsenal of weapons lined the hay bales outside the training field. Barrels popped, overloaded with spears, containers filled with swords and bows and arrows flanking either side. Instead of targets and weapons, wagons filled the training field. A few women moved from wagon to wagon, painting layers of green and brown stain on the coverings, mimicking the forest. Every detail seemed accounted for.

I stepped into the commotion, barely able to skip out of the way as people passed me, arms loaded with goods. Moving to the side of the road, I looked up and saw just as many people racing on the bridges above. Leaves swirled around me, falling to the ground whenever a careless step on a bridge displaced them. Even through the traffic of the crowd, I found Arrow easily, hunched over his maps at the opening of his tent.

"Arrow," I said, running towards him. "This is crazy!"

"Good morning!" His smile belied the weariness on his face. Dark circles sank his eyes, and dirt smudged his cheeks.

"Didn't you sleep at all?" I asked, already knowing the answer.

"There was too much to do," he said with a shrug. After a quick pause and a final look at his maps, he rolled them up and offered me a slice of bread. "Let me show you what we've been doing." He led me down the center of the path, pointing out the supplies.

"How did this all happen in one night?"

"It's like you said, we've been preparing this for years, and when we heard about you we started putting the final pieces in place. This here is just the start. They'll continue once we've left," he said, biting into the bread.

"So all of this is for us? That seems a bit overkill."

"No," he said, laughing. "This is all for the first teams that are heading out. Our supplies are over here." He led me back to the quaint white cottage near the entrance to the Grove and opened the front door. "I figured since we'd be leaving today, it's better to have our things out of the way. Our trip will take longer than some of theirs, and we want to time it right."

I barely heard his words as he droned on about preparations. The worn cottage drew me in. Flecks of ivory paint fell beneath my slight touch, revealing the dilapidated stonework beneath. Ivy cascaded down from the roof, framing the darkened windows. Even when I cupped my hands to the glass, I couldn't see through it.

The old wooden handle creaked as I pressed down on it and walked into the dark room. It took a moment for my eyes to adjust to the dim light coming in from the small openings in the ceiling. I walked further into the building, crossing my arms for warmth and peeked over boxes and around the back of the door. Everything I'd listed seemed accounted for.

"This is it?" I asked, hearing his footsteps crunch in the leaves. The small collection surprised me.

"It's everything you asked for, plus all the items I could think of. Why? Do you see something missing?" He opened the tops of the boxes, nodding as he counted items.

"No, I see everything I asked for, but it seems so little in comparison." I shrugged and blew warm breath into my hands.

"Anything would seem small in comparison to what we're preparing in the streets."

"That's just it. Will this be enough for our team?"

Arrow smiled and rubbed his hands over mine. The heat warmed me. "We'll be fine," he said. "I'm actually not sure if our horses will be able to carry this entire load."

I looked over at him, tilting my head. "We'll be fine? How many people are on this team?"

"You're looking at it."

"You're kidding? Right?"

"We'll be fine. Between my skills and your knowledge, we'll make it through anything."

"But is that safe?" Even if everything went according to plan, danger was guaranteed.

"Don't worry, I'll protect you." He grinned and squeezed my hand.

"Arrow, I'm serious." I pulled my hand back and walked around the supplies.

"I'm being serious too. What do you expect to happen once we get to Berkos' castle? Can a larger team make it through?"

I narrowed my gaze but thought about what he said. "No, you're right. It doesn't make sense to have more men. They would either get in our way or slow us down in the castle."

"Yes, the fewer people with us, the smaller our chance of getting caught."

Or killed, I wanted to add.

"So, it's you and me...and a couple of horses," he said. "I have to run back to get them and give the final instructions to General Amos and General Tanner. Is there anything else we might need?"

"No. As far as I can tell, we're ready," I said, surprised that my voice remained so calm.

"I'll be right back," he said, stopping at the threshold to look back at me. "It's going to all work out."

"Our next adventure," I said, forcing a smile.

He grinned, then turned around and hurried back into camp.

"Just me and you," I said to myself, picking up a roll from one of the leather bundles. Something strong nagged at me, something more than the imminent danger we faced. I didn't want to admit it, but the thought of being alone with Arrow for a week scared me. Even after our night in the trees, all of this was new. I didn't want to ruin things.

I closed the door behind me and leaned against the cottage. Dried paint sprinkled the ground as I nervously picked at the wall. How long ago had it been since we walked through the hidden gate into the Grove? Not as long as it felt.

"Hey, Alex!" an angry voice cried out. "What do you think you're doing?"

I turned at my name, confused. I hadn't seen anyone this morning, let alone done something wrong. Melody strutted towards me, her dark eyes glaring beneath a wave of black locks. My heart fell. Maybe that's why she was mad.

"Melody," I said, smiling, meeting her at the trail. "I'm glad you found me. I looked for you but didn't see you." A little white lie never hurt anybody.

Her face softened, and she winked. "That's because I was saying goodbye to General Tanner."

"Ah, I understand," I said, biting a nail as she adjusted the fringe and feathers on her vest.

"But you wouldn't have left without saying goodbye, would you?" she asked.

"Never." I shook my head and bit my lower lip.

"Then get over here and say goodbye properly," she said. "But no crying! Heroes don't cry."

I gave her a small smile. "Maybe not, but friends do," I tightened my grip around her.

"No more of that," she said, pulling back and glancing behind me. "Are you ready?"

"It looks like it," I said. "Arrow certainly packed enough for us."

"Well, I hope there's room for a couple more things. I brought presents." She dangled two items in front of me.

"What are those?" I leaned in, trying to grab them.

"Not so fast," she said, hiding them behind her back. "Is he here?" she asked, peeking over my shoulder.

"Who? Arrow?"

"Yes, silly. Is he here?"

"No, he went back to grab the horses. Do you want to wait for him?"

"No," she said. "These are for you."

"What's going on?"

"I just wanted to make sure you were taken care of. He doesn't always think of things the same way as we might. I wanted to give you these." She unpacked a roll of freshly cut vines and handed me two necklaces.

"Aren't these from the tables yesterday?" I asked, pinching the leather string around the pouch etched with black flowers.

"I know you said you didn't want anything to do with dragon weed, but it's one of our most powerful defenses, and I thought you might need some. That's the powder, and the vial is full of its essence. Make sure none of that gets on your skin, though. It can burn through anything if it sits there long enough."

"Perfect," I said, cringing as I hung them around my neck. "Thank you. You didn't have to do any of this."

"Of course I did. You're a friend...and as a friend, there's just one more thing." She hesitated. "It's about Arrow."

I arched an eyebrow. "What about him?"

"I need you to promise that you'll take care of him," she pleaded, reaching for my hands.

"Of course. You know I will."

"Not just make sure he doesn't get hurt. No matter what happens out there, we need him back. I know he's determined to save the queen, but we can't afford to lose him. Do you understand?" She tightened her grip.

"I do, and I promise he'll be fine," I said.

"Take care of us, too," she added, more softly. "One thing this rebellion has taught us is that you never know how much time you'll have. There's no time for games or hesitation. We live and love full. So, even though we just met, I want to let you know that you'll always have a friend here."

"I feel the same," I said, feeling tears start to well up again.

"And Alex? If you see my dad…" she said gravely.

"Uh-huh?"

"Make him pay."

I nodded, feeling a lump rise in my chest. Unable to speak, I watched her run back into the crowd, passing Arrow on her way.

Arrow gave her a curious look before turning back to me. On each side, he led a horse, complete with saddles and pack bags.

"What'd Melody want?" he asked, tying the reins around a branch.

"She just came to say goodbye," I whispered.

Arrow nodded and disappeared into the house.

I walked over to one of the horses. Sharing my breadcrumbs, I looked the steed in his eyes and wondered what we were getting ourselves into. How did I go from playing a game to leading a rebellion? What if I was wrong, what if things were different? I thought back to Marix's manor, and the small things that had tripped me up. A guarded castle held more danger than a baron's estate. I leaned against the horse, trying unsuccessfully to push the negative thoughts from my mind.

"I think this is everything," Arrow said, coming out of the old house, arms loaded with boxes and bags.

I laughed and helped him load the horses. To my surprise, everything fit.

"That's the last of it. Are you ready?" he asked, strapping the final bag to my horse.

I nodded, not wanting my voice or words to give away my concerns.

He strode to my side and wrapped his arms around my waist, looking into my eyes before lifting me on the horse.

"Don't worry," he said. "This will all be over soon."

What if that was my biggest worry?

"But before we go, it appears some people wanted to say goodbye." Arrow nodded behind me and turned his horse.

"What, who?" I asked, following Arrow's nod.

I gripped the reins tightly. An unsettling feeling burned in my chest. Everyone in the Grove had stopped their preparations to see us out. A level of solemnity surrounded us, squeezing the breath from my chest.

In the front, General Amos and General Tanner stood at attention, faces unreadable. Others knelt or bowed their heads. Cale removed his hat and blew a final ring of smoke in our direction. Boris stood at his side, eyes closed. Around him, some of the other men from Flourin followed suit. I scanned the crowd, memorizing faces and the expectations painted on them.

My gaze lingered on a small group of young girls. They giggled behind their hands, tossing braided vines at us. Bracelets of red scars marked their wrists. Their faces, now free of dirt and welts, wore smiles, and their eyes held hope.

"What's going to happen to them?" I asked.

"Thanks to you, they'll have a chance at life."

"It's all worth it then. Let's do this." I tightened my lips and let the memory of freeing them slip away. It no longer stung.

Arrow clicked his horse forward, taking the lead. The long braided vines and fabric at the entrance parted around us, revealing the hidden trails of the forest. I turned around for one last look at the Grove, but it camouflaged seamlessly into the rest of the forest. A sense of loss I hadn't expected hit me.

Arrow must have seen my face or heard me sigh. He slowed his horse to my side and tightened the restraints across my legs. "Is everything all right?" he asked.

I nodded and bit my lower lip. "I just realized that I won't see the

Grove or its people again."

He furrowed his brow and gave me a sad smile. There was nothing he could say to diminish the truth. Melody's warning came back to haunt me. Leaving was going to be much harder than I ever imagined.

"Let's ride. It's a long way to the castle, shortcut or not." Arrow nudged his horse forward.

Content to follow his lead, I fell in line behind him, winding through the narrow trails. The normalcy of the forest compared to the Grove threw me off. The trees moaned with the wind, bending under its force. Without the bridges holding them steady, they flailed against one another, dropping leaves and branches without concern.

The burning in my chest subsided after we'd ridden for a few minutes. Something about the fresh air brushing my hair back relaxed me and replaced my nagging worry with pleasant thoughts. We rode all morning without stopping.

When he did slow, allowing me to catch up, I barely recognized him. Dark circles dominated his face, and he could barely keep his eyes open.

"Arrow, you need sleep. We should stop," I said, looking around at the overgrown forest around us.

"No, we can't stop. I can sleep while we ride. I just wanted to make sure you knew the way before I dozed off. The horses should guide us straight along the path, but if they stray, just bring them back. We take this path to the base of the mountain. You can wake me there."

I raised my eyebrows. "Are you sure?"

"Come here." He pulled his horse next to mine and kissed my forehead. "Stop worrying. This is the easy part of our journey."

With that, he closed his eyes and slumped forward in his saddle.

I rode beside him, watching the tightness around his eyes disappear.

I settled back into the saddle and kept a safe distance behind his horse as it led us along the trail. We moved at a slower pace, but that didn't bother me. The rhythm of the chirping birds guided our steps. The synchronicity of it all put me at ease. Maybe this was what Arrow had meant about the joy of adventure.

All my doubts couldn't be erased though, and in the back of my mind, I worried about more than the battle ahead. I had given myself to this cause and to Arrow's people willingly, but the more invested I became, the more painful the end would be. I looked over at Arrow's peaceful face and sighed. Complications that I'd never imagined clamped my heart.

As the hours stretched out, the forest slowly changed. The dark green leaves lightened with sprinkles of snow, and its dense foliage opened to meadows and flatlands as we approached the mountains. Sharp crags replaced the lush vegetation, and the dusty trail choked out the few wildflowers that had tried to bloom.

"Whoa." I slowed my horse and tightened my ponytail. The trail ended, but when I looked over at Arrow, he still slept. The horses stopped at the junction, sniffing the ground for the sparse remains of withered grass. A twisted tree marked the intersection, and weathered signs hung haphazardly from the gnarled limbs. Faded paint identified a dozen forgotten paths. I didn't recognize any of the names.

"Arrow," I said, shaking his leg. "We're here."

"Hmmm," he mumbled, opening his eyes.

I smiled and poked his leg. "We're here."

"Already?" He sat up and looked around, disoriented.

"Well, you've been asleep for more than a few hours. Which way do we go, left or right?" I reached into my bag and threw him a roll.

He caught it with a smile. "We go straight."

"You want us to go through there?" I asked, nodding at the darkened canyon nestled between the two towering mountains.

"Hey, you're the one who wanted to take the shortcut." He smirked, taking a bite of the roll.

"To the castle, not to my death," I said, feeling the oppression of the dark canyon settle over me.

CHAPTER TWENTY-EIGHT

The sinuous path up the mountain gave way to a steep and treacherous route. Sharp drop-offs edged the sides of the trail, if you could even call it a trail. Slippery roots entangled our steps as trees crept closer, shrinking the path to a single-file road.

Arrow led the way, pulling his horse up and over the spindly roots. As the trees crowded together, the ground turned into a web of roots, each limb knotting around the other. My gaze didn't leave the ground, afraid of the inevitable slip ready to send me over the edge. There were countless ways to die in Lockhorn, and I feared my own clumsiness topped the list.

"I'm not so sure about this anymore," I said, my voice quivering as my grip tightened around the reins.

He took one look at my pale face and white knuckles and slowed his gait. "As long as we stay on the trail and are careful, we should make it through the mountains and Shadow Alley without a problem."

"Shadow Alley?" The name sent shivers down my spine.

"There are reasons people don't take this path, Alex, and it has nothing to do with how steep the trail is. This is just a small part of what we're going to face. Shadow Alley is a place I didn't want to show you. Almost nothing is, from this point on."

I nodded and bit my lip. I had to suck it up. Arrow had chosen this path at my insistence, and I had to accept these unknowns. No matter how much they made my skin prickle.

I kicked my horse and followed him up the steep trail. The wool cloak barely kept the cold out, and my breath mixed with the fog, clouding my vision as we went higher. Icicles broke when I hugged the interior side of the trail. Crystal daggers clung to the ragged edges of the cliffs.

Then we breached the fog barrier and stepped out into sunlight.

"How is this possible?" I gasped. The air shimmered, birds flittered around us, and trees swayed gently in the breeze.

"Anything is possible when you rise above the storm."

"But this—"

"Is spectacular."

"I thought you said there wouldn't be anything beautiful up here." I swiveled from side to side, taking in every angle of the panorama.

"I said almost. Nothing is ever complete darkness. Beauty always finds a way through. Sometimes when you least expect it." He dismounted and walked to my side, patiently waiting as I unhooked my legs from the saddle and tethers.

I nodded, unable to find any words to adequately express what I felt. Beautiful seemed too small a word to capture the grandeur around us.

Streams of sunlight broke through the clouds, casting their rays on the falling flakes at a perfect angle to make each piece glitter. Gusts of wind altered the snow's slow descent, making it swirl until it coated the trees. A weighed-down branch tipped over, dropping the snow in a cluster and snapping back into position.

Stretching my hand out, I ached to catch the snowflakes. The frosted crystals landed, hesitating a moment before melting. Another snowflake collected on my hand and then another, until my hands burned red and a pile of snow built up along my cloaked arm.

Arrow watched, amused, as I stuck out my tongue on impulse. "Are you done playing?"

"Never," I said, leaning my head back, feeling the cold prickles of snow speckle my face.

"I don't know what to do with you." He shook his head, hiding under his cloak.

"That's part of the adventure, right?" I winked and went back to catching snow.

He took that opportunity to let the horses rest, and once I had caught enough flakes to satisfy me, we watched the snow fall to the ground in silence. Unlike the silence I had subjected my mom to for the past month, this was pleasant, like the world didn't want to breathe and break the beauty. It was a comfortable moment where speech came second to experience. Those didn't occur often, but the longer I was with Arrow, the more of them I seemed to have.

"I could stay here forever." I reached for one of the icicles dangling off the branch above us and missed, pulling a branch and a puff of snow down on top of me.

"It's tempting. You still need to be careful though. They're beautiful but dangerous." He pulled me to his chest and out of the way as a bigger branch gave way beneath the weight of the snow. Ice chunks sprayed outward, and glassy shards dropped where I had stood.

"How did you know it was going to fall?" I asked, liking the way his arm wound around my waist.

"I've become pretty familiar with things that are both beautiful and dangerous." His heart sped up beneath my palm.

"That's a good thing," I said, resting my head on his shoulder.

We didn't talk. We no longer needed to, content to marvel at the falling snow as we walked. The silence echoed around us, only broken by the soft shuffling of the horses and our own feet.

Being this close felt right, and I was tired of hiding behind the excuse that I was afraid. I couldn't deny the feelings surging through my body. Every inch of me trembled at the thoughts running through my head. Thoughts I had never had. Never felt. Was this what love was supposed to be like? Anything I'd felt before seemed small, insignificant, almost laughable in comparison.

I bit my lip, looking at him. How would I even begin? I had been afraid for too long. I thought about my regrets, moments in the past when I hadn't acted. If I had simply talked to my parents, the anxiety of moving might have been calmed, or if I had really listened to Brian, maybe I would have realized long before that I deserved better. Apprehension and anticipation clawed for a way out.

"Arrow," I said, surprised my voice was strong. Quiet, but steady.

"Yes?"

"I, uh, I think I'm falling—"

"I'm falling too." He tilted my chin up. The look in his eyes twisted my insides. He leaned forward to meet me, and I closed my eyes.

A loud crack sounded, jolting my eyes open. The ground shifted beneath me, and then smaller cracks popped in sequence, like dominoes falling, each movement propelling the next.

"Oh crap. Arrow, I'm falling!"

The ground between us gave way. My fingers slipped through Arrow's, catching the edges of the falling icicles. I hit the ground with a thud, pressing into the soft ledge of snow below. Ice crystals scratched my hands, digging into me as they reflected the light into rainbows. Beautiful, dangerous, painful.

I pulled the ice shards from my hands, thankful that I'd missed the large chunks glistening by my head. Arrow looked down at me, his forehead scrunched up as he leaned over the edge.

"I'm fine," I yelled before he could ask.

My hands burned bright red as I clambered up the soft ledge. I tucked them under the cuffs of my sleeve and warmed them with my breath. The climb back up the trail went slowly as I tested each step, cringing as the snow crunched beneath my weight.

Thundering echoes shook the icicles clutching the cliffs. I closed my eyes and hugged the interior wall. When I opened them, I saw Arrow's leather boots, darkened from the saturating snow, and his outstretched hand.

"Are you hurt?" he asked, looking me up and down. "You have to stop scaring me like that. I can't lose you."

269

I nodded, not trusting my voice.

We stood an inch apart, my eyes searching his face. "Arrow, I…"

"Me too," he said, leaning towards me.

The heat from his hands warmed my back, possessively pulling me closer. A fleeting shudder rippled through me as the snow melted under my shirt, lost under the heat of Arrow's embrace. My fingers wound around his hair, pulling him closer. I eagerly kissed him, letting everything around me disappear.

He pulled away slowly, tracing the outline of my jaw. My lips parted in anticipation. When nothing happened, I opened my eyes and saw the sadness in his. The haunted look on his face chiseled away at my heart. He pulled his hand away and dropped his gaze to the ground.

"I'm sorry," he whispered. "I was wrong. We can't do this."

"What is it?" I asked, alarmed. "What did I do?"

"It's nothing that you did. But I can feel it now. It's different than before. You believe, don't you?"

"Believe what, about all of this? Yes! Yes, I do. What's wrong with that?" I asked, reaching out for him.

"Because seeing you fall like that, I finally realized that I'm going to lose you. Whatever I want, whatever you want, it can't happen. It's like you said before, none of this is real." He avoided my hand and turned to walk back up the trail.

"No, no, no," I said, following him, twisting him around. "You can't just walk away from me like that and say this is done. I don't understand why we can't be together."

"Because this isn't real," he said.

"Yes it is!"

"Maybe what we feel now, but there's no future in it, in us. You don't belong here."

"But what about that kiss?" I asked. "You can't tell me you don't feel it or that everything you've said isn't true."

"It can't be," he said.

I turned away and clenched my jaw before tears could fall and stared at the ground where he had thrown my heart. I swallowed hard, releasing my tears, and turned to face him.

His hair fell over his eyes, covering but not hiding his obvious longing. The hollowness of his words echoed in my head. They were nothing more than a preventative bandage. And even though I knew my heart would shatter when it ended, not letting it happen at all would be more painful.

I stepped forward and took his hand. He met my gaze, confused.

"But we can't," he said.

I covered his lips with my fingers. "I don't want to lose this chance."

"But we have no future," he said. I saw the fight in him dwindling.

I felt his hesitation and conflicting emotions. In my mind, Melody's warnings against hurting him echoed. "I know, but I love you." I whispered.

He gave in, cupping my face in his hands. "All right, Alex," he whispered. "I don't need a future. I want now."

"Now," I said, leaving no room for protest. I rose onto my tiptoes and hooked my hand around his neck, pulling him close.

He met my kiss with his own, pressing me against the mountain wall. Snow melted behind me, but I hardly noticed anything except his cold fingers holding me close, keeping my legs from giving way beneath me.

CHAPTER TWENTY-NINE

The tingles left by Arrow's lips lingered. I puckered, refusing to open my eyes and face reality. Even 'now' had an expiration date, and I heard it ticking. Arrow must have sensed my unease and pressed his lips against my forehead. I relaxed. Worry would do nothing but steal precious seconds, and I had already lost too many.

Pulling back from the warmth of Arrow's embrace, my gaze strayed between his eyes and his soft lips. "What do we do now?"

He brushed a snowflake off the tip of my nose with a kiss. "Nothing's changed. We just continue."

"Nothing's…changed?" I asked. He was right and yet so wrong. It had never been so obvious to me that everything was different.

"Nothing for me has changed, Alex. You stole my heart the moment you soared through the air and pummeled that giant. I knew then that everything I thought I understood or wanted was a soft whisper of what I needed. I need you, and now that you're here, committed, I plan on holding on as long as I can. We're doing this together."

Together. I liked the sound of that. My negative reaction to reliance on someone slipped away, replaced by a measure of comfort and reassurance. My tongue tripped over the words I wanted to say, but it didn't matter. The swelling in my chest poured out of me, and I knew it showed in my eyes.

"Together," I whispered, and pulled him close for another kiss.

He reluctantly pulled my hands from around his neck, kissing each as he lowered them between us. "We still have a long way to go, and I don't want to risk these steep cliffs for much longer. Once we round the top of the mountain, the terrain should even out, and it'll be easy riding until we descend into the foothills."

"Easy?"

"Well, straightforward at least. After these cliffs, we'll go through Shadow Valley and then down the foothills."

"What happens then?" I asked, looking down at our hands entwined under the long sleeves of the cloak.

"Then…" he said. "Then, we're almost there."

"Oh," I said, wishing I hadn't asked.

"But that's still a ways off, and we don't need to think about it right now. Now is about you and me, right?" He grinned mischievously.

"Yes it is," I said, grabbing his hand as we began the long walk back up the trail.

A trance of new love covered us as we hiked back to the horses and rode through the mountains. Snow glittered in the air, and birds twirled in a majestic dance, their neon feathers streaking across the blue sky. But more captivating than the panorama was the man riding at my side. My eyes drifted over to him, no more than a few feet away, and I smiled.

The hours blended together and, sooner than I expected, we had unloaded and set up for the night. Camping in the mountains proved a challenge, with the only patches of dry ground pressed up against the bases of trees. Even after clearing an extra few feet of snow and widening the area for a fire and the horses, our quarters were tight. I didn't mind.

I leaned back into his arms, finding the curved spot at the nape of his neck. The warmth from the fire and his skin melted me against him. I sighed. "This is nice."

He smiled. "I'm glad you stopped fighting. I was beginning to worry that I had lost my charm somewhere."

"Oh no, your charm was always there. I just didn't know what to do with it."

He chuckled and tossed a green branch into the dwindling flames. Rich, thick smoke floated around us as the leaves crinkled and hissed, succumbing to the heat. "I'm glad we figured it out."

"You know what I haven't figured out yet?" I asked.

"What's that?" He looked down at me with raised eyebrows.

"Promise me you won't laugh?" I scrunched my nose and turned to face him.

"I promise," he said, even more intrigued.

"Okay, how do I phrase this..." I hummed. "There are certain similarities between the game I played and this world."

"Go on," he said, trying to hide a smirk.

"Well, some of the people I've met are similar, the animals too...in the game, there were even fireworks when I completed a level. Since I've been comparing this world to what I knew from the game, I wondered...how do I compare to your history and the legend of the Golden Hero?" I bit my lower lip and gazed ahead into the fire, almost afraid to hear his answer.

"Ahhh, I knew you had been comparing me to the game!"

"No, no, not you," I said in a rush. "I never saw you in the game, I promise. I would've remembered." Heat rose to my cheeks.

"Alex," he said, turning me to face him. "I don't know what has caused you to doubt yourself. Nothing I've seen from you in your actions, words, or convictions deserves such skepticism. I wish you could see yourself as we do, not just as the Golden Hero, but also as Alex."

"Oh, I've seen what they thought of me. Cale and the other men made it pretty hard to forget."

"Don't stop your memories at that initial meeting or gloss over the admiration and respect you earned afterwards. Our people trust in you. I trust in you. Not because of a title but because of your action and commitment. That's what matters to us, and hopefully to you."

"You're right," I said and leaned back against him.

"But you asked about the Golden Hero. Let me tell you some of the stories I heard as a boy. Granted, most of these were told by entertainers in the castle, so I can't vouch for the authenticity." He rested his head against the tree, and I resettled into his arms. "The first time I heard about the Golden Hero, I was five. A traveler from the north visited the castle with silks woven with the brightest gold. My mother loved them, and when she asked him his secret, do you know what he said?"

"Hmmm?"

"He said his thread was spun from the head of the Golden Hero. Naturally that had me hooked, and I hid in the shadows behind the marble pillars, hoping to remain unnoticed."

"Did you?"

"Oh yes, they never found me, but that poor man..." Arrow stopped his story to shake his head. "He underestimated our love for heroism and, before he could recant his story, he was thrown out of the castle. He never peddled furs in Flourin again after that."

A deep, rich laugh shook me. I covered my mouth.

"And then a few years later..."

I closed my eyes. The deep, rhythmic timbre of his voice lulled me to sleep. His words mingled with pictures in my mind, and reality and my dreams seemed to blur.

The sun crested the mountains, sending a stream of light onto Arrow's face. I watched his reluctant waking. The fluttering of his eyelashes quickened, and his shoulders slumped at awkward angles as he exhaled slowly and stretched. His right hand settled along the curve of my waist, and a contented grin appeared on his face before he opened his eyes.

"I could get used to this," he said lazily, tightening his grip on me.

"I could too," I said, nuzzling closer to him and pulling the cloak up over my shoulders, hoping to stop my involuntary shivering in the morning wind. "I wish it would warm up a bit though."

"It will soon enough, I promise. Speaking of..."

"Don't say it." I cringed, already knowing what he wanted to say.

"Not saying it won't change it."

"I know, and I know we have to go, but give me a few more minutes just sitting here."

"Anything for you," he said, reaching for the travel bags at my side. "Can you grab some food?"

The rolls and jerky were on top, and I handed him a few pieces before grabbing two for myself. "What are the chances you packed anything besides rolls and jerky?"

Arrow laughed and took a bite. "Not very good, I'm afraid. We're stuck with this unless we find something along the way."

"Somehow I doubt we'll have such luck."

"You never know. I've seen stranger things happen in these mountains," he said.

"I thought you hadn't been up here before," I said with a quizzical expression.

He looked at me with his crooked grin. "I haven't."

I threw a roll and him, then hastily grabbed it back. "I'm not strange," I said, biting into the bread with an exaggerated pout.

"Ah, Alex, you're strange in the most wonderful of ways. It makes me smile."

I looked away and hid my grin beneath another bite of bread, but a flush filled my face. He made me smile, too.

We ate in silence, our eyes carrying on their own conversation until neither one of us could put it off any longer. We had to go.

We packed everything up silently and continued riding along the narrow path. The trail inclined steeply, passing miles of jagged crags. Behind the stone walls, on both sides, fog blocked the view.

"Shadow Alley," I mused, looking at the outline of the ridges and the darkness above the canyon.

Arrow frowned in the direction of my gaze and nodded.

At the top of the first ridge, he jumped off his horse and motioned for me to follow. My legs wobbled as I landed. Riding all day took some getting used to. I followed slowly as he descended over the ridge and disappeared behind a large outcropping of rocks.

"What is that place? That's more than shadows," I said, ducking behind him as translucent creatures floated towards us, materializing from one cloud and blending into another. I swallowed hard. An unending haze of fog filled the crevasses between the mountains.

"That's our shortcut. It's the one place I've never wanted to explore."

I looked at his guarded eyes and then back at the wisps of darkness covering the sky.

"We need to be careful when we're in there. There's a spell that keeps most shadows off the path, but one shout or false move," he said, raising his eyebrows, "and it'll be broken."

"What happens if it gets broken?"

"I don't know for sure, but they say that the shadows will devour you, making you one of them, cursed to remain in this valley forever."

"Game over," I whispered. Dread prickled down my spine. "So how do we get through it?"

He looked at me for a moment and winked. "Why don't you tell me? The shortcut was your idea."

"That's not funny, and you know it," I said, squeezing his hand.

His good humor soured. "You're right, but I honestly don't know. Not many people attempt this route. We're on our own in here. All I can promise is that I'll be by your side through it all."

My heart beat uncontrollably as his rough lips brushed my cheek. It wasn't quite the reassurance I was hoping for.

"Let's go," I said, pulling away and tucking the cuff of my sleeve over my wrist. I clambered back on my horse. I needed to go before my nerves caught up with me.

The stillness haunted me like the eye of a storm. Whispers of wind pressed against me, and the pit in my stomach dropped. The top layer of snow slithered off the pathway, swirling in mysterious symbols before dispersing with the breeze. Our footsteps disappeared as the wind picked up, moaning. Strong gusts sent my hair flying, blinding me as white crept in from every angle.

The mist rolled in, claiming every blade of grass and shrub beneath its shimmering shadow. I watched the landscape change, trying to memorize the twisting path.

"Stay on the path, right behind me. And don't make a sound," he warned. "You'll see their shadowy figures and hear their cries, but they aren't allowed to touch you unless you scream."

His tense tone alarmed me. "I'll be right behind you," I said.

"They're fast but not stealthy." He pointed towards the first of the ghostly figures approaching us. "If you listen closely, you'll hear them rattle as they move."

Sure enough, when I slowed my breathing and quieted my mind, I heard the tell-tale rattle. "They're like rattlesnakes," I said, giving Arrow a small smile.

"What's a rattlesnake?"

"Just something from my world," I said, hurrying to shrink the distance between us. Barely into the canyon and I had already slipped behind.

"You can tell me all about it when we get out. Hand me your reins. I don't want the horses to get spooked and run off with you."

I dismounted and handed the reins to him. Normally I wasn't claustrophobic, but as the fog crowded around us, the air tightened and my chest refused to breathe deeply. I didn't notice that I had stopped walking until Arrow became a faint shadow in the distance. The fog surrounded me, and I jumped ahead before he disappeared.

I had to stay focused. That was twice in such a short period of time that I had almost lost him.

A rattle jumped out on my left, followed by a pale, disembodied face. Arrow's warning flashed in my head, and I choked back the scream in my throat. I squinted, hoping I could forget the hollow eyes and sunken cheeks, and walked around, making sure she didn't follow me.

By the time I turned back to the path, it was empty. Arrow had gone too far ahead. My heart raced as I looked around at the nothingness.

"Arrow?" I whispered.

The mist clung to me like a spiderweb, shrouding me in its cloak of mystery. I brushed at my shoulders, feeling the viscous substance grope at me. The metallic taste of blood filled my mouth as I bit into my cheek. I wanted to scream for Arrow to find me.

The white crept up from all angles until I couldn't see anything. Not the shadows, not the snow, not Arrow. My stomach knotted, and I dropped to my knees, watching my hands disappear under the layer of snow. I looked around, not knowing which way was up.

"Arrow?" I whispered, afraid to awaken the creatures. Rattles surrounded me, quicker and closer the longer I waited. Something cupped my left shoulder, and a stab of ice burned down my arm.

"Arrow?" My voice creaked as I stumbled to my feet and ran. Another hand grabbed me.

Disoriented, I stumbled forward, not knowing which direction I was going or even if I was staying on the path. I wavered back and forth, avoiding each disembodied rattle. I never knew white could be so dark. Lurching over hidden branches and rocks, I fell to the ground and silently screamed.

The chill radiated from my shoulder down to my fingertips and over to my face until my chattering teeth bit my tongue. Had that brief contact been enough to turn me into one of them?

Tears froze on my cheeks as I sat on the ground, arms wrapped around my knees, rocking back and forth, dreading the transformation. New faces popped in and out of the mist, ghoulish visions, malnourished and maimed. What would Arrow or the rebellion do if their hero was cursed in the shadows?

I didn't want to believe I had failed, but as the cold spread, my doubts grew. Suddenly, another hand—a warm hand—grabbed my shoulder. Warmth. I saw the concern in Arrow's eyes.

"I'm fine, I'm fine," I said, grabbing his hand to stand up, willing the tears to stop, though the redness around my eyes was proof enough.

"You're cold," he said, furrowing his eyebrows. "Whatever you do, don't let go. We have to get you in front of a fire." His hand grabbed mine as he pulled me forward into the white shadows. "Put these in your ears."

"A roll?" I watched as he broke the roll apart and used the soft insides to create small balls, pressing them into his ears.

I followed his example and was amazed at how much it helped. The wind's deep moans were dulled, as were the shadow creature's rattles. I wished he had a way to fix the ice building in my bones. We walked the rest of the way in silence, until the shadows lightened and I fell to the ground, coughing up blood.

CHAPTER THIRTY

Arrow helped me up, his gaze lingering on the splattered blood behind me.

"I think we can rest here. We're not quite out of the shadows yet, but we should be far enough out of the main canyon to rest. What happened?" He wrapped an arm around my shoulders and leaned in to hear my trembling voice.

"I'm not sure," I said, trying hard to keep the tears from falling. The concern in his eyes didn't help. "One minute, I was right behind you, and the next, you were gone."

"Shhh… it's going to be all right. I'm here now." He tightened his arms around me and rocked gently back and forth. "You're so cold and pale. Did you see them?"

I nodded, wishing the mention of them didn't invite them back into my mind. Horror like that was hard to forget.

He stopped rocking and looked at me. "Did they touch you?"

The tears I'd held back flowed, freed from the control I'd tried to exercise over them. "One did," I whispered, biting my lip.

Arrow let go of me and ran to where he had secured the horses, grabbing something from the bag before rushing back to my side.

"Do you think I've been cursed?" I asked, trembling, putting my biggest fear into words.

"I'm not sure," he said calmly, but his hands shook as they worked to untangle the package of vines. "If you were cursed, I think there'd be more blood, but I don't know for sure."

"Arrow, I'm scared," I said, covering the vines with a hand as he tightened them.

He gave me a sad smile. "I know. Try not to think about it. We should be safe now. Let's just let the vines do their thing and make sure you're not too hurt before we continue." He handed me another roll. "You wanted to take the shortcut," he said.

"Probably the last I'll ever take again," I mumbled. I held up the roll. "Did you pack a whole bag of these?"

"You're joking—that's a good sign," he said. "And as a matter of fact, yes, I did. Right after I change those vines, I'm going to find some wood."

"No!" I yelled. I covered my mouth.

Our eyes darted around us, watching the burgeoning fog, waiting for a rattle, but nothing came. He dropped to my side and crossed the vines over my shoulder.

"You can't leave me," I whispered, reaching out with frozen fingertips.

"You need a fire," he said. "Just relax. I won't go far, but there's no wood on the trail. Try to relax, and warm yourself up in my cloak."

"But you'll need it."

"Right now you need it more. We've made it this far, and we'll make it the rest of the way when you're feeling up to it."

"How will you find me?" I asked, looking at the white mist rising around us.

"Hey. Don't worry," he said, his voice softening as he pulled me close. "I'll always find you."

I watched him disappear into the mist, and the spot where I caught my last glimpse of him became my sole focus. My chest burned as I held my breath for his return. Silence. With my tongue, I traced the gouges I'd made in my cheek. I needed a new nervous habit. My nails weren't long enough to bite, so I settled for ripping the bread to shreds before eating it. I took small bites, noticing the metallic taste slowly disappear, but the tenderness inside my mouth remained.

What would happen if he didn't come back? The thought of being cursed in the shadows took away my breath. I couldn't think that way. Arrow would be back; he had to be back. He promised.

When his head broke back through the fog's veil, I almost screamed, tasting the blood fill my mouth again. His face had paled, and his lips were colorless. I jumped up and ran to him, wrapping my arms around his neck.

"Did they get you? You're so cold."

"N-not cursed. Jus-st c-c-old," he stuttered. A few of the logs fell out of his arms, and he let the rest go as he wrapped his hands around my waist. I tucked my face into the crook of his neck and breathed a sigh of relief. I felt the chill from his hands through my shirt.

"Let's get that fire going," I said, picking up the wood and creating a cabin of logs near where I had sat.

We both needed the fire. Once I finished stacking the wood, he started the fire by slamming two luminance rocks together. A small flame blossomed from the spark, eating its way along the larger logs. The flames entwined and danced, captivating me. Through the fire, I caught Arrow staring.

He moved to my side. My face flushed as he looked at me. I hoped he didn't notice. I could blame that on the heat of the fire. But I had no way to explain the way I trembled.

Luckily, I didn't have to. Arrow took my hands in his, warming them with his breath.

Prickles of pleasure shot down my leg where the outsides of our thighs met. I settled into the warmth of his arms and listened to the calming beat of his heart next to mine. We watched the fire until no more embers popped and the last coal turned dark.

I looked up at him and tucked my lips together. He matched my gaze. Neither one of us wanted to be the one to speak up.

"It's time," I said, clasping my hand in his and pulling him up. "I want to get out of these shadows for good."

"You do know where we're going, right?"

I shot him a look. Of course I did. "Yes but at least there I can't be cursed to live in shadows."

"No," he said, shaking his head. "If we fail, we'll only die."

I grabbed the reins to my horse and climbed on.

"I'm right behind you."

Once the fog lifted, I realized that the mountain trail was lengthier than I'd thought. Shadow Alley was only the midpoint in a serrated mountain range. Snow-covered cliffs and valleys dominated the horizon. Our journey wasn't over yet.

"Don't stop here," Arrow said, passing me. "We still have a long way to go, and it'll be safer once we crest these next few ridges. Let's put this canyon far behind us." He kicked his horse.

I followed suit, content to ride behind him.

The next several days merged together, ridges and mountains blending into one another. Despite my reluctance for time to pass, I threw myself into each moment, recognizing it for what it was. A gift. We rode in quiet contemplation of our surroundings, watching the terrain change as Arrow had predicted.

The steep cliffs softened into wider paths and easier turns. Clumps of heavy snow fell from the trees, the sun's warmth melting the fragile flakes. The magic I felt in the mountains wore off as we began our descent.

After a week of conquering the treacherous terrain and my own feelings, I realized how much I had lost by hiding behind fear. It stole something irreplaceable: time. I had wasted too much of it, wallowing in my own insecurities, and if I had only shed that crutch earlier, Arrow and I would've had more time together. Shielding myself from an imaginary pain hadn't made me stronger.

What I would've given to hit restart, to have known this from the beginning…but I couldn't. All I could do was cherish every moment left in our adventure.

"So what can you tell me about these woods? I know you haven't been here, but are there ghost stories or—" I stopped and pressed my shoulder blades together as clumps of snow fell down my back.

I looked up at the pristine trees and spun to see Arrow, eyes wide and hands raised in exaggerated fashion. I jumped off the horse and knelt to make a snowball from the pile gathered by the base of the nearest tree.

"Don't you dare!"

"Or you'll what?" I asked, taunting him by tossing the snow between my hands.

"Or this," he said, sweeping in and throwing me over his shoulder. The snowball fell, but I slapped his back with my frozen hands until he dropped me.

"Ouch!" I protested, but I couldn't keep from giggling as he rolled to my side and brushed flakes of snow off my cloak.

"Ah, you're tougher than that," he said.

"Trickier too," I said, pummeling him with handfuls of snow and skittering out of reach.

Arrow chuckled and fell back onto his knees. "I give up—I'm at your mercy."

I peeked from behind a tree and squinted. It was almost too easy a shot, but I took it anyways.

He fell back as the last snowball hit him square in the chest. "You win, Goldy, you win."

"That's all I wanted to hear you say," I said, tromping back to his side.

"It's good to hear you laugh again," he said.

"It felt good." I leaned my head on his shoulder. He knew exactly what I needed.

Arrow cocked his head to the side and covered his lips with a finger for silence. "Do you hear that?"

"What? Is it your heart shattering from losing?"

"No," he said, smiling. "I think our luck has turned." He jumped up and crept to the nearest tree, peering up through its branches.

"What do you mean?" I asked, listening for sudden movement or an indication of what had alerted him, but I heard nothing.

"I think it's time for something new for dinner." He unhooked the pack on his right side and pulled out a quiver of arrows and a bow.

"Don't joke with me about that," I said, unable to hide the excitement in my voice.

"I wouldn't dare. Look at these tracks," he said, pointing to triangular puncture holes in the snow. "Snowbirds, I believe."

"Snowbirds? I haven't seen any—what do they look like?" I asked, picturing the species I had seen here.

"Well, they're hard to see," he said. "Their white feathers blend into the snow almost perfectly, and they're stealthy, making little sound as they bound through the brush and trees. But their meat…it's worth the effort of catching them. They're a delicacy, and will be the perfect way to end our journey."

My words caught in my throat. I hadn't realized our time together had dwindled so quickly, or that we were so close to Berkos' castle. It didn't feel like nearly enough time. My stomach growled. The idea of fresh, warm meat moistened my mouth and sent tingles along my tongue.

"I'll take that as agreement." He smiled and tied our horses to the nearest tree. "If you want to hunt in the trees, I can search among the brush.

The thought of climbing exhilarated me, and I untethered a bow and quiver of arrows from the side of my horse. I balanced atop the saddle and reached for the nearest branch, pulling a pile of snow down on top of me.

"You look just like a snowbird," Arrow said, jumping down from his horse and tethering it to the nearest tree.

"Let's hope that helps. How will I find one?" I asked, shaking the snow off my arms and climbing onto the first branch.

"Hmmm…I'm not sure exactly. Look in the clumps of snow. They use them for camouflage."

I looked up and saw snow falling from the branches above me. Squinting, I saw something shimmer and jump forward, disappearing into the higher branches.

"I got this one," I said, balancing on the saddle again and climbing onto the closest tree limb. Scampering up the tree, I chased the bird through the maze of variegated branches. The nimble bird jumped along at high speeds, knocking bumps of snow down behind it, then stopped at the edge. His head, crowned in a thick bush of white and pearlescent feathers, bobbed from side to side in deliberation.

I pulled an arrow out, centered my aim, and released. The air whooshed, but I missed. The bird didn't waste any more time and jumped forward to the next tree, knocking down more pristine tufts of snow.

I kept my sight trained on the bobbing creature, lest it disappear within the trees. The slight branches would not hold my weight, so I climbed higher to a sturdier limb. I smiled as the flakes glittered, suspended, before succumbing to gravity. They settled slowly, dropping by my horse, no more than a small dot below me. A wave of disorientation hit me as I looked between the horse and the bird. I couldn't go much further without risking my safety.

The snowbird perched at the edge of the branch, mocking me with its still pose. Its head fluttered as I drew a new arrow. I inhaled, pulling back and aiming for its chest, and released the bowstring.

The arrow wobbled, spearing through tufts of snow and landing with a solid thud. I jumped with excitement. Snow inundated me, slipping between my cloak and tunic. I shook off the chill and bounded down to retrieve my spoils.

Surprise and disappointment hit me when the bird fluttered off the edge, dropping a lump of snow with it. What had I hit? And what sparkled back at me? I stared at the edge of the branch, waiting for a flutter of opalescent feathers, but nothing moved. Inching closer, I clutched the branches above me, careful as they bowed with my weight. A brief reminder of how high I had climbed flashed in my mind. I weighed the risk of falling against the draw of whatever glistened at the edge of the branch and cautiously stepped forward.

Could it be, here, in the middle of the forest? I reached forward and brushed off a small pile of snow from atop an engraved box. Carvings marked all its sides, equally as impressive as the others I had already found. Golden paint twisted around silver stems, and etchings of circles and starbursts covered the front where the golden latch glittered. My fingers rested on the small handle as I pondered what was inside. And then I let it go—it had a destination beyond my needs.

A rattle of coins sounded as I placed it back on the edge of the branch and carefully added a layer of snow on top. A smile grew as I looked back and saw it camouflaged. No one but the person it was intended for would know it was here. My fingers strayed, taking time to trace their way back to the branch, and as my gaze lifted, I noticed a change in the forest along the horizon.

Arrow was right. We had reached the foothills. The leveling out of the trees and the way the white faded back to green made it impossible to ignore. And even though Arrow had already warned me, the transformation of the landscape made it real. Seeing the end of our journey saddened me.

I looked back down at the base of the tree and saw Arrow swinging a pair of birds by their talons.

Securing the bow and arrow, I climbed down the trunk, straddling the branches as I went.

"Looks like you got some. Good job. No luck for me this time," I said, putting my gear back on my horse.

"That's not a problem. I had enough for the both of us," he said with a smile that stretched from one side of his face to the other.

I reached to hold his hand, but changed my mind at the last moment and stretched forward for a full embrace, knocking him to the ground. Warmth filled the space between our bodies.

I liked the thought of what he'd said: together only one of us had to be lucky for us to succeed. But I also had an inkling that together, we'd have more than enough of everything. As his arm encircled me, I realized that "together" came with a lot of perks.

CHAPTER THIRTY-ONE

The slow pops of the fire woke me. Glowing embers flew around Arrow's face as he poked the half-burned logs with a long stick.

"What are you doing up so early?" I asked, pulling my cloak up under my chin.

He gave me a sad smile and poked at the fire again.

"Arrow, what is it?" I asked, propping myself up onto my elbows.

"I was just thinking about how peaceful you look when you sleep. I was trying to memorize your face."

"Oh," I said, lying back down. "I thought it was something serious."

"It is serious. We'll be there either tonight or tomorrow, and I don't want to forget what you look like."

I sighed. This was not how I'd intended to wake up. But I recognized the worry rising within him. I felt it too. Ever since we passed through Shadow Alley, I'd known I only had one last challenge to face.

I sat up and wrapped the cloak around me before resting my arms over my knees. "If it makes you feel better, I feel the same way."

"Really?"

"This may come as a shock, but this hero thing is not my normal job." I stuck my tongue out at him.

"You seem pretty good at it to me."

"Well, that's because I have skills." I laughed. "Really though, you might see a calm exterior, but inside, I'm shaking. I'm ready, but

I'm not."

"What do you mean?"

"I mean that I'm ready to save the queen… but I don't know if I'm ready to leave Lockhorn yet. I know I've spent so much time here trying to leave…but that was before…"

"Before?"

"Before you."

He smiled and reached over to pull me into a hug. "It's a good thing I'm going with you then."

"Stop it! Seriously though, this is too much, too early. We're going to have to face all this later. I just want to have breakfast in peace."

"That, I can do," he said, jumping up to put another log on the fire. "Leftover snowbird?" he asked, holding out the skewered remains.

"Sounds perfect," I said and adjusted my stick over the fire. Arrow hadn't lied about the flavor of the bird. The meat melted in my mouth, and, even reheated, it surpassed all the other meals I'd had here.

"Arrow, I just wanted to say thank you," I said after I devoured the leftovers.

He raised an eyebrow and poked the fire, breaking the logs apart. "For breakfast? Anytime."

"Not for breakfast." I rolled my eyes and started rolling up our bags and putting the supplies away. "For everything else. As much as I was determined to do this on my own at the beginning, I couldn't have done any of it without you."

"I wouldn't have wanted you to." He grabbed my hand. "But speaking of…"

"I know. It's time to go," I said, brushing off the dirt from my leggings as I stood. "Lead the way."

"No, before we go, there's something I want to do."

I cocked my head.

"It's for luck," he said. "My brother and I used to have a

tradition before he went off hunting."

I sat back down and turned to face him, wrapping my arms around my knees, giving him my full attention. "What do we do?"

He squinted at me like he'd expected me to protest, but when I didn't falter, a boyish enthusiasm overcame him. His eyes lit up. "Stay here." He left my side and ruffled through the horses' packs. "Don't laugh," he said, coming up beside me.

I raised an eyebrow. "You know that's just asking me…oh, wow."

"I asked you not to laugh," he said, hiding the item behind his back.

"You're right," I agreed, tightening my lips. "What do I do?"

He pulled it out slowly. "You promise?"

"You have my word," I vowed, lifting my fingers up in a scout's signal.

"All right, so I told you about my pet horned-bit." He raised an eyebrow as I stifled a giggle. "Well, even though it didn't last long, my brother was amused by my determination and rounded it up after it impaled me. This is its foot. It's supposed to be a reminder to never give up. You know, for luck." He rubbed his hand over the fur and handed it over to me.

I petted the lucky horned-bit's foot and handed it back to Arrow. "I like traditions," I said. "Thank you for sharing that with me."

"We can use all the luck we can get. Thank you." He tucked the treasure back into the bag and nodded for me to join him.

Arrow was unusually quiet and pensive, careful of the terrain's new threats. Severe changes dotted the landscape when we descended from the mountains into the foothills. The frequency of trees increased, choking off the great expanse of sky. Crumbling leaves replaced the crunch of snow as we rode, similar sounds that provoked infinitely different feelings. I pulled my cloak tighter as we rode deeper in the forest, but the chill remained.

I hadn't noticed how long we'd ridden until we crested the last hilltop and the moon lit our path. On the horizon, melting into the approaching twilight, a dark castle wavered like a mirage. I didn't realize how comforting the cover of the trees had been until I couldn't avoid the view of Berkos' castle.

A familiar beat hammered in my chest. It was time to play the game again.

Everything changed when we started down the final hillside. The crowded forest stifled me, and the trail darkened into shadows. The hairs on the back of my neck stood on edge as the birds stalked our movements.

My gaze drifted to Arrow, who ducked under branches and stepped around the withered brush with ease. But even his movements slowed as the brambles tangled our legs. The shadows accentuated the heaviness in his eyes and the deep lines carved in his forehead. Worry pulled him down.

"We need to stop," I said, yelping when the branches snagged my hair. "It's getting too dark."

He sighed. "These woods aren't the best place, though."

"I don't think we're going to find a good spot from here on in," I said.

He started to argue, but one look at me stopped him. I could almost picture the disappointment that painted my face. I'd spent weeks trying to forget my mission; the moment we crested that hillside and saw the castle, reality hit me. The pressure of rescuing the queen, the awareness that I might be going home soon...a bittersweet sadness filled me. I never thought I would feel that way about going home.

"You're right; there aren't a lot of places. We can stay here, but we'll need to break camp early," he said, jumping off his horse to help me dismount. The wind pushed me into his arms.

"I understand. I want to get out of here too. Not that I'm looking forward to where we're going, but I definitely won't miss this place."

"You certainly haven't seen the best parts of our world."

"I saw the Grove," I said.

"Yes, but not for long enough," he said, giving me a warm smile. "Maybe another time."

A rush of heat rolled over me, and I bit my cheek to stop the tears from collecting in my eyes. There wouldn't be another time, and we both knew that. I turned away and focused on setting up camp, unrolling the blankets and preparing a small feast of jerky, dried fruit, and rolls.

I focused on each task, knowing it was for the last time. Assuming our journey went as planned, tomorrow everything would be different. For Arrow and for me. I couldn't deny it now.

"Alex! You have to come see this," he yelled from behind me. The excitement in his voice startled me.

"What is it?" I asked, dropping a roll to run to his side.

"Look at this." He jumped ahead and pulled down a charred paper that had been nailed to the tree. He shook it and handed it to me. "We're doing it."

I shook my head in confusion. "What do you mean? We haven't done anything yet."

"Not us. The rest of the rebellion. Look at this...and this," he said, running ahead and pulling papers from the next few trees.

He came back and handed me a pile of worn parchment. Blowing off the withered moss and dirt, I saw crudely drawn pictures of Arrow's generals and other men I recognized from camp.

"I don't understand. These are wanted posters. How is this a good sign?"

"Don't you see? Berkos didn't know of these men before. If General Tanner is wanted for treason, he has succeeded in his part of the plan. We're making him take notice."

"That's great," I muttered.

"It is! I've been worrying about that for a while now," he said, riffling through the paper. "When we decided to take the shortcut, I knew we'd be cutting down time but also losing communication.

News may travel fast here, but nothing makes it through these mountains. These posters put me at ease."

I frowned. I had been so preoccupied with my own internal struggles that I hadn't even thought about how the generals were faring. I coughed to get some fresh air.

"Are you all right?" he asked.

"Yeah…no," I said. "I'm not all right. It's finally hitting me. All the plans and preparations are coming together like you hoped."

"That's a good thing. The more it comes together, the fewer people will get hurt."

"I know. It's just like I said, things are real now." I frowned again.

"What's wrong?"

"I don't know. Seeing the men described this way, it makes me sad." I grabbed the stack of papers and flipped through them again. "General Tanner—traitor, General Amos—traitor, Boris, Cale. They're all traitors."

"Don't take it too seriously," Arrow said.

"But these rewards are sizeable. I hate to think of the danger they're—" I stopped when I flipped to the last poster and saw a familiar face smile back at me. "Oh no!"

"What is it?" Arrow peeked over my shoulder. "Do you know him?"

"This is Pipes. He's one of the first people I met in Lockhorn. He helped me through the marketplace. Without him or Deakon…I don't know what would've happened."

He furrowed his brow and squinted. "What does it say?"

"Pipes—traitor, rogue performer, dissident. Wanted for crimes against the crown, espionage, and aiding the escape of a known enemy. Do you think that means me?" I asked.

"Could be," Arrow said. "You are Berkos' biggest threat right now, and he did help you."

"I didn't know they were risking their lives by helping me."

"They did," Arrow said, tightening his lips. He settled on a portrait of a woman I had not seen before.

"Is that her?" I asked.

Arrow nodded. "Queen Elin, although this picture doesn't do her justice."

I grabbed the worn parchment, taking care not to damage the edges that had crumbled off into ash, and stared at an image of the queen. The portrait, hastily drawn, pulled at me. Under a mop of curls, sharp cheek bones contradicted the softness in her eyes. They glistened with pain and sorrow, feelings I couldn't perceive when playing the game at home. The charcoal smudged my fingers when I traced the image. I wiped my hands on my leggings and focused on the page. She was a stark contrast to the pixelated pink princess I had saved so many times. Regardless of the burned paper she was drawn on, I saw why everyone fought to free her. She was more than just a queen; she was the hope of a kingdom. She had to be saved.

"Thank you. This is exactly what I needed." I wiped a tear off my cheek and leaned into his arms.

CHAPTER THIRTY-TWO

"Wake up Alex," Arrow said, gently kissing my forehead and grabbing my cloak so I couldn't pull it up over my head.

"It's too early!" I rubbed my eyes. "The sun's not even up yet." I propped myself onto my elbows and looked down the hill to the darkened valley.

"That's what makes this the perfect time to go, before they start watching for us." He gave me another kiss and started packing up camp. "There's no good coverage going down the hill, and I wanted us to get as close as possible before the sun rose."

I huffed and leaned back down. "You should have told me that was what you were thinking. I could have given you a couple more hours of rest. We don't have to worry about cover because we're not going in through the main entrance. We're sneaking in through the graveyard on the other side of the castle."

He stopped packing for a moment. "We have to go through the graveyard? No one goes through the graveyard."

"And no one goes through Shadow Alley either, but we did." I yawned.

"And you almost became one of them…"

"Arrow, one of us has almost been killed every step of the way, and yet we're still here. Nothing about this rebellion has ever been safe. Toss me a roll?" I stretched, resigned to the fact that I was awake. "Anyway, the fact that no one goes there is kind of the point. No one will think to look for us there."

"Are you sure?"

"It's the only way I know." I nodded as I bit into the roll. The last level started in the graveyard.

Arrow nodded, put the last of the blankets and supplies in the bags, and leaned them against the tree where the horses waited. I grabbed an extra roll before handing him my bag and kissing his cheek.

"Are you ready?" I asked. "I mean, really ready? This is it. There's no going back from here."

When he looked me in the eyes, a range of emotions hit me, but behind them all, I recognized honesty. "I can't go back, regardless, but with you guiding me? We have a chance. I'm ready."

I hesitated, then threw my arms around his shoulders, stifling the tears I wanted to shed. He might be ready, but a shiver of dread shot through me. If something went wrong, it wouldn't just be game over. It might very well be the end of the rebellion, me, and my only chance to get home.

He pulled back and smiled. "You should trust yourself too. Didn't you say you beat this castle over a hundred times?"

I choked back a laugh. "At least, if not more." I wiped the tears away with the back of my hand.

"Then stop worrying. We'll take this one step at a time."

"One step at a time," I said.

"And, apparently, our first step is into the graveyard. Not what I would have chosen, but you're the hero..." He beckoned me forward with his hand. I appreciated his attempts at joviality. It would be a hard day. Grabbing his outstretched hand, I climbed onto my horse. We wouldn't be able to take the horses all the way down, but they could carry us a couple miles closer before we were on our own.

Twisted branches interlocked with other trees, hiding the sun in their struggle for dominance. Empty limbs hung low, grabbing at our clothes and bags as we passed by, slowing our descent. The forest seemed dead; no animals scurried out of our way, no birds chirped from above. The ground remained as dark and empty as the branches above. Nothing grew along the sun-starved trail. The only green I saw came from the moss clinging to the crumbling bark.

I shook my head and reached out for Arrow's shoulder as he ducked beneath the nearest branch. "Be careful of the moss here," I said. "Actually, just don't touch anything white or light green, even the branches. It's all poisoned." I pointed at a dark ring of burnt ashes and feathers on the ground at the base of a nearby tree. "Berkos doesn't want anything in these woods to live," I whispered.

He brought his hands closer to his body and nodded.

"We'll have to leave the horses soon," I said. "We don't want them to be noticed by any guards wandering these hills. Do you think they'll be able to find their way back to the Grove if we let them go?"

"You want to let them go?" he asked incredulously.

"I think it's for the best. There's poison here; we can't tie them to the trees, and I don't know how long we'll be. I thought I'd be in and out of Lockhorn in a couple of hours."

"I, for one, am glad you stayed longer," he said, his voice thick with emotion. He pulled the reins towards himself and tightened his hands around my waist, hugging me close. "Would you stay if you could?"

"Don't ask me that. You know it's not possible." I bit my lip as my heart sped up. The truth was, I didn't know how to answer that question anymore.

"You're right," he said, helping me down. "I'm sorry. We should focus."

"Besides, you don't have to worry. We still have a long way to go together, and I plan on making every moment count," I said, trying to lighten the mood.

I pulled away, but he resisted, tightening his grip on me and pressing me against the tree. His lips teased mine as he held me captive. My legs grew weak, his kisses becoming more demanding.

"Arrow," I said, gently pushing him away.

"Mmmm," he mumbled, nibbling on my lower lip.

"You have to let me go, or I'll never want to go save the queen," I said.

"If I must." But his hands remained interlocked behind my back.

"Stop!" I laughed. "We still need to organize our supplies." I nodded to the bags at our feet. "We won't be able to take all this stuff. Will you help me?"

He sighed loudly, finally releasing his grip. "What do we need?" he asked, emptying the supplies on the ground.

I rubbed my forehead and scrutinized the items strewn in front of me. I knelt by his side and emptied my own bag next to his. "Geez, you weren't joking about packing a bag of bread!"

He took a bite of one roll and handed me another. "I knew we'd have to keep our energy up."

I shook my head and bit into the bread as I sorted the other items into categories.

"We can leave the food here. We won't need it on the inside."

"What about when we're done?" he asked, stopping mid-bite.

"If we need to, I'm sure we can raid the kitchen." I stuck my tongue out at him, afraid to give voice to the thoughts running through my head. One way or another, I would be gone by then.

"What about the rest of this stuff?" Arrow asked, holding up his bundle of vines and the whip.

"Bring it, as much as we can carry. We'll need it all." I secured my dagger and reached for the broadsword, deciding at the last moment that it was too big. I hesitated before attaching the electric whip to my right leg and strapping a quiver and bow to my back. I stuffed my pockets with packages of luminance powder and double-checked the necklaces of weed pollen and oil. I felt more like Renaissance Rambo than the little hero from the game.

I looked at Arrow and took a deep breath. "Are you ready?"

"I'm about as ready as I'll be."

Adrenaline surged through me, amping up my steps as we bounded down the hill in the darkness. The hillside flattened into the valley, then melted into the dark and desolate lowlands, hidden under a layer of haze.

When we reached the graveyard, light crested the horizon.

I wiped my forehead with the back of my hand. Thick, hot plumes of steam jutted up through hidden vents in the ground, obscuring my view.

I tucked an ear device in and marveled as the rush of steam confused everything else. Quick pulsating bursts of static threw me off balance. I yelped as I tripped over the broken stones, scraping my shin. I pulled the device from my ear and shook my head at Arrow. He would have to listen for us while I kept my eye on finding the secret entrance.

Stone markers outlined the graveyard, even and symmetrical, except for the occasional scattered stone. I weaved through them, trying to find something familiar to pinpoint where to start.

Letters and symbols stained each slab, but I could discern no order or pattern. I traced the stones, surprised when a viscous substance stuck to my fingers. It was like the putrid muck from the pits all over again. I cleared my hands of the slime in the dirt and moved to the next marker. More lettering greeted me, but nothing made sense.

I started shivering—from nerves more than cold—but pressed on. Arrow and the rebellion were counting on me. The entrance had to be here somewhere. I just had to navigate the differences between the game and the real world.

A pebble hit me in the back as I traversed the third row of grave markers. I turned and saw Arrow tapping his ear. I threw the ear device back in and heard a strange new sound. A steady beat thumped behind the rush of steam. I dropped behind the nearest pillar, watching as Arrow ducked behind a gravestone. I held my breath, hearing the rhythmic *thump* collide with the staccato beats of my heart.

We waited, casting glances in all directions, watching for an intruder. The thumps grew louder, and then stopped abruptly before scurrying off. I turned and saw tail feathers ruffle in the wind. My exhale sounded like a storm. I took the ear device out and rested my head in my hands. This was only the beginning, and I was already teetering off the edge. I needed to keep my head in the game.

Tension grew across my forehead, and I rubbed the pressure points at my temples. I didn't expect it to take this long to find the marker. Arrow's hands rested on my shoulders, and then he helped me up. Deserted graveyard or not, I didn't want to risk being out here too long.

I skipped forward, running past the stationary markers into a darker region of the cemetery that hid in shadows, larger statues and mausoleums blocking out the sun. Walking around statues of fallen angels, stepping over their broken wings and fallen scepters, I felt hidden, more at ease. The cool marble slid under my hands as I caressed its edges.

The garden of tombs stretched out of view. Flustered, I turned around to find Arrow, only to see two grotesque gargoyles flanking a granite archway. Beyond the arch, mausoleums lined up on either side of a pathway. Their open doors haunted me, until a moment of déjà vu hit. Of course! I knew one of them marked our entrance.

A rock thumped ahead of me, and then another hit me in the back. I turned to glare at Arrow and tripped over a marker. Bits of gravel dug into my palms and knees, leaving impressions and dots of blood. The hearing device dangled next to my ear. I listened, waiting for a thump of footsteps, and then heard something else, something constant beneath the bursts of static. My head shot up as Arrow approached me.

"Is that what I think it is?" I asked, feeling something like hope.

He pulled the hearing device out of his ear. "It sounds like water to me. Is that what we're looking for?"

I nodded and put the device back in. The smooth gurgle was undeniable. I pulled it out again and smiled. "That's our way in. Help me up! I know where we have to go now."

I ran back to the stone archway and counted off the mausoleums, stopping in front of the third one on the right side. The stone tomb terrified me. The morbid symbolism of gaining entrance to the king's castle through death's chamber…well, it was unnerving, to say the least.

I jumped when Arrow's voice sounded behind me. "Is this it?"

Without removing my eyes from the dark building, I nodded. Ten stairs led up to a half-open door where columns held up decrepit angels. I swallowed hard and grabbed Arrow's hand.

"I can't go in there alone," I whispered.

"You don't have to face any of this alone," he said, squeezing my hand as we started up the stairs.

At the top of the stairs, a green rectangular box lay on the ground like a welcome mat. I shrugged at Arrow and knelt, examining the marker. I brushed off the top of the metal, revealing spiral etchings at each corner. Spiderwebs and dirt stuck to my palm.

It was reminiscent of the money boxes in the forest. A familiar feeling ran through me as I traced the designs. I had found something special.

My fingers ran over hidden bumps along the outer edge, identifying a set of hinges.

"This has to be it," I said, gripping with my nails around the edge. Sweat dripped down my forehead as I pulled, but nothing budged. Arrow knelt beside me, but even our combined strength didn't help.

"It won't open. What do we do now?" he asked.

Ideas flowed through me as I played the level in my mind, trying to relate its two-dimensional features to this world. In the game, I entered through the tomb and descended through the tunnels.

The tomb. I shuddered and gazed behind at the darkness peeking in from the doorway of the mausoleum. "We go in there." I sighed.

The door creaked when we pushed it open. Warm, still air mingled with the dust sitting on every surface, choking my breath. Arrow covered his mouth with his cloak as he entered.

An oppressive silence consumed us. The tomb, dark except for the sliver of light at the doorway, scared me. Nothing seemed right about the place. My breath quickened.

Arrow tapped me on the shoulder and pointed to the far end of the room. Against the back wall, poised between the two blown out candles, a metal wreath marked the wall. I walked closer and saw the leaves of the wreath—a pattern of spirals.

"They're the same as on the marker outside," I said, reaching forward to touch the scrolled metal.

"I think they are." He coughed.

"Ouch!" I jerked my hands back and brought my fingers to my mouth. The metal had burned me. Small blisters popped up along my fingertips.

"Do you need a vine?"

"No, save them," I mumbled, shaking my hands through the air, annoyed that I had already bruised my shins, scraped my palms, and burned my fingers, and we still weren't inside the castle. "Be careful, it's hot," I said, wrapping my hands inside my cloak before grabbing the metal wreath again.

It creaked, giving way reluctantly as I pulled it away from the wall. Now it looked more like a wheel for a hatch opening than a decorative fixture. I slid my covered palms along the metal wheel and nodded to Arrow for help.

He placed his hands alongside mine. The metal stung, even with a fabric barrier. I hoped the burn wouldn't be deep enough to blister. We twisted the wheel, moving it no more than an inch each time.

Sweat coated our faces when it finally released, and a blast of steam shot up from outside.

I looked behind us and saw the green box standing open in the doorway. Squealing in delight, I ran to it and fanned the steam out of the opening. The heat of the steam burned me, yet I shivered.

"We did it!" I jumped up and down and grabbed his hand. "Now, don't forget to stay close and have your luminance handy. The tunnels will be dark." My words raced together in my excitement.

"You want me to go in there?" Arrow asked, waving his hand through the warm cloud.

"This is the way in," I said.

"You never mentioned tunnels. I...can't do that, I don't like being closed in." He stepped back from the entrance.

"This isn't a time for fear. It's the only way I know of to get in. We don't have another option." I reached forward, grabbing his wrist to keep him from sprinting down the stairs.

"But—" he protested.

"But nothing. You knew we weren't going to walk through the front door." The finality of my tone broke through his reservations. We had come too far to let anything stop us now.

"I, er, I know, but I didn't expect this. This wasn't in the plan."

"Didn't you say you embraced adventure? Here's a new one for you. It's time to drop every notion you have about this castle. What we saw in Marix's manor is nothing compared to what lies ahead." I reached for his hand one more time. Relinquishing control, running towards the enemy, it all went against our natural instincts. "I asked you before, but I'll ask again. Are you ready?"

"No." He gulped and held up a hand. "Wait, I think someone's coming. Shh…" He furrowed his brow in concentration, cupping the ear device with his hand. His jaw tightened, and he pushed me back into the tomb. "Stay in the corner and don't move."

I fell back to the ground and watched him race around the stone doorway. His tone scared me. I didn't understand what was going on, but I knew it was serious. Then I heard the electric hum. Crawling to the door of the mausoleum, I pulled myself up against the doorway and peeked around the edge.

Silent screams rattled my heart.

A sharp gasp escaped me. At the base of the stairs on the mausoleum opposite, five guards stood in a semi-circle around Arrow's body. His head hung forward onto his chest, and a drop of blood fell from the corner of his mouth. Blood matted his hair against his cheek, and I saw a large welt appear around his left eye. His arms draped lifelessly at his side.

I bit my fist to keep the sobs from echoing in the darkness.

Around his body, black marks charred the stairs. A buzz swarmed in the air as the guard standing furthest from him snapped a whip. Sparks and dust sprayed off the stone staircase, leaving a crack in the ground. His next attempt didn't miss. Arrow's body shook, flailing as the whip connected with him. I watched in horror as his body jerked with electric shock.

Tears fell down my cheeks, and I wiped them away. Every piece of me screamed to turn around and not watch, but I couldn't. Each crack of the whip struck me. When they threw their heads back in laughter, they mocked me. They finally dragged him down the stairs and back through the graveyard, taking away my heart.

I shook, dropping in a heap at the base of the stone doorway, a crumbled mess. My heart boomed in my chest as visions of Arrow's lifeless body flashed in my mind. The way he hung in the guards' hands, the blood dripping from his fresh wounds, the blank expression as he stared at the ground.

In all the scenarios I had envisioned, losing Arrow never entered my mind. He seemed invincible. And he sacrificed himself for me. That debt couldn't go unpaid. No matter what doubts I had, regardless of the fear rushing through me, I knew one thing for sure. I would do the same for his people.

I had to save the queen. If not for the rebellion or my way home, for Arrow. I wouldn't let his death be for nothing.

I shifted the bag across my back and double-checked the straps. Wiping the fresh tears with the back of my hand, I willed my emotions to settle into a comfortable numbness. I put on my game face. It was time to save the queen.

CHAPTER THIRTY-THREE

Steam rolled out of the open tunnel and down my cheeks. I hesitated for a moment before jumping into the darkness, flailing as the searing water attacked me. The current took control, submerging me in the river.

I gasped for air as I rose to the turbulent surface. Water splashed over my head, the current dragging me down the narrowing tunnel. I spat out water, reaching for the walls, surprised when my fingers slipped along the smooth edges. Nothing could slow my descent.

Except for the occasional light flickering through vents from above, the tunnel was bathed in darkness. I couldn't see quite enough to get my bearings, but I knew I was in trouble. Water covered over half the tunnel. Every time the current changed directions, I plunged underwater. I relaxed my body and followed the river's course, knowing that the harder I resisted, the more the water would force its will on me. The game hadn't steered me wrong yet; I had to believe it wouldn't here either.

The rush of the water deafened me. This was no sweet gurgling stream, but a domineering roar, forcing me down its path. I struggled to keep my head above water in the shrinking tunnel. My legs floundered, twisting me as I swam. I lost track of where I was, how long I had been there, and what direction was up, but I knew it had to end soon.

But what if I'd taken the wrong tunnel? Had I counted correctly and chosen the right tomb? While I considered the possibility of miscalculation, the water beneath me suddenly dropped away. I floated for a moment in empty space before the freefall down.

My scream echoed in the darkness until the water silenced me. Pinned beneath the force of the waterfall, I fought to resurface, gasping for air as the current pulled me downstream.

I flipped onto my back and kicked my way over to the side, savoring my breath. The tight confines of the tunnel widened until the sides disappeared into darkness, leaving me with the feeling that I was suspended in a void. If it weren't for the flashing dots on the ceiling, I would have been concerned that I'd hit game over. As it was, the flickering lights reminded me of the busy skies back home.

Home. Even in a world away, it still found me in the smallest of details, calling out with bittersweet memories. Some things never fade away. Isn't that what Arrow had said in the Grove?

Thinking of Arrow summoned tears to my eyes. I let them fall, hiding them under the splashes of water. I wished he was still with me. I wished. I wished. I was tired of wishing. That hadn't worked when I first arrived here, and it didn't now.

I flipped over and swam. I couldn't focus on that anymore. Not now anyway. The end was too close for me to lose my focus.

The slow pull of the current directed me down a narrowing tunnel. Thick strings of algae and slime hung from the walls, hiding spiraled carvings in the stone. The stench of decay from the walls intensified as I paddled closer to look at the designs. I plugged my nose to keep from getting sick. Not that it would have mattered here, in the bowels of the evil kingdom.

The carvings on the walls continued until the room split into three pathways. A symbol crowned each of the corridors. I looked at the three: a serpentine branch, a dragon's head, and the Great Oak. Without a second thought, I swam towards the passage that flowed under the tree.

The current, now just a strong suggestion, directed me through several narrow corridors lit only by a faint light streaming in through ceiling vents. The further I swam, the fainter the pull of the water grew, until it stilled completely. The tunnel became shallower and the water thicker and more stagnant. I trudged through, keeping away from the edges where dark bubbles and algae swirled at the surface.

The tunnels branched off again, and each time I followed the tree until the stench of the water became unbearable and the corridor narrowed into a sliver of space no wider than my arm span.

A wave of excitement rushed over me when I turned a corner and saw a wall of stones. I sloshed through the shallows, the dark water and guck splashing over me. At this point, it didn't matter. I was already soaked, and I wanted to get out of there.

The wall, a roughly constructed stack of river rocks, towered over me. If not for the small sliver of light peeking in from the top, I would've thought it was a dead end.

I slipped my hands into the rough crevices between the rocks and climbed. Rock fragments and dirt loosened my grip, and the water dripping from my clothes weighed me down, but I pressed on. Nothing was going to stop me from reaching the top.

When I'd scaled the wall, I pulled myself over the edge and into the narrow passageway. My heart drummed as I crawled through the hallway, holding my breath as the full weight of the castle seemed to bear down on me. When the room finally opened, I rolled over onto my back, breathing deeply. If I hadn't played this my entire life, I would have second-guessed my choices. The narrow passageways did not inspire hope.

But I knew that hope was not the intention of this castle. A labyrinth of chambers, hallways, guards, and traps, this place signified death and torture. I really hoped I could skip those last parts.

I rolled into a sitting position and dumped a small river out of my boots. Leaning the still-saturated boots upside down against the wall, I sat back and rummaged through my bag. I formed a small pile of sticks and struck my luminance balls together. The fire was small but intense, and I basked in its heat. I sat back and waited. I wasn't going anywhere until the boots and my clothes dried. Their wet prints would lead the guards directly to me.

The puddles of water at my side called to me. I fluttered my fingers through the pool, watching the edges of the water roll onto the dry stones in a feathered pattern.

I leaned forward and dipped my finger in, and then brushed them on the dry stones to my right, watching the slow transformation. My strokes became quicker and more fluid as I recalled an image in my mind. The water didn't dry at a consistent speed, creating depth in the shadows of the portrait. I worked intently until a picture of the queen stared back at me.

When her image waned, drying in the heat of the fire, I painted again. Conjuring a different memory, I deepened my strokes, angling the edges more sharply. I drew in a trance until I sat face-to-face with Arrow.

I bit my thumb. Frozen in a moment of happiness, this was the Arrow I remembered. I traced his lips, raising one end in mischievous defiance. If only I could see that smile again. The image faded as quickly as it had been made, and I grabbed my boots, ignoring the dampness at my toes. They were dry enough to leave no marks.

I needed to get out of there. The small chamber was closing in on me.

I unsheathed my dagger and walked ahead, careful of the empty corridors and growing shadows. No matter how abandoned the subterranean vault seemed, danger lurked everywhere. A moment of complacency would kill me here. Now that I was on my own, I needed to be more aware.

The hallway ended at a spiral staircase brightened by evenly hung torches. Charcoal ash stained the walls and floor, and, in between, an even layer of dust covered the worn stones. I ran up them as quickly as I could, but four unending flights left me breathless.

Stumbling out of the stairway, I leaned against the wall, cooling my forehead against the metal rungs that hung beneath dead torches. When I managed to look up, a sense of familiarity rolled over me.

The corridors on this level all seemed the same. Dilapidated dark stones lined each wall with only a small opening at the top for light. It felt oppressive. I struggled to breathe as I ran down corridor after corridor, leaving a small set of footprints on the dusty floor.

Red doors flanked either side of the narrow hallways. I tried to ignore them. Most of the doors remained closed, hiding their traps, but a few were open, teasing me with bright lights and melodic music. I scurried through the halls, blending into the shadows. I didn't have the time or inclination to explore. I wanted out of this place.

On the other side of a half-open door, the guards' rhythmic march sounded. I skidded to a stop and threw myself backwards against the wall, hoping they hadn't seen me. I tried to keep from hyperventilating as I risked a quick peek around the corner. Their march grew to resounding booms.

Crap. They were headed towards me. It didn't matter if they had already seen me or not. If I didn't move, they'd catch me for sure. My grip tightened on my dagger.

What was I doing? Who did I think I was, taking on an entire army by myself? I wasn't cut out for this. The future of Lockhorn depended on me, and I only had one shot. I had to play this smart.

I ran in the opposite direction, counting the doors that I passed. Getting lost here would be certain death. Assuming this was like the game, I knew half the doors would bind me in a trap, and the others would send me spiraling back to the beginning. I couldn't risk either.

Skirting the corner into the fourth room, I rested against the back wall and regarded the roomy surroundings carefully. Grand golden frames trimmed with diamonds lined the walls, decorating paintings of human sacrifice and torture. I bit my cheek and slunk through the shadows. Statues of Berkos and his supporters, some of whom I recognized from Marix's manor, leered at me. Intermixed between the statues, gargoyles perched atop tall pillars. Their hollow eyes seemed to follow me.

At the far end of the gallery, a portrait of King Berkos stared me down. In a room full of gold and gaudiness, the onyx frame shimmering around his image seemed to bleed evil. My arms prickled with the sensation that I was being watched. I looked around, but only the painting watched me. Feverish black eyes met my gaze, and the edges of his lips were turned up in a mocking smile.

I took a deep breath and shook my shoulders, but the hairs on the back of my neck wouldn't settle. I jumped forward, anxious to leave that hall. Not all art tempted me.

Before I could prepare for the next challenge, the room shook. Three distinct blasts jolted the ground and rattled the portraits behind me. I waited, and ten seconds later the three booms sounded again. A lump tightened in my chest.

"Pounder," I said, wiping my palms on my leggings and reaching for the pouch of dragon weed around my neck. If this matched up to the game, I knew the only way to defeat the mutated dragon would be with fire.

My fears were confirmed when I turned the corner. Pounder, a hybrid between an alligator and a dragon, half-slithered, half-crawled across the floor, blocking my path. Drool dripped from the fangs hanging over its long, narrow snout. Behind the elongated nose, spiked ridges ran along its muscular body and encircled the lean, whipping tail. The slits of its eyes turned in my direction, its eyes flashing and fading to white. A long forked tongue uncoiled, snapping as it flicked the ground.

Sweat beaded on my forehead, and I knew it smelled me. I ducked behind the nearest pillar, listening as the jingling from its collar announced its approach. The spiked tail snapped, shaking the pillars with its force. Acid steam burst from its nostrils as it gnashed its teeth, leaving a slick trail across the floor.

Its forked tongue flickered and snapped against my hand, sticking for a moment before releasing my skin. I fumbled with the opening to the pollen pouch and felt the burn sizzle on my wrist when grains of the powder wafted out of the package. The acid on just one grain was enough to burn through the top layer of skin. I hoped they had enough strength to burn through Pounder's thick underbelly. Large chunks of pollen dropped from the bag, falling into the seams between the marble tiles around the base of the pillar. I had underestimated its speed, but I knew it would follow my scent.

It deserved its name—its tail, once engaged, pounded in three continuous snaps, pulverizing anything unfortunate enough to be in its path. The moment its snout rounded the pillar, I blew a burst of pollen in its direction and somersaulted to the right.

Its tail thumped the ground three times, and then it jumped, snapping and snarling as it landed where I had scattered the pollen. Its tail thumped again, and I ran, throwing the vial of dragon weed oil behind me. After the next two thumps, Pounder thrashed wildly, knocking over the stone pillars.

I ran out of the gallery and around the corner, opening the second door on the right. Pounder's muffled thumps faded. I leaned back against the door and waited for my heart to slow. Small blisters bubbled up on my skin where the pollen grains had landed. I was more flustered than I wanted to admit; my hands shook as I tucked the blisters under my sleeve.

The hallway seemed to lengthen the further I went. Torches lined the walls, but only one in every three bore light. I ran forward, glancing back over my shoulder as I counted the doors. When I twisted the handle to enter the next room, the door behind me opened.

Crap. A set of guards had found me.

Stealth ceased to be important. Speed became my only tool, and, unfortunately, my head start diminished as soon as they broke into a run.

I opened and slammed doors, going through some and back through others, careful to keep track of where I was. The thought of avoiding one danger by falling into another terrified me. If I died, it didn't really matter how it happened. Death in the king's castle would be final, and the rebellion would fail.

I ran through the next door and slammed into one of the guards. Glowering at me from below the tufted helmet, his obsidian eyes shifted to my hand. He growled and chomped his rotted teeth, tightening his grip around his mace.

I spun around and ran. It wasn't the right direction, but that didn't matter anymore. The walls crowded in, imposing, dark, and void of any warmth. The thought of imprisonment made me shiver. Terror choked me, taking my breath hostage in my throat.

The metallic clomp of his footsteps echoed through the halls, and it grew louder the further I ran. When I turned around, three more guards had joined him, marching in synchronization. The rhythmic beat of their boots on the hard stones chilled me to the bone. They weren't in any hurry to get me; it was inevitable.

The cruelty in their eyes startled me as they bore down with deadly intent. All the other dangers I'd faced had hinted at death, but this was the first time I feared torture.

My feet slipped out from under me as I slid around the corner. The crumbled stones skinned my face and palms. Forgetting about the dangers lurking behind each door, I opened them all as I fled for my life.

The roar of flames burst through one door behind me, and shadowy creatures lurked in the entrance to another. The guards didn't miss a beat, walking through the flames and ignoring the shadows as they systematically closed each door and shortened the gap.

I reached down and halted as my hand strayed to the dagger. That wasn't enough to protect myself from the guards. I hesitated before uncoiling the whip from my belt. The weapon I hadn't wanted to bring was my only chance at escape. I arched it through the air, surprised at its fluid movement. The guards hesitated at the first crack of the whip, and then sped forward towards me. I twisted the lever controlling the power level to low, feeling the buzz vibrate through my hand.

The blue flame empowered me, and I clenched my jaw. I charged forward, snapping the whip. I missed more than anything, but every spark of the whip when it cracked against the wall inspired fear in their eyes. My inexperience added to their distrust. I tightened my grip, keeping the whip from falling out of my hands as it struck each guard in turn. The electric current shook violently when it hit the metal breastplates. Their yells were like whispers above the deafening vibrations of the whip. I spun wildly, and I didn't stop until every guard lay unconscious on the edges of the corridor.

The smell of burnt skin permeated the narrow passageway. I stepped over each guard before turning the whip off. My hands still shook.

I closed my eyes, reorienting myself to my position in the castle. Where had my frantic running taken me? I knew that several doors looped back to previous locations in the castle. The doors in this hall and the proximity to the room guarded by Pounder told me I was closer to the end than I'd thought. Re-securing the whip to my belt, I passed through the third red door on the left. Then, after passing the third hanging torch, I walked through the second door. On a map, this linear approach didn't make sense. Only one thing in Lockhorn ever had, and now he was gone.

The stones crackled as I moved further down the hall, scattering pebbles to the edges. Uh-oh. I crept forward, reaching out to the walls on either side of me. Bigger chunks of rock dissolved around my feet. I stopped, holding my breath, hoping the stone would hold. Somehow, I had miscounted the doors.

The red door seemed miles away, out of reach. My arms strained against the walls on opposite sides of the hall, hoping to lighten my steps. The tentative touch of my left foot proved too much. The stone cracked, disintegrating beneath me. My screams echoed as I fell.

CHAPTER THIRTY-FOUR

Pain rippled down my side as I landed on a pile of stones. I blinked, watching the flecks of dust settle. The only light flickered through a narrow crevasse in the ceiling, where the floor of the hallway had been. Barely enough light to see beyond my hands.

I wanted to cry, to give up, but I couldn't. Not with everyone counting on me. Maybe a hidden trap didn't have to mean game over. Maybe this was just a restart.

I pushed myself up, nearly screaming when my dislocated ribs popped back into place. My breaths quickened, and a rush of nausea hit me. I rolled to my knees and pulled myself up. Rough stones scratched my face while I fought to control my breath.

The ground groaned as rocks and debris settled. When I stabilized, I heard another moan.

"Who's there?" I pulled out my dagger and watched its tip waver in the faint light. I steadied my trembling hand and took a cautious step across the room.

The floor gave with each step. Rocks blocked my path, tripping me as I stumbled along the uneven surface. I struggled to find a suitable place for my feet while keeping an eye on the dark lump at the edge of my vision.

The hunched creature moaned again. It reeked of burned flesh and sweat. A moment of panic choked me. I looked down at my dagger and reconsidered. I didn't want to get that close to whatever they had left in here to die. Reaching back, I unhooked my bow and poked the back of the creature with its tip. It didn't stir.

Morbid curiosity drove me closer. I poked again, harder, moving it forcefully. An arm slid down, revealing a battered face and chiseled jaw.

"Arrow!" I dropped to my knees and framed his face in my hands. My tears dropped onto him. I leaned over and kissed them off, wiping his skin clear of dirt and ash. I felt sick when I saw how his pale skin had been darkened by bruises and welts. His moans broke my heart.

"I thought I had lost you forever. It's me," I said, peeling his hair away from his forehead. "I'm not going anywhere."

His hands fumbled up his chest until they reached my hands. I bit my tongue, trying to keep myself from sobbing. I let the silent tears fall. He moaned again.

"I told you we were doing this together. I still mean that," I said, tightening my lips. "I'm not going anywhere, I promise you, but I have to get my bag on the other end of the room."

I let his hands go and ran to where I thought my bag had fallen. After what felt like an eternity, I found it, hidden between rocks and debris. The leather ripped when I yanked it out, but I didn't care. I ran back to Arrow's side. His hands warmed one of mine while I rummaged through the bag. I emptied the contents in my lap, rolling the unneeded items out of the way. One of the luminance rocks rolled against him, brushing against the skin on his arm.

His groans deepened into agony.

"Oh crap! I'm so sorry!" I said, grabbing the ball of light and placing it on the stone next to me. I hadn't thought about the heat of the ball radiating through him. I shook my head, cursing myself for my thoughtlessness.

I dug further into the pile of items in my lap and grabbed the final scraps of tangled vines.

Melody's last-minute gifts had now saved me twice.

"It'll be okay soon. I have the vines. Just sit still so I can place them." I unrolled the vines and slid my dagger along the interior seam of the plant. The crisp smell hit me, and I almost smiled.

I laid the cool interior of the vines across his chest, cringing as he shook in pain. He knocked them off his chest.

"Does it hurt?" I asked.

"No," he whispered, trying to turn away from me.

"Then what are you doing? You need these!" I grabbed the vines off the ground.

"No," he said. "You said it yourself. The whips are deadly. Don't waste your vines on me. You might need them."

I bit my lower lip. I couldn't deny the danger from the whips, and I knew I might not be able to heal him. But I also knew I couldn't leave without him. I forced a smile into my words and repositioned the vines across his chest.

"Oh no, I'm not saving them for me. You'd be proud of me, getting to this point with nothing more than a few scrapes and bruises. I have another set in the other bag, but these are for you." I hoped he would forgive the lie.

He didn't argue.

"Arrow?" I asked, shaking his shoulder. Tears of frustration and anger boiled over, spilling onto my cheeks. I splayed the vines and spread them evenly across his chest, covering the slashed ribs and bruises. I looked at the diminishing pile at my side, hoping I had enough. "You're not leaving me again." I ripped more vines open, draping them across his forehead and up and down his arms.

His moans deepened and then relaxed, and his breathing grew slow. Too slow. Rocks dug into my knees as I leaned over him, listening to the sluggish beat of his heart. I couldn't be too late.

"Arrow," I wept. "Open your eyes. You can't leave me. I don't want to do this without you. Don't leave me." I wrapped my arms around my knees and rocked back and forth, watching the slow rise and fall of his chest.

I'd never been one for waiting. In fact, the longer it took for something to happen, the less interested in it I became. Instant gratification, my mom called it. I called it common sense. Life went by too quickly to waste time waiting on something when you could have something else instead. As I watched the soft flickering of his eyelids, I begrudgingly admitted that some things were worth waiting for.

That didn't make it easier though. Stuck in the darkness, time stretched to an agonizing pace. I had no way to judge how long I had been in there or how long Arrow slept. When I looked up, I only saw the soft flickering of the torches, and I wondered if I would be stuck in this pit for eternity.

I leaned back and rested inside the niche of rocks I had sculpted into a chair next to Arrow's body. The tips of our fingers touched before I closed my eyes. I don't know if I slept before a fit of coughing startled me. I jumped up, one hand dropping to the hilt of my dagger.

Arrow's body shook. He groaned as he pushed himself up, covering his ribs with his wrapped hands. And then he turned, and I saw his weary eyes.

"Arrow?" I blinked the happy tears back. "No, no, don't get up," I said, helping him lay back down.

"Alex?" he asked in a deep, raspy voice. "What are you doing here?"

"I'm the Golden Hero, remember? I'm here to save you," I said lightly, falling to the ground at his side.

He half-laughed and grabbed at his ribs. "I thought we were done saving each other."

"I don't think we ever will be," I whispered.

His hand grabbed the cuff of my shirt, pulling me closer. My heart pounded as I looked into his eyes. The darkness could not hide his raw emotions. "Alex, thank you." His hold on my shirt grew stronger, and his other arm encircled me from behind, pulling me in for a kiss.

I sensed sadness in his kisses, and I saw it in his eyes when he pulled back.

"I'm sorry I dragged you into all this," he said.

"What are you talking about?"

"If my brother hadn't called you here, you wouldn't be stuck. You'd be out there, in your own world, free of the burdens we've placed on you. Free from this dungeon. And the way I treated you in Flourin—"

"Hey, stop that. I may not have asked for this, but it hasn't been all that bad." I squeezed his hand. "In fact, it's been better than I ever imagined. This world, and you," I said, holding his gaze, "have shown me what I've been missing. I've learned to not shy away from adventure, or from love..." I let that thought trail off and bit my lip. "You sound like you're giving up, and we can't do that. It's not too late to get out of here and save the queen. There has to be a way."

I stepped away from him and patted the walls, looking for something to grab ahold of.

"I'm just trying to be realistic," Arrow said. "I don't see many options here; there are no doors, stairs, or exits in here. I mean, think about everything we've seen. My men didn't even make it out of Marix's manor. How are we going to break out of here?" He looked up at the crevasse above us.

"There's always a way out, we just need to find it. Don't underestimate me now." I moved from wall to wall, unable to find a grip to hold on to.

"Do you know something I don't?"

"No, but it's way too early to give up hope. Just let me think." I wasn't going to give up.

"Let me know if you come up with something. I'm going to look for a forgotten slice of bread."

"There's none. I already checked." I blushed. "You were asleep for a long time."

He sat back and sighed, looking up at the ceiling.

"We'll find a way out," I said. "I promise."

"Don't make promises you can't keep. I've already made too many of those." He swore and threw a rock.

"You only promised what you could—that you would try. There's no fault in that."

"I promised much more than that. I promised a future of hope and possibilities and a chance to live without wondering who was on your side."

"You haven't broken those promises yet. We can still find a way. Stranger things have happened."

"You keep on hoping. I'll check the bag again for a magic wand," he said, shuffling to where I'd dropped my bag.

"We don't need magic," I said.

"If we had some, we could make our own way out of here instead of going around in circles talking about impossibilities."

I jerked my head in his direction. "What'd you say?"

"Magic wands? Impossibilities?"

"No, you said we could make our own." I felt a smile grow on my face. "We'll make our own way out. You're a genius!" I ran to his side and gave him a quick kiss before scouring the pile of items from the bag.

"How do you expect to do that? Neither one of us knows any magic."

"We don't need magic when we have this." I pulled out the last pouch of luminance powder and emptied half of it into his hands.

He looked at the pile of glimmering dust in his palms. "What am I supposed to do with this?"

"Help me find the way out. These traps were always built with an exit. We just need to find it. There has to be a trap door, staircase, moveable blocks, I don't know. Something. I'm sure of it." I pinched the dust and threw it up in the air, watching it settle.

He shook his head like I had lost it, but followed my example.

Golden flakes filled the room, shimmering on the ground like hidden treasure. The pile of powder shrunk more quickly than I'd expected. I glanced at Arrow, pacing along the other edge, empty-handed. Now what? I threw the last bit at the wall.

The flakes settled around my feet. Deflated, I looked back at Arrow, who had walked to my side. "Maybe I was wrong."

"Or maybe not," he said, pointing to one flake lying suspended in mid-air.

I dropped to my knees and scooped up more of the golden dust, tossing it at the floating flake. I squealed as several flakes landed next to the first, and others came to rest above it on a slight angle. The dust now clearly defined a hidden staircase.

"That can't be," Arrow said, throwing more.

"It is! And you know what that means. We're getting out of here."

I climbed up the illuminated staircase, digging my nails under the layer of powder.

When I reached the top of the stairs, I slithered across the smooth stones of the hallway, keeping my eyes focused on the red door at the end of the hall. The stones cracked under my weight, sending a new wave of panic over me.

"Run!" I yelled behind me, throwing the door open and crashing through it. Arrow tumbled over me.

I winced and pushed him off me, cradling my ribs. "I told you we'd find a way out of there."

"I'll never doubt you again. What do we do now? Save the queen?"

I looked behind him, down the dark hallway lined with red doors. A shudder ran down my spine. "Now we kill the king."

CHAPTER THIRTY-FIVE

Dread settled over me the moment the words left my lips. The hair on the back of my neck stood on edge, my stomach tightened, and my hands lost their grip. Everything popped with heightened sensitivity.

I jumped when Arrow tapped my shoulder. "Don't do that," I said, catching my breath.

He raised his hands in surrender. "I didn't mean to startle you. I just wanted to stay by your side. In case..." He let the thought trail off.

I looked at him, daring him to continue. "In case you needed to be saved again?" I offered.

"That's exactly what I was thinking." He smiled. "Do we have a plan?"

"Just the same as it's always been: Find a way through this maze of a castle, and then you can take care of the king."

"That easy?"

"I never said it would be easy." I gave him a hard look. "Are you sure you're ready to do this?"

He patted his ribs. "I'm as good as new, thanks to our overabundant supply of vines."

"Who would have thought my clumsiness would come in handy?"

He winked at me. "There you go, underestimating your worth."

I rolled my eyes. "Let's just hope our luck holds out. We've used the last one." I ran my hands over my bruised ribs, hiding the intense pain. "Get prepared. There should be a pile of guards around this corner. I don't know if they'll still be knocked out or not." I lowered my voice to a whisper and wrapped my fingers around the hilt of my dagger as we turned the corner. "They're gone," I said, surprised.

"What?"

"The guards. I must have stunned at least three or four of them before I took the wrong turn."

"Or right turn, depending on who you ask."

"You're right." I smiled back at him. "I just thought they would still be here."

"That's good though, that means you didn't kill them."

"I guess you're right." I kept my hand on the dagger.

I counted the doors and took us down the right hallways until we entered a larger corridor. From the outside, it seemed the same as the others—dark, dismal, and bare. But to me, it was different. I knew that the true darkness waited at the other end, behind the last red door.

That door became my sole focus, and the rest of the hall faded as I examined every inch of it. Unlike the others around the castle, this door glimmered in perfection. Its red paint glistened, and the polished golden knob reflected the wavering torchlight framing it on both sides. Light pulsed at the bottom, like a quiet siren.

The dagger slipped in my sweaty hand as we walked closer.

"This is it," I said, reaching down, making sure the whip stayed coiled at my side. The words seemed to carry a different message to Arrow than they did to me. As I assessed my weapons, he gave me a sad smile.

He grabbed my left hand and pressed it to his lips. "Alex, whatever happens in there, I want to thank you. I couldn't have done this without you." His gaze deepened.

I couldn't find the right words to say before he turned and strode through the door. What did he think he was doing? I ran after him, skidding to a stop as I turned the corner. Déjà vu.

The throne room was an exact replica of the final scene from the game. My eyes skimmed the sterile white walls, bare except for the red drapes that seemed to bleed around the windows. Marble pillars lined the expansive room and curved behind the golden throne. Vases of dragon weed fluttered on either side of the garish seat.

King Berkos drummed his fingers along the edge of his throne. Fear constricted my breath. "Arrow, wait!" I whispered, barely recognizing my own voice. I wanted to run to Arrow's side, but my feet refused to listen to me.

The two men, poised on opposite sides of the throne room, mimicked the setup for the final battle. I shook my head and dismissed the thought. This wasn't a game.

"It's about time, dear boy. I've been waiting all day." Berkos' deep voice echoed off the marble walls. "I hope you've found the accommodations to your liking."

"Hello, Berkos," Arrow responded with a steady voice.

Berkos tsked. "Ah, so formal. Is that any way to greet your uncle?"

"Any familial ties between us were severed long ago," he said. He unsheathed the sword from his side and stepped closer.

A deep laugh broke the tension. "That's the spirit. I hoped these last few years had toughened you up a bit."

"You know nothing about me. You never did."

"I knew enough to see a spoiled child running about the castle, playing at being prince—as if you had any inclination or ability to lead the kingdom." He sneered. "Even your dear brother lacked a backbone when it came down to it."

"Leave my brother out of it." Arrow clenched his jaw and tightened his grip around his sword.

"Oh, you don't need to worry about that. He's been long since forgotten. The moment I killed him, he became meaningless."

Arrow's face matched the pallor of his knuckles. "What's the point of this?"

"Oh, there's no point, just some idle chit-chat while I wait for your gift to be ready," he said, looking behind us towards the back door.

"Gift?" Arrow asked, following his uncle's gaze.

"I wouldn't be able to call myself a host if I didn't present you with an offering."

My stomach flipped at his choice of words. "Arrow, I don't like the sound of this," I whispered, walking to his side. "It's some sort of trap."

"We don't have much choice. We're not leaving without the queen."

"Ah, such a sweet sentiment," said Berkos, "I'm sure she'd appreciate it if she knew. Unfortunately, she doesn't get out much these days. And I have an inkling you won't be joining her." He paused as Arrow lurched forward. "And about the gift, I must insist. It's been prepared especially for you."

"Don't let him get to you," I said, pulling him back. "He's just trying to goad you."

"The hero speaks such words of wisdom," he said, turning his attention to me. "It's hard to imagine that someone as tiny as you could have created this uproar." His calm words and demeanor contradicted the burning hatred in his eyes. Heat rose to my face as I tried to maintain eye contact.

"Leave her out of this," Arrow said, stepping in front of me.

"It's hard to ignore such a creature. You seem to have that problem as well. Tell me, how is it, working with this thing?" He pointed at me.

I looked at the ground, trying to stay out of it. My blood boiled, but I needed to keep my cool. We were too close to the end to lose it now. I reached for Arrow's arm and shook my head.

"She's not a thing," he said.

"What is she, then? She's not one of us. That much is certain."

"Her name's Alex," he said, brandishing his sword. "And she's here to save the queen."

Oh boy. I lifted my gaze, hoping I looked braver than I felt.

"This is priceless. I wish more people could witness this." Berkos stood, the black velvet robe unfurling behind him as he descended the stairs. Slow, deliberate steps echoed through the hall.

My face paled and I gripped the knife tighter. I knew I couldn't beat him by traditional force. He was an obvious threat even without a weapon. I hoped my fear didn't show. If it did, no one noticed. Arrow and Berkos locked in on each other.

"There's nothing you can do to stop us now." Arrow said, pointing the tip of his sword at his uncle.

"Surely you're not going to harm me when I come bearing gifts." He snapped his fingers, and one of his guards entered from the back. "What has it been? Five years? I thought one per year would be sufficient. If it's not, though, let me know. I have plenty more I can give you." His chuckle reverberated in the chamber.

The guard kneeled and presented an oddly shaped bag.

"Ah, perfect." He waved off the guard and peeked inside. "I love that smell—fresh, cloying, and definite."

"Arrow, don't take it," I urged. I pointed the dagger at the king.

"Don't listen to her. It's just a little gift, just something to show you how I feel about your little game of rebellion. Please, go ahead and open it."

Arrow glanced between me and the king. I saw it in his eyes, anger and desperation. If he opened it, nothing would stay the same.

"No!" I yelled, knocking the bag from his hands as he reached for it.

I screamed as head after head rolled out, staring at me with their blank eyes. Even in death, their faces constricted in pain, their final screams frozen. Behind the empty stares, I saw young faces, void of scars and wrinkles, guilty of nothing. I thought back to the boy in Flourin, so eager to fight for freedom. And then I saw the familiar face of Pipes, and my heart went cold. I sheathed my dagger and grabbed the whip, my grip now surprisingly steady.

"You sick, deranged—" I snarled, jumping for him. Arrow grabbed my arms, pulling me back to his side.

"Flattery gets you nowhere with me, my dear. Trust me, you

would have to do a lot more to impress me."

"I'm going to kill you, you monster." I lunged at him with a guttural yell. The king deftly twirled to the side, dodging my first strike. I nearly dropped the whip as it chipped a chunk of marble off the pillar.

I raised the whip and refocused, ignoring the pain vibrating through my palms. A smirk grew on his face as he stared at me. "The little girl wants to fight! How precious. I thought I had seen it all from the queen, but apparently this new generation doesn't do docility. A blessing and a curse."

"I'll show you a curse," I said and blew a strand of hair out of my eyes as I ran towards him, sliding across the smooth floor, swinging at his ankles.

The blue flames from the whip singed the black velvet of the king's robe. His smile faded when he glanced back at the scorched garment. "This is your last chance to save yourself, little girl. None of this pertains to you. If you leave now, I will spare you."

"You're wrong, Berkos," I said, walking to Arrow's side, clipping the whip to my belt. "This does involve me. More than I ever thought possible."

"Don't say I didn't warn you." He unclasped his robe, the velvet dropping in a heap around his feet. A quick snap of his fingers and a team of guards marched in, tossing him a black sword and shield.

"Attack!" The ground shook with the guards' approach.

Fear flashed in my eyes as I looked at Arrow, but his gaze had already hardened with an intensity of focus. I turned in time to see the closest line of guards running towards me. I ran to the outer edge of the room, searching for a plan. I saw the drapes and thought about swinging, but I didn't know what that would accomplish. Swinging out the window wouldn't work here. My heart raced as their feet came closer. I had used the last of the dragon weed on Pounder, and the luminance powder would do nothing for me here. My mind drew a blank, and my chest burned from running. I had to come up with something quick.

"Flowers, use the flowers!" I heard Arrow yell.

What was he talking about? I had already used up the dragon weed. My mind raced until I saw the fresh flowers fluttering by the window.

I looked back in time to see him engage two of the guards, the red stamps on the back of the first disappearing under a stream of blood. The next second he turned and swung at the other, slicing off an arm at the elbow.

Behind me, I heard swords unsheathe, and my hesitation disappeared.

With a burst of energy, I ran towards the windows and grabbed the vase, careful to keep the pollen from hitting me. That flower had burned me enough. I twisted the red drapes around my wrist and forearm and jumped, pushing off the wall, turning in mid-air above them. I yanked the flowers from the vase and scattered them, watching the golden pollen fall into their eyes and between the plates of their armor. While they screeched and scratched at their faces, I pounded the vase against their heads, knocking them to the ground.

I wiped off the scattered pieces of pollen and looked around for Berkos. He sat back in his throne, watching Arrow fight with casual indifference. The calm stroking of his mustache enraged me. I tightened my grip around the handle of the whip, feeling my temper rise.

Arrow's voice interrupted my thoughts.

"And now, Berkos, it is your turn." He faced the king, his sword dripping with the guards' blood as he walked forward.

"At last," the king chuckled. "It's time to put an end to you and your pesky followers. I've been dreaming of this day."

"Then it's time to wake up. Your days of ruling are over."

"And who do you expect to take over after me? You?"

"No," Arrow said, adjusting his sword. "Lockhorn will continue to be ruled by the true monarch, Queen Elin."

Berkos sneered. "You think a shrew trapped in a dungeon can rule a kingdom better than me?"

"Anyone with a heart could rule this kingdom better than you. You're a disgrace. True leaders don't need to rule through fear and bribery."

"That, my dear boy, is why you were never king and never will be. Weakness cannot hold a kingdom together."

"Who is weaker? The man who opens his heart to help others or the one who only cares about himself?"

"I've had enough of this bickering." Berkos stood and reached for his sword.

Something shimmered against his thigh. I narrowed my gaze and gasped—the keys. I needed to get those without being noticed. I tiptoed along the outer edge of the wall, fading into the shadows.

Berkos walked down from his throne and stood across from Arrow. Beneath Arrow's dark matted hair, sweat dripped down his forehead. He wiped it with his shoulder, the muscles in his arms rippling. I had no idea who would win.

Berkos stabbed first, a quick jab, easily blocked. A smile grew on his face as he thrust forward again. His movements seemed playful, although his smile dripped with animosity. Their swords crashed against each other as their moves increased in speed and ferocity.

Sweat dripped down Arrow's face, and his jaw tightened with concentration. His arms twisted as he met and deflected every thrust of the king's.

Berkos' grin faded, and his face glistened with exertion. "I have you now," he said, knocking Arrow down over the body of a fallen guard. Arrow rolled out of the way just as Berkos' sword cracked the plated armor at his side. Arrow jumped up and deflected the next swing, maneuvering around the other guards. Berkos kicked the fallen men and slid through the puddles of blood around them. His smile turned sinister.

"You may have learned a trick or two, but you're still no match for me."

"You're right, I'm not your match. I'm better." Arrow flipped through the air and kicked out with his feet, connecting with Berkos' chest. The king flew back, landing against the far wall.

Berkos shook his head and stood, his hand on his ribcage. "That's the last hit you'll get."

"So you say," Arrow said, running forward, his blade whistling through the air as he sliced at Berkos' head.

Berkos redirected the hit and smacked him with the side of his blade. The shallow cut streaked blood across Arrow's face. He covered his face, paling when he saw the blood drip off his hand.

I slid around the room, pressing against the wall until I stood behind the throne. This had to end before Berkos maimed Arrow. Once in position, I waved my arms.

Arrow saw me and pressed forward, forcing Berkos back, thrust after thrust. I tasted the metallic twinge of blood in the air and flinched with every crash of the swords. He came at me quickly. I barely had time to strategize before I saw the swing of the keys and heard the whirling of the swords.

I leaned forward from behind his throne, reaching forward tentatively to avoid the moving blades. Berkos grabbed my wrist and twisted it until I spun in front of him.

His warm breath on the back of my neck sent shivers down my spine. He twisted my wrist until the pain forced me to release the dagger. With his other hand, he grabbed it and held it against my throat. The jewels sparkled along the hilt. I trembled despite my best efforts.

"Arrow," I said, my voice quivering.

He glanced between me and the king and raised the tip of his sword. "Let her go. Your fight's with me and the rebellion, not her. You said so yourself."

"Ah, yes, I did. But I also gave her the chance to leave," Berkos said, his voice rising in a manic cackle.

Tears trailed down my face, blending with the blood dripping from the tip of the blade as it slid down my neck and under my shirt.

Berkos wiped it with his finger and licked it. "I generally don't believe in second chances. But maybe an arrangement can be made," he said, releasing the pressure against my neck. "What are you prepared to give up for her?"

He looked at me and then back to the king. "Name your price."

"Arrow, you can't," I pleaded. "Think of the queen and the people depending on you. I'm nothing."

"She makes a passionate plea. But let me ask you, dear boy. Is life worth living without the one you love?"

"Don't listen to him. Don't give up what you have worked for these past few years for what we've shared in only a couple of weeks."

"You know what these weeks have meant," Arrow said.

I did. That made this choice so much more difficult. I saw the pain in Arrow's eyes, the guilt as he weighed my life against the lives of the others. No matter which way he chose, doubt and regret would haunt him forever. The sword shook in his hand.

I couldn't save him or the rebellion and win the game. I had to choose between what I wanted and the greater good. Looking between the two men, weighing the options in my mind, I realized my choice was clear. And it didn't have anything to do with being a hero. It had to do with being me.

I looked over at Arrow. "Please don't. I'm not worth it. The rebellion may want me, but they don't need me. They need you."

"They may not need you, but I do. Let her go!" he yelled.

The reverberation of his sword hitting the ground shook me to the core. I closed my eyes.

"I'm sorry, Arrow." I dropped the keys to the ground. A stray tear slid down my face, blurring his image as I pressed my right leg against Berkos' leg.

"Game over," I said, twisting the lever on the whip up to the highest level.

Berkos jerked his head down, confusion flickering to fear as he realized what I had done.

"No!" Arrow's screams blended with my own. Waves of electricity shook my body. The hum vibrated through me, climaxing in a gray blur as my vision failed.

My world disappeared into a limbo. Everything hid behind a veil of light, and loud ringing drowned out all sound for what felt like hours. I slowly regained my senses as spasms flared down my side. I couldn't move.

The outline of the window lit up with the flash of fireworks. I tried to move again, and my arms buckled. Tears puddled around my cheek as I stared helplessly at the body in front of me.

King Berkos stared back, the sneer frozen on his face, his eyes glinting with hatred. Stuck in the same place I was, hanging to the threads of life, I saw his fingers inch forward. Between us, the whip buzzed, leaving charred scars across the marble floor.

Pulling the energy from every inch of my body, I moved my hand forward in a last battle of wills. The handle hummed through me as I grasped the cold metal and pulled it to my side. Berkos flinched as I flicked the power lever off, and the hum fell silent.

Before I closed my eyes, I saw Arrow creep up behind him. Sadness haunted Arrow's face. Deep circles I hadn't noticed before highlighted the red splotches around his eyes. I wished I could see him smile, if only for a last time. Berkos stole his attention. Bursts of fireworks glinted off my dagger as Arrow held it high above the king. I closed my eyes.

Berkos' scream echoed in my soul.

It was done. Arrow had killed the king, and all I could do was cry. Strong arms wrapped around me. He cradled me to his chest, rocking back and forth.

"This wasn't supposed to happen like this," he whispered, kissing my forehead.

"Y-you did it," I stuttered, slowly forming the words.

"We did it. I never could have gotten here without you." He brushed a strand of hair out of my eyes.

I bit my lip, wishing the tears would freeze like the rest of my body had. "Keys."

"What?" He looked behind me at the discarded ring of keys.

"I don't know how much longer I'll be here. You still need to

- *Dreamscape: Saving Alex* -

rescue the queen. She's down below, in the stairway behind this room. You should be able to find it without a problem."

"I'm not worried about any of that right now," he said, rocking me again. "I'm staying here with you."

"But…"

"I'll be here for as long as I can. I'm not ready to let you go."

I smiled up at him, wishing the sadness in his eyes wasn't a reflection of the grief he saw in me. "I wanted an adventure," I breathed. "You gave me an unforgettable one."

He gave me the smile I had hoped for, the one that had stolen my heart. I looked away, watching the fireworks fade into the darkness. The sky separated into a pixelated mosaic of colors.

Soft golden flakes blew in from the window, landing on my knee. I lowered my eyes, watching the golden dust swirl around me. Energy hummed through my body.

I looked up at Arrow, his eyes wide in disbelief. An overwhelming sadness filled me.

"It's time," I whispered.

He nodded. His quiet acceptance broke my heart.

"I don't want to leave you," I said, tightening my grip on his vest. My voice disappeared beneath the barrage of whirling flakes.

"You never will. I'll always be here. You know where to find me."

"In the game? I want more than that." My chin trembled.

"No, I'm not just in the game anymore. I'm right here. Always." He pointed to his heart.

I looked down at our hands, mine now covered in golden light, his pale. "But I'm not ready to go."

"We're never ready. There's never a good time say goodbye."

He leaned forward, kissing me one last time. I closed my eyes and responded to his lips. His fingers traced the outline of my jaw, and a soft sigh escaped me. In that moment, everything disappeared except him and me and the feelings we shared.

Then a rush of electricity ran through me, and I felt the golden light rise from my legs over my elbows until the sensation of our kiss disappeared under the control of the rhythmic hum.

A whirlwind of golden flakes separated our hands, tearing us violently apart. My heart ached and my chest heaved as Arrow disappeared behind the golden storm.

"No!" I whispered, wishing I had the strength to scream.

CHAPTER THIRTY-SIX

"No!" I jumped up, wiping the fuzz from the corner of my eyes. Everything blurred under the bright light of the sun. My head pounded as I recognized the familiar song in the background.

"Arrow?" I asked, rubbing my eyes harder.

"Hmm?" An unexpected but familiar voice grumbled. Natalie.

"Not yet. I'm not ready to go," I murmured, closing my eyes, knowing even as I said it that it wasn't my choice. There was no going back after game over.

Natalie mumbled something incoherent, then tapered off into silence.

I ignored the grumbles and concentrated on the song in the background, memorizing the endless loop of music, holding on to the last piece of Lockhorn I could. I knew reality waited when I opened my eyes, but I wasn't ready to let go. So I kept them shut.

But no matter how much I wanted to hold on to my memories of Arrow, I couldn't ignore the soft blankets at my side or the lingering fragrance of cinnamon. No matter how much I fought it, I couldn't deny the truth. I was home.

The pang of disappointment surprised me.

Home. That word held so many conflicting meanings for me now.

I wasn't ready to be back. After months of fighting to stay here and weeks—in game time, at least—of trying to get back, this was the last place I wanted to be. It didn't seem fair. Where was the happy ending I wanted?

This wasn't it. That realization stabbed me.

What I'd thought I wanted now seemed minor in comparison to what I knew I could have. I wanted more. I didn't want a moment from my past or an adventure to dream about, I wanted to live it. But that meant opening my eyes.

Could I do that? Open my eyes and accept whatever reality awaited me? I didn't know, but I had to try.

I exhaled deeply and gripped the blanket at my side, waiting for the haze to clear. Even through the blurriness, I recognized the familiar shapes of my trophies and the pictures covering the wall. Everything was the same as when I'd left. Boxes lined the far wall, and, above them, my old photos stared at me. The fights I had gotten into for those torn images now seemed pointless.

My surroundings felt strange, memories of a lifetime ago. Their familiarity didn't bring the comfort I'd come to expect, just a pit in my stomach. The mosaic of colors I had prided myself on seemed dull. Artwork from the past filled the spaces that should have been left for future projects.

I clutched the blanket and lifted it to my mouth to muffle my scream.

Natalie grumbled on the floor again, tucking her head deeper into the sleeping bag in protest. The tips of her long hair curled out, half-hiding the pile of toppled cinnamon popcorn at her side. I watched breathlessly, waiting to see if she moved, but besides the slow rise and fall of the bag, she remained still.

I sighed and dangled my feet over the edge of the bed, careful to avoid waking her. Natalie usually slept in later than me, and today I was counting on it. I wasn't ready to jump back into real life yet.

Pins and needles shot through my feet as I dangled them over the edge of the bed. I rubbed my ankle, doing a double take at the red lines crisscrossing up my shin. The indentations of the blankets looked oddly familiar. Dismissing what had happened as a dream seemed absurd. Every place, event, and person was imprinted on me.

I shook my head and walked to the nearest wall, cursing when I tripped over the stack of unused boxes lying half-hidden beneath my dresser. Hopping on one foot, I hobbled over to the wall where the bulletin board full of familiar faces smiled at me.

The sides of my mouth inched up as I unpinned the closest picture. An old photo of Natalie and me after the first game she cheered at. My uneven pigtails looked misplaced beside her perfectly coiled curls. That's what we were, two odd pieces that fit together perfectly. I remembered that game. We'd had a sleepover afterwards, and the next morning we each ate half a dozen doughnuts. The photo dimmed compared to my memory.

I grabbed the photo next to it and peeked at the inscription on the back: *Halloween, 7th grade.* That was the year of the big sleepover at Melissa's house. There was no way I could forget that or the midnight swim in our mermaid costumes. I bit my lower lip as a grin grew on my face.

I looked at the next photo and the ones behind it, all memories I hadn't forgotten. In fact, every photo on that board seemed a pale comparison to the stories I remembered.

After one last look at the photos in my hand, I dropped them into the half-filled moving box at my side. The photos flipped over in all directions as they fell, but that didn't matter. I didn't need to see them to remember those moments in my heart.

My fingers itched for action. It was like traversing the dark forest all over again. After the first step, the rest came easily. Posters came down, followed by my artwork. Everything found its way into the box, and then I settled back on the edge of my bed.

I could no longer filter out the endlessly looping song in the background. Tucking my knees inside my white shirt, I thought about the game on the screen. I glanced around my room, stopping at the red door that led to the hallway. Then I glanced down at the pile of stale cinnamon popcorn around Natalie's head and settled my gaze on the indentions on my leg.

What had happened to me? Which was more absurd, believing that the game was real or that I had dreamed it all up? Was it even possible to dream so vividly that I feared death and fell in love? I traced my lips. I didn't know which option I wanted to be true. Both seemed inadequate to answer the questions racing through my mind or settle the tremors in my heart.

But it was my choice. What did I want to believe?

I screamed into the pillow and hurled it across the room, nearly hitting the flashing screen. Then I crawled to the edge of the bed, almost falling off onto Natalie as I picked it back up.

The screen flashed again, and the final scene of the game repeated itself. I held my breath, watching. The key to the dungeon opened the cell door. My chest burned as I watched the little pink queen stand and twirl in victory. Fireworks burst at the top of the screen, and a slow march of golden letters along the bottom announced the end of the game.

"Arrow," I murmured. "You did it. You saved the queen." Tears stung as they filled my eyes.

"Stop that," Natalie grumbled behind me.

"What?" I turned, surprised.

She rubbed her eyes, smearing the last of her mascara down her cheek. Her exasperated look spoke volumes. "No crying this early in the morning. You're not leaving until this afternoon."

"No, you're right," I said, wiping my eyes with the back of my hand. "No more tears."

She looked around the room at the empty walls and full boxes and arched her eyebrows. "How long have you been up?"

"Not too long. I couldn't sleep." What else could I tell her? "I had too many things going through my mind."

"That makes sense. It looks like you packed a lot." She stared at me like she wanted to say more.

"What is it?"

"I'm not sure. I can't quite place it. You just seem different this morning, that's all."

After a moment, I said, "Last night was fun."

She propped herself up on her elbows. "It was. I haven't played that game in years. I can't believe you still remembered all of it."

"There's a lot that I think I missed. Are you ready to play again?" I asked, tossing her a controller.

"Seriously, this early? What about packing?"

"There'll be time later. Worst case, I'll let my mom finish it. It's just stuff, right?"

Natalie stared at me and finally shook her head.

"What?"

"Nothing, you're just different from yesterday. Happier..."

"I guess I finally realized there were more important things to do than hold onto the past. Like this," I said, nodding towards the screen. I settled back into the groove of blankets and closed my eyes, letting the rhythm of the song reach my soul. As I punched in the familiar start code and saw the golden tornado swirl across the screen, I turned to look at Natalie.

"What do you say we don't take the shortcut this time?"

She shrugged and settled in next to me. "Are you sure we'll have enough time for that?"

"Yes," I said, urging the little green hero into the dark forest. "There's always time for an adventure."

ABOUT THE AUTHOR

Kirstin Pulioff is a storyteller at heart. Born and raised in Southern California, she moved to the Pacific Northwest to follow her dreams and graduated from Oregon State University with a degree in Forest Management. Happily married and a mother of two, she lives in the foothills of Colorado. When she's not writing an adventure, she's busy living one.

Website: www.kirstinpulioff.com
Facebook: KirstinPulioffAuthor
Twitter: @KirstinPulioff

Published Works
Middle Grade Fantasy
    The Escape of Princess Madeline
    The Battle for Princess Madeline
    The Dragon and Princess Madeline
    Princess Madeline Trilogy

YA Fantasy
    Dreamscape: Saving Alex

Short Stories
    The Ivory Tower
    Boone's Journey

Made in the USA
Charleston, SC
16 May 2015